HELLHOUND

LOU YARDLEY

To Emily
I hope you enjoy the story!
Lou

Published by

Lou Yardley / Y Books

www.louyardley.com

First printed April 2018

ISBN: 978-1-9996452-0-5

DEDICATION

This one is for everyone who gives me any kind of encouragement when it comes to my writing. Whether it's in person, online or by buying and reading my stories, it means a lot. Thank you.

CONTENTS

ACKNOWLEDGMENTS

First of all, I need to thank my family. Mark, Mum, Suz, and Nan, thank you acting enthusiastic whenever I mentioned this book .

Secondly, there's my friends. I would mention you all by name, but I know that I'd miss someone and then I'd be in trouble. So, thank you all. Drinks soon, yeah?

Thirdly, I have to thank my amazing Beta Readers. Ange and Luke, you have no idea how grateful I am for all of your time, effort and passion for this project. (Ta very much for picking up on all of the typos I put in on purpose!)

Fourthly, I need to thank the extremely talented and fantastic Racheal Gater for creating the cover art for this book. You can check out her stuff here: http://www.rachaelgater.com/

Fifthly, I'd like to give a quick shout out Ben Galley. Not only is he fantastic author, but he also gave me some brilliant self-publishing tips. Visit Ben's website here: https://www.bengalley.com/

PROLOGUE

Many years ago.

Warmth spread across the child's back. Sunlight poured down, so bright it was near blinding, but the boy didn't notice, his attentions were elsewhere. Drawn to the shadows, the child's eyes flickered this way and that, eager to find something hidden just out of sight.

+ *Are you afraid?* +

At first, the voices startled him. But fear soon gave way to curiosity.

'No.' he said, his voice bold and in complete contrast with the tiny, almost sickly, body it emerged from.

+ *Then step into the forest.* +

Ten-year-old Daniel obeyed the voices happily, following the shadows deep into the dark forest that backed onto his home. Excitement covered his face and he smiled so much he thought his cheeks might split. His parent's dried blood felt tight and cracked on his skin. Daniel had no need to be afraid; there were no monsters out to get him.

He picked up his pace and started to skip. Birds sang above him, and his cape fluttered behind him. The cape was made from a portion of his father's back, his skin still smelt familiar.

Bloodied and insane, Daniel skipped into his destiny.

+ *Om grutt* + the voices chanted, thrilled to have such a young protege. + *Om grutt* +

PART ONE

CHAPTER ONE

Present day.

The pavement was so hot, Kit Byers reckoned he could have fried an egg on it. But who would want to do that? Imagining the germs that could infect such an egg made Kit cringe. *No, thanks*, thought Kit. His stomach lurched at the thought. A man and his dog walked past, and Kit pitied the dog. Not only was it covered in fur, but its feet were constantly encountering asphalt. The dog, however, seemed to be putting on a brave face, never wincing and never complaining.

English summers were not supposed to be like this. They were meant to be drenched in rain and overcast, giving the British public everything they needed to complain. If complaining ever became an Olympic sport, Britain would bring home the gold. They excelled at it. Over the centuries, they'd developed a variety of tones, swear words and eye-rolls to help communicate their irritations. The combinations they could create with these tools were almost limitless. This summer, however, had been very different. The British public had still complained, but for very different reasons. Hell's mouth had opened and it had exhaled its sulphurous heat directly over Surrey. Some people were loving it, basking out in the sun at every opportunity, running around in as few items of clothing as possible while guzzling beer and ice cream. But not Kit. Kit preferred a colder climate, one where he wasn't permanently coated in a layer of sweat. His pasty complexion didn't fare well under the strong sun. That unforgiving fireball in the sky didn't tan him, it left him looking like a boiled lobster.

Each step along the pavement was torture. Using a sweaty and tired hand, Kit loosened his tie. The tie felt almost slimy - a disgusting serpent coiled around his neck, trying to choke him. Buttons popped off his shirt as he ripped the top of it open. He needed to feel the air on his skin and he could always buy a new shirt. Water, he thought, feeling like a dying man in a desert. *I need water.*

He stumbled through the door of the nearest shop and his skin rejoiced as it took full advantage of the air conditioning. After spending a bit of quality time in the chilled section (long enough to cause some concern for the shop assistant), Kit grabbed an overpriced bottle of water, paid for it and re-entered the furnace outside. The water felt divine as he gulped it down, feeling it flow through his throat and down into his stomach. Crunching the empty plastic bottle in his hand, Kit looked around for a bin. As luck would have it, a bin sat a few feet away, swarming with flies. They buzzed around excitedly as he drew closer and gingerly dropped the bottle like a sacrifice into their kingdom before backing away. Kit hated flies.

Hydration made the walk a little easier, but it still couldn't be described as enjoyable. His mind raced with a thousand thoughts; each one competing for his attention. He'd fucked that job interview up. He knew it. And he knew exactly where he had gone wrong. What sort of question was *"what kind of animal are you?"*? An important one, apparently, and "*worm*" just hadn't been the kind of answer they were hoping to hear. Kit's heart had sunk as he looked at the faces of both interviewers when he answered. The moment they stopped happily scribbling into their notebooks he knew it was over. That was never a good sign. Why on earth had he said "*worm*"? Kit still couldn't decide if he was just trying to be funny, or if it was all his stressed little brain could come up with.

Worm.

Who the fuck said "*worm*"? Is that how he saw himself?

It had been his third job interview in two weeks and, rather than getting used to the interviewing process, his meagre skills were declining. His nerves refused to settle, and he stumbled over his words. Nerves and humidity ganged up on him, making sure his armpits and brow were always sweaty. Nobody wanted to shake the hand of a sweaty man. No-one would ever hire him at this rate.

Kit paused at the crossing of the crossroads. Ahead, a multitude of bars and clubs awaited him, each one ready and willing to help him drown his sorrows and forget his troubles in exchange for a couple of handfuls of his rapidly disappearing savings. Well, probably more than a couple of handfuls, Kit thought. The price of a pint was ridiculous these days. Home waited to the left, while a park and another residential area lurked to the right. A beer sounded bloody good, but Kit knew he had to save his money. Without a regular salary, his savings were dwindling at an alarming rate. Kit needed a job, and fast. Turning his head up to the sky, as if praying to Heaven and a god that didn't seem to have any idea that he existed, Kit waited a few moments. No divine entity revealed itself. No answers. No help. Only the sun's searing heat burning his already sunburnt face.

'I just need a job.' he said to nobody in particular. 'I'd sell my soul for a fuckin' job.'

Unnoticed by Kit, or anyone else around, the shadows cast by the buildings, people and vehicles started to darken. Somehow, they were becoming more whole. Shapes began to form. Vaguely humanoid, they looked to one another before making an exit; destination unknown. God may not have been listening, but someone was. Someone was always listening.

A woman stared at him, trying to work out if he was using a hands-free kit and having conversation with someone elsewhere, or if he was just crazy. The modern-age had made it incredibly difficult to pick out the weirdos from the general population. The woman, seemingly convinced that the sweaty man was indeed crazy, increased her speed and gave him a wide berth, doing everything she could to avoid eye contact. Kit just smiled and went back to his thoughts. Who cares if she thought he was crazy?

A car horn sounded, and brakes screeched. Without realising it, Kit had wandered into the centre of the road, cars swerved around him, trying to avoid getting blood and guts on their bumpers. After all, that was a bugger to clean off. Now he jumped out of the path of one car, only to find himself in the path of another. His breath caught in his throat. His bowels threatened to let go. The second car just missed him, but he felt the air move next to him as it sped past.

Standing at the centre of the crossroads, Kit breathed a sigh of relief. That was close; he'd felt certain that his time was up. He really needed to pay more attention to what he was doing. His body, only just realising what had happened, started to shake.

Now I need a stiff drink AND a job, he thought to himself and decided that perhaps going to a pub was a good idea. Probably the best idea he'd had all day. Besides, one drink would help to settle his nerves. Two drinks would be a commiseration prize for not getting that job. And Kit could easily find excuses for any other drinks that he decided to consume while in there.

Making sure to the look both ways, Kit crossed the remainder of the road and headed to the first pub he could see. Several people stared at him, but quickly averted their eyes when he looked back. No-one wanted a confrontation with the crazy dude who talked to himself and played with traffic.

The pub's door creaked open and Kit half expected its clientele to pause their conversations and turn to look at him. Instead, nobody paid him any attention whatsoever. This wasn't one of those old Westerns when the outsider walked into the bar and caught everyone's interest. Nobody stopped playing a jaunty tune on a piano to turn and look at him. Hell, there wasn't even a piano. To Kit's surprise, the pub stood half empty. It seemed that maybe other people were not drawn to a pub at the first sight of sunshine, or maybe they just had planned to cool off in another drinking establishment. Either way, it meant that Kit had a choice of tables to sit at. He chose none of them. Kit planned to prop himself up at the bar for the duration of his stay.

'Can I help?' the barman asked, again ruining Kit's expectations. The barman didn't ask him *'what'll it be?'* as he should have done to fit in with Kit's internal Western movie.

'A pint of Hobgoblin and a shot of whiskey, please.' Kit said, pulling his wallet from his trousers.

'Any particular whiskey?' the barman asked as he started to pull Kit's pint.

'Whatever you've got.' Kit said, and the barman nodded.

Kit paid for his drinks, thanked the barman and started to study the pub. A song played just loud enough for Kit to hear, but not so loud to interrupt any conversations. Music at the perfect volume. Sadly, it was not the perfect song, it was one of those ones that just kept repeating the same lyric over and over again making you want to scream or drive a screwdriver through your own eardrum. Or both. So, Kit pulled out his MP3 player and popped one of the earbuds in, leaving the other earbud-free, in case someone should need to talk to him. Although unlikely, someone may want to ask him to move out of the way.

The song playing in his left ear was *"The South"* by *The Cadillac Three*; one of Kit's 'go to' songs at the moment. Had a bad day? Stick *The Cadillac Three* on. In a great mood? Must be time for *The Cadillac Three*!

Kit knocked back his whiskey, enjoying the burning sensation as it ran down his throat. Now he felt even hotter, but at least there was air conditioning in the pub. As he took a small mouthful of beer, Kit began to relax and immerse himself in his music. The song sang about living and dying in the same town, making it sound romantic. While *The Cadillac Three* were singing about the American south, Kit felt that the phrase could also be applied to Croydon, Surrey. But nobody wrote songs like that about Croydon. Croydon wasn't inspirational like that. It was the kind of place you tried to escape from. Known by many as the 'Arsehole of London', Croydon became known as a ‘shithole’. So, while Kit was born here and was likely to die here, it wouldn’t be by choice. Nobody stuck around inside an arsehole by choice. Even the most stubborn of turds eventually vacated. Except for Kit. Kit was destined to stick around forever.

Vibrations from his phone grabbed his attention, so he checked the screen. Without unlocking it he could see it was a text from his mother. Not only was this obvious because her name popped up on the display, but also because of the first two words: *'Hi Bernie'*. His mother always insisted on calling him by his real name or, at very least, a variation of it. Much to his annoyance, Kit's real name wasn't Kit, it was Bernard. And he hated it. Thankfully, since the age of eight years old, most people had called him Kitt due to his rather unhealthy obsession with *'Knight Rider'*. At some point over the years he’d decided to drop the final T. Kit's mother was not most people. She'd named him 'Bernard' and she stubbornly stuck to it. Besides, she thought calling him 'Bernie' was cute. It wasn't. It really wasn't. Other people may have been fine with the name, but Kit felt like it didn't suit him. At least, not in the way that 'Kit' did. He'd often wondered if everyone should be named after stuff they liked. Wouldn't that make more sense than the current system? Perhaps. Perhaps not. It would mean that there would be a lot of nameless babies hanging around while their parents waited to see what toy, music, book or TV show they gravitated towards. No, maybe that was a terrible idea.

Returning his attention back to his phone, Kit still refused to read the whole text. He had an idea of what it would say anyway. His mother would want to know how he got on at the interview and Kit didn't want to disappoint her. Kit was one of the middle children in a family with four kids. His older brother had become a successful lawyer, his younger sister had worked hard to be a doctor and his youngest brother owned his own restaurant. His whole family oozed success, with the exception of Kit. Kit felt like a failure.

In fairness, he still hadn't received a call about the interview to confirm either way, but Kit was a realist leaning towards becoming a pessimist. If he had got the job, he would have heard by now. Besides, who would hire a worm?

Kit downed his beer and looked up the bar to get the barman's attention.

'Same again?' the barman asked.

'Absolutely.' Kit replied, stifling a belch. He handed the barman some more money and waited for his drinks. If he continued like this, he'd be slaughtered by teatime.

'Are you OK?' the barman said as he handed Kit his change. ‘I hope you don't me saying so, but you look like shi-... I mean, you look... er... worried.'

'Yeah,' Kit said, taking a sip of his pint. It tasted just as good, if not better, than the first one. 'You must be good at picking up on that kind of thing working in here. Does everyone burden you with their problems?'

The barman nodded and began wiping down the bar. 'They tell me a lot, but I don't mind. It kinda feels nice to help, y'know?'

'I guess.' Kit said with a small smile. 'Personally, it would drive me mad.'

'It's fine. I don't let it bother me. It comes with the territory.' The barman placed yet another pint in front of

Kit, but instead of walking away, he remained in front of him on the opposite side of the bar. 'Got anything you want to talk about?'

Kit wasn't big on talking about his problems. People said that a problem shared was a problem halved, but that didn't make a lot of sense to him. He could tell this barman about his troubles, but they'd still be there. It wouldn't and couldn't change anything.

'Nah,' Kit said. 'I'm cool.'

'OK, let me know if you change your mind.' the barman said, a reassuring smile spread across his face and then he started to move away. 'I'll be here if you need me.'

Kit let him walk away. Complete strangers who wanted to listen to the bitching and moaning of others were weird. Unnerving in a way. Kinda creepy. Still, he supposed, some people were like that. Some people were very odd indeed.

The drinks kept coming as the day wore on. At some point before the evening rush, Kit found himself wanting to open up. As promised, the barman stood by, ready to listen to him. Kit started to tell the barman - for he was still just a barman, Kit hadn't even thought to ask his name - all about his failed interviews and his money troubles. It felt like he talked for hours and the barman barely said a word, only interjecting words full of wisdom at random points. Kit had to admit that even though his confidant hadn't taken his problems away, or even offered any advice, he did feel a whole lot better. He didn't even bother to pick up when his phone rang; his interviewers could tell his answerphone that he didn't have a job. He didn't need to listen to their half-hearted feedback about how he only just missed on the post because another interviewee had more experience or had given them a better answer than 'worm'.

Sometime later, a young woman entered the pub. She ordered a drink and then buried herself in her phone, actively ignoring anyone who looked in her direction. Maybe she was waiting for someone, or maybe she just wanted a quiet drink by herself; with no way of knowing, it would have to remain a mystery. Not without asking her, anyway. The newly open and ready-to-share Kit thought about talking to her, but her body language screamed '*FUCK OFF!*', so he refrained. Instead, he signalled to the barman for another drink. Both his liver and his wallet were taking a beating, but those were problems for Future Kit; Present Kit planned on getting drunk.

'How badly do you want a job?' the barman said, handing over Pint Number Eight... or was it nine? Kit's hands reached for it greedily.

'You got a job for me here?' Kit's slurred speech failed to embarrass him now. Too much alcohol danced in his bloodstream for that.

'Something like that.' the barman said. 'So, how badly do you want a job.'

'I'd give anything.' Kit's mouth had trouble forming the words, so he took a couple of gulps of beer hoping they'd fix it. They didn't, but they didn't seem to make it any worse. Not that he could get any worse now.

'Anything?' the barman said, raising an eyebrow.

'Yeah, anything.'

That's when everything stopped for Kit and his body lay passed out on the pub's beer-soaked floor. Not for the first time that day, strangers stared at him and cast judgements.

CHAPTER TWO

The cab wouldn't arrive for another hour, so Christine decided to kill some time in a pub; it had to be better than melting outside. From outside, The Hound & The Philosopher Inn seemed like a welcoming kind of place and a sticker on the window promised air-conditioning and free Wi-Fi, while a small poster declared that food would be served until 10pm. It seemed just about perfect.

Inside the half empty pub, a small smattering of people scattered around, drinking contentedly. Most were confined to the booths and tables, carefully studying newspapers, books and phones or having subdued conversations, but one had perched himself against the bar. This one looked rough. He looked like he should have stopped drinking hours ago, but he still knocked them back with enthusiasm. Impressive really, since it was still technically only early evening. Dark circles covered eyes with dilated pupils. Yellow sweat stains lurked under his armpits. Christine easily imagined how he smelt without even being close to him.

Due to the layout of the pub, Christine had no choice but to stand near him at the small bar to order a drink, thus confirming her suspicions. The man smelt vile. A gag-reflex inducing bouquet of stale sweat, stale alcohol and a hint of desperation. Christine wondered how he could have let himself get into such a state, but she also supposed that he was past the point of caring. He certainly looked like he didn't give a shit.

While she waited for the barman to notice her, she fiddled with her phone; glad to have her personal People Avoidance Device in her pocket. The idea being that anyone looking at her would understand that she was busy and not to be disturbed. Everyone in The Hound & The Philosopher Inn seemed to understand this. Everyone except Drunk Guy. Drunk Guy kept staring at her, his mouth opening and closing like a goldfish while he tried to find something to say. Unsuccessful in his search for words, the guy shut his mouth, but continued to look in her direction.

As if sensing her discomfort, the barman looked over to her and smiled. The smile seemed to say *'Don't worry, I can help. I'll be with you in a moment'*. Christine didn't know how she could get all that from a smile, but that was how it was. Christine buried her head in her phone again and waited for the barman to finish serving the drunk man.

THUD.

The drunk guy lay in a heap on the floor, beer soaked his shirt. He lay still, possibly unconscious.

‘Should we call an ambulance?’ Christine asked the barman, as he peered over the bar. His face suggested a lack of concern, maybe even some amusement. Perhaps this was an everyday occurrence in The Hound & The Philosopher Inn. Maybe this was just how Drunk Guy rolled.

‘Nah, don't worry.’ The barman said. ‘I know him, and he'll be fine. He just needs to sleep it off.’

With that, the barman came out from behind the bar and grabbed the man under the armpits, apparently not caring about the abundance of sweat that resided there and Christine hoped that he’d wash his hands before he served her drink. The drunk guy offered no resistance as he dragged him across the floor and through a door that said, *“Staff Only”*. Christine tried to sneak a peek through the door before it closed behind them, but only darkness appeared to await them on the other side. Something about the whole situation struck Christine as being odd, but at the same time she felt completely at ease.

Soon enough, the barman returned. Again, he wore that reassuring smile.

‘Can I get you anything?’ he said, as he washed his hands, much to Christine's relief.

‘Are you sure that man is OK?’ Christine said, looking at the *“Staff Only”* door as if she hoped to see through it. Unsurprisingly, she hadn’t developed x-ray vision in the last ten minutes.

‘Yes, he's fine. Don't worry about it.’ The smile appeared again. ‘Would you like a drink?’

‘Yes, please. A rum and coke.’ She said, the drunk guy already forgotten. Under normal circumstances, Christine probably would have called an ambulance regardless of what she had been told, but she didn't feel the need to here. Everything was under control. She had no doubt of that.

‘Single or double?’ he said as he grabbed a glass.

‘Single, please.’ Christine said, and the barman nodded. While he made her drink, Christine studied him. The thing that struck her the most about his appearance was how incredibly average he was. Average height, average build, neither particularly good looking or ugly. He was as middle of the road as you could get. And, yet, it was this that made him stand out. Christine found that, despite knowing she had to leave soon, she wanted to talk to him for hours.

‘Anything else?’ he said as he gave her the drink and Christine fought back the urge to tell him her whole life story. She'd never met the man before and yet she wanted to tell him everything. Instead, not trusting herself to speak, she shook her head.

The barman looked around and, content that nobody needed his help at that moment, made his way back to the *“Staff Only”* door. *He must be going to check on that man*, Christine thought. At least he hadn't just been forgotten. If anyone would know what to do, she felt like the barman would. He seemed the trustworthy sort. Even though they had only exchanged a handful of words, Christine felt like she shared a connection with him.

Now that the barman had disappeared, Christine felt abandoned. The urge to stick around for hours on end dissipated. It left her feeling disorientated and alone. Checking her phone, she realised that she only had a few minutes left until her cab arrived. Time seemed to fly by in this pub. Christine downed her rum and coke and made her way to the door, allowing herself the briefest looks over her shoulder to see if the barman had materialised from the *“Staff Only”* door. Disappointment nagged at her when she saw he hadn't, so Christine continued on her way.

Walking through the door back onto the street felt like passing into another world. An intensely uncomfortable heat hit Christine immediately. Noise erupted around her. She hadn't realised how quiet the pub had been. Hovering in the open doorway allowed Christine to experience both worlds at the same time and the calm of the pub called to her. It would be easy to go back inside. She could cancel the cab and hang around for as long as she wanted.

Then her phone buzzed. A text appearing letting her know that her cab awaited her, and it gave the car's registration and description so that she could find it easily on the busy street. With a sigh, she stepped forward and let the door close behind her. The door closed slowly, as if reluctant, creaking and groaning its discontent. She understood how it felt; she didn't want to leave either. But, she knew that she couldn't stay there forever, so she walked away.

A noise nagged at her during that first step. Something like a scream, but without the urgency. Only idle curiosity tugged at her thoughts and she looked back through the window into The Hound & The Philosopher Inn. The same selection of patrons was there, each going about their own business, but none of them seemed interested by the scream. *Maybe I imagined it*, she thought. *I did drink that rum pretty quickly*. The rum's warmth still worked its way through her, as if trying to prove her hypothesis. Deciding that this was enough of an explanation, Christine set about searching for her cab. It didn't take long, and she was on her way home in no time.

The uneventful journey home gave her time to think. Even as she moved away from it, The Hound & The Philosopher Inn still had some kind of hold over her.

The only difference being that now her concern for the drunk guy kept increasing. What if he needed medical attention? What if the barman couldn't get him home?

But, the question that bugged her most during that journey home was the one that was going to haunt her for the rest of the night, preventing her from falling asleep.

What if she hadn't imagined that scream?

***

+ *We* +

+ *are* +

+ *always* +

+ *watching,* +

+ *listening,* +

+ *waiting...* +

CHAPTER THREE

Goosebumps covered his flesh. Cold claimed his body. This wasn't right. The middle of a heatwave shouldn't be the time for Kit to feel cold. He shivered and curled into a ball in an effort to retain some body heat. That's when it occurred to him that he was lying on the floor. A vague recollection of sitting at the bar and then falling backwards flashed across his memory. Well, at least that explained the headache.

A tightness clasped Kit's head, its vice-like grip getting tighter and tighter, convincing Kit that his head might pop at any moment. Moving slowly, Kit touched his forehead. It was hot and sweaty; feverish. Meanwhile, his fingers were like icicles. None of this made any sense.

With no small amount of effort (in fact, it felt like he was on an expedition to the peak of Everest), Kit opened his eyes to be greeted with darkness. Waving a hand in front of his face revealed nothing. Kit had no idea that darkness could be this complete, this absolute. An oppressive, heavy force that threatened to crush him. His pulse quickened. His heart pounded in his chest.

Lying on the floor made Kit feel vulnerable, so he jumped to his feet and immediately bashed his head, increasing his headache tenfold. Fighting to hold onto consciousness, Kit clenched his teeth and groaned. Wherever he was, it had a bloody low ceiling. Kit sat back down and that's when he realised he lacked any kind of clothing. Nothing at all. He sat there completely and utterly starkers. He also realised that the floor wasn't carpeted, and it wasn't wood. It wasn't even lino. Pure earth lurked beneath him. Mud and grit scratched against his butt cheeks. The sensation wasn't entirely unpleasant, but what the hell had happened?

Since sight was out of the question, Kit started to pay closer attention to his other senses. The earthy smell of the place flooded his nostrils, along with something else. An animal scent covered everything, invading his nose and he could feel it on his tongue. The taste lingered on his taste-buds. It reminded Kit a little of a wet dog, but not quite. It felt more than that. It felt different; dangerous and bestial. A predator had been here recently. Perhaps this was its lair. A thought started to emerge in Kit's aching head. Was he prey? His already shivering body shuddered again with the thought.

Deciding that he wasn't going to sit around and wait to be eaten by some murderous creature, Kit started to search for a way out. If he got in here, then it stood to reason that he should also be able to get back out. His hands moved in frantic movements against the walls made of stone and earth. They were alive, full of things growing and living on them, adding to the earthy scent. At one point Kit thought his fingers brushed up against a worm. The Universe's idea of a joke was not lost on him.

It felt like he had been walking for hours; time moved in odd ways in this void. Without his sight, Kit couldn't be sure if he was stuck in a tiny little box room, or if he wandered lost in a vast labyrinth. Darkness played havoc with his sense of direction, turning him around in circles. He needed a better plan and he couldn't shake the feeling that he was running out of time; whatever lived in here was bound to return sooner or later. He paused, straining his ears to listen. Faintly, as if hundreds of miles in the distance, Kit could hear voices. Voices mingled with laughter and the clinking of glasses. Testing the walls again, he realised that he could reach both sides with his outstretched arms while he stood in the middle. Guiding himself in this manner prevented him from spinning around. Every step he took felt like real progress. Every step took him away from the cold. Kit headed in the direction of the merry voices.

Some time later the tunnel started to shrink and Kit had to start crawling, the walls began to close in. Kit had never been one to be bothered by small, enclosed spaces, but claustrophobia gripped him. What if he got stuck? He could be trapped here for days. Or, worse, whatever lived here could rip the flesh from his bones and take its time with consuming him and there would be nothing he could do about it. Kit crawled and shuffled along faster and almost smiled when the tunnel broke off into two directions. The tunnel on the left contained the sounds of people and the smells of alcohol. The tunnel on the right presented him with the sounds of traffic. Both tunnels carried the stench of animal. Neither way felt safe.

Kit's first thought had been to head towards the voices; towards civilisation. He could already picture the scene that awaited him; the pub (because somehow, he now knew his location), happy faces, a welcoming atmosphere and a stiff drink. Maybe more than one stiff drink. Maybe even some food. Something stopped him from running in that direction, even though his stomach rumbled. What if they weren't as friendly as he had hoped? Someone had dragged him into that tunnel. Someone had stripped him. Someone had left him there as a snack for whatever called that cold, dark, damp place home. What if that someone was currently knocking a few pints back with those other voices? What if they were waiting for him right now? Hell, they could all be in on it. What kind of pub was this?

Kit skulked back into the tunnel, like a small rodent avoiding detection, and crawled along the other tunnel. Warm night air awaited him, and a slight breeze tickled at his bare skin. He stood at the back of the pub, in an area likely used for deliveries. It was empty now, much to Kit's relief.

The yard contained several barrels and a collection of boxes, all stacked meticulously. Apart from one. One lonely, beaten up cardboard box sat in the middle of the yard. On it, written in thick, red marker pen sat one word: *KIT*.

Seeing his name like that stopped him in his tracks. They (whoever *'they'* were) had known that he would come this way. He was playing right into their hands, following their script. A script he had never read. A script where he couldn't even guess at the ending. Kit felt like he was performing his role for an unseen audience. His skin prickled as he stood there, imagining mysterious eyes looking over his flesh. He felt exposed.

Despite likely doing exactly what they wanted him to do, Kit walked over to the box. For a brief moment, he thought that he might open it to find a severed head or something equally terrifying, but the contents of the box turned out to be completely mundane. The box contained his clothing and possessions, the clothing neatly folded, but still dirty with the day's grime and stale beer. Why strip him naked only to give him back his clothes? None of this made any sense.

As if scared that someone planned to snatch the contents of the box away, Kit dressed in a speed that he never knew he possessed, pulling on his smart, yet filthy black trousers and sweat stained white shirt over his shivering body. His clothes felt strange against his skin, scratchy and uncomfortable, as if they belonged to someone else, but he was certain that they belonged to him. After all, it seemed unlikely that another guy called Kit had an outfit stashed in a box outside a pub. Then again, all this swelled under a cloud of unlikeliness. A wallet, a set of keys and a mobile phone were shoved into his trouser pockets. Kit didn't even bother to open the wallet and check to see if everything was there. It didn't seem important at the moment and he wasn't exactly rolling in cash anyway. He also didn't bother to check his phone. Kit just wanted to get away from this place as fast as possible. He shoved his feet into his shoes. Shoes that were uncomfortable and tight, but a glance down told him that they were the exact same shoes that he had worn to the interview earlier that day. Had he had a growth spurt? Was it even still the same day? The idea that he had been unconscious in that tunnel for longer than a few minutes scared him almost as much as the idea of being eaten by the nameless animal. Anything could have happened in that time. They could have done anything to him and he still didn't know who *they* were. He pulled the phone back out of his pocket and checked the date on the screen. Much to his relief, it was still today. This meant that his feet had grown too big for his shoes in a couple of hours. He didn't know if this was a good or a bad thing.

Kit hobbled along the yard towards a gate. An unlocked gate. One that allowed Kit to just step out onto the street. A sense of normalcy accompanied the street. The sounds of cars and people lifted his spirits and the glow from the street lights and shop and bar fronts provided a relief after being stuck in the tunnel. But, the best thing of all, was the smell. The street smelt alive. It reeked of people. It stank of gasoline. Under normal circumstances, Kit probably would have found it revolting, but it smelt divine compared to the animal stench he'd been living with recently. The smell of the street may not have been pleasant, but at least it didn't smell dangerous. It didn't smell like it was going to kill and devour him. It just smelt... *normal.* Awesomely, fantastically, normal.

Now that Kit had escaped immediate danger, he took a moment to think about that. He'd never thought of smells being dangerous or safe and he'd never been able to smell people in the way that he detected them now. In the last couple of hours, something had heightened his sense of smell and made his feet grow. As he hobbled home in shoes that now felt at least a size too small, he wondered what other changes were waiting for him. Maybe he would awaken tomorrow morning to discover that he had superpowers. A montage of superhero movies danced through his mind as he walked, leaving him convinced that any superpowers he possessed would soon reveal themselves and that he would soon be able to use them to save the planet. He wondered what his superhero name would be. Did you get to choose your name, or did you have to wait for the press or the general public to assign one to you? What would he be? Bigfoot Man? Heightened Sense of Smell Man?

Finally, he reached the house that he shared with four other people. Kit couldn't afford to live alone, so this was the next best thing. Besides, right now the thought of walking into an empty house would have been unbearable. Kit needed to be around people. He needed to be around life. On the flip side, he knew that he looked awful, so he would need to try to sneak past everyone and freshen up first. He wanted to be around his housemates and have normal conversations with them. He didn't want to talk about where he'd been or what had happened to him. Hell, he didn't even know what had happened to him, how could he hope to explain it to someone else?

Sounds and smells rushed at him as he opened the front door. The sounds of one of his housemates cutting her toenails in the upstairs bathroom were instantly detectable, followed by the sound of someone stirring a cup of tea in the kitchen. Kit could also hear someone else tapping away at a keyboard in one of the bedrooms. Sniffing the air told him that one of his companions had eaten fried chicken earlier that day, while another had devoured some sushi.

Without calling out a greeting, Kit made his way to his bedroom, being careful not to tread on the creaky step on the staircase. The plan remained the same: clean up first, then come back down and talk to everyone.

In his room, Kit grabbed a pair of tracksuit bottoms and a clean t-shirt. Remembering the toenail cutter, he abandoned his journey to the bathroom. If he was going to freshen up quickly, he had to do it in his room. Since a shower was out of the question, Kit settled for spraying himself thoroughly with antiperspirant and running his hands through his hair. He looked in the small mirror that he had nailed to the wall. He didn't look brilliant, but it was already a vast improvement on five minutes ago. The clean clothes really finished the look off.

The reflection of his face in the mirror stole his attention for a while. His face, while still clearly recognisable as his own, looked different for some reason. Something discreet enough to avoid immediate detection, but different enough to disturb him. A doppelganger looked back at him, an almost perfect doppelganger. One mistake, one difference continued to heckle him. Hiding just out of reach. Several moments passed while he examined the image in the mirror in front of him, squinting at it, trying to read it. After a while, his efforts were rewarded.

Kit's usually blue eyes were flecked with bits of yellow.

CHAPTER FOUR

The barman wiped the bar down. There were always more spillages as the night wore on, and the drunken behaviour of his customers always amused him. After all, the more alcohol they consumed, the chattier they became.

The more they talked, the more he learned.

The more he learned, the better he knew his clients.

All this helped him towards finding out one crucial piece of information:

It meant that he discovered their price.

And, as the barman knew all too well, everybody has a price.

CHAPTER FIVE

The comfortable bed embraced her, but Christine couldn't sleep too long or too deeply. Exhausting all her usual tricks (one foot out beneath the blanket, fan on, window open, sheep counted), she got up and walked to the window. Outside, despite the late hour, there were still people milling around, in various states of intoxication doing whatever people do in the very early hours of the morning, at the point where 'tomorrow' turns into 'today'. Aside from the odd shout or lone car horn, the night was peaceful; the outside providing no reason why she shouldn't be able to sleep. Those reasons hid inside her head. Her mind just couldn't let go of the events of the last few hours. The scream – real or imagined – weighed heavily on her mind, anchoring her in wakefulness. Going back to bed would be pointless, so Christine turned to check the clock radio on her nightstand to see if it was a reasonable time to make coffee and start on breakfast. Darkness stood in the place where red digits usually waited.

That's odd, she thought. *Must be a power cut or something.*

Bare feet paced across the room and she tried the light switch. It didn't work. No change - not even a flicker - happened after she'd clicked it on and off again half a dozen times. *Maybe a fuse has blown*, she thought.

Glad to have something to do, Christine crossed back to her nightstand, opened the drawer and pulled out a torch. A big heavy thing that took a seemingly infinite supply of those huge batteries. Sometimes she thought about replacing it with something more compact, but she liked the idea of having it close to her at night. Christine lived alone, and she thought the torch might prove itself to be a useful weapon if anyone chose to break in. Not that it could do much damage, but a decent swing to the head with enough force behind it might slow any wannabe attacker enough for her to make a hasty escape.

The space in front of her immediately illuminated as she hit the power switch. Christine couldn't remember when she had last replaced the batteries, but the light held bright and strong. As she swung the light around her bedroom, she wondered if any passers-by would mistake her for a burglar. She dismissed the thought almost as soon as it had formed. Of course, no-one would. Nobody would be remotely interested. You could be bleeding from every orifice and screaming like someone insisted on inserting a very large, very sharp metal pole up your rectum and nobody would even bat an eyelid. Everyone here was too involved in their own business. In many ways, this was one of the things that Christine liked about her current location; she had anonymity here. It also nagged at her. What if the hypothetical attacker did break in? She'd be on her own. The big torch filled the role of being her first and last lines of defence.

With the torch tightly gripped in her left hand, Christine carefully made her way down stairs. The fuse box was just by the front door, almost directly in front of the staircase. She'd look inside and with a quick flick of the switch there would light and radio alarm clocks. Her hand touched the door of the fuse box, but, before she could open it, she noticed something amiss.

It felt like she was being watched.

Her heart quickened in her chest. Was this it? Was the hypothetical attacker real? Faking nonchalance, she slowly turned around.

A face stared back at her, the whites of its eyes wild.

It took Christine a long moment to realise that she was looking at her own reflection in the mirror on the wall. She smiled, even though part of her that thought that the reflection wouldn't do the same. Her eyes locked with the mirror image. There was nothing unusual here, her reflection only looked sinister due to the dark shadows caused by torchlight. Nothing to worry about. There were no ghoulish apparitions in the house. Everything was fine.

That's what she told herself.

But that feeling of unseen eyes studying her remained, making her skin prickle. Frantically, she looked around, trying to take in every bit of her surroundings. She knew this house, she'd lived here for seven years, so she could account for every shape and every shadow. *Maybe I'm just shaken because of what happened at the pub*, she thought, reasoning with herself. She turned back to the fuse box.

Knock...

Knock...

Knock...

The knocking was quiet, but intentional. It didn't need to be loud, she was standing right next to the door. Whoever stood on the other side waited just a few inches away, separated by a lump of wood. Christine hoped it was a very strong, very secure lump of wood. If she concentrated, she could hear breathing. Ragged, feral breathing. More animal than human. *This is stupid*, she thought, but it didn't stop her from tightening her grip on the torch even more. Cramp threatened to take her hand hostage. Knuckles whitened with the effort.

For a moment, Christine couldn't move. She wanted to flick the switch in the fuse box and she wanted to check the peep hole, but she did neither of those things. At that time, those things were impossible. Christine stood perfectly still, feeling like any movement would betray her, and tried to remember how to breathe. She'd been breathing for years, surviving perfectly independently… Why couldn't she do it now?

Finally, she convinced herself to move. Slowly, carefully and as quietly as possible, she moved towards the door. Her hands touched the wood panelling and her face closed in on the peephole. The little round hole revealed the world outside.

There was nobody there.

I'm imagining things. I must be sleep deprived.

After she had examined the view through the peephole for a little while longer, her eyes persuaded her that nobody had come to visit. Almost. Christine may have been sleep deprived, and she may have been paranoid, but what was the saying? *Just because you're paranoid, it doesn't mean they're not after you.* Having confirmed that there was nobody outside her front door, Christine decided to return to her original task. She aimed the torch back at the fuse box and stepped back over to it. She took one step. Then another.

Then the torch died.

Darkness swallowed Christine. A feeling of panic started to grow inside her. Starting in the pit of her stomach, it forced its way up into her throat. Asphyxia wrapped its claws around her. She took deep breaths, trying to calm herself. This was stupid; a grown woman shouldn't be afraid of the dark. Besides, she could work out which switch needed flicking by touch. She'd be basking in artificial light in no time at all. Her left hand refused to let go of the torch – the thought of the hypothetical attacker still firmly lodged in her mind – so she used her right hand to feel its way around the outside of the fuse box. Soon enough, she found the small handle and opened the box. The small door omitted a high-pitched squeak as it opened, making Christine cringe. If an intruder stalked around the house, they would have heard that. Still, she needed to open that little door, it was the only way that she was going to get any light. Once again, her hand reached forward, aiming for the area where she thought the rows of switches started.

Then she paused.

What if there was something in the fuse box? What if her hand plunged into a massive spider web? What if a creature with thousands of legs now reached out for her hand as her hand reached for the switches? Christine swallowed, trying to force the revulsion that she felt back inside. She was being irrational.

Christine reached out, pushing the thought of touchy-feely little creatures from her mind. Slowly her hand closed the distance. Her fingertip touched a corner of the first switch and then moved to the next. No critters touched her, and nothing bit her. Christine methodically continued with her task. She allowed herself to calm down and breathe more easily. She was fine. Everything was fine.

Knock…

Christine's heart nearly leapt out of her chest.

Knock…

She turned her head towards the door. Anger replaced terror, violently pushing it out of the way. An idiot teenager probably waited on the other side, thoroughly enjoying their idea of a joke.

Knock…

Stopping her task once again, Christine almost threw herself towards the door. She peered through the peephole, expecting to see nothing or, at very least, the sight of someone running away, laughing at her expense. Neither of those visions met her eye.

Outside stood a man wearing a dark suit.

And sunglasses.

At night.

He stood there with an air of authority. His demeanour didn't suggest that he was involved in a prank and his stance certainly wasn't that of a drunk. Christine felt compelled to open the door, but she held back. Who the hell was he and why the hell was he here?

'Christine.' The man said softly, but loud enough for her to hear on the other side of the door. 'I know you're there.'

Christine held her breath and continued to watch.

'I just want to talk to you. I have something important to say.'

The man's words were met with silence and stillness.

'It's about The Hound & The Philosopher Inn.'

This got Christine's attention. 'What about it?'

Her quiet voice must have been muffled through the door, but the man appeared to hear it perfectly. 'Open the door and I'll tell you.'

Christine knew that no matter what, she shouldn't open the door. Keeping that door shut ensured her survival. Nothing about this situation felt safe. She lived in an area where nobody gave two shits about their neighbours, in a house on her own, in the dark, with nothing but a dead torch for protection. All that was bad enough even before you considered the strange man on the other side of the door. The man that Christine was now starting to think of as a creepy James Bond. There was no doubt about it, the rational side of her brain knew that she absolutely shouldn't even consider opening that door. The trouble was that the rational side of her brain was in complete disagreement with the curious side of her brain. This man might be able to give her answers. If she had answers, then maybe she could sleep.

Christine opened the door and brandished the torch like a baseball bat, hoping that it would put creepy 007 off attacking her.

'Hello Christine.' He said, not at all bothered by Christine's choice of weapon. Christine noticed this and immediately found her torch woefully inadequate. 'Sorry to bother you at this hour.'

'It's fine.' She said. It wasn't. How could it be?

'Fantastic. I didn't want to disturb you.'

'You said that you wanted to talk to me about The Hound & The Philosopher Inn?'

'Yes,' the man said, taking a step forward. Christine immediately took a step back. 'You were there a few hours ago, weren't you?'

Christine nodded.

'I've been lead to believe that you may have seen or heard some things that you weren't meant to.' He said. 'We're going to need you to forget all about them.'

'What things?'

'You know what things.'

'Who are "we"?'

'You don't need to know. You just need to forget.'

Before Christine knew what was happening, the man had moved even closer and grabbed her arm, completely ignoring her weapon. His grip was strong, and Christine knew that her arm would be bruised come morning.

'Stay away from the pub.' He said. 'Do not mention it to anyone. Do you understand?'

Christine nodded.

'If you were to talk to anyone – and I do mean anyone – about what you think you've witnessed, things will end very badly for you. Do you understand?'

Christine nodded again. She had no doubt that some tragic end would befall her if she disobeyed the man.

'I know…' the man said, smiling at having come to some kind of decision in his head. 'I'll give you a taster of what you can expect. Pay close attention now.'

'No… please don't hurt me!' Christine twisted in the man's grip, unable to escape. It was like he possessed a superhuman strength. 'I understand. I won't say a word! I promise!'

The man held his free hand in front of Christine's face. At first, she thought he intended to hit her, but when no hit came, she focused her attention onto the hand, unsure of what else to do. As she stared, the man's index finger started to stretch unnaturally. She could hear the bones inside it creak and crack and grow and alter their shape. Not only did the finger grow in length, but the knuckles widened, and the skin turned grey. At the finger's tip, a talon-like claw began to form. The claw looked deadly, and sharp as a knife.

Christine screamed.

Nobody seemed to notice. Nobody came to her rescue.

With a nauseating slowness, the man guided his hand to her arm and plunged that deadly blade-like claw into her flesh. Blood pooled around it and dribbled along his hand. The man let go of Christine, but she stayed still, transfixed on the monster in front of her. While he knew that he had her undivided attention, the man licked her blood from his deformed finger. The man's predatory smile widened. Making him even more sinister. Making him look like a wolf.

***

After the man had left, Christine sat on the floor in the dark for a long time, leaning against the now closed front door. Why had she ever opened that front door?

Gradually, she forced herself up from the floor and made her way to the fuse box. Soon enough, she flicked a switch and then felt around for the light switch. Instant palpable relief coursed through her as she turned it on and light filled the hallway and illuminated the objects in it. Most of the shadows vanished almost instantly, but some lingered a little too long like they didn't want to leave. Christine decided that she must have imagined it. She was in shock.

***

Once back in bed, she fell asleep almost instantly, barely noticing the shadows closing in around her, clawing at her bed clothes. Her sleep was so deep she almost didn’t notice the words whispered into her ear.

***

+ Don't +

+ say +

+ a +

+ word +

CHAPTER SIX

After grabbing two Grande skinny lattes from her favourite coffee shop, Shannon Hackett embarked upon her short journey to her usual lunch spot, trying to work out if she'd made the right decision in not getting a cake as well. Every Wednesday when the weather allowed it, Shannon went to the same park bench overlooking a beautiful pond and met her best friend Christine. Together, they put the world right, drank coffee, ate sandwiches and watched the ducks. The fresh air and the abundance of life of all kinds was the perfect respite from office life. And, even though the road ran by it, the park still felt like a little slice of nature, separate and independent from the day-to-day world.

As expected, Christine waited on the bench when Shannon arrived. Usually her friend would be studying something on her phone or reading a book, but today she was just staring into space. She didn't even notice Shannon walking towards her.

'Hey Chrissie!' Shannon called as she got closer. At first Christine didn't answer. Instead, she just continued to stare straight ahead. Her eyes were unfocused, not even taking in the scene of a duck and her ducklings in the pond in front of her, something that would usually fill her with excitement and have her reaching for her phone to take photos and videos. Her Instagram followers lapped that kind of stuff up.

'Chrissie? Hello?' Shannon said as she sat down and held out one of the coffees to her friend. 'Are you in there?'

Christine looked up, her eyes were tired, both from exhaustion and from crying. Her voice was scratchy and raw as she spoke. 'Hi.'

It seemed like that single word took a lot of effort and that anything more would have caused her pain.

'Christine, don't take this the wrong way, but you look awful. What's wrong? Here, have a coffee.'

Christine took the coffee, and, for the first time, Shannon noticed that her friend was shivering. Sutton was still in the middle of a heatwave and Shannon was pretty sure that parts of her body that she didn't even know existed were sweating and yet Christine shivered like a leaf in a blizzard. The shaking woman gripped the warm takeaway coffee cup like a lifeline, stealing its warmth through her hands.

'I'm scared, Shan. I don't think I've ever been more scared in my life.' Christine said after taking a delicate sip of the coffee. Shannon put her own coffee down on the ground and slid along the bench to be closer. Christine didn't seem to notice and didn't even react when Shannon put her arm around her. Even though her body was there, her mind had wandered somewhere else.

'You're starting to scare me now. What happened? Do you want to go somewhere more private?'

Christine looked around as if only just noticing where she was.

'No, it doesn't make a difference.' she said. Not only did she look scared and tired, she also looked defeated. A brief silence filled the gap after Christine spoke, and Shannon took the opportunity to take a proper look at her friend. Her hair was a mess, her skin pale, and her hands still shook. Her lips were split, and dry blood covered them; Shannon couldn't tell if this was due to exhaustion or illness, or if Christine had been self-harming. Maybe it was some kind of stress relief? Whatever had happened to her had affected her a huge amount. Anything that could affect Shannon's usually grounded friend in this way was worth worrying about and Shannon certainly was worried.

'Christine,' Shannon said softly. Now her voice was shaking. Fear was contagious, easily infecting anyone in a close enough range. 'Please tell me what happened.'

Christine swallowed nervously and nodded, resolving herself to telling her friend everything.

'I went to a pub yesterday...' Christine began.

'Did someone touch you? Do you want me to call the police?' Shannon interrupted before making herself bite her own tongue. She knew she needed to shut up but seeing her friend like this was too much. She just wanted to help her. 'Sorry... you continue. I'll ask questions at the end.'

'There was a weird drunk guy there.' Christine said, continuing her story, and Shannon felt sure she knew how this story would end. She'd wait for Christine to finish telling her story and then she'd track down this rapey scumbag, rip his cock off and make him eat it. Then she'd make sure that Christine got the help that she needed.

'Nothing like that.' Christine said, apparently reading the expression on her friend's face and, apparently, her mind. ‘I know what you're thinking. The guy didn't even talk to me - there was no contact whatsoever, so don't worry about that.’

Christine paused, thinking about how she should continue. Suddenly it all seemed rather ridiculous. The idea that her best friend might not believe her started to gnaw at her, nibbling at the edge of each of her thoughts. But, she'd gone too far now, she couldn't just brush this off as nothing. She knew that Shannon wouldn't let it go.

‘This is going to sound weird.’

‘Don't worry, you can tell me.’ Shannon urged her on, wanting to get to the bottom of this.

‘The guy was drunk.’

‘Like you said.’

‘Yeah, like I said. And, it looked like he was about to say something to me, but he didn't. He got another drink from the barman instead and then just collapsed.’

‘That doesn't seem so weird.’ Shannon said. ‘Drunk people fall over all the time. Do you remember me at Morgan's party last year? I drank so much that I passed out next to the toilet.’

‘I know... that's not the weird part." Christine continued. "After he fell, the barman dragged him away.’

‘Maybe he was just taking him somewhere to sleep it off.’

‘Yeah, that's what I thought. And, while I was in the pub, it all seemed pretty normal. But, as soon as I walked outside, I started to think that it was pretty odd. Why wouldn't the barman just call the guy a cab - or an ambulance - why drag him out back?’

‘Umm...’ Shannon thought about this. ‘Maybe he knew him. Maybe they were friends. Or maybe they were related. They could be brothers or something. It could be that this happens a lot to this guy and the barman was used it.’

'Maybe...' Christine replied. 'But... then something else happened.'

It didn't seem possible, but even more colour seemed to drain out of Christine's cheeks as she contemplated the next part of her story. Her skin became almost translucent. Whatever had happened was causing her to fade away. Her body shivered.

'What happened?' Shannon asked, starting to feel a chill herself, even though the temperature hadn't changed.

'When...' Christine started to talk. Her words came out slowly, as she chose each one carefully. 'When I left the pub, I heard a scream.'

'Okay...'

'But no-one else seemed to hear it. Or, if they did, they weren't bothered by it. I was sure that it came from inside the pub, but when I looked back inside, nobody had moved. Nobody looked scared. They all just continued to nurse their beers and chat about whatever they were chatting about.'

'Maybe you imagined it?' Shannon said, wondering why this had freaked her friend out so much.

'That's what I thought... at first.' Christine said. 'But, why would I imagine it? I thought about it a lot in the cab on the way home... and even more when I got home.'

'You've probably worked yourself up over nothing. You need to get some sleep. Call into work and go home. You'll feel better after you've slept.'

'That's the other thing; I have slept. Or, at least, I think I have.'

'What do you mean? You've either slept or you haven't.'

'I know... I had some really strange dreams. I think they were dreams... I *hope* they were dreams.' Christine tried to explain. Shannon didn't like the way this conversation was going. Was her friend having some kind of mental breakdown? Did she need professional help? Would Shannon have to call someone - some professional - against Christine's will? Shannon didn't like the idea of that.

'What were the dreams like, Christine?' Shannon asked.

'Someone came to my house...' Christine began. 'In the dream, I mean. Because it had to be a dream. This person came to my house. It was like something out of a movie or something from TV. The guy was dressed like a weird kind of FBI agent. Like he was on *The X Files* or something.'

'Was it the drunk guy from the pub?'

'No, this was a completely different man. He was dressed in a black suit and tie. He looked... professional. Focused.'

'You know we don't have the FBI in England, right?'

'Right... so, he was... whatever the FBI UK equivalent is. He looked like James fuckin' Bond. Double O seven.'

'Ok, got it.'

'Except his eyes... They were wrong.'

'Wrong?' Shannon felt herself getting sucked into the story. 'Wrong how?'

'They were a yellowy colour. Amber. They were really unnerving.'

'And that's what's upset you? A dream about James Bond with creepy eyes?' Shannon said, feeling her sympathy starting to slip away. What the hell was going on with Christine?

'No. Well, not just that.' Christine said, annoyed that she was now having to justify her fear to her best friend. 'He told me to forget what happened. That it didn't matter.'

Christine paused, expecting Shannon to say something, but Shannon stayed quiet. She didn't know what to say without upsetting Christine. Christine took Shannon's silence as permission to continue.

'I told him that I would. I told him that I'd never tell anyone about it, but I don't think he believed me. He must have seen it on my face or something. Or maybe he could read my mind. I suppose that's possible. It was a dream, right?'

Shannon nodded slowly.

'But that's where that theory starts to fall apart.'

'What do you mean?'

'Dreams can't hurt you, can they?' Christine said. 'But, this one did. Like I said, this guy - James Bond - didn't believe me. So, he grabbed my arm and squeezed it tight. I thought he was going to rip it off... but he didn't. But, something else happened. I looked at his hand and watched as it... as it... started to transform...'

'Transform?'

'Yes, I told you this was strange.'

'How did it transform?' Shannon said, intrigue getting the better of her.

'One of the fingers - the index finger - started to grow and change. The nail seemed to harden and sharpen. And... it was even sharper than it looked. It was a weapon. It cut into my arm with ease.'

At this, Christine rolled up her t-shirt sleeve to reveal her bicep. A painful looking red line, deep and angry cut across it. Whoever had inflicted the wound had meant business. But, it wasn't the wound itself that worried Shannon the most, it was the person responsible for it. Had Christine done this? After all, she'd said it herself: dreams couldn't hurt you.

'Then he said that if I didn't let this go, he'd be back. I get the feeling that it'll be much worse if he returns.'

Satisfied with her story, Christine sat back, leaning against the back of the bench and drank the rest of her coffee. Shannon looked at her, wondering what to say next.

'So...' Shannon started, hoping that the right words would somehow fall out of her mouth like magic. Christine looked at her, waiting for her to continue. 'So, what now?'

'Good question.' Christine said. 'I think the smart option would be to just forget about it.'

'You're probably right.'

'... but I can't do that. I think someone killed that drunk guy. I can't just let that go.'

'What?'

'I'm going back to that pub.'

***

+ telltale +

***

Shannon hadn't wanted to leave Christine on her own after that conversation, but her friend had insisted that she wanted to be alone. Shannon had let her go only after having her promise that she wouldn't go to the pub by herself. If she wanted to go back there, she could go after she'd slept for a while and then only if someone - preferably Shannon - went with her. All that had taken place around two hours ago now, and Shannon was still kicking herself for letting her friend walk away. She was almost completely sure that Christine had lied to her. There was no way she was going to just go home and forget about it. There was no way that she was going to wait until there was a time that was convenient for Shannon to go with her to the pub. Shannon should have known that from the start. She could have kicked herself at her stupidity.

Now two hours had passed, and Christine was nowhere to be found. She wasn't at home (Shannon had considered it to be an emergency and used her 'emergencies only' spare key) and she wasn't picking her up the phone. No matter how hard she tried, Shannon couldn't remember the name of the pub that her best friend had talked to her about. In fact, she couldn't even remember if Christine had told her its name. So, Shannon was left with a few facts, and none of them filled her with any joy.

The first was that no matter what happened the day before - and the jury was still out on that one - Christine was in a bad place. She looked haunted. The second undeniable fact was that Shannon had no idea where Christine was. And the third was that Shannon was worried sick.

People say 'worried sick' all the time. It was a phrase that Shannon had used on numerous occasions over the years, but it was only today that she truly began to understand what it actually meant. The more she thought about Christine's plight, the more she found herself running to the bathroom and retching into the toilet. She was too worried to eat and, even if she had wanted to have a snack, she never would have been able to keep it down. Her worry felt like a solid ball of lead deep within her stomach drawing heat and energy from her.

The final fact was that, until she heard back from Christine, there was absolutely nothing she could do but wait. The waiting was the worst part. But, at least she wasn't alone. Shannon had those incredibly intense and unrelenting feelings of helplessness, regret and panic to keep her company. That ever-attentive trio didn't leave her alone for a second. They didn't let her sleep. They didn't let her distract herself with television, books, music or even alcohol. They were ever-present and constant, gnawing into her brain and churning up her gut.

That had been the longest afternoon of her life. Shannon firmly believed that hours couldn't pass any slower. That was until night came and darkness fell. Then the hours started to drag - stretching longer than any hour had business stretching, and her feeling of hopelessness increased with every moment. Those hours were torture.

Shannon checked her phone so much that in the rare moments when she wasn't scrolling through messages or holding the phone to her ear to listen to it ring as her friend didn't answer, her hand felt weird. It was as if the electronic device had become an extension of her own body. Every time she tried Christine's number, the phone rang out. There was no option to leave a message and she never picked up. Even though she listened to it again and again, never hanging up until it had rung off just in case her friend answered, the ringing gave her no answers. There was no clue as to where Christine was. There were no hints about her state of mind. There was nothing to say if she was safe. The deeper into the night that Shannon got, the more she became convinced that some dreadful fate had found her friend. Maybe she was lying in a ditch somewhere. Maybe she'd gone back to that pub and the answers she had been looking for had found her first. Those thoughts chilled Shannon to the bone.

At some point during the night, Shannon decided that she had to do something. Pacing around her flat in an attempt to work off her nervous energy was no longer an option, and she was fairly certain that she had worn track marks into her carpet. Shannon had always been a productive person and she needed to do something productive now. Reaching for her jacket and her keys, Shannon decided that she would go back to Christine's house and wait for her there.

Or, at least, that's what she had intended to do. However, all her plans collapsed when she looked at the time. It was fast approaching midnight. Shannon wasn't a suspicious person but seeing that minute hand creep steadily towards the twelve to join its little brother, filled her with dread. Didn't bad things happen after midnight? Wasn't that when the monsters - supernatural or human - slipped out from their hiding places and stalked the streets. Wasn't this when murders happened? Shannon hated herself for thinking like this. It was stupid and was the result of a lifetime of being told that women shouldn't go out late at night on their own, for those nights never ended well. Shannon rarely bought into that crap, but tonight her nerves were on edge. Tonight, it felt like the stories of bogeymen and modern-day Jack the Rippers could be very real.

So, instead of heading out into the night to be the kind of heroic friend that she wanted to be, Shannon stayed put. Instead of going to Christine's house, Shannon returned to her mobile phone. She unlocked the screen and started to make a call. For the first time that night, this time someone answered. It wasn't Christine, but then, that was no surprise as the call wasn't to her. It was about her. When it was Shannon's turn to speak, she said seven words, powering through the sentence even though her voice had started to crack.

'I need to report a missing person.'

CHAPTER SEVEN

The Hound & The Philosopher Inn took on another persona in the dark. By day, it was a welcoming, if slightly empty pub, but by night it came alive. Not in the same way that other pubs and bars in Croydon came alive. It wasn't crawling with young twenty-somethings on a mission to get drunk and get laid, each one doused in cheap vodka and even cheaper perfume. No, The Hound & The Philosopher Inn was very different. It crawled with something else entirely. Something far more malevolent. Christine stood across the road from it, trying to work up the courage to go in; she'd been standing there for about ten minutes, her muscles refusing to move, her joints locking themselves into place. It was as if they knew something that she didn't. Looking at the pub now, it felt like the building was alive and, if she walked through that front door now, she'd be swallowed up by it, never to be seen again. Somehow, that just added weight to her theory.

Something bad was going on beyond that front door and something bad had happened to that drunk man. Christine had never been surer of anything in her life. She also knew that it was down to her to do something about it. Her best friend hadn't believed her so it was unlikely that anyone else would have, even if she'd had the courage to go against the freaky 007's warning and tried to tell them. There was no way around it, Christine was on her own.

Ignoring the missed calls from her friend, Christine checked the time on her phone. 9.32pm. The night was still young. She could just walk into that pub, order a drink and act like everything was normal until the time came to prove that it wasn't. It wasn't much of a plan, but Christine didn't have anything else. She put her phone back in her handbag, took a deep breath and walked across the road. Her heart pounded in her chest, the beat intensifying with every step. Sweat broke out across her brow and under her armpits. For some reason, this reminded her of a time when she was fifteen and she'd had to give a presentation at school in front of her entire year group. Christine had discovered there and then that public speaking really wasn't her forte. Back then, fear and nerves had stolen her voice, hiding it somewhere out of reach so that she just stood there, dumb and sweaty, in front of a room full of people. That had not been a good day. But, Christine would have happily relived that moment half a dozen times if it meant that she could skip right by this one. Resigning herself to whatever fate awaited her through the door, Christine entered the pub.

As previously, on the surface, the pub looked relatively normal. No masked axe murderers propped themselves up against the bar and no monsters sat at the tables. A feeling of ease swept over her, like it had when she had spoken to the barman in here before. For a moment, Christine wondered why she had ever thought anything was wrong. But, that in itself was wrong, wasn't it? How could she now feel so relaxed about a place that minutes ago terrified her? It didn't make sense. It was starting to feel like nothing made sense.

She approached the bar, figuring that she may as well order a drink if only to try to blend in. Before she had even reached it, she had gained the barman's attention.

'Hello again.' he said. His voice was friendly and reassuring. It should have put her even more at ease, but it didn’t, and he seemed to realise that his charm wasn't working. 'Are you okay? You look worried about something?'

A sudden urge to talk to the barman about everything crashed over her. It seemed absurd that the barman would be able to help her, let alone want to listen to her possible paranoia, but the desire to talk to him about the drunk man and the evil 007 that had shown up at her house, was strong. Christine bit her tongue. After all, there was a chance that this barman was caught up in all this. Whatever 'all this' was.

Christine wasn't sure, but the barman may have said something else to her. Her head felt foggy, making her feel somewhat separated from the rest of the world. She blinked slowly, trying to regain her focus. The barman looked at her, head cocked at an angle, like an inquisitive spaniel.

'Oh... er....' Christine said, knowing that she should say something. Words evaded her. It was like that school presentation all over again.

'Drink? Do you want one?' the barman asked, sensing she was struggling. A small smile teased the sides of his mouth, but he kept it in check. Even through the fog in her head, Christine managed to spot his attempt at concealment. It could be that he was trying to spare her embarrassment as he tried not to laugh at the confused woman in front of him. Or it could be a sign of something else. Paranoia started to push away any lingering feelings of ease. Christine decided to go with the worst-case scenario. Whatever all this turned out to be, Christine was willing to bet that the barman was in on it.

***

The barman sighed. It was always so much more difficult when they caught on. Equally fun, if not more, in the long run, of course. But, more difficult in the beginning. The bit that he had to deal with.

The barman had been on the job for years. Most of his life, in fact. In the beginning, he had found it difficult. He had wrestled with his conscience with every person he took, but now it felt natural. Even enjoyable. The barman wondered what this meant for his soul, if he had one. The barman acted as a middleman, between his employers and the pub's patrons. The patrons tended to fall within one of three groups: recruitment, disposables and those who were left alone. It was rare to be asked to add to the first group, but it happened from time to time and he envied every single one of them. The second group was far more common and the third was a necessity. If, for whatever reason, everyone who entered the pub never walked back out again, word would spread, and no new customers would ever turn up. That would be terrible for business, on every level.

Meanwhile, the woman in front of him had started to succumb to the drugs pumped through the pub's aircon. The barman had no idea what these drugs were, and he had no intention of ever asking. Ignorance, as they say, is bliss. He was immune to their effects due to taking the antidote every day. Other than that, all the barman knew was that the drugs tended to make the patrons relax, they made them more susceptible to whatever fate he had in store for them. They made his life easier.

He recognised the woman from the evening before. She'd been there when he'd grabbed the latest entrant into his employer's world. She should have been warned off by now. She should have been scared away. And yet, here she was. Defiant and a bit wobbly, but defiant nonetheless. That made her interesting and his employers liked to know about things of interest. Once he'd given her a drink - laced with more drugs, of course - he'd give his employers a call. They'd be impressed with this. With the plan set out in his mind, he asked for a third time what she'd like.

'Umm... never mind.' She replied, an unreadable look flitted across her face. 'I just realised that I have to go.'

It should be noted that unreadable looks are only unreadable by those who do not have the code to decipher them. One of the perks of the barman's job was that his employers had provided him with such a code. He couldn't read minds per se, but he was always able to get a general idea of what was going on in a person's head; whether he wanted to or not. The mind-reading trick was fine while he was at work, but if he was out somewhere, trying to relax, it became an annoyance. Seriously, who wanted to know when their neighbour was fantasising about someone they shouldn't be? As a result, the barman didn't have much of a social life. The way he saw it, he saw enough people in the pub, he had no desire to seek them out elsewhere. Besides, he never had been any good at making friends. He was one of the world's eternal misfits.

As it was, he was at work now, so he got to put his gifts to good use. Not only had the woman announced that she needed to leave, the barman could also read fear in her eyes. She knew something wasn't quite right. And, irritatingly, she had also concluded that the barman was involved. That was unfortunate. The barman usually liked to play a 'good guy' role, but that would have to change on this occasion. Still, he was nothing if not flexible.

'But, what about your drink?' he said, his words freezing the woman to the spot. She looked like a deer caught in headlights, the poor thing.

'Don't worry about it,' she said, in a voice not much louder than a whisper. 'I'm going.'

As she turned away, the barman nodded to a group of men at one of the tables between the bar and the door. The men nodded back, almost imperceptibly. As one, they stood, and a fight broke out between them. The barman knew it was all staged - after all, it was a plan he had held in place for years - but it gave him the excuse to come out from behind the bar and walk in the direction that the woman was walking.

***

It felt as though she was wading through treacle; every step was an effort, every movement away from the bar was a battle. Then the fight broke out. Fists flew, glasses were smashed, insults were exchanged, and noses were bloodied. It looked vicious and savage, but Christine couldn't shake the feeling that this was for her benefit; that it was a distraction. As her brain joined the pieces together, she remembered what - or who - it was that she should have been focused on. At the same time, an arm wrapped around her body and a hand clamped tightly over her mouth. An involuntary yelp escaped from the barman, as she kicked into his shin with her heel. It was a high-pitched noise, perhaps one that the barman would have been embarrassed by, should anyone have been listening. Fortunately for him, everyone else was too preoccupied with the fight to notice his difficulties. Christine wasn't sure if her actions had hurt the barman, surprised him, or both. It didn't matter, she had to act quickly if she was going to use this to her advantage. With a banshee yell, she twisted out of his grip. Now they were face to face and the barman was almost unrecognisable. Gone was the friendly guy, eager to listen to the problems of strangers. The niceness had been replaced by rage. Or, maybe it was never there in the first place.

Christine realised that she had a choice. She could either launch an attack on the barman or run. Fight or flight. Part of her wanted to fight; she had no doubt that the barman deserved any pain that she could inflict on him. But, the more sensible part of her wanted to run; to live to fight another day. Even though the bar fight still raged on beside her, she still felt outnumbered. She was also lacking on anything that could be used as a weapon. So, she listened to the sensible part of her brain, turning and racing towards the door.

Even though it stood only a few feet away, Christine may as well have been on Mars. She ran as fast as she could, arms outstretched, reaching for the elusive door handle. It was so close. So very close. Her fingers grazed against it. The cold metal shocked her, but she also found it inviting. It signalled escape. It signalled freedom. It signalled safety. These were things that Christine hadn't really thought too much about, but now she hungered for them. She needed them. All she had to do was open the door and run into the muggy night outside.

Her fingers gripped the handle and her heart leapt into her throat, wanting to get the hell out of that pub just as much as the rest of her did. She could sense the barman behind her, feeling the unwelcome warmth of his breath on the back of her neck, but everything else faded into the background. The scuffling and yelling from the bar fight felt like it was far away. The street outside may as well have been on another planet.

She pulled.

The door started to open.

Warm air blasted into the cool, air-conditioned pub.

Then everything just stopped. No warning, no pain. It just stopped, like someone flicking a switch.

CHAPTER EIGHT

Morning came all too soon, and the night had robbed him of sleep. No, that wasn't quite right. Kit checked his phone. He had slept straight through the next day. Why the hell did he still feel so tired?

Kit hadn't been able to talk to his housemates the night before, so the opportunity to have any kind of taste of normality had passed him by. Instead, he had found himself staring at his reflection for hours on end. His eyes weren't just yellow as he had first thought; they were made up of different yellows, ambers and oranges and the colours taunted him, moving and dancing as he watched them.

But it wasn't the changes in his appearance that had caused his tiredness.

Every time he closed his eyes, he felt like he needed to be somewhere else. Like there was someone waiting for him to arrive, but he didn't know who wanted him or where he was supposed to be. The most infuriating thing about it was that the knowledge was there, somewhere in his brain, but exhaustion made it impossible to think clearly. It had been a very stressful day. And night.

As he lay on the bed, trying to work out who he was supposed to meet and how stressful his day had been, he realised that he probably should have spoken to the police about it. Kidnapping was illegal, right?

But something stopped him from reaching for the phone.

He wasn't supposed to tell anyone about what happened. He knew that without knowing how he knew that. In fact, his body physically hurt whenever he thought about talking to anyone about it. Kit wondered if actually saying the words out loud would cause his spleen to rupture or something. He also found himself wondering what his spleen looked like and realised that, up until this moment, it wasn't something he had given a lot of thought to.

Every muscle in his body groaned in protest as he sat up. It was like he'd been hit by a very large, very heavy truck, and then thrown down several flights of stairs. But, it wasn't his muscles that were causing him the most discomfort; a sharp, searing pain shot through his neck, making him clench his teeth to keep himself from screaming. Kit tentatively touched the back of his neck with his fingers, probing the area gently. Judging by what he could feel, there seemed to be a circular wound there, around the size of a fifty pence coin. The skin around it felt puckered, as if it had started to heal already, but it was still raw to the touch. How he had missed this injury was a mystery, but, then again, yesterday had been a very odd day.

In spite of his body's reluctance, Kit climbed out of bed. As he stood, his stomach growled hungrily, and Kit felt like he hadn't eaten in weeks. The kitchen downstairs called to him, so he pulled on a clean t-shirt and a pair of jogging bottoms and headed down the stairs. Switching to auto-pilot, he set about his normal morning routine. The espresso machine powered on, bread flew into the toaster and he looked at the fruit bowl even though he knew full well that he had no intention of consuming anything from it. Soon enough, he was sat at the kitchen table with a coffee and two slices of toast and strawberry jam. Yet, despite his hunger, he couldn't bring himself to eat it. The thought of eating the sweet jam repulsed him, so he pushed the plate to one side and focused on drinking the coffee. His body seemed to accept this, but his stomach's constant noises told him that he was going to need something more substantial.

He went to the fridge, opened the door and stared inside it for a few moments, waiting for inspiration to hit him. He had no idea what he was looking for, he was just hoping that something would jump out at him and say, "eat me". Nothing did. But there was an open packet of wafer thin ham that didn't make him feel nauseated to look at it, so he took it back to the kitchen table. The ham didn't belong to him, so Kit made a mental note to replace it. Consuming the ham didn’t take very long; the thin slices disappearing into his mouth within a few seconds. They didn't satisfy his hunger, but they did make him feel a little bit better. He stared at the empty plastic packet thinking that he could eat a thousand of them. Kit needed to go food shopping, he hated going food shopping. Supermarkets were like Hell on Earth.

His stomach growled again, as if reminding him that there was no getting out of it. Kit pushed himself away from the table with a sigh and went back up to his room to get ready. It was going to be a tough morning.

CHAPTER NINE

As expected, the supermarket resembled one of the circles of Hell. Probably the worst one. Was that the one in the middle? Kit briefly wondered if the circles of Hell were concentric, or if they were a collection of circles, dotted around the underworld. If it was the latter, were they the same size? Did they overlap? Regardless of their layout, he was sure that at least one of them looked like this. It just made sense. Kit half expected a demon to creep up behind him and poke him in the arse with a trident. Did demons use tridents? Kit wasn't sure.

The supermarket was a grotesque combination of fluorescent lighting, screaming children and dawdling shoppers. It was a monster to rival Frankenstein's most famous creation. Kit wanted to grab what he needed and get out as soon as possible. Without realising it, Kit found himself in the meat aisle. Various joints and slabs of meat found their way into his basket; the thought of eating anything else just felt wrong. Almost as an afterthought, he dropped a packet of wafer thin ham into the basket, remembering that he needed to replace what he took for breakfast. Convinced that he had everything he needed, Kit headed to the checkout to pay.

The queues on each of the tills were ridiculously long, even though it was a weekday and most people should have been at work. For Kit, this was just further confirmation - as if he needed any - that he was in a version of Hell that did 'buy one get one free deals' and price-matches. As he made his way to one of the self-service checkouts, a smile tugged at his face as he wondered if the Devil would do a price-match on a packet of biscuits.

If supermarkets were Hell-on-Earth, self-service checkouts were a particularly sadistic form of torture. They were stubborn machines, determined to make even the most techno-savvy user look like a complete imbecile. They also sensed fear. If you even thought that they may not work properly, they'd play on those doubts. They'd make the scanning of each item an ordeal. They'd make you question if you really wanted to buy these items anyway. Did you need them? Were they necessary? Perhaps the government wanted people to spend less money. Make it so difficult so that people would just give up and walk away. Annoyingly, Kit needed his items. He needed to eat. And soon. He was starting to feel a bit weird.

By the end of the process, after having numerous 'unexpected items' in his bagging area, Kit decided that having his eyelids ripped off would be a more comfortable way to spend ten minutes. But, his torment wasn't over just yet, he still needed to get out of the building. As if from nowhere, a herd of people with trolleys and buggies appeared in front of him, moving at a snail's pace and blocking his exit. A combination of frustration and unprecedented rage started to build up inside him. Kit could feel it lurking there, throbbing just behind his right eye. His eyeball ached, and his vision started to do crazy things.

Out of the corner of his eye, Kit could see shadows. Malformed creatures, darker than a black hole. Somehow, he knew that these shadows were not simply the product of something blocking a light source, but something else entirely. Not only did they not look like any object or living thing that Kit had ever seen, they felt full and solid; they had mass. Without knowing how he knew, Kit felt sure that these shadows were beings in their own right. They were beings full of sadistic malevolence and a cold intelligence. Something about them felt evil. Not 'comic book super-villain evil', but real evil. The kind of evil that would defile your body and soul just for shits and giggles. Their twisted limbs reached out towards him, branch-like fingers clawing at him. His anger rose as they started to close in, almost shutting off his vision completely, leaving him in darkness.

The trouble with darkness was that it made it damned hard to see where the darkness ended, and the shadows began. Which meant they could be anywhere. He was under attack and it was only a matter of time before they made their move. Kit didn't want to think about what the shadows would do if they got their unnatural fingers on him. Somehow, Kit knew that their touch would be cold. Cold like a crypt.

He caught the sound of a growl escaping his throat; a low and dangerous noise, animal and wild. Kit felt like a dog that had been backed into a corner. Nowhere to turn and nothing left to lose. His muscles were so tense that they had started to ache and burn, and his teeth were bared. Kit had never reacted this way before in his life, but it felt so natural.

So natural, in fact, that he couldn't understand why people were screaming and shouting.

Then he realised.

Apparently, it wasn't normal for a man to be stood in a supermarket, snarling and growling at nothing.

'Shit... look at his eyes!' thc panicked, yet excited voice of a shop assistant brought Kit back to the present and the shadows finally receded. Kit's anger dissipated, falling away as quickly as it had come on; washed away as the shadows made their exit. The anger was replaced by embarrassment and Kit looked to the floor to avoid eye contact with anyone in the store, lest they follow the shop assistant's suggestion and looked at his eyes. Even though Kit could not see his reflection, he knew what they'd see.

He knew that his eyes were now completely yellow.

He also knew that he had to leave. Gripping onto his bag of groceries, Kit marched out of the store, barging people out of the way in the process. He didn't care if he appeared rude; he had bigger things on his mind. Like worrying about what the hell was happening to him.

With no other options revealing themselves to him, Kit knew what he had to do. He had to find some answers and there was only one way that he was going to be able to that.

Kit was going back to the pub.

.

CHAPTER TEN

The quest to replace his housemate's ham now forgotten, Kit took his shopping bags and headed in the direction of the pub. Just as it had been during his previous visit, the day was hot, sticky and loud. The meat in the bags would soon spoil in this heat. His senses took in everything around him. Kit could see the slightest movement and hear a pin drop. If someone was close enough, he could hear the sound of their sweat running over their skin. It was a sound that he'd never thought about until now, but now it was all around him. It was a slithering, wet sound. He wasn't sure if his heightened senses were a blessing or a curse.

The heavy carrier bags dug into his hands, but he didn't notice the plastic handles doing their best to cut off the blood supply to his fingers; Kit's mind was elsewhere. The shadows had returned.

The sights and sounds around him started to merge together, leaving Kit feeling like he had taken a dive underwater. Only the shadows were left with any clarity. They were currently stood together, moving slightly, like a writhing black hole in the middle of the pavement. Kit was rooted to the spot; unable to do anything but stare. A tundra-like cold crept across the space between Kit and the shadows, fighting off the heat and claiming the air as its own. Goosebumps rose on the flesh of his bare arms and legs as the penetrating cold brushed against him. Taking this as their cue, the shadows started to move, and a limb broke away from the overall mass. Finger-like tendrils reached for Kit and he held his breath as if trying to stop time. He knew that the cold from the breeze would be nothing compared to the sensation from those fingers. If they touched him, he would never be warm again. If they touched him, it would be 'Game Over'.

The shadow hand moved closer, teasing him. It wouldn't be long now. Kit held his breath and waited for the inevitable. Just as he was about to surrender to the shadow's wintry touch, strong arms grabbed him around the waist from behind and dragged him backwards. Kit's shoes scraped against the concrete and, as the world around him started to move, Kit realised where he was being dragged. The familiar scent of stale beer hit his nostrils and confirmed his suspicions.

He tried to talk, but the words stuck in his mouth. The shadows were still creeping towards him, unperturbed by their prey's attempt at escape.

'Almost there.' a familiar voice announced, as Kit was dropped to the floor. A wave of pain shot up through his back, making him groan. 'Suck it up, Kit. It's about to get a lot worse than that.'

Kit turned his head to looked at the owner of the voice. The barman looked back at him and smiled. Kit supposed the smile was meant to be reassuring, but Kit didn't feel reassured. Kit felt scared. Especially now that the shadows were making their way into the pub, oozing their way through the closed door.

'What's going on?' Kit asked, wondering why the barman was no longer keeping him away from the advancing shadows.

'*Om grutt*' the barman replied, leading Kit to wonder if he was losing his mind. What the hell had this guy just said?

'Seriously, what's happening?'

'*Om grutt*.' the barman repeated.

'What the fuck is an *om grutt*?' Kit asked, as he scooted across the floor backwards, on his arse. It wasn't the most dignified of ways to travel across a pub, but Kit didn't really care about that.

'It's probably better if I explain that afterwards.' The barman replied as he casually propped himself against the bar. The man looked like he didn't have a care in the world. Kit, meanwhile, was sweating profusely from every pore, unable to comprehend what was happening to him.

'AFTER WHAT?' Kit growled through gritted teeth. The barman remained silent, instead choosing to nod at the approaching shadows as if in greeting. It was almost as if they were old friends reuniting for a drink.

Kit continued to scoot across the floor but found that he was trapped. His back was, quite literally, up against a wall. The shadows drew closer, their shapes becoming more defined.

'You've gotta help me.' Kit tried to appeal to the barman. 'Don't let them get me.'

'There's no stopping it now, Kit.' The barman replied, distracted by a bit of dirt under his nail. The man's apparent disregard for Kit's situation was getting on his nerves. Just as he was about to use one of his favourite insults to let the barman know this, one of the shadows touched him.

That touch was everything Kit expected it to be and more. Freezing cold fingers caressed his forehead, sending permafrost through Kit's body, the cold rippling out like ice breaking in a pond. Kit looked at his hands and saw that his fingers were turning blue. His face felt numb and he imagined that his lips were following the example of his fingers. His breath clouded out in front of his face. He looked towards the barman and saw that he was still engrossed in whatever was under his fingernail. Kit was turning blue and the barman didn't care.

A pain shot through his chest and Kit imagined that his heart was turning into a lump of ice, useless and cold. He tried to speak, he tried to scream, but nothing happened. Even the clouds of breath clouding in front of him were getting smaller. Kit firmly believed that he was going to freeze to death and there was nothing he could do about it. The barman continued to study his fingernail, as if Kit's plight was the kind of thing he witnessed on a daily basis. Suddenly, the world went dark and silent. Trying to focus and trying to move was impossible. Everything was eerily still. The pain was gone, everything was gone. Reality had vanished. Kit didn't even feel numb; it was simply like he had ceased to exist. He was adrift on a sea of nothingness. An indeterminable amount of time passed by.

Gradually, sensation started to return to his body, followed by pain. Not as much pain as previously, but it was still there. Then he could hear the barman breathing and shuffling around. He could hear the muffled sounds of the street outside; of people going about their lives. But, as expected, he couldn't hear the shadows. Were they standing over him, marvelling in his pain and discomfort? Had they retreated? Were they getting ready for round two? Kit didn't want to open his eyes and look. He didn't want to know. He didn't *need* to know.

No, he wouldn't look.

He refused to.

But, alas, curiosity is a funny thing. He would allow himself a peek. Just one little peek. One tiny, little peek. With no small amount of caution, Kit slowly opened his eyes. The pub's interior was all around him. Wooden panelling, old tables, chairs and bar stools. Everything that Kit could hope to see in a pub was there. The door stood ahead of him, almost mocking him. It was so close, but Kit was in no shape to walk out of it. And there was something unusual about it, something wasn't quite right. Allowing himself a few moments to study it, Kit realised what was wrong. Looking through the glass window in the door, the world outside was in darkness. Night had fallen. Even as a child, Kit had never been afraid of the dark, but now, lying on the floor of a pub whilst being tormented by shadows, he felt like he had reason to be. Kit tightly closed his eyes again, as if closing them would turn back time, or remove him from the situation entirely.

'C'mon, buddy. Don't be like that!' The barman's voice penetrated Kit's ears. 'Open your eyes. You'll miss everything otherwise.'

Kit sensed a trap, but he opened his eyes anyway. As soon as he did, he realised that he should have known better. Another face looked back at him. A face made of shadow and darkness. Empty eye sockets seemed to stare at him and he stared back. Inside those sockets he could see the nothingness that he had been trapped in before. As he stared, Kit couldn't help but think of the Friedrich Nietzsche quote. *'If you gaze long into an abyss, the abyss also gazes into you'.* The shadow - the abyss - was certainly gazing into him now. Not only was it gazing into him, but it was also reading him. Dissecting him.

'Dissecting' felt like a very apt word, as what felt like a dozen invisible blades sliced through him. But, no blood leaked from the invisible wounds. Pain threatened to consume him.

Curling into a ball on the floor, Kit felt his body shutting down. He was going to die on the floor of a pub. Hell, he'd already received a taster of what was to come! Nothing! For all eternity! What a way to go! Just as he was about to resign himself to this fate, the shadow that had touched him originally bent over him. Unable to move, Kit just watched as its ghost-like hand touched him once more.

\+ *Om grutt* + said a voice inside Kit's head. It was a voice that Kit had never heard before and one that he hoped that he would never hear again. If Kit's body had been behaving itself properly, it would have set his nerves on edge, like nails on a chalkboard.

With those words, everything changed; it was like he had been hit by a lightning bolt. His heart went into overdrive, beating faster and pumping harder than it had ever done before; the pounding in his ears threatening to deafen him. Fire spread through his veins, coursing through his body at an alarming rate. His deadened limbs sprang into action and his body developed a mind of its own. Before he knew it, Kit was on all fours in the centre of the pub floor. He could feel the barman's eyes on him. Finally, he was more interesting than a dirty fingernail.

Just as he was about to stand, his arms and legs started to feel like they were being stretched. Kit watched as his hands changed into new shapes and his own fingernails hardened and elongated into claws.

Once again, he tried to talk. He needed to know what was happening. He needed to hear something other than '*Om grutt*'. But, further changes were happening in his throat and mouth, preventing the words from forming. Blood filled his mouth as his gums split open. Sharp teeth started to protrude from the newly opened holes, and blood and saliva drooled from his lips. His body emitted a symphony of creaks, groans and moans. Coarse, black hair started to grow all over his body. His face started to stretch. Kit didn't want to think about how he looked now, he had more pressing matters on his mind.

+ Om grutt... Om grutt... Om grutt +

Kit could hear the voices of the shadows in his mind. They were chanting, a sound that was more sinister than joyous. Kit tried to concentrate on those voices as a way of diverting his attention from the pain. It seemed to work and, as he focused, he found that the sinister tones started to change; they started to feel comforting. For a moment, he forgot that he was unable to speak, as he tried to chant along with them. Instead of chanting the nonsense words, the only sound to escape his throat was a low growl. The sound of it almost shocked him. Almost.

As unbelievable as it seemed, Kit knew what was happening to him; he had seen enough horror movies to come to the correct conclusion. It was ridiculous, far-fetched and nonsensical, but when considered alongside the most recent events of his life, it felt real. He was becoming a werewolf. As if sensing that his mind was coming to terms with the change, his body started to stand.

No, Kit wasn't just a werewolf. He had become a wolfman. Kit didn't know whether to laugh or cry. He decided to do neither. An eerie howl seemed more appropriate. Looking around the pub, Kit studied his companions. Both the shadows and the barman seemed to approve of Kit's new form and, for a moment, Kit felt something akin to happiness. Feeling like he belonged to some secret club, Kit howled again. This time the howl was cut short, as a pint glass flew into his snout, stunning him slightly. It smashed on the floor, shattering into tiny pieces. Kit looked in the direction the glass had come from and made eye contact with the barman. The shadows had grouped around him, as if pledging their allegiance to the barman. They were showing him that he wasn't quite part of their gang. Not yet.

'Quit howling, would you?' the barman said, anger flashing behind his eyes. It was the first time that Kit had seen anything negative there. 'Do you want everyone to know about us?'

Kit didn't answer; he couldn't. Instead of using words, he whined like a dog who had been scolded by its owner. His tail fell between his legs, making him realise that his clothes were gone, ripped and ruined beneath him.

'Don't worry, we'll get you new ones.' the barman said, as if reading his mind. 'We'll get you a lot of things. You'll see.'

The barman's words seemed kind enough, but Kit wasn't sure if they comforted him or worried him. He didn't have long to worry about it though, as a vice-like pain gripped his head. Apparently, his torture wasn't over yet. Just like a vice, the pain gripped tighter and tighter, building a pressure that was more intense than anything Kit could have imagined. Surely his head couldn't take this kind of punishment? Kit was sure that his eyeballs were going to pop out of their sockets at any moment. He was waiting for his skull to crack like an egg, spilling his brains.

That moment never came.

***

Hidden from view, on the other side of the pub's window, a figure stood, bearing witness to the monstrosity taking place within.

So, the figure thought, *they've taken another one.* That changed things. Not a lot, it just increased the amount of work that needed to be done. It was a slight inconvenience.

The figure watched as the wolfman gripped the sides of his head with clawed hands. Or was 'paws' a more accurate description?

'*Om grutt*, indeed.'

The figure walked away, not needing to see anything else.

***

The barman watched as the final stage of *Om Grutt* took place. He looked at the man - Kit - with a mixture of approval, disgust and envy. The barman had worked for his employers for years, but the possibility of *Om Grutt* had never been offered to him. It was the one thing he wanted more than anything; he deserved it more than anyone.

Out of the corner of his eye, he noticed one of the shadows becoming restless, its attention diverted from the writhing form of Kit. Trying to follow its gaze, the barman looked to the window. Nothing but the night and his own reflection looked back at him, but he still felt uneasy. Initiating the *Om Grutt* in the bar was a bold move. Perhaps one that was a little too risky. The so-called 'normal people' would have no interest in the pub while the *Om Grutt* was being performed. No, they would be kept away by the wards the shadows had put in place years ago. But, that wouldn't stop other prying eyes from looking in. The barman considered the possibility of being observed by an unknown voyeur and found that the thought both scared and excited him. The shadow turned back to Kit, telling the barman that any threat - real or imagined - had passed. Disappointment nagged at the barman as he followed the shadow's example.

***

Having thought that the transformation was over, Kit had started to relax. How wrong could he be? The pain in his head was increasing by the moment and there was nothing he could do to stop it. For a second, he even thought that death would be preferable to his current situation. But then, things changed. Kit lost control.

The transformation had been out of his hands anyway, but this was a brand-new situation. Before, the pain and the changes were something that were happening *to him*, but now it was like he was on the outside, looking in. He was still in his body, but he was separated from it. A hunger started to rise within him. He growled without even realising that he was going to do it; his body was reacting on its own. He had become a basic creature, caring only for sustenance and survival. He watched in horror as he turned to the barman, eyeing him up, thinking he looked a lot like dinner. Kit was sure that the barman probably deserved whatever he had coming to him, but the thought of having his flesh between his teeth made Kit feel ill. Human Kit probably would have retched, but Human Kit wasn't present. Instead, Wolf Kit was here, and Wolf Kit was hungry, and the barman looked like prey.

'Easy there, fella.' the barman had, to his credit, read the situation perfectly. From his spot in the audience, Kit couldn't help but shake the feeling that the barman had done this before. He seemed like an expert in... whatever this was. 'Wait there a moment.'

The barman held up his hands slightly, as if telling Kit to stay, and walked away. He disappeared through the *"Staff Only"* door. At that moment, Kit could have run. He could have escaped and done whatever he wanted. Instead, he stayed where he was, proving himself to be the loyal and obedient dog that the barman thought him to be. Besides, the shadows would likely track him down wherever he went.

The barman returned after only a few minutes, holding a pigeon. The pigeon thrashed around in his grip, determined to free itself, but not having any luck. It viciously pecked at its captor, aiming for the eyes wherever possible. Its efforts were in vain, but it didn't give up. *Its putting up more of a fight than I did*, Kit realised with no small amount of embarrassment. Wolf Kit, on the other hand, was not feeling embarrassed, Wolf Kit was still feeling hungry.

The barman barely had enough time to launch the pigeon into the air and dive out of the way, before Wolf Kit had launched at the prize. The bird was torn apart in a matter of seconds by Kit's razor-sharp teeth and claws. Its organs and flesh devoured eagerly. Internally, Kit was repulsed. Sure, he'd eaten plenty of animals in his time, but they were always cooked and never consumed like this. The sound of crunching and snapping bones disturbed Kit from his thoughts and he found himself back in the moment again, ready, yet unwilling, to witness whatever this new version of him did next.

Wolf Kit looked toward the door, knowing lots of warm, fresh flesh waited beyond it. If Human Kit had control of the body, he would have shuddered.

+ *Not yet. Soon though. Soon.* + the unearthly voice of one of the shadows said.

CHAPTER ELEVEN

The howling woke her. It woke her from a sleep that she didn't even know she was having, from a dream that she didn't even realise she was dreaming. Once awake, she couldn't remember the dream, but the memory of it lingered on the edge of her mind, teasing her. It hadn't been a good dream, but she couldn't be sure of what kind of nightmare her subconscious had just witnessed. Her inability to recall it was frustrating, but she had more important things to think about. Like where the hell she was and what the fuck was happening.

As her eyes started to adjust to the gloom, Christine began to take in her surroundings. She was in some kind of tunnel, it was damp and cold, and little did she know that it was a different section of the same tunnel that her Drunk Guy had been in before. Christine shivered and wished she'd worn a hoodie or a cardigan, even a long-sleeved shirt would have been good. Her area of the tunnel was lit by a handful of small candles, their flames flickering, hypnotising her, almost managing to lull her into a false sense of security. She needed to get out of here. She needed to call for him. Reaching into the pocket of her denim shorts, she found nothing. Her phone was gone. Everything was gone, her pockets were completely empty. Christine felt alone and abandoned. Without her phone, her lifeline was gone. There was no chance of anyone - not the police, not Shannon - coming to save her. She would have to save herself.

Aside from the howling, Christine could hear muffled voices. Or, at least one muffled voice. Although she couldn't work out exactly what was being said, she thought she recognised it. The barman. It was his fault that she was here, she knew that much.

But, where was 'here' exactly?

She focused again on the tunnel. The floor was dirt, the walls were a combination of more dirt, moving along to red and brown bricks, the colours reminding her of blood. Spiders and other tiny creatures - some of which Christine knew the name of, some of them she didn't - occasionally crawled across those bricks. They didn't seem bothered by her presence. Maybe they were used to strangers in the tunnel. Maybe Christine just wasn't very threatening. Either was possible.

Christine had no idea how long she'd been there, but she was now sick of the tunnel. It was time to act, time to move. The barman's voice continued in one direction, occasionally it was interrupted by a howl. Those otherworldly howls, hollow and harrowing. The tiny hairs on the back of her neck and the bare skin of her arms and legs stood on end whenever she heard them. Sweat broke out on her skin, her palms moist despite the lack of warmth in the tunnel. Her teeth bit into her bottom lip, refusing her the ability to scream along. No, going that way was walking into mortal danger. Her primal brain, the one locked away behind miles of facts and figures, knew that. It was something more than knowledge, it was reflex.

The other direction was a mystery. If she was to choose a book or a movie, Christine would usually pick a mystery of some sort. However, she wasn't in the mood for a hard-hitting *Whodunnit* at the moment. Instead, she just wanted to be at home, safely tucked up in bed. Then again, she wasn't keen on the idea of running into the barman again. He clearly had something planned for her and she didn't want to stick around and see what that was.

So, with the lack of any other options, the Tunnel of Mystery won. Slow, cautious steps took her down the tunnel, and she was unable to shake the feeling that she was acting like one of those idiots in a horror movie. But, in fairness, either direction was full of risks. The further she walked, the more she became aware of two things. The first was that she was not alone. The second was that she had made a terrible decision. Maybe she should have headed towards the sound of the barman's voice and that tortured howling. What was it that they said? It's better the devil you know.

The unmistakable sounds of footsteps echoed around her, confirming her fears. The echoes made it difficult to determine how far away her incoming company was, but Christine wasn't about to delude herself into thinking that she had plenty of time. *Shit*, she thought, too scared to say the word out loud. Holding her breath, she forced herself to be as flat as possible against the tunnel wall. It was a ridiculous hiding place, given the candlelight, but

Christine was out of ideas. Besides, even if they didn't see her, they were sure to hear her heart pounding. There was no way around it, she would have to face them. Whoever they were. She bit into her lip again, drawing blood and not noticing it drip down her chin.

Stepping away from the wall, she placed herself in the centre of the tunnel, fists raised and a hard determination in her eyes. She could only try her best, and she could only hope that her best was good enough. Her body wanted to hyperventilate, so she forced to herself into steadying her breathing. Now was not the time to show any kind of vulnerability.

She waited.

As far as she could tell, the footsteps were getting ever closer and closer. Sweat broke out on her brow, defying the tunnel's chill.

And closer.

Two figures emerged at a bend in the tunnel. Both were sharply dressed, and both had spotted her, there was no doubt about that. Recognition flashed across her face. One of them was 007's evil twin. His yellow eyes met hers and a smile spread across his lips as he looked her up and down. Christine had never felt like she was being treated like a piece of meat quite as much as she did at that moment. There was a hunger in that stare. The only thing was that Christine didn't think there was anything sexual about it. 007 desired her the same way that she desired pizza on a Friday night. He licked his lips and Christine shuddered, this time it wasn't because of the cold.

'Christine!' he said, as if greeting a fond acquaintance. 'So lovely to see you again.'

'Ah, Peter, is this your new... er... *friend*?' The second man's voice had a slight accent, but Christine couldn't place it. Then again, she'd never been that good with accents.

'She is indeed.' 007, or Peter, replied, still smiling. He was well-spoken and articulate, and held himself with confidence. 'I tried to warn her off, but she just couldn't stay away. Maybe it's my irresistible charm. Was that it, Christine? Oh, do you prefer Chrissie?'

Christine didn't reply, but she didn't look away. She was transfixed by Peter's yellow, predatory eyes. They drew her in and she felt powerless against them. Every cell in her body screamed at her, warned her of the danger standing in front of her, but her body refused to move. She was paralysed and at the mercy of Peter and his friend.

'She doesn't say much, does she?' Peter's friend said, his head cocked to one side. 'The curious ones are usually a little more talkative. Still, it's nice to have a change.'

'That it is.' Peter replied, still refusing to take his eyes off her and break the spell.

'How -' Christine started to talk, but she found that her words stuck in her throat, painful and uncomfortable. Fear still had her in its clutches.

'Go on, dear. You can do it.' Peter said, his voice condescending. 'Use your words.'

'How do you know my name?' she said. It was still an effort to talk, but somehow, she was managing it. The rest of her body still refused to co-operate.

'We know many things.' Peter said, still holding her gaze. 'We know everything that we need to know. How we come about that information is none of your business.'

Christine looked at the strange man standing in front of her, this time studying his eyes, working past their unusual yellow colouring. It was then that she realised that it wasn't just the colour that had her on edge. Peter's pupils held a darkness purer and deeper than anything she had ever seen. The darkness hinted at places beyond this one. Places that Christine had no desire to go visit. At the same time, the darkness held a certain familiarity. She knew it and, more importantly, it knew her. Even though she still wasn't sure on the details, she had a feeling that it had something to do with the dream she couldn't remember. The dream the howls had woken her from.

The howls.

The howls had stopped. Was that good or bad?

The two smartly dressed men in front of her seemed to notice the silence too, as they exchanged a glance, but managing not to give anything away. It was impossible to know if this new development worked in their favour or not, so Christine decided to make it work for her. Now that Peter's eyes had broken their hold, Christine found that she was able to run. Before she'd even thought about it, her legs had made the decision for her. They ran. They ran in the opposite direction down the tunnel. They ran towards the new, empty silence. Christine had never been what would be described as athletic. She wasn't overweight or particularly unhealthy, but any kind of competitive sport was out of the question. Until now. It turns out that running for her life was Christine's sport. She excelled at it, her feet eating through the distance faster than she could think. So, she stopped thinking. Or, at least, she tried to. Trying to forget the imminent danger behind her, she concentrated on what was directly in front of her. Instead of focusing on the threat of death, she focused on putting one foot in front of the other. It was working.

Christine kept running, she was fast, but reckless and she stumbled more than once. To her surprise, no hand clamped itself on her shoulder and nobody tackled her to the ground. Allowing herself a split second to look behind her for the first time since she started running, she noticed that her sharp dressed men were not directly behind her. Nor were they running. Instead, they were gaining on her at a snail's pace, taking a leisurely stroll through the candlelit tunnel, seemingly without any cares or concerns. Their lack of interest was alarming. Christine redoubled her efforts, now even more determined to get away. Even more determined to survive.

Once again, she ran, her breath coming out in desperate gasps.

Soon enough, she came to a set of steps, concrete, cold and clinical. She mounted them with gusto and burst through the unlocked door at the top of them, almost knocking it from its hinges. The impact knocked her off balance, but she didn't want to stop. Using her forward momentum, she half staggered, half crawled the next few feet until a perfectly timed kick to her side sent her sprawling. She fell in a heap, somehow managing to knock both elbows and both knees against the hard floor, the sudden pain momentarily stunning her.

'Ah,' said a voice Christine recognised as belonging to the barman. Instantly she realised that she was back in the pub again, her nostrils breathing in the smell of stale beer and sweat... and something else. Something metallic. And something animal. Something deadly.

***

The barman watched with absolute glee as the woman realised what kind of situation she was in. Although she hadn't quite put together all the pieces, he could tell that she knew that she wasn't safe. The look in her eye reminded him of the look on the pigeon's face as Kit threw himself at it. He wondered if she would fight as hard as that little fella had. He wondered if she would scream. He hoped that she would, it would be more fun if she did. If he were a werewolf, he'd make sure that his prey screamed.

'Is it that time already?' he asked as two men walked through the now open 'Staff Only' door, his smile broadening. Sure, he was jealous of Kit, but the barman loved his work.

'No, not quite.' Peter said. He looked around, surveying the scene in the bar. The barman couldn't tell if he approved of what he saw or not; Peter had never been easy to read. 'It won't be long now, though. Not long at all.'

The shadows next to the barman almost seemed to quiver with excitement.

Wolf Kit snarled and stalked towards the new prey that lay in front of him, blood dripping from his jaw and feathers stuck out from his teeth almost comically. Christine looked up, unwilling to believe what her eyes were showing her. It just wasn't possible. Her vision started to cloud over and turn grey. Her eyes rolled back, and she willingly slipped into unconsciousness once more.

Peter held Wolf Kit in his gaze and walked over to Christine's prone form. Under his new master's command, the wolf stood still. Sufficiently convinced of the wolf's loyalty, Peter turned his attention back to the woman at his feet. 'Be a dear and tie her up.'

Nodding at his employer's request, the barman disappeared behind the bar to find something suitable for the job.

CHAPTER TWELVE

This time, the sound of voices nudged her back into consciousness. Christine kept her eyes closed, not wanting to let her companions know that she was awake. She was still alive, they hadn't killed her yet, so she must be useful to them. For what, she wasn't sure, but she had to make sure that things remained that way. Gradually, the voices gained focus and she was able to understand what was being said. The more she knew, the more valuable she could make herself. Knowledge was power and all that.

'Ah, you're awake!' the barman's voice said almost cheerfully. How could he know? She hadn't even opened her eyes or murmured. Had she?

'Er... yeah...' a groggy voice said, and Christine realised that the barman's statement hadn't been directed at her. Apparently, there were other unconscious people in the room. Christine imagined that the room may look like the aftermath of a college party. ‘Er... what’s going on?’

Christine heard footsteps moving around the room, possibly the barman getting closer to the tired man. ‘What do you remember?’

‘Not much.’ the voice said. ‘Had some pretty vivid dreams though, they almost felt real.’

She heard shuffling, as if someone was trying to sit up on a bed. Memories of her own bed, in her own home, flooded into her mind. She would give almost anything to be there now. A sense of longing filled her.

‘Wait... what is she doing here?’ the groggy voice said. Christine couldn’t resist it any longer, she opened her eyes. Not much, just a sliver. Just enough to have a look, a bit like when you’re trying to peek at the neighbours through a gap in the curtains. Just enough to see if she was the ‘she’ the groggy voice referred to. With no small amount of relief, she noticed that the barman had his back to her, but the owner of the groggy voice looked directly at her partly opened eyes. Shared recognition passed between them; it was a sober version of the Drunk Guy. The one she had been worrying over. The whole reason why she was in all this mess in the first place. She closed her eyes again, not knowing if he was friend or foe, and hoping that he’d think he had imagined her being awake.

Kit had some vague recollections of seeing the woman before, in the pub after his job interview. During their fleeting glance, Kit had noticed that her eyes had been full of terror. That look, along with the zip ties around her wrists and ankles, told him that she wasn’t here voluntarily.

Then a flash of a memory overwhelmed him. His ears rang, and pain ripped through his head. He clenched his jaw, as if that action alone would drive the pain out. He hadn't just seen her after his job interview, he'd seen her more recently too. He'd seen her in his dream.

But, if she was here, it couldn't have been a dream, could it?

Kit opened his eyes and stared at his hands, as if expecting them to be covered in fur... or blood... or both. Now that he thought about it, he thought he could smell her panic, her disbelief. Kit looked back down at the woman, but she didn't meet his eyes. She had locked herself away behind her eyelids, a futile attempt at safety. Kit felt like he knew how she felt. Although she wasn't safe there, she could at least pretend it wasn't happening.

'So, you do remember a bit then?' the barman probed. He seemed to be enjoying this.

'I... I don't know...'

'Do you need me to jog your memory?'

'I...' Kit didn't know what to say next. What *could* he say? Did he really want to know what had happened? Did he really want to know what he had become?

'Let me help you.' the barman said as he positioned himself directly in front of him, gently putting a hand on both of Kit's shoulders. '*Om grutt.*'

'Fuck.' Kit couldn't manage to say anything else. It had all been real. Those two nonsense words had the power to confirm everything.

'I can tell you what *Om grutt* is now. You wanted to know about that, didn't you?' It felt like the barman was mocking him. 'I can tell you all about it.... or have you changed your mind now? Has something left a bad taste in your mouth?'

Kit's tongue ran around his mouth, as if following the barman's suggestion, finding scraps of... something... between his teeth. There was a weird taste there, but Kit had a feeling that he knew exactly what it was. In front of him, inches from his face, the barman smiled. It was as if the man could read his thoughts. He didn't want this strange man running around inside his head.

'That was from when you were feeling peckish last night.' he said, that shit-eating grin now firmly plastered on his face. 'Get it? Peckish? It was a bloody pigeon!'

The barman started to laugh, clearly pleased with his own joke. Meanwhile, Kit wasn't finding anything about this funny at all.

'Lighten up, bud.' the barman said, finally unclasping Kit's shoulders. 'It's the dawn of a new day. A new beginning! Can you feel it, Kit? Are you excited?'

Kit thought about the barman's words. It did feel like he was on the cusp of something. It certainly felt like something was about to happen. However, given the kidnapped woman on the other side of the room, Kit wasn't convinced that it was necessarily a good thing. Good things rarely started with kidnappings.

'I'll take your silence as a 'yes', shall I?' the barman said, apparently not caring either way. 'So, what was I talking about? Ah yes! *Om grutt*! The *Om grutt* is your official entrance into wolfhood. Oh, don't look so surprised, Kit. What did you think was happening? Don't tell me that you always tear into live pigeons with your teeth.'

And with that, everything became crystal clear. As unbelievable as it was, Kit had become the stuff of B-Movie legend. He was a werewolf.

'What does *Om grutt* mean?' Kit said. He had thousands of questions, but it felt like this one was a good place to get started.

'Damned if I know.' The barman said, a look of disappointment on his face. 'My employers and I have an agreement. I don't ask, and they don't tell me. Only those who have completed the *Om grutt* understand the language.'

'Then why don't *I* understand it?' Kit was already finding flaws in the barman's words and this gave him hope. Maybe this whole thing was an elaborate hoax. An elaborate hoax that was in very poor taste if the bound woman was anything to go by.

'Good question, Kit. I'm glad you're paying attention.' the barman said. The smile was back again, but not as intense as before. The man seemed to like it when he was able to impart wisdom. 'You don't understand it, because although you have started the *Om grutt*, there's still something else to do before it's completed.'

'What? Like dotting the i's and crossing the t's?' Kit's eyes rolled as he asked. He was getting sick of this bullshit and he just wanted to go home.

'Something like that...It's almost time to get things started.' the barman said as he checked his watch and nodded. 'Yes, not much longer now.'

As if hearing their cue, footsteps sounded in the corridor outside the room. Kit assumed that he was still in the pub, but he had no real way of knowing, except for the familiar smell of stale beer that seemed to have saturated into everything. Now that was something that he was having a hard time trying to explain away. How had he ended up with an enhanced sense of smell?

Someone twisted the door handle and slowly pushed the door open.

'How's everything going in here?' said a voice, the owner of which was now entering the room. The man was smartly dressed in a black tailored suit and his dark brown hair was neatly cropped.

'Everything is running according to schedule, sir.' the barman replied. There was a glint in his eye, Kit noted. This was a man eager to please and hoping to be noticed by his superiors. Kit suddenly realised that the barman wasn't at the top of the food chain.

'And what about you, Kit? How are you feeling?' the man said, his blue eyes looked at Kit like a doctor appraising a patient. Meanwhile, Christine listened intently. She couldn't be sure, but she thought she recognised this voice. Was it one of her friends from earlier? Was it Peter? She fought against the impulse to open her eyes.

'I'm fine.' Kit said. 'Confused though.'

'Yes, that's to be expected.' the man said. 'Now, I'm sure that our friend here has been filling you in on what's going on and what *Om grutt* is, but I'd like to take a few moments to make sure that you've been properly brought up to speed. So, I may go over some things that you've already heard, but I feel it's important to be thorough. Is that alright, Kit?'

'Yes, that's fine. In fact, anything you tell me would be useful. This guy hasn't really told me anything.'

The smartly dressed man looked at the barman, a look of amusement flashed across his features. 'Is that so? I think we'll need to discuss that later. You may leave now.'

The barman gave a sombre nod and then scuttled out of the room. Kit was amazed at the amount of power his new companion had.

'Now... where were we?' the man said and sat down on the bed. His hand brushed an imaginary piece of fluff from his immaculately pressed black trousers. 'I think the best thing to do is to start by introducing myself. I've been terribly rude so far, haven't I?'

'Er... don't worry about it.'

'Right you are. My name is Peter Smedley and my colleague here, Mr Lawson, brought you to our attention as someone who may benefit from being part of our very unique organisation.'

CHAPTER THIRTEEN

After his terrifically productive meeting with Kit, Peter didn't want to be getting a stern telling off from his colleague and, yet, here he was. It was bound to happen sooner or later, Peter thought. Poor old Erik had been stewing over Peter's little transgression for three whole days. He must be fit to burst by now.

'So, what's the big plan? How are we getting out of this one?' Erik was angry, that much was clear. He was so angry that Peter almost felt nervous; his companion was usually such a mild-mannered individual. But, at the same time, Peter also wanted to laugh. You see, when Erik was agitated, he had the habit of slipping in and out of his native German accent. The funny part was that Erik didn't just switch between German and English, he also dipped in and out of accents of every place he'd lived during his lifetime, and that was a very long list indeed. Erik picked up accents like most people pick up the sniffles.

'We? Don't you worry about it, Erik. There's no 'we' here. It's my mess, so I'm cleaning it up.' Peter said as he walked over to the bar. The men were back in the main bar room of the pub. It was still empty, but it still retained all the delightful human smells that bars have. Pouring both himself and Erik a shot of whiskey, Peter looked back at his friend. 'Relax. Everything will be fine. You'll see.'

Erik crossed the room in a couple of strides. Even his walk was angry. The man was a bag of nerves hidden inside an expensive suit. Apparently, those anxious nerves had now had enough of being hidden and burst out through the man's mouth in a shout. 'HOW.... HOW CAN YOU SAY THAT?'

'I said to relax, Erik. This doesn't sound like you're relaxing now, does it? This still sounds angry.' Peter held out on of the shot glasses. 'Here, have this. It'll make you feel better.'

Erik looked at the glass warily, as if it contained poison, before shrugging slightly, grabbing it and knocking it back. The whiskey's warmth filled his throat almost immediately. As much as he was loathed to admit it, Peter was right; it did make him feel a bit better. The alcohol did nothing for him, but the taste reminded him of a time when it did. He was still angry. He just felt slightly better about it. After a few moments, he had pulled himself together and allowed himself to speak again. 'How will everything be fine?'

'I've got myself a patsy.'

'The guy going through the *Om grutt*?' Erik said, intrigued.

'That's the one. He doesn't know it yet, but he will take the fall.' Peter explained, pouring himself another drink. This one was celebratory.

'I don't know...' Erik held out his glass for another shot. 'The Council is bound to see through it.'

'Ah, the Council. They're not all-seeing, all-knowing, Erik. It will be fine.' Peter flashed what he hoped was a reassuring smile at Erik. Erik, meanwhile, didn't seem to be buying it.

'Fine...' he said, pausing to find the right words. 'But did you actually clean up? ...And I mean literally clean up.'

'No, it's still a mess. It looks like a crime scene. Which I suppose it is, isn't it!?' Peter said with a laugh. 'Besides, I want them to find it.'

'The Council? What kind of game are you playing?'

'No, not the Council. People, Erik. I want normal people to find it.' Peter downed his shot. 'They need to see it.'

Erik may have said something at this point, but Peter didn't hear him. He was too busy reliving his transgression in his mind's eye.

CHAPTER FOURTEEN

Life was what happened while you were busy making plans. Or so the saying went. And that's exactly how Lynn Morton felt as she sat nursing a glass of red wine on the sofa. She and her husband Nathan were spending the evening how they spent most of their evenings; planning their future while drinking wine and watching TV. As tonight's show was one of those property development things, they were now discussing what their future home would look like.

'That one's nice.' Nathan said, gesturing at the TV, wine glass in hand. 'I could live in that... but I'd want to move it and put it somewhere hot and sunny.'

'Hmm-mmm.' Lynn said. It was her standard, non-committal response. It had been one of 'those' days at work. Annoying and long. So very, very long.

'It would be nice to live near the coast as well, wouldn't it?'

'Hmm-mmm.' And so, the evening, and the bottle of wine, went on. It was just like any other night. By ten o'clock, everyone - including their nine-year-old son, Evan - was tucked up in bed. It was, after all, a school night.

Silence covered the semi-detached house like a blanket. The street outside was empty and still. Even after nearly twelve years, this was something that Lynn still hadn't got used to. Having grown up on a council estate, she was used to hearing noise at all hours. Cars speeding. Car doors slamming. People talking. People shouting. Children playing. Dogs barking. Loud music. Loud TVs. There was never a quiet moment. But here, on this suburban street with its large, green trees down the side, things were different. The neighbours were respectful to each other and the atmosphere was calm and collected. Even though the neighbours had no idea of Lynn's past, she couldn't shake the feeling that they thought she didn't belong there. It still felt a little bit too posh for her. Or, she felt she was a little too common for it. Either way, she felt like she stood out like a sore thumb.

So that was why the mundane sound of a twig snapping startled her. There was someone out there, breaking the silence that she still wasn't used to. She looked at her husband. 'Nate...'

Nathan snorted in response before rolling over. Even though he wasn't awake, Lynn continued to whisper. 'I heard something. It was probably nothing, but I'm just gonna have a little nose out the window.'

This time Nate didn't respond at all; the man was a deep sleeper. Lynn carefully got out of bed and padded over to the window. The previously hot day felt like a lifetime ago and the temperature had dropped so much that her bare feet felt like ice. The world outside glowed orange thanks to the several streetlights that stood on guard along the road. Everything was still. There was no movement. No breeze. It was just like looking at a photograph. Just as she was about to chalk up her unease to an overexcited imagination, something moved. She caught it out of the corner of her eye. It wasn't a big movement, just a slight shift. Enough for her to know that someone was out there. Turning her attention to that area, Lynn squinted into the twilight. There, just next to their well-pruned hedge was... something. Whatever it was, it seemed to sense that she had spotted it and it retreated into darkness. Now that it was swallowed by shadow, identifying it was next to impossible. All Lynn knew was that it was big.

Regardless of its size, it didn't appear to be hurting anyone or causing a nuisance, so Lynn decided to go back to bed. She walked back across the carpet, not bothering to creep because Nathan wouldn't hear her anyway and crawled back into bed. The blankets once again accepted her as one of their own. As she lay there, trying to reconnect with sleep, she thought about her nocturnal visitor. Was it some kind of rare animal? Would it return tomorrow night? Lynn wondered if she could get one of those wildlife cameras to record it. If it was a rare animal, surely footage of it would create quite a buzz on the internet. Lynn decided to investigate buying a camera in the morning.

She closed her eyes not knowing that she would never sleep again.

***

Evan awoke to the sound of the back door opening downstairs. He had thought that both of his parents were in bed, so he snuggled deeper under his blankets for protection. It felt safer underneath them and he didn't want to know what was down there. It was a false sense of security. While he wasn't scared of the dark and hadn't been for at least a year as he kept telling his parents, he still wasn't completely comfortable with it. If he was older, he would have said it was the fear of the unknown and the fact that the unknown could get really fricking close to you in the dark without you even noticing. It could sneak right up to your bed, wrap a bony hand around your ankle and drag you out before you even had the chance to look at it. That's what scared Evan. Darkness wasn't scary; the things that lurked inside it were.

Despite not wanting to know who was downstairs, his ears strained against the night, searching for clues. Was the tap running? Was Dad getting a snack out of the fridge? Was Mum going to switch the TV on because she couldn't sleep?

But, there was nothing.

The lack of any noise scared the boy more than if there had been footsteps coming up the stairs. The lack of noise meant that someone was trying very hard to be as quiet as possible. There was a strong chance that it meant that they weren't supposed to be there. The thought that it could just be his mum or dad trying to be quiet and not wake anyone never crossed his mind. Sometimes you just know when something's not right. And things were starting to feel very wrong.

Evan started to try to come up with a plan. He wasn't a particularly brave or heroic child - in fact, he had once got scared in an episode of *Teenage Mutant Ninja Turtles*, but the less said about that the better - so, he didn't think about trying to warn his parents of their impending doom. In addition to his cowardice, there was also the fact that he could be wrong, and he didn't want to appear foolish. Not again, anyway. The *Turtles* incident had been quite enough, thank you very much. His hands gripped the side of his bed as if it were a raft and he was adrift at sea. But, he knew that lying there wouldn't help him, not if there was a burglar or monster somewhere downstairs. All they'd need to do was come up and look in his room and they'd find him immediately and then it would be *'Bye bye, Evan'*. No, he needed a better hiding place than that. Without moving from his sanctuary, Evan started to think of suitable hiding places. The trouble was that he was pretty much limited to just two. The first was under his bed, which he had already ruled out as being a bad idea, mainly because he was still a bit scared of anything else that might hide under there. The second was inside his wardrobe. The wardrobe won. The only thing was that he now needed to summon the courage to leave his patch of safety. Taking a deep breath, he rolled out of bed, taking the blanket with him, wearing it like armour. He was torn between being fast and being quiet, so he tried to combine the two, uncertain if he was successful in achieving either. The wardrobe door creaked slightly as he opened it, making him wince. The noise made him pause for a few seconds. Had someone heard him? The trouble with making noise was that it made it difficult to hear if anyone else was also making noise. It made you vulnerable.

No other noises were forthcoming, so Evan carefully clambered into the wardrobe, fighting all his usual clumsy tendencies as he did so. Once he had taken a seat on top of some plastic storage boxes that contained some of his toys, he gently closed the door. The door creaked once again, but Evan was thankful that it didn't make any more noise than that. Then there was nothing left to do but wait.

***

Just as Lynn had closed her eyes again, a noise disturbed her. She couldn't quite place what it was, but it seemed somewhat familiar. She strained her ears against the night, like her son was doing in the next room unbeknown to her. For quite a while, there was nothing. Then, as she was starting to relax, she heard Evan get out of bed and open his wardrobe. She'd know that door creak anywhere. What could he be doing at this time of night? She would have to investigate. Sighing, she sat up and got herself out of bed for the second time that night.

'Don't worry, Nate.' she said, out loud this time. 'I'll go see what he's up to.'

In truth, she didn't really mind that she was getting up again. The strange creature outside had spooked her more than she realised, and she was grateful for the distraction. Not only that, but she was intrigued. What was Evan up to?

As she walked around the double-bed, with Nathan still snoring in it, she tried to picture what was going on in the next room. Was he hiding? Did he just want to try sleeping somewhere else for a change? Was it a bit like camping? Was it part of a game? Evan was always dreaming up complex games with his imaginary friends.

She reached out her hand to pull open the bedroom door -

- and the door burst open on her, slamming against the bedroom wall and waking Nathan in the process. Nathan jumped out of bed like a flash, fear and confusion filling his eyes.

***

The sound of the door crashing open seemed huge from Evan's hiding place. It felt world shattering. Deafening and final. Evan peered through the small gap in the wardrobe doors, eager for information, but afraid of what he'd find. The darkness beyond his sanctuary told him nothing; its lips were sealed.

There was no way that the sound of his parents' bedroom door crashing wasn't real. He'd heard it with his own ears and its vibrations had reverberated around the house. Even so, Evan wished that he'd imagined it completely. He wished for this more than he'd ever wished for anything in his life. He wished for it more than he wished that he would get an XBox for Christmas. But, tonight was not the night for being granted wishes. Instead, he heard more crashing, mixed with screaming and something else. Was that a growl?

***

Nathan leapt in front of his wife, desperate to help her, but having no idea of how he was going to do it. The thing - because that's what it was, a thing - was massive, easily a foot taller than Nathan and he was hardly a short man. If that wasn't enough, it was covered with muscles. This thing had muscles that neither Nathan nor Lynn had ever seen before, let alone knew the name of. Somehow all this managed to fly through their heads in the precious few seconds that the thing stood still in front of them. After that, it was like the gates of hell had opened. The beast lashed out with a heavily clawed hand (or was it a paw?) and swiped Nathan out of the way. He crashed into the wall, catching his forehead on the radiator. In a bid to avoid blacking out, he focused on the sticky sensation the blood on his head gave him and started to struggle to his feet again.

Never one to stand idly by, Lynn grabbed the nearest object to her - a bedside lamp and held it like a weapon.

Had Evan seen her like this, he would have remarked on how she held that lamp like an orc would hold a warhammer she thought. Evan loved stuff like that. Lynn would have given anything to feel as powerful as the orcs looked on Evan's computer games. Instead, she felt tired and frightened, and was fairly convinced that she was going into shock. Who could blame her? It wasn't every day that a wolflike beast invaded your bedroom and attacked you. Hoping for the best, she swung the lamp at the beast's massive head and then ducked out of the way, dragging her dazed husband with her. Together, they collapsed in a heap on the floor, barely out of reach of their attacker. The beast wasted no time in closing the gap between them. Lynn looked into its black eyes and knew instantly that it was out for blood. This was one of those 'kill or be killed' situations. She could only hope that they could find some way to overpower it. They probably had a better chance of winning the lottery.

With a horrific guttural growl, the beast snapped its jaws at them. Its breath was putrid and fowl, decaying flesh of some other unfortunate victim was caught between its deadly looking teeth, making Lynn turn her face away. Vomit threatened to escape, but she pushed it down. There was no time for that. Between them, Lynn and Nathan took it in turn to lash out at the creature. Several punches and kicks found their target, but none seemed to have any kind of effect. This thing appeared to be invincible.

‘RUN!’ Nathan screamed as he attempted another flurry of punches. The beast let each one make contact, seemingly entertained by the couple’s efforts. It was toying with them, that much was clear. Its black eyes stared deep into Nathan’s own and, as it moved in for another attack, Nathan could see the level of intelligence lurking within them. Somehow, this made it worse. It was one thing to be attacked by a mindless creature that was just following its instincts, it was another to know that it knew exactly what it was doing. It knew exactly what level of pain it was inflicting. It was revelling in the fear it had created.

Lynn managed to make it a few steps before she heard the noise. Nothing in the world had ever seemed so final and defeated as that noise. It was a combination of a whoosh, a smack, and a slimy, sticky wetness. Turning slowly, she braced herself for what she was about to see; for she knew what her eyes would be greeted with. Nathan still stood, dressed only in his boxer shorts, but the beast had now stepped away from him, making sure that Lynn could see what had happened. Apparently, it didn't want to obstruct her view. Her husband's hands were pressed tightly over his belly, in a futile attempt to hold his insides in. His intestines had other ideas and they snaked between his fingers, flopping onto the carpet below. Even though he could feel his life slipping away from him, Nathan had the ridiculous thought that he had just ruined the carpet. It was only a couple of months old.

CHAPTER FIFTEEN

The sound of his companion sighing loudly shattered Peter's daydream. It was a hideous and obnoxious sound, due to both the interruption and because Peter knew what was coming next: more lectures. More holier-than-thou judgement and condescension.

On the whole, Erik was a good egg, as far as werewolves could be considered 'good eggs'. He followed the rules imposed by the Council to the letter, even if he did do everything he could to avoid that organisation, and always made sure that his debts were paid on time. Until he met Peter, and subsequently brought him into the club, Erik had been the poster child for all things werewolf, aside from one or two slip ups. Peter had changed all that. He liked to bend the rules and push the boundaries. He was a welcome gust of fresh air in a claustrophobic dank tomb. Or, at least, he had been. These days Erik was starting to worry that his protege was more of a liability and the wayward werewolf's most recent escapade did little to contradict that hypothesis.

'They'll have your head for this.' Erik knew that he had disturbed Peter from his recollections.

'I'd like to see them try.' Peter didn't even remotely seem to be bothered about the situation he had left them in. 'Our friends, *"The Six"*, are so out of touch. As I said before, they can't and don't watch our every move. They're never going to know if it was me or the new boy back there. Well, not unless someone takes it upon themselves to tell them.'

The younger man's stare promised violence and bloodshed and Erik found himself answering him hurriedly. He hated that the younger man made him feel like this. How had he let him garner so much power over him? 'No, I wouldn't say a word. I wouldn't dream of it. But, we need to be more careful. Just because they're not watching our every move now, I don't want to encourage them. Getting ourselves on their radar is the kind of scrutiny that I could do without.'

'If everything goes to plan, we won't need to be careful.' Peter said with a sly glint in his eye. 'If everything goes to plan, we'll be free.'

'Here we go again,' Erik rolled his eyes and his fear of the other man disappeared. This was a discussion that they had danced through on numerous occasions over the years. It was Peter's recurring daydream. 'I'm sure we talked about your plans for a revolution only the other day. Are you sure it's time to go through it again? Is it really that time already?'

'Yes, it is.' Peter's tone suggested that he was offended. Peter was dangerous when he was offended. 'But this time is different.'

'Different? How so?'

'I've taken action this time, haven't I?' Peter said, snarling. 'Or have you forgotten the whole reason for this argument? Don't you remember my delightful little slaughtered family?'

'No, of course I haven't forgotten your latest victims - or are they cries for attention? Either way, it doesn't matter, we still have time to tidy this mess up. We'll go with your plan on that one; we'll use your new fall guy. There's just no need to start a werewolf social justice movement. We are not being oppressed. Peter, dear, we are at the very top of the food chain. We cannot get any higher.'

'We can.' Peter said, stubbornly. He reminded Erik of a petulant child who wasn't getting his own way. Unlike most petulant children, however, he was in possession of a fairly compelling argument. '*"The Six"* are higher than us.'

Erik didn't want to admit it, but the younger man had a point. For as long as Erik could remember, he had been governed by the Council. Despite effectively being in place to keep a rather large, and rather widespread, pack of wild animals under control, the Council was a well-ordered and well-maintained organisation, with multiple individuals who could be considered to be employees. Although, they were rarely paid in a conventional manner. As with any large, multinational corporation, there were those who sat at its head. In the case of the Council, these were known as *"The Six"*. Even though the names and faces of those at the top changed rather frequently, their number never grew nor dwindled. No matter how many challenges or schemes to gain power littered the Council's history, *"The Six"* remained. At present, *"The Six"* consisted of three women and three men, but this wasn't by design. At various points over the centuries, "*The Six*" had been all male, all female or a combination of both sexes. It all depended on who had it in them to fight the longest and hardest at the time.

'You're going to make a bid for power.' Erik said, realising that Peter was actually serious about taking action this time. 'Who are you going to assassinate to claim your place in "*The Six*"?'

'Power? Yes, but I'm not planning on joining that ridiculous little club. No, *"The Six"* has had its day. What I'm planning will be its extinction event. You say that we're top of the food chain - let's make sure that the world knows that. I'm taking us public. In fact, we may already be in the mainstream consciousness. Be a dear and turn the TV on.' He said, waving a hand at the wall-mounted TV. 'I want to watch the news and see if my little project has been discovered.'

A low growl crept from Erik's throat. Any other protege wouldn't have the audacity to tell their elders what to do, but here was Peter, bossing Erik around like his own personal butler. For the briefest of moments, Erik's self-restraint threatened to slip. A flash of red danced across his eyes as he fantasized about what it would be like to rip out the other man's jugular. Although he had a certain fondness for his companion, such a turn of events was a long time coming. Erik had often wondered how he had managed to put up with the stubborn young pup for quite so long. Perhaps he was going for a martyrdom of some kind, although he didn't relish the thought of dying for his cause. No, that wouldn't do at all.

But, still, in spite of all that, Erik was curious and found himself switching on the TV. An explosion of light, sound and colour erupted from the small box and made him wince. That was the problem with heightened senses, you became ridiculously over-sensitive to just about everything. Some days, the only thing you could do was sit in a darkened room in complete silence.

Nobody ever mentioned such inconvenience to the newbies of course. That would have been terrible for morale.

The newscaster's voice made Erik inhale sharply. You'd think that after all these years that he would have become used to light and sound and all their delightful little effects, but there was something about TVs and other digital devices that still threw him off. There was a coldness to them that he was never quite ready for; they were keen blades, ready to slice right through him. He wondered if other werewolves experienced the same thing, but he never wondered enough to actually ask anyone - not even Peter. Especially not Peter. To do so would be to admit to a weakness. It would threaten Erik's position in the pack. Not that Peter saw him as anything more than his equal anyway. But it was nice to keep up appearances.

'Here we go!' Peter said, sounding like a child who was just about to meet Santa in a shopping centre. 'Are you ready for my five minutes of fame?'

'I can't wait.' Erik said, being sure to withhold any enthusiasm. Truth be told, there was a certain excitement here. If everything went according to Peter's plan, the world as they knew it would change forever. Hell, it wouldn't just change for them - or even werewolfkind as a whole - it would change for everyone. Things would never be the same again. There was no turning back. For better or for worse. Erik became aware that he was holding his breath and swung a look at his companion. Peter hadn't noticed, his eyes were fixed on the box, enraptured on the talking head encapsulated within. The newscaster covered a variety of topics, each one holding little significance to Erik and Peter, but there was nothing about Peter's adventures. Not even the smallest of hints. Erik wasn't sure if he was pleased or disappointed.

'Hmm...' Erik said, trying to choose his next words carefully.

'Ah well,' Peter said, clapping his hands together in a decisive, confident manner. 'Not to worry, maybe it'll be on the next one. What is it that they say? Good things come to those who wait, right? The pay-off will be even sweeter when it finally arrives.'

Erik nodded, feeling a little dumbfounded. Somehow, Peter had managed to snatch victory from the jaws of defeat. Had things been the other way around, Erik would have sulked for days. Peter was different. He was smiling, for fuck's sake. His plan - or, at least, part of it - had unravelled before his eyes and, yet, here he was, smiling like the cat that got the cream. It was like they were all just playing parts in a film that he had seen countless times before. Somehow, he knew what was going to happen in the end, so he didn't particularly care about the journey. What did it matter how you got there, if you knew you were heading straight for a happy ending? Erik couldn't help but admire the younger man. No-one could, really. It was all part of his charm. It was what made him the perfect werewolf. However, his over-confidence also made him a natural disaster. Peter walked a fine line daily; tightrope walking between sense and pandemonium. In some ways it was a thrill to watch - you just had to forget that your life also hung in the balance. It was a bizarre suicide pact. But, hey, what's a little hara-kiri between friends?

'Yes, actually this is even better.' Peter was still talking, his enthusiasm already starting to infect Erik like the insidious plague that it was, gradually wrapping its eager, yet methodical tendrils around his thoughts. 'Let the bodies rot a bit. It will add to the shock value when they're finally discovered. The more horrific it seems, the better. Don't you agree?'

And Erik did.

In spite of his better judgement, Erik found himself firmly on board with whatever scheme Peter had in mind. It was complete insanity, of course. But, if there was ever going to be someone to pull off such a feat, it was Peter. Erik decided that he may as well get a front row seat to whatever carnage ensued. Whether it was their blood or that of "*The Six*" that was spilled, Erik would have the best seat in the house.

'I imagine it will be pretty spectacular.' Erik said, having come to terms with his decision in the dark recesses of his mind.

'You've changed your tune.' Peter said with an almost predatory smile. The raised eyebrow suggested a hint of surprise, but his tone betrayed him. Peter had known that this would happen all along. Maybe the cocky arsehole could see into the future.

'Yes, in a way. I'm interested to see what happens.' Erik said as he turned the TV off, trying not to squint as its brightness assaulted his retinas. It was like it was trying to get one last dig in before he pulled its plug.

***

As Peter and Erik had discovered, there was nothing about Peter's transgression on the news. That didn't mean that the crime scene was going to go undiscovered for long.

Back in sunny suburbia, Denise rang the doorbell for the third time in as many minutes. It wasn't like Lynn to stand her up and she would usually call or text if she was running late or needed to change the plans completely. Denise's phone revealed no more information than it did two minutes ago. It was ridiculous. It was like the woman and her entire family had just got up that morning and disappeared from the face of the earth.

'Excuse me.' the voice made Denise jump out of her skin. She hadn't even heard anyone walk up the gravel driveway, so to find this woman in a trouser suit and dark glasses standing on the doorstep with her was a shock to say the least.

Denise put a hand to her chest and laughed nervously. 'Oh, sorry. You scared me... I didn't know you were there.'

'Don't worry about it,' the woman said. 'You seemed very engrossed in your phone there.'

'Yes, I'm trying to get in touch with my friend. I was meant to pick her up this morning.' Denise had no idea why she was telling this stranger so much information, but she felt compelled to. 'She's not answering my calls. She hasn't text me and no-one's opening the front door.'

'I know, Miss... er...'

'Denise. You can call me Denise.' A horrible sinking feeling came over her and began its heavy descent into the pit of her stomach.

'Denise, I'm with the police and there has been an incident. Please can you come with us? My colleague will need to speak to you. I think you'll be able to help us with our investigation.'

'Yes... Yes, of course.' Denise said, her mouth agape. Something terrible had happened.

'This way, please.' the woman said, leading Denise back down the gravelly path. At the end of the driveway, Denise noticed a line of 'DO NOT CROSS' police tape.

'How long has that been there?' She asked, pointing at the tape.

'Oh, for most of the night.' the woman said.

Denise frowned. It certainly hadn't been there when she'd first arrived.

CHAPTER SIXTEEN

Kit found himself in a different room. This one was above the pub and more luxurious than his previous accommodation. Briefly, his thoughts drifted back to the woman who was still likely trapped in that room, bound to the bed stained with fuck knows what and wondering what the hell she did to deserve ending up there. The thoughts and concerns faded as he reclined on the comfortable double bed. The sheets were clean; not only were they lacking in any visible stains, but Kit's heightened sense of smell picked up on the detergent almost immediately. His eyelids felt heavy, so he let them drop. It didn't take long for him to fall asleep.

The dreams that came were strange. Not necessarily because of their content, although that was certainly strange enough, but because Kit had the feeling that he'd lived these events before. In fact, he knew he had; he had the scars to prove it. Dream Kit found himself naked and back in the tunnel, only this time, he wasn't alone. This time two men stood close to him, dressed in suits, yellow eyes blazing. Recognising them as the men he had seen earlier, Kit tried to remember their names. He had only spoken to one of them, Peter, but he seemed like a different man in this tunnel. When they'd had their chat, he'd been friendly and calm. Now he seemed bloodthirsty and cunning. Kit was witnessing the other side of Peter's complex, but effective coin.

'Hold him down.' Peter said as he nodded slightly in Dream Kit's direction. Not knowing what was happening, but sensing that it was something awful, Dream Kit screamed. Peter didn't seem to be bothered. Someone else - the barman - appeared from the shadows and did as Peter asked. 'Do you have it?'

The other man in a suit nodded and handed Peter a small glass vial. 'Of course.'

Dream Kit tried to look up, he was in equal parts intrigued and terrified by the contents of that vial. Whatever it was, he knew it could be nothing good, and yet he found that he wasn't resisting. The barman didn't need to hold him down, he would just lie there and accept anything that happened.

'Now,' Peter said, crouching down next to Dream Kit and whispering in his ear. 'It's my first time doing this - well, it's the first time any of us have done this for a while - but, don't worry, I've heard it's quite straightforward and I've got my friend here to guide me. He's an expert, so I'll soon get the hang of it.'

The glass of the vial glinted in the candlelight. The colour of the contents was unmistakable; it was blood. Dark, red and thick. Inside the blood, something moved. Something small and pale squirmed inside the liquid. It seemed excited, its excitement growing as Peter held the vial closer to Kit.

'It's time.' Peter said, his words spurring the barman into action again. Now that he knew that he didn't have to hold Kit down, he was free to complete his other tasks. As he was face down on the floor, he couldn't see what the barman was doing, he could only watch Peter's smiling face and listen to the movement that was happening behind him and above him. Suddenly, one of the barman's hands clamped hard on his shoulder.

'Now, this may sting a bit.' Peter warned. "Sting" was an understatement. Something - Kit wasn't sure what - plunged into his neck. He was immediately paralysed, unable to do anything except endure the pain. Something warm and wet cascaded over his neck and pooled on the floor beneath him. He didn't need to look to know that he was bleeding.

Although he was unable to move, Kit still had the ability to feel everything that was being done to him. A shiver wanted to run through him as he felt fingers pulling the wound on his neck open. His imagination ran away with itself as it thought of the gaping wound that lurked there. Then he heard the unmistakable sound of a cork being popped; only this wasn't champagne. The vial was now open. The thing inside it started to thrash around, desperate to be out. Kit could only watch as the other man passed Peter a pair of tweezers. Peter accepted them with another smile and used them to pull the creature from the vial. It was a washed out mix of pink, grey and white and it wiggled enthusiastically the closer it got to Kit. Kit now realised how ridiculous the universe was. The thing - the ugly, repulsive creature - was some kind of worm. For a moment, he felt like he was the butt of some cosmic joke. But, it only lasted for a moment. After that all he felt was pain. Someone - Kit imagined that it was Peter - had dropped the worm into the open wound in the back of his neck. Kit felt it wiggle and burrow deeper into him. He felt it scrape against bone and toy with his nerves. He screamed. Again.

Through his pain, he heard Peter stand and walk away. 'He'll pass out soon. When he does, see to it that he is sewn up. Maybe clean the wound a little too. We wouldn't want it to become infected.'

'I thought you guys could heal.' the barman's voice replied.

'That we can, but it's very early days for our friend here. He's just a baby.' Peter laughed at that. Kit didn't think it was very funny.

'Okay, you've got it.' the barman said. His tone hadn't changed, he obviously hadn't found Peter's joke very funny either. 'What do I do then? I mean, I've only done this a couple of times before and that was years ago... and we never did it like this. They were always... y'know... willing.'

'A fair point.' Peter said. 'Once he's all sewn up, leave him here to sleep it off a bit. Put his clothes somewhere where he can find them.'

'Then what?'

'Then let him be on his way.'

Kit couldn't believe it, they were letting him go.

'Aren't you worried that he'll run off? Is someone going to follow him?' the barman seemed to be as shocked at Peter's decision as Kit was.

'Don't worry, he'll be back. Trust me, I know exactly what I'm doing.' Peter said. And he did. After all, he'd been in Kit's place before. He knew about the magnetic pull that would guide the young man back to the pub. Back to his maker.

***

Kit's eyes snapped open and he raised his hand to gently rub the back of his neck. The texture of the scar was immediately obvious, but even now it was fading. It definitely felt less pronounced than it did when he'd last touched it. But, the scar was the least of his worries. There was a worm.

Inside him.

Bile threatened to escape, so Kit clamped his hand over his mouth. Even though Peter and his friends had kidnapped him, assaulted him and let a worm take up residence in his body, for some reason he didn't want to ruin the decor in this bedroom. Taking a deep breath, he calmed himself down. Okay, so there was a worm in his neck. Well, he was assuming it was still in his neck. What was to stop it from travelling around, doing whatever it wanted? Kit had no answer to that question and the thought made the vomit rise again, so he decided that the best thing to do would be to stop contemplating it completely. He switched his focus.

The woman.

She'd been in that room with him. Maybe she had also been implanted with a worm. Maybe she was also going through these changes. But, that didn't seem quite right. She definitely hadn't been receiving the same kind of treatment as he was, and she'd looked terrified when she'd seen him turn. Maybe he should find her.

Stretching, Kit rose from the bed and, as quietly as possible, crept across the bedroom, his bare feet taking full advantage of the luxurious carpet his captors had supplied. Now that the initial violence was over, they seemed to be doing their best to make him want to stay.

And, Kit couldn't deny it, he did want to. For the first time in a long time, he felt like he belonged. The trouble was, he just wasn't sure what it was that he now belonged to and if it was something he wanted to belong to in the first place. He had so many questions. When was the Peter guy coming back? When they'd last spoken, he'd done little except for introduce himself and hint at the possibility of a job. Kit wondered if all the confusion was intentional, something to keep him on his toes and second guessing everything.

He reached the door handle and tried it. It twisted easily. He wasn't locked in. Apparently free to do as he wished, Kit left the room, but he shut the door very carefully and quietly behind him. Even if they did trust him, drawing unnecessary attention to himself just seemed careless.

The interior of the rooms above the pub, did not match the establishment below, and they certainly didn't hold any resemblance to the rooms and tunnels below that. The pub below had wooden, worn floors combined with mismatched furniture and several coatings of stale beer. This place, on the other hand, looked like the kind of place that nobility from the 1800's would want to spend time in. Not that Kit knew anything about nobility from the 1800's, or any era for that matter. All he knew was that he felt very out of place there, but not entirely uncomfortable. He could certainly get used to the furnishings given a bit of time. He just didn't know if he would stick around long enough to test the theory.

Letting himself relax, he started to explore. Upon leaving the bedroom, he had found himself in a room that looked like a sitting room come library. A couple of leather chairs and a table acted as a focal point in the room's centre, and an assortment of books lined the shelves. Peter and his friends were obviously big readers. A large, flat screen TV hung on the wall, looking a bit out of place. The room smelt of the furniture cleaner that his grandmother used to use, and he found himself smiling in spite of the confusion and fear. Peter looked to be relatively young, certainly no older than his mid-forties, yet he seemed to have the tastes of someone much older. That was, of course, assuming that this place belonged to Peter. Kit wasn't sure what to think any more. Things made less sense the more he thought about them.

Kit decided to open the next door that was closest to him. It creaked slightly as it opened out onto a small landing area and a staircase. His keen ears picked up the sounds of the pub below. Closing the door, he decided his time was better spent exploring the rest of the upstairs rooms. He walked across the sitting room to where three more doors stood. The first one was open and revealed a small, yet clean kitchen. The next was locked, as was its neighbour. Kit didn't have as much freedom as he first believed. He was still being kept on a leash, it was just a longer one than before. Standing in front of one of the locked doors, Kit pressed his ear against the wood. If the woman was up here with him, he should be able to hear her. The only thing to greet him was silence. He tried the same process with the next door with the same result. Although he was disappointed at not finding the woman, he was glad that something else had been confirmed. Peter and his friends were not around.

Kit was alone.

CHAPTER SEVENTEEN

The solitude became tiresome quickly and Kit lost count of the amount of times that he had paced from room to room. He'd examined the contents of any cupboard that wasn't locked, and he found... Nothing. The rooms that Kit found himself confined to were decidedly dull.

Then, a realisation came to Kit. He wasn't confined. He was free to walk down to the pub whenever he wished. The pub could provide him with drink and maybe he could find out where that woman was. He could also get something to eat. His stomach growled at the thought. Looking around the sitting room, he searched for a reason to stay. Finding none, he made his way to the open door and down the stairs, holding on to the rail to support him. His palms were sweaty, his grip tight. Despite now being kept in comfort, Kit was still well aware that he was being *kept* and the thought of doing something to anger his prison guards worried him.

Not because he wanted to please them, but because he didn't want to face the consequences of pissing Peter off. Absently, he rubbed the back of his neck, the worm within twitched. Angering Peter would be a bad move.

The door to the pub was well-oiled, opening with barely a squeak into the beer and whiskey-soaked room. As with his first visit, nobody looked up at him when he entered. This still wasn't a western.

The only person to notice him was the barman and he stood smiling on the other side of the bar, drying a pint glass with a raggedy tea-towel. 'Good to see you up and about, Kit.'

Kit nodded, no longer drawn into the smile. Kit know knew that the smile that once suggested friendship and safety was merely a mask for brutality and torment. It was just an illusion, and Kit saw straight through it. He saw through it, but it was too late.

'Drink?' the barman said, still doing a wonderful impression of a normal barman despite having sliced open a neck in the not-too-distant past. 'Beer? Whiskey? Rum? Cider?'

'Umm... Beer.' Kit said. '... and a shot of whiskey.'

'Good choice.' The barman said as Kit reached into his pocket and pulled out his wallet. 'Don't worry about that. It's on the house. You're part of a very exclusive club now, so you drink for free.'

'Thanks.' He said, not trusting himself to say much more. The beer and the whiskey were drank quickly and in silence. The barman didn't seem to mind or take it personally.

While Kit was no stranger to a drink or two, he did usually notice a slight effect after even just half a pint. A warming of the blood. A slight feeling of wellness. This time was different. This time he felt nothing.

'No buzz, eh?' the barman said, as if he knew exactly what was going through Kit's head. Perhaps he did.

'No.' Kit said, disappointed that the barman knew more about this than he did. He could ask him about what was happening and what Peter had in store for him, but he knew that he wouldn't trust a word that came out of the barman's mouth.

'Don't worry, you'll get your kicks in other ways.' the barman said, that knowing smile plastered across his smug face still. 'You'll see soon enough.'

'I want to ask you something.' Kit said, changing the subject completely. The barman nodded. 'There was a girl in the room with me - the other room, I mean, not upstairs. Do you know where she is?'

'Of course.' he said. 'She's still in there. Go through the *"Staff Only"* door, through the room and follow the corridor. You'll find some stairs leading you down to the tunnels. Then just... er... follow your nose. Or you could always go out back and go in the way you left last time.'

Nodding, Kit was surprised at how easily the barman divulged the information, but unsurprised at the revelation that he had been watched the last time. 'Can I see her?'

'Go on then. Why do you think I told you where she was? You're free to do as you wish, Kit.'

'Okay.' he said, his voice flat and quiet. He still didn't trust this man. He didn't think he ever would. Before the barman could say another word, Kit walked away from the bar and headed towards the door. The same door that his unconscious form had been dragged through on the day of his job interview. Kit, however, didn't remember that at all. The door opened onto what looked like a normal staff room. There was a sofa, a TV, a kettle and a microwave. A dirty cup, possibly owned by the barman, sat next to the kettle, waiting for its owner's next break. Choosing not to concern himself with any of that, Kit chose to walk straight through and opened the door at the other side. As promised, a corridor waited for him on the other side. At least the barman wasn't lying about that. Perhaps Kit would find the woman after all.

But, what would he do if he found her? Save her? If so, how?

With no plan to guide him, Kit settled on following the corridor as the barman had told him to do. Surely, a plan would come to him once he'd found her. If he found her. There was still the chance that the barman was lying, and nothing was in the tunnels. Or, maybe he was walking himself straight into another perverse surgery. What creature would they shove into him next? A spider? Kit hoped it wasn't a spider, he hated spiders. Too many legs. Too many eyes.

Eventually, the corridor came to an end and a door awaited him. Without further thought and without pausing, Kit walked through it. He was doing exactly what the barman - and probably Peter - wanted him to do, but he didn't care. His heart was set on finding that woman. He was unable to say why, but he thought she was important for some reason. Kit couldn't help but think that she held some answers for him. The stairs on the other side descended into darkness, but Kit didn't need to turn on the light; he could see perfectly well now, his amber eyes handling their duties with perfect ease. The tunnel must have run for miles, with multiple rooms - or cells - leading off from it. It would have taken days to search the entire thing, but Kit didn't need days. The barman was right once again; Kit just followed his nose.

***

Christine had been left alone for hours. Or, at least, she thought it was hours. It could have been days since they'd led the formerly Drunk Guy away, but it was impossible to tell. After they'd left, they'd turned the light off and then the darkness had swallowed any sense of time that Christine possessed. She'd tried to sleep, but with limited success. She may have drifted for a while but sleep never truly claimed her and she couldn't relax no matter how much she'd tried. This little prison, perhaps unsurprisingly, was not the most calming of environments. Sooner or later, however, the body will find ways to get what it needs, and Christine's body needed sleep. The shock of recent events had left her exhausted, so she dozed. When she awoke, she wasn't sure if her eyes were open or closed, the darkness was so absolute. So complete. For a moment, she tried to sit up before remembering where she was and being reminded by zip ties around her wrists and ankles that she was bound in place. *Great*, she thought. *It wasn't a nightmare.*

Then she remembered why she'd woken up. A noise. Laying still and breathing as quietly as she could, Christine listened to the dark, dank world around her. For a while, only silence screamed back at her. Then the noise came again.

A footstep.

A scuff of a shoe.

An exhale of breath.

The darkness suddenly didn't seem so lonely.

The urge to call out 'hello' gripped her, but Christine had no desire to go hunting for a horror movie-esque death. Then again, whoever was out there probably knew where she was anyway, and they were likely going to be entering her cell very soon. As Christine battled between the choice of calling out and remaining silent, the footsteps stopped.

Whoever it was. They were outside the door. She just knew it. She could feel it.

Her breathing started to quicken, and a scream built up inside her. Panic had set in. She bit her bottom lip to keep the scream in.

Silence. She had opted for silence.

Christine could only hope that she'd made the right decision.

***

The scent was almost overpowering. Fear. Kit had never realised that fear had its own smell until that moment. It was an animal scent, something that centuries of evolution couldn't destroy or change. His stomach and his throat growled in unison and completely against his will.

+ *Don't fight it.* +

At least one of the shadows was down here with him. He should have known. Was he ever truly alone now?

+ *Remember Om grutt.* + it said, + *Brace yourself.* +

Without realising that he was doing it, Kit tensed almost every muscle in his body. Visions of the dismembered pigeon flashed upon him. He knew what was about to happen and no amount of tensing was going to prepare him for it.

+ *It will get better with practice.* +

Kit took little comfort in that as he growled again. It was a low, bestial sound. One that could easily be heard on the other side of the door. Christine started to struggle against the zip ties. Kit couldn't see her yet, but he could hear her every move, even if he was still otherwise distracted.

Muscle, flesh and bone all began to mutate. Kit could feel every moment of it. He could hear it. The cracking and the stretching echoed through his head. He tried to scream, somehow imagining that the scream would alleviate some of the pressure that had built up inside him. The only thing to exit his mouth was a howl. He was right about one thing though: the pressure was gone.

As the sound of the howl filled the room, Christine continued to struggle against her bonds. Miraculously, one of them chose this moment to snap. Her left arm was free. Christine was so happy she like she could cry. The happiness faded as she realised that her other three limbs were still tied up. She could wave at the wolf thing when it came through the door - as the howl left little doubt in her mind about what was out there - but she couldn't run. Somehow, Christine didn't think that waving was going to do a lot to save her life.

She continued to struggle. The beast continued to howl.

Her efforts to break the remaining zip ties were proving fruitless, so Christine changed up her tactics. Rocking from side to side, she tried to use her momentum to overbalance the cot-like bed. At least if she was on the floor and the bed was on its side, she wasn't being offered up to the wolf thing on a platter. The bed toppled, and Christine's second miracle had taken place. It turns out that such miracles could also temporarily wind a person, so she remained still for a moment, able to do nothing but listen to the sounds on the other side of the door. They were sounds that she would never forget for as long as she lived.

Wet cracks sang choruses alongside moans and growls, while howls soloed over the top. It was the most grotesque symphony she had ever heard. A morbid melody. A song for the insane.

Then there was a brief silence. A beautiful silence.

Then breathing.

Deep, heavy, heaving panting.

Whatever was going on outside the door was over and Christine knew that could only mean one thing. She was the subject of the wolf thing's attention once again. She fought and battled against the three remaining zip ties, succeeding only in injuring herself even more than she already was. Frustration had her in its clutches. There was nothing she could do.

The door slammed open.

No light chose this moment to come flooding in. Christine was still in the dark, but she definitely wasn't alone. Her eyes took their time adjusting to the dark, but when they did, she wished she had remained blind.

She screamed. It wasn't a scream of terror, although she could feel plenty of that inside her body. It was a scream of defiance. A banshee wail. A war cry. If this was to be her last stand, she wasn't going down easily.

PART TWO

CHAPTER EIGHTEEN

The scream registered somewhere in his mind. It raced through the synapses in Kit’s brain, firing up the necessary connections, sending the message to the relevant places. Wolf Kit may have been taking centre stage, but regular, normal, run-of-the-mill Kit was still in there. Not quite locked away, but certainly pushed to one side. For a moment, a feeling of accomplishment swept through him: he had found the woman. He had done what he had set out to do. She was right there, laying on the floor in front of him.

Screaming.

The woman was screaming like her life depended on it. That wasn't right, was it? He was there to save her. Surely, she should be thanking him if anything. The scream tore through him, setting his nerves on edge, making him gnash his teeth.

+ *Feed* +

The shadow voice interrupted his thoughts, bringing Kit's crushing reality with it. The reality was dark.

He was no longer Kit, he was a monster. He was the reason why she was screaming. Words refused to form as Kit tried to talk, thinking that if he could reason with her and explain that he was just a regular bloke who'd had a worm dropped into an incision in the back of his neck and could now transform into something from your nightmares at inconvenient times, that she'd calm down. But, his story would have been difficult to explain at the best of times. When your vocal chords have morphed into something unrecognisable, it was impossible. Instead, he growled and howled and snarled at the woman, like a creature possessed, achieving nothing apart from making her scream and yell even more. It was hopeless. Just as his disappointment and failure threatened to swamp him, the shadow voice came again.

+ *Feed* +

It was just one word; no more, no less. No elaborate instructions and no demands. Was it an order or a suggestion? Either way, Kit was repulsed.

But only for a moment.

His stomach started to rumble, betraying its master. There was no denying it, Kit was hungry. No, *hunger* didn't quite cover it. *Ravenous* was a better description. He didn't think he'd ever been this hungry. The woman's eyes - brown, and full of a cocktail of anger and fear - stared up at him. There was nowhere for her to go. She couldn't run. She was trapped, and she was his for the taking. It would be easy.

***

Christine looked up at the monster. It was the same thing that she'd seen tear apart a pigeon the night before.

At least, she assumed it was. She didn't want to consider the possibility that there may be more of them. The only difference between last night and now was that she had replaced the pigeon and the creepy 007 guy was nowhere to be seen. He'd saved her last time, hadn't he? Christine had a vague recollection of him saying that it wasn't the right time. Did his absence mean that the right time was now? Despite having no-one around to confirm her theory, Christine thought that it did.

The monster seemed to pause above her. It hesitated as if trying to come to some kind of decision. Christine didn't know when, or if, she would get another chance. She had to do something. But, what could she do? Options were thin on the ground. The last few moments since the monster burst in had offered no further solutions. Christine felt well and truly fucked. She also felt that this was the appropriate term to use when in this situation. *Fucked.*

In the absence of any other ideas, Christine did the only thing she could do. Struggle and then struggle more. She pulled and twisted against her bonds, all the while aware of the beast that looked upon her. Hot, putrid breath beat down on her, assaulting her nostrils and making her gag. Christine had discovered something that only a select few know: werewolf breath makes dog breath smell like roses. She continued to fight, both against the urge to vomit and against the zip ties that were keeping her in place. Hope was in short supply, but it was the only thing she had. Sharp plastic dug into her wrist and ankles, while she frantically used her free hand to tug at the zip ties. Her binds ripped into her skin. Blood pooled around them, gradually dripping onto the floor below her.

Drip.

Drip.

Drip.

Each drip felt like a part of a countdown. It was like her body was counting down until the moment it expired. Or until dinner time for the beast. Christine closed her eyes, having lost any desire to see what was going on in the world around her.

No, she thought. It can't end like this. What happened to fighting?

With renewed energy, she thrashed against the rickety little bed. There was a snap. And then another. Then another. These zip ties weren't meant to break that easily, were they? It didn't matter either way. All that mattered was that she had freed herself. Now she could fight. Or run.

I won't do it! Kit screamed inside his own head. *I won't eat her!*

But the shadow voice was insistent.

+ *Feed* + came its stubborn reply. What had started as a whisper was increasing in volume each time it had to repeat itself. + *You must feed.* +

NO! Kit replied, again within his own head. The only thing the woman on the floor below him heard was another hungry growl. *YOU CAN'T MAKE ME!*

+ *We don't need to make you.* + said the shadow voice. Although it was louder now, it was still calm. It was the kind of voice that sounded like nothing could ruffle it. It was the kind of voice that belonged to someone who was always in control. In a way, it reminded Kit of Peter's voice, even though they had only had a short conversation. But it was older. Much, much older. + *You need to feed, otherwise you will die.* +

Then I'll get myself a sandwich, thought Kit, marginally pleased that he was able to be sarcastic in a moment like this. I don't need to eat her.

\+ *Maybe not her, but you do need to eat someone.* +

There it was. One little word that could fill Kit with dread: the shadow voice had said "Someone". Not "something". Not "anything'. It had said "someone".

\+ *It's good that you're catching on so quickly. It takes others much longer. I believe you'll meet some of those soon enough.* + the shadow voice said. Kit could have sworn that he detected a hint of pride in its voice. + *You're right, it needs to be someone. You need human flesh.* +

Oh god, why? Kit's words were a sob, even in the confines of his head.

\+ *God? No, there's no god here. At least, not in the way that humans have been lead to believe. There is a higher power though and for you, at this moment, it's me.* + Its tone was matter-of-fact rather than boastful or teasing. Somehow, that made it worse. + *You need human flesh to complete the transition. Without it you will die.* +

Can't I sleep on it, thought Kit, hating the pleading sound of his internal voice. *Do I have to do it now?*

\+ *No, time is running out. This is why it's better when new recruits are willing. They have all this explained before the process begins. It saves a lot of time and effort.* + In spite of the situation, Kit hoped that someone was in trouble. Perhaps Peter. Or the barman. Or that other guy who dressed like Peter. Kit didn't care who got in trouble, but if he had to suffer then it felt good to take some other deserving party with him. The woman on the floor was not a deserving party though. She was innocent - just like he had been.

I can't, thought Kit. *I can't do it.*

+ *You won't know until you try.* + the shadow voice said, sounding like a parent encouraging their child to learn a musical instrument. The difference was that most music lessons didn't involve murder and cannibalism. Was it still cannibalism when technically you were a werewolf at the time?

Kit made his decision. It was simple, he would just have to die. Death by starvation didn't seem particularly pleasant, but nothing over the last couple of days had been pleasant. Besides, it was the right thing to do. It meant the woman would live. Or, at least, she wouldn't die by his hands. Or teeth.

Just as his mind was made up, something happened to change it. There was a smell, something fresh. Something appetising. The shadow voice was surprisingly quiet, as if it knew what was going to happen next and it approved. A metallic tang swept through Wolf Kit's senses, intoxicating him. His resolve started to fade as baser instincts took over. All Wolf Kit knew now was that he was hungry. And there was food within reach. Thick saliva dropped from his maw.

As he went to bite into his prey, a pale arm swiped at him, catching his elongated nose and stunning him slightly. It was more the shock of the movement, of the defiance, that stunned him, rather than the force of the blow, but it still paused him for a few seconds. The sound of stumbling footsteps receded from him. Panicked breaths teased his eardrums. A terror-stricken heartbeat stampeded through his mind. His prey was on the move and, as much as it meant that dinner would be delayed a bit longer, Wolf Kit found that he was relishing the hunt.

If normal, run-of-the-mill Kit was still around, he either had nothing to say on what was about to happen, or he was no longer given a say. The conversation with the shadow voice had come to an end, and the shadow voice had been right. Kit needed to feed, and he needed to feed soon.

The woman's footsteps started to disappear, and Wolf Kit realised that it was time to act. He'd given her a head start and toyed with her slightly, now it was time to give chase. Just as he heard her trip, he loped off in her direction.

***

Fear. It's such a short, simple word. One so simple, that you think you know its meaning. Christine thought she knew what it meant, but as she ran for her life down that dark, dirt-floored corridor, she realised that she had no idea. Until now. Fear was not a word with a simple definition. Looking it up in a dictionary wouldn't give the reader the slightest indication of what Christine felt at that moment. It couldn't. A dictionary can't feed the reader the smell of fear. Or its taste. Or the way it makes your insides want to melt and then evacuate your bowels, when really you'd rather use that kind of energy running from whatever it was that scaring the shit out of you in the first place. Dictionaries didn't give you that. The only way to truly know fear was to live it, and Christine wished that she had never met it. It was a cruel, unrelenting creature. One that wouldn't let her think straight. If she could only take a moment to think logically, then she stood a chance at getting out alive. Instead, she was just running. For all she knew, she was running in the wrong direction.

***

Wolf Kit's run had turned into more of a gallop and he closed the distance between the cell and the woman in a matter of seconds. He leapt on her from behind, not caring that it wasn't a fair fight. She'd lashed out at him once before, he didn't want to underestimate her. Wolf Kit had decided that he would never underestimate prey again, and with that, he sank his teeth into the area where the woman's neck met her shoulders. The taste, the feeling of her warm blood running down his throat and over his chin, was divine. Before Kit's life had been chewed up and shat out by Peter and whoever else he was working with, Kit had been to a fancy restaurant. Apparently, the food there had been to die for. Whoever had said that was wrong. They had clearly never bitten into a human being while their heart was still beating.

***

The beast's jaws felt hot and wet on her skin. Sharp, deadly fangs tore into her like filthy, rugged knives. Bizarrely, she found herself thinking about the number of bacteria that was currently making itself at home inside her newly acquired wound. Somehow, despite being pinned face down to the ground, Christine managed to turn her head slightly, her eye managing to make contact with that of the beast. For some reason, a large part of her wanted to look at her killer. On some level, she wanted to know the reason – and know the creature behind it - why she wouldn't get to wake up tomorrow morning. Or any other morning. The beast's eye locked with hers. Maybe she was imagining it, but there seemed to be a glimmer of intelligence in that glowing eye. While the orange eye was monstrous and alien, there was still something hauntingly familiar about it. Christine just couldn't put her finger on what it was.

The initial pain started to fade, and Christine was just left with a sense of resignation. It hung over her like a dark cloud, singling her out. There was no walking away from this. A shape caught her attention, for that's all it was. In fact, it was barely a shape. It was the kind of thing that you saw out of the corner of your eye and then dismissed as nothing. But, Christine knew that it was more than that. Maybe the things that you saw in your peripheral were things worth paying attention to after all. As she stared, the thing started to come into focus and a ghostly phantom stood - or hovered - just over to the beast's left. The phantom looked like it spent its eternity in an old sepia photograph. Its only colours were browns, yellows and, to some degree, blacks. Its eyes were hollow sockets and its mouth was a gaping hole. Despite its hideous appearance, Christine was more curious about it than afraid. When you have a werewolf eating you alive, you don't have much else to fear.

Except one thing.

Shit, she thought. *Now that I've been bitten by this thing, won't I become one too?*

Slowly, almost imperceptibly, the sepia phantom moved, shaking its cowled head from side to side. Did that mean what she thought it meant? Did it mean what she hoped it meant? Hope was a dangerous game to play, and one that hadn't worked out too well for her so far.

+ *You're fine* + a voice said. The sepia phantom's vacuous mouth hadn't moved, but Christine sensed that it was the one doing the talking. Of course, there was always the chance that her body and brain had given up and thrown in the towel, and this was an odd and surprisingly vivid hallucination. That did seem to be the more realistic option. Then again, up until the last two days, Christine hadn't thought that death by werewolf was a particularly realistic option. Anything was possible now; the rule-book had been set on fire and chucked out of a window.

Temporarily, Christine forgot that she was being eaten and tried to talk with vocal chords that were already on their way to being digested. The action brought about a renewed wave of pain and dismay.

+ *Don't worry* + the voice said, and Christine now didn't care if it was real or not. She wanted to believe the grotesque monochrome phantom, lurking over the shadow of the werewolf that was consuming her. She needed to know that it was there to offer her some comfort. She needed it to be telling the truth. + *You'll be alright. It will be over soon. You won't turn.* +

What's next? she wondered.

+ *Oblivion* + replied the voice.

Compared to her current situation, oblivion seemed like paradise. With that, the phantom flickered out of her view. Although it would return, Christine would never see it again.

Knowing it would be over soon, Christine looked back into the eye of her killer. Oblivion may have been waiting for her on the other side but given half the chance she would destroy this fucker.

***

The woman's eye locked with his and wouldn't let go. As a surprise to both regular Kit and Wolf Kit, the eye didn't appear to be pleading with him. It was like she wanted him to know that she was resigned to her fate, but she wasn't happy about it. The look in her eye at that moment suggested that, if ghosts were real, she could take great pleasure in haunting him and tormenting him for the rest of his days. And why couldn't ghosts be real? Werewolves were. Wolf Kit paused mid chew, debating internally with regular Kit. Should it continue?

+ *It's too late to change your mind* + the shadow voice said, and it was right. The woman's eyes had glazed over. She was gone.

There was no point in wasting a perfectly good piece of meat, so Wolf Kit devoured her entirely. Regular Kit sat back and waited it out. It was like the shadow voice had said, there was nothing he could do now. The damage was well and truly done. That didn't mean he was happy about it. Far from it. But, he would have plenty of time to contemplate what had happened.

Unlike Peter's crime scene, Wolf Kit ate everything. No bone, tooth or internal organ was left when he was done. All but a few strands of hair appeared to have escaped his jaws. Wolf Kit had certainly been ravenous. Starving, even.

And, in truth, that was what werewolf kills were meant to be like. They rarely left leftovers behind. That was, of course, unless they wanted to make a statement.

+ *Sleep now.* + the shadow voice said. Wolf Kit didn't need to be coerced. Collapsing on the ground amidst blood and gore, he fell into a deep, soothing sleep.

CHAPTER NINETEEN

The TV chatted away to itself in Peter's flat above the pub. Neither Peter nor Erik were paying any attention to it, but it didn't seem to mind. Inanimate objects tend not to.

'I hear he's done it.' Erik said, still undecided about if he should be excited over Peter's plan. 'He's completed the *Om grutt*.'

'He has indeed.' Peter said. Things were going well for him, but there was still nothing about his homicide on the news. He was sure of this because all he seemed to be doing was watching the news. Or read the news on his phone. Or read the news in an actual newspaper. It didn't matter where he looked or for how long he searched, there was no mention of it anywhere. Not even a hint. It didn't feel right at all. It felt like someone had thrown a very large spanner into the works, and it had collided full force with his head.

‘I thought you’d be pleased.’ Erik said, noticing his friend’s mood. ‘What’s wrong?’

‘It’s odd, isn’t it?’

‘What is?’ Erik asked, noticing that Peter was rubbing his neck. He did this whenever he was trying to work something out. It was as if he was rubbing a magic lamp, waiting for a genie to appear and answer all his problems. Or probing his worm. Maybe he thought that it should come up with some ideas.

‘I thought we would have heard something by now. I mean, my work should be all over the news. Even if they think they’ve caught the killer… or if they think it’s a deranged animal attack… there should still be something. But there’s not. There’s not even a hint. I don’t even feel like they know something and have been told to keep it quiet. It’s odd.’

And it was odd. In fact, it was downright eerie. Like a house that’s too quiet. Erik realised that this could mean one of two things, and he knew that Peter knew it too. Either no-one had discovered Peter’s work of art, which seemed unlikely given that they lived in a residential area and would have been missed at their respective places of work or education. Or, it meant that they were currently stood in the eye of the storm and the Council had already got wind of it and had performed their own cover-up. Although the likelier option, Erik didn’t want to think about what that meant for them. It wouldn’t take the Council long to work out who was culpable and, as was always the case with the Council, justice would be served. And justice would be painful.

‘Shall we check on Kit?’ Peter said, striding across the room, apparently bored of talking about the oddness of their current situation. ‘I wonder if he’s awake yet.’

Peter seemed excited again and any onlooker would have thought that he didn’t have a care in the world. Sadly, for Peter, that couldn’t have been further from the truth. Like Erik, he had worked out what the lack of news coverage could mean, and he wasn't exactly revelling in the prospect. His veins already felt like they were burning as he thought about the punishment that the Council was likely to inflict on him. It wouldn't be swift, but it would be thorough. The Council were known for their thoroughness and attention to detail. They'd certainly make sure that they dotted the i's and crossed the t's. Silver would be pumped through his veins, sending pain throughout his body - and that was just for starters. The main course didn't bear thinking about. Whether or not they'd stop the process before he died or not, he couldn't guess. It depended on the mood of *"The Six"*. The idea that his life was in their hands was not a comforting one. While they were methodical beyond compare, they were also evil incarnate. He would have preferred it if Van Helsing made the decision, the fan of the supernatural that he was. If he were real.

'Erm… yes.' Erik said, rising from the armchair he had been reclining in and sweeping the foggy confusion from his mind as he did so. It was hard to keep up with Peter sometimes; he jumped from idea to idea, never really allowing those who he was with to bridge the gaps in between.

The two friends left the flat and made their way down to the pub. Several hours had passed since Kit last spoke to the barman and began his journey into the tunnels. Night had fallen outside, and the pub's patrons were intoxicated either due to alcohol or the drugs that were constantly pumped into the establishment, or both. It was usually both.

'Good evening, gentlemen.' the barman said, even more chipper than usual. He was obviously pleased that Kit had done as they wanted him to. New recruits were always difficult; especially when they hadn't volunteered for their new way of life. Some were stubborn and fought the process every step of the way, but - even though he had been a bit doubtful and reluctant - Kit had been a relatively quick study. It had almost been pain free - for everyone apart from Kit... And the woman. And that pigeon from the night before. But, other than that, it was pain free. 'It's a wonderful evening, isn't it?'

'You seem rather pleased with yourself.' Peter said, locking eyes with the barman.

'Well, yes.' he responded, suddenly not quite so sure of himself. 'Is there something wrong? Did Kit fail? Is he a disappointment?'

'That's for us to decide.' Peter answered, continuing to stare. 'You'd do well to remember your place. You're not one of us, you're an employee. Remember that.'

The barman opened and closed his mouth once, wanting to say something, but knowing that he'd never find the right words. Meanwhile, Peter stalked away towards the "*Staff Only*" door.

Erik lent across the bar and whispered as if sharing a conspiracy theory, 'Don't worry about him. We really do appreciate all that you do for us, it's just that... Peter's got a bit on his mind at the moment. Try not to take it personally.'

Nodding in reply, the barman still didn't trust himself to speak. Erik lent across even more and gently patted the man on the shoulder before turning away and following Peter through the door.

The barman felt a dribble of warm urine trickle down his leg as he remembered just how dangerous his employers could be, and just how close to the line he often danced.

***

‘Can we get rid of him?’ Peter asked as soon as Erik walked through the *“Staff Only”* door, to Erik’s surprise, he had waited for him.

‘I thought you liked the man. He was your pick.’ Erik could still remember the day that Peter had appeared at their old home, after about two months away. His excitement for coming up with the perfect plan was infectious. Peter was always coming up with perfect plans. Although, in the case of the barman and the pub, Erik had to admit that Peter was onto a winner. They’d never gone hungry and none of the locals had ever suspected a thing. ‘You’re just having a bad day.’

‘The kind of day that I’m having is irrelevant, Erik.’ Peter spat the words, forcibly hurling them towards his companion. ‘He thinks he is one of us. He’s not one of us and he will never be one of us.’

‘I don’t think he wants to be-’ Erik began, before Peter cut him off.

‘He does. I can see it in his eyes. The jealousy in his eyes as Kit was going through the *Om grutt* was ridiculous.’

‘Okay, yes, I’ll give you that. He did look ever so slightly disappointed that it wasn’t him. He never used to want it though. That’s only a recent thing. And, besides, what difference does it make if he does want to be one of us? We don’t have to change him? The Council will never change him. It’s just a dream. It was part of his agreement when he joined us, he would never go through the transformation. You remember that, don’t you?’

‘Yes.’ Peter sighed.

‘And, he’s a good worker. He does a job that we can’t-’

‘We can.’

'Okay, he does a job that we can't always do… and, to be quite honest, I rather like that someone else picks out my prey and brings them to me now. Why should we give that up? I remember how difficult it could be before you found him.'

'Someone else could do it. We could pick just about anyone. I'm bored of him.'

'That's hardly a reason to kill him. That is what you meant, isn't it? I've never known the phrase 'get rid of' to mean anything else with you.' Erik was desperately trying to be the voice of reason.

'Maybe you're right.'

'So, you won't be killing him any time soon?' Erik couldn't hide his pleasure at Peter acknowledging he was right. It happened so rarely these days.

'I really want to rip his smug face off though.' Peter almost moaned. There were times when he was like a petulant child.

'I know you do.' Erik put a brotherly arm around Peter's shoulders and started to lead him out of the tiny staff room. 'We all do sometimes.'

Finding Kit didn't take long at all. He was still sprawled across the floor in the tunnel, naked apart from the odd smear of blood. Erik was disappointed that he'd missed the transformation back into human form. It was always an oddly captivating experience. It was incredibly uncomfortable for anyone going through it but fascinating for anyone who chose to watch. And Erik did like to watch.

'WAKEY WAKEY' Peter called as he nudged Kit's sleeping form with his foot. 'RISE AND SHINE! UP 'N' AT 'EM!"

Kit groaned and tried to roll over to go back to sleep. If he knew where he was or what had happened, he showed no sign.

‘WAKE UP!’ Peter shouted, already tired of his own little game and clearly out of ways to wake a sleeping person. Kit jolted awake and sat up. A look of shock ran through his features, his eyes were wide, his mouth open and his skin paled. His hair was ruffled and streaked with blood.

‘What…. What happened?’ he asked, looking around for something to cover his intimate area with and eventually settling on using what was left of the woman’s torn t-shirt. He looked at the bloodstained piece of cloth that was resting on his genitals. ‘What did I do?’

‘Ah, don’t play coy!’ Peter said, enjoying himself once more. ‘You can’t tell me you can’t remember a thing. I think you know exactly what you did, don’t you?’

‘I…. I….’

‘Don’t try to lie to us, Kit. Remember, we’ve all been there.’ Peter’s tone was teasing, and he waggled an index finger at the bloodied man to further drive home the point.

‘I… I can’t believe that really happened. I really did that, didn’t I?’ Erik watched as the reality started to sink in. If you weren’t willing - or even if you were, sometimes - that first human kill was always a toughie. It took a while to come to terms with the fact that you were playing by a completely different set of rules. Some mastered it faster than others. It had taken Erik a few kills before he finally accepted himself for what he was. On the other hand, Peter was fine with the way things had to be almost immediately. It was like the man had been born for this life. Some days, Erik thought, the younger man enjoyed it a little too much. He had a habit of playing with his food - something that Erik had never been okay with. You either ate it, or you let it go.

'Yes, you did!' Peter said, a huge genuine smile splitting his face. 'You've completed the *Om grutt*, Kit. How do you feel?'

'I've just murdered someone, ...and I've eaten their flesh-'

'And bone!' Peter interrupted cheerfully. 'Don't forget the bone! Oh, and teeth... and most of her hair from the looks of it.'

'Are you done?' Kit said, not caring if he caused Peter any offence. He was well aware that the man was unhinged and that he could probably kill Kit before he had even had the chance to stand up, but, at that point, Kit didn't care. He'd been through hell and he'd dragged an innocent person along for the ride with him. 'I feel awful, if you must know. I doubt you'd understand though. Empathy doesn't seem to be your strong point.'

'Empathy?' Peter said as he laughed. 'Why ever would I want that? What a complete waste of my time.'

While Peter was amused at the suggestion of empathy, Erik wasn't. In a lot of ways, Erik was Peter's complete opposite. The yin to his yang. He crouched down next to Kit and lowered his voice. 'I know what it's like. I know exactly how you feel. We can talk about it later, if you want.'

Kit nodded, not noticing that Peter had adopted a smug grin again. Erik may have been being sincere, but Kit seeing him as some kind of kindly uncle figure, could come in handy later on. It was amazing how things fell into place without Peter even trying. He'd been told, on multiple occasions, that he was not the centre of the universe, but it was hard to argue otherwise when things always seemed to go his way. Well, they almost always went his way. There was the small matter of the Council and "*The Six*". On thinking about them, the sense of urgency that had haunted him before crept up on him once again.

'We have so much to show you.' he said to Kit, while Erik was still crouched next to him. 'We shouldn't dilly-dally.'

As much as Erik wanted to help Kit come to terms with his new life, he realised that Peter had a point. They'd turned Kit for a reason and they could have the Council breathing down their necks at any moment.

'Come on, Kit,' Erik said softly. 'Let's go.'

'What about my clothes?'

'I'll find you some more.' Peter said. They'd had the foresight to keep a few outfits in a cupboard in the cell where the woman had been held. Leading the way, Peter marched ahead. Erik signalled for Kit to follow. Reluctantly, Kit stood and walked slowly behind Peter, his head hung low. If Erik didn't know better, he'd think that there was something interesting hidden in the muck on ground. But, Erik did know better. He'd been there before, and he'd be willing to bet that he'd felt exactly how Kit felt now.

***

Victorian London.

The world had been very different when Erik had been turned. Like Kit, he hadn't had much say in the matter. Instead of being dragged into the back room of a pub, Erik had been snatched from the streets of Victorian London. If he had known what Kit thought of the decor of the flat upstairs, he would have smiled. Back then, in the 1800's, Erik hadn't been a man of means. At least, not until he was transformed. Until that point, he had been a vagrant, wandering from street to street, stealing and cheating to survive.

Like Kit, Erik had two makers. Only his were a man and a woman.

The cobbled streets had been cold and hard against his backside and he had to keep shuffling around to prevent cramps. He'd been sat there for hours that evening, holding out an old piss pot in the hope that someone would feel sorry for him and drop a couple of coins into it. To add insult to injury, it had also been raining. It felt like it had been raining for years.

Just as Big Ben informed London Town that it was now midnight, a figure emerged out of the fog. He wore a long dark coat, a top hat and held a cane in his right hand. The cane must have served some other purpose, rather than being a walking aid, as the man didn't lean upon it once. Despite looking as if he was richer and more powerful than most of the people on the street at that time of night, the man moved furtively. Perhaps his wealth was why he was so nervous. Any vagabond wanting to try their luck could have found a blunt instrument to knock him over the back of the head, but no-one did. It was as if the man gave out a signal of some kind, making everyone stay away. Erik certainly felt it, which was why he recoiled as the man walked towards him.

'Good evening.' He was well, but quietly spoken; polite and perhaps a little nervous. His cane tapped a short rhythm on the ground, as if the man just wanted to expel a small amount of excess energy.

'Evening, but I don't see what's so good about it.' Erik replied, unable to resist the joke he told anyone who said good evening, morning or afternoon.

The man raised a quizzical eyebrow. 'You're not from around here, are you, Mr...er...?'

'Erik. Just call me Erik. There's no need for formalities when you're wearing clothing that stinks of other people's piss.'

The man sniffed the air. 'Yes... quite. You're not from London, are you?'

'No.'

'Where are you from?'

'Not London.' Erik said, something about the man's interest in him disturbed him. And his German heritage was of no consequence to the stranger anyway.

'Hmm...' The man didn't seem to put off by Erik's response and seemed to mull it over for a while. 'Fair enough.'

A silence stretched out between the pair. 'So... er... Is there anything I can help you with?' Erik asked, the strain of the silence getting to him. The other man, however, seemed to be perfectly comfortable. He looked like the kind of man who lived most of his life in silence, Erik reckoned. Even his voice seemed surprised at being used in their short exchange.

'No,' said the man. 'I don't think there is actually.'

With no further explanation, he turned and walked away. As far as obscure midnight encounters went, this one was one of the more intriguing and, before he realised what he was doing, Erik had abandoned his dented piss pot and was following the stranger into the night. Erik had looked back on this moment at many points over the years and wondered if he would have behaved any differently had he known what was to come. The answer he gave himself changed from day to day.

In a foolish move that was entirely out of character, Erik followed the man's silhouette into a darkened alley. The man was a fast walker and was already a fair way in front of him. As Erik approached him, he became aware of voices. The stranger was not alone. Erik paused and stared at the pair in front of him, wondering just what he'd got himself into.

‘I thought you said you changed your mind.’ A woman said to the man in the top hat.

‘I did.’ the man replied. ‘I mean, I have.’

‘Then why is he here?’

For the first time, the man seemed to realise that Erik was there. ‘Why did you follow me, Erik?’

‘Curiosity.’ Erik said without hesitation. ‘You appeared out of the mist and spoke to me like a human being, rather than a piece of filth like most of your lot do, then you just disappeared. I wanted to know what you were up to.’

‘You don’t want to know.’ the woman said and there was a hint of melancholy in her voice. Erik got the feeling that she didn’t really want to know what they were up to either. ‘You should go.’

‘Go where? I have nowhere to go.’ Erik should have left then. He should have walked away and gone to look for his piss pot, but he didn’t. He never saw that piss pot again. Looking back, he was never sorry about that.

The man mumbled something that Erik couldn’t hear. Judging by the way the woman scrunched up her face, she hadn’t heard it either.

‘Maybe.’ the man said, apparently repeating his mumble.

‘I guess you’re right.’

‘Right...’ Erik said, joining in. ‘I’m glad you’re both now in agreement, but what are we doing? Where are we going?’

‘You’ll see.’ the man said. ‘You’ll understand everything soon enough.’

‘Understand what?’ Erik said, feeling more confused than ever.

‘Follow us.’ The woman said. Erik did so without argument. At no point during the walk from the alley to the townhouse was he forced to walk with them. He was never held under duress and he was never harmed. It was only once they were inside the house and the front door had been locked behind him that anything changed.

Even though he was walking into the unknown, Erik still took some time out to marvel at the house it was exactly how he would have decorated, had he owned a house to decorate. Some of those old tastes still followed him today.

'You have a lovely home.' he said to the couple, as they helped him to remove his coat and hung it on the coat rack.

'Thank you.' the woman replied, seeming slightly embarrassed for reasons unknown. 'We haven't lived here long, but we're starting to settle in.'

CHAPTER TWENTY

Present day.

The sounds of the three men's footsteps echoed around the tunnels. Peter lit candles as they went along, whistling while he worked, although they were all perfectly capable of seeing in the dark. One of the many benefits of werewolfism was superb night vision. Peter just liked the ambiance of the light. It added a certain drama. There was something about that which appealed to him; he was a firm believer that life was a stage. Didn't someone famous say that? Peter couldn't remember who it was. And nor did he care. It didn't affect him, so it was unimportant. The sound of Kit's shuffling followed him.

'Come along, Kit.' Peter called down the tunnel, feigning impatience. He was actually enjoying himself. 'You don't want to catch a cold.'

He laughed at that. The idea of a werewolf with a cold was just too ridiculous. That was another benefit of being a werewolf; you no longer gave a shit about temperature. Neither extreme cold, nor extreme heat was a problem. It wasn't even a mild inconvenience. There was also the bonus of being immune to most diseases, you could walk through a room full of plague ridden peasants and not develop so much as a sniffle. Unfortunately, they were not spared the wrath of *all* diseases.

Gradually, Kit and Erik caught up with Peter. In the time that it had taken them to reach him, Peter had already entered the cell and grabbed some clothes, and now stood with a pair of blue jeans and a black t-shirt folded in his arms. No underwear was in the pile, there was no point. It would just be more clothes to get ripped and ruined during Kit's next change. Peter knew it would take him a while to get used to disrobing before transforming.

As if frozen, Kit stood in the doorway of the cell. The damaged door lay in several pieces on the floor in front of him. Dried blood decorated the overturned bed - which looked more like one of those camping beds to Kit - and the floor around it. A bloodied hand print was smudged across the door-frame. Kit sniffed the air. It smelt charged, electric even.

'You can feel it, can't you?' Peter said.

'What is that?'

'Leftover energy from the attack.' Peter said. 'It happens a lot with particularly violent ones, but you grow used it. The first time is interesting, but… like most things… it becomes wearisome after a while. You can have too much of a good thing, you know. But, the first time is good. In fact, I'd say that the first few decades are sublime. You're a lucky boy, Kit.'

Kit made a sound that could have been the result of choking on air, but it was probably meant to be a laugh. Or a snort of derision. 'Lucky? I am anything but lucky.'

'You just don't see it yet,' Peter said. 'But you will, soon enough.'

Kit snatched the pile of clothes from the man's arms. 'Give me some privacy.'

'Why? We've already seen everything.' Peter laughed. 'Besides, what's the magic word?'

'Peter...' Erik said, motioning for Peter to leave Kit alone. 'Let's wait outside.'

'Don't worry, I've got no desire to watch him dress.' Peter said to Erik, and then turned to Kit. 'The room's all yours. Enjoy!'

And, with that, Kit was left alone.

***

Outside the cell, Erik led Peter away from the open doorway, dragging him out of earshot. 'You know he isn't lucky, don't you?'

For a moment, Peter looked confused. 'Of course he is. He's a werewolf, what could be better than that?'

'Yes, but...' Erik continued. 'he won't be one for long will he?'

'Well, then... he's lucky for us. He's like one of those rabbit's foot keyrings that people carry around with them.' His answer made it sound like that is what he meant all along, but Erik knew better. Either Peter was warming to Kit and wanted to keep him around, or he had forgotten his plan entirely. Worryingly, there was a strong possibility that it was the latter. Over the last few decades, Peter had become increasingly forgetful. It was little things here and there - like the date or the details of some minor dinner plan that they'd had - but it was getting worse. For all his charm and wonderful ideas,

Peter's brain was falling apart. Whenever Erik had brought it up, Peter had dismissed it as nothing. He was around one hundred years old (you lost count after a while), of course he was going to forget things here and there. At those points, Erik didn't want to point out that he was the older of the two and his memory was still intact. Frightfully so, in fact. He could still remember specifics from events that happened at the time he was transformed. Worst of all, he could remember the events following it.

***

Victorian London.

The procedure - for that was what the couple had continually referred it to as - had been surprisingly quick and, relatively painless. Apparently, the man was a doctor - a surgeon of some kind - and he was good at his work. Erik generally liked to keep a clear head, but when it became clear that he wouldn't be able to walk away from what the couple had in store for him, he agreed to the man's offer of opium readily.

The event that Erik was currently recalling took place a couple of days after the procedure. He was propped up in bed in the nicely decorated house. The restrains that had held him in place before and during the operation had been removed and, in theory, Erik was free to move around as he wished. Just as he was thinking of moving, there was a knock on the bedroom door.

'Can I come in?' the muffled voice said on the other side of the door.

'Of course.' Erik said. 'It's your house.'

The door opened, and the man entered. For the first time since meeting him, Erik was able to take in the man's appearance. He was taller than average, with wide shoulders. His hair was cut short and a thick scar started at his temple and ran towards his ear.

'It's a childhood injury.' he stated, sensing Erik's curiosity. 'I don't like talking about it.'

'That's fair.' Erik said.

'Yes, and in the interests of fairness, I need to tell you what's happening. I need to tell about what you are now.' the man began. Erik remained silent, at least some of his curiosity was about to be sated. 'What I'm about to tell you is quite complex and really quite unbelievable. In fact, I'm finding it difficult to decide on a place to start... I suppose it would be best to start at the beginning... In that case... My name is Jack Harrison... and I'm a werewolf.'

***

Present day.

The electricity in the cell seemed to crackle around him. Dressed in the borrowed clothes, Kit stood in the centre of the cell, in pretty much the exact spot that he had stood previously, as he had moved to attack the woman. Tiny blue flashes of lightning whipped around his head, biting into the air next to his ears. At first it was alarming, but now Kit was starting to warm to it. Peter was right, it was an experience. But he still didn't feel lucky. The look on the woman's face as he'd sunk his teeth into her flesh, was burnt into his mind. It didn't matter if ghosts existed or not, she would haunt him forever. His guilt wouldn't let it be any other way.

***

Victorian London.

'Are you insane, Mr Harrison?' Erik asked.

'No... well, maybe I am. But, not because I think I'm a werewolf. That's a fact. I am a werewolf. And so are you.'

Erik started to put the pieces into place. 'The procedure...'

'Yes.'

'But you didn't bite me. Or did you?'

'No, that's not the way it works. Don't believe in fairy tales. Well, not all them, anyway.'

'So, how does it work exactly?'

'I don't know how much you remember, but I made an incision in the back of your neck.' Jack began without preamble.

'I remember.'

'Into that incision, I inserted a worm.' Jack continued, and Erik's eyes widened with shock. 'Yes, I know it sounds unusual.'

'There's a worm inside me?'

'Yes. It's a special kind of worm. It resembles a tapeworm in appearance, it shares the tapeworm's pale and flat body, but it also has a mouth of sharp teeth. It is called the Lupine Serpent, which seems like a rather grand name for something so small. But, when you can consider the things that it is capable of, the name doesn't seem grand enough.'

'So... what kind of things can it do?' Erik touched the back of his neck, fingering the wound that resided there.

'It completely changes the physiology of its host. After what I've told you regarding what I am, and considering the name of the creature, I'm sure you can work out what happens.'

'Understood.' Erik said, nodding once. 'So when will I change?'

'Your first change will occur at some time today.' Jack said, moving across the room and then perching on the edge of the bed. 'It's already started in some small ways. You might start to notice a few abnormalities over the next few hours. Try not to worry about them. It's all part of the process.'

'How do I control it?' Erik said, still not believing the words coming out of Jack's mouth. It was more likely that the man was suffering some kind of malady of the mind.

'You don't. Not yet. The process still has some steps before it is complete.'

'What kind of steps?' Erik said, taking a moment to look over Jack's shoulder towards the door. He hadn't seen the woman since the procedure. What was her role in this? Given that Jack had clearly lost his mind, had he murdered her?

'Well, you'll need to transform into your wolf form. Then, when you're a wolf, you'll need to feed. The final part of the process is for you to eat a human being. Don't worry, I've located someone who won't be missed.'

'Like I won't be missed, I suppose.' Erik suddenly realised why Jack had chosen him.

'Yes, in a way.'

'So, you've brought me here to turn me into a murderer.' It was a statement rather than a question. With that, the bedroom door opened again, and the woman entered.

'Not quite.' she said, not caring that she had been eavesdropping or that she was now interrupting. 'You're here so that we can create a pack. You're going to be part of our family. Family is important.'

'Your both insane.' Erik said, climbing out of the bed. 'Werewolves aren't real. You're out of your mind. Next, you'll be telling me about vampires and monsters and ghosts. I don't buy it. Not a single word of it. And I won't be part of your pathetic little family.'

Jack sighed and looked towards the woman. 'Ida...'

'Don't worry.' she replied and took a couple of steps towards Erik. 'Erik, my dear... look in the mirror.'

Erik didn't flinch as the woman - who he now knew to be called Ida - gently put a hand on his shoulder and led him to a dressing table on the other side of the room. A large mirror sat waiting for him in the centre of it.

'Look in the mirror.' she said. 'Tell me what you see.'

At first, Erik had no idea what she was talking about. Except for being a little rougher around the edges, as anyone would after going through an ordeal like his, he looked the same as he always did. Ida was as insane as Jack. As if sensing that he was thinking about her, Ida lent closer to him, until her lips were nearly touching his ear. 'Look closely.' she whispered.

Being unused to having a woman at such a close proximity, Erik did as he was told. He studied the familiar image in front of him, looking for any possible abnormalities. It was easier than looking either Ida or Jack in the eye.

Then he noticed it.

It was his eyes.

They were changing.

CHAPTER TWENTY-ONE

Present day.

The leaflet was thrust into the woman's hand at such a force that she nearly ended up with a collection of paper cuts. The Staffordshire Bull Terrier that was walking by her side barked furiously.

'Shush,' the woman said softly and stroked the top of his head. 'Good boy.'

As she examined the now slightly crumpled document, she realised that 'leaflet' was perhaps too generous a description for the thing she held in her hands. It was a hastily written photocopied document, that was clearly a copy of a copy of a copy. Of a copy. She highly doubted that it had ever even seen the same room as the original version.

The piece of paper declared that those that read it could be saved in big, bold capital letters. It should be added that this wasn't normal, lowercase saved. Like the kind of ‘saved’ a person might use if they were attempting to convince others to save money. This was the big, biblical kind of SAVED. It was another one of *those* leaflets; propaganda for a god that didn’t exist. The woman sighed and crumpled the piece of paper into a ball. In seeing the action, the dog wagged its tail and yelped with delight, clearly anticipating a game of fetch. Meanwhile, it did occur to the woman that a werewolf doubting the existence of another supernatural being may seem odd, perhaps even short-sighted, but she felt that she had been around long enough to know what existed and what didn’t. However, the leaflet had been right about one thing: she could be saved and, after hearing about a certain suburban massacre, she knew exactly what needed to be done.

Scrunching up the ball even more, the woman threw it and smiled as the dog happily chased after it.

CHAPTER TWENTY-TWO

The vice-like pain squeezed tighter and tighter, making Peter feel like his brain had been crushed and was now trying to force its way out of his eye socket. Werewolves couldn't get ill in the conventional way, but they could get headaches. Well, Peter could anyway. He'd never heard Erik complain of a headache in all the years that they'd known each other. Closing his eyes, he waited for it to pass, glad that Erik had decided to go back for a further pep talk with the newbie. The headaches never lasted for long, but they were brutal when they showed up. Soon enough, the pain faded, and Peter was able to function again. Something wasn't right. Peter knew that, but he still did nothing about it. It wasn't like he could go to a doctor.

He opened the "*Staff Only*" door and stepped back into the pub. Chatter and laughter filled the air, the patrons all seemed to be in high spirits. It was funny to think that just a few hours earlier and a few feet below this very room, that someone was being torn apart and eaten. Parts of the woman's body were still probably working their way through Kit's digestive system. Peter's thoughts were disturbed as he became aware of the barman walking over to him.

'What is it, Mr Lawson?' Peter said. The barman was approaching him like someone would approach a dangerous wild animal. Which, in all fairness, Peter was.

'Umm… there's a… I mean, er… someone…' The barman began, inwardly beating himself up for appearing so weak in front of his boss. The truth was that Peter had scared him earlier. Mr Lawson had been working for these men for so long that he had forgotten what they were. He knew that they were werewolves, but it had slipped his mind that they could kill him whenever they felt like it. He supposed he had just become comfortable in the arrangement. But, that had now changed. The barman now felt very uncomfortable. He had even considered running away and never returning, but he had the feeling that Peter would have just hunted him down to prove a point. The point being that he was a psychopathic arsehole.

'Spit it out, for fuck's sake.' It was Peter's way of encouraging his employee to speak his mind.

'Er, yes… right. Sorry.' the barman said, beginning to babble again. Clearing his throat, he began again. 'There was a phone call while you were… er… downstairs. Someone called Daniel Griswold. Does that name ring a bell to you?'

'Griswold? Griswold?' Peter muttered the name to himself for a bit. 'No, it doesn't ring a bell with me. Are you sure it wasn't for Erik? Or a wrong number?'

'No, sir. He definitely asked for you.' The barman decided that throwing a "sir" in there would help him to win some brownie points. He held out a piece of paper with the mysterious Daniel Griswold's number on.

'How very curious.' Peter said, taking the scrap of paper. 'Thank you, I'll give him a call.'

Folding the piece of paper, Peter walked away from the barman and headed up to his flat above the pub. As he walked up the stairs, he repeated Daniel Griswold's name a few times, trying it out on his tongue. There was something familiar about it. It was definitely a name that he had said before. Perhaps even numerous times. By the time he reached the top of the stairs, he realised that he did know a Daniel Griswold and that he absolutely did not want to call him back. But, even for an immortal, life wasn't that fair, and Peter knew that he'd be making that telephone call sooner rather than later. He sighed and flopped into one of the leather armchairs.

His sigh was for a collection of reasons. It was despair at having to call an old, but powerful, acquaintance. It was dread because he knew that the headaches and the forgetfulness added up to something very unpleasant. And it was exhaustion. The suburban murder, Kit, his health - they were all things fighting for his attention. As much as he was loathed to admit it, life was taking its toll on him. It wouldn't surprise him if this was yet another symptom of his disorder. Peter liked to think of it as a 'disorder' rather than a sickness or a disease, because he was mistakenly under the impression that a disorder could be re-ordered, and he'd be fixed. This went against everything that he'd been told about his condition.

Although the forgetfulness had been around for a lot longer - hell, Erik had tried to talk to him about it more times that he could count… or remember - it was around twenty years ago when he found out what he had. Back then, he was in the midst of another scheme. He was in the process of doing what he had told Erik that he would never do. Peter was trying to join the Council. More specifically, he was trying to become one of "*The Six*". It was at this time that he had first met a woman called Kathryn. She was, and still continued to be, one of "*The Six*". Somehow, Peter had got her to take a liking to him and, even though she often spoke to him as if he was a pet or a child, she was still willing to help him with his bid for power. Peter believed that she saw him as a bit of a project and had no doubt that he would need to side with her on various things once he was in, but it was a small price for what he was about to receive. It was a price that he would gladly pay.

But, Kathryn was perceptive. Peter had managed to pass off a few bouts of forgetfulness as 'one of those things', but after the third or fourth, she'd stopped buying it. The more they worked together, the harder it became to hide the headaches. She'd caught him out and worked out what was going on. Luckily, she took pity on him. It became clear that, although he was aware of his symptoms, he had no idea what they meant. It wasn't like he was intentionally trying to hide something deadly serious from her.

And, that was the thing… it was both deadly and serious.

Even though there were many things he couldn't recall, he could still remember the day she confronted him about it.

***

Somewhere in America, in some year Peter had forgotten.

Sunlight streamed through an open window and, although Peter could remember the moment, he couldn't remember the year, or even the country. All he knew was that he was discussing plans and schemes with a beautiful woman called Kathryn, while jazz played in the background. Kathryn F. Hartmann was a strong, powerful woman, with a strong American accent. The world beyond England was still new to Peter, so he found it difficult to identify her origins purely from the way she pronounced words, but he had a feeling she was from the south, possibly Texas. Peter was smitten. He had been drawn to her immediately, hooked on her confidence and the fact that Erik - the man who acted as his friend, brother and father - had warned him to stay away from her. Even going as far as to make Peter promise that he wouldn't even speak to Kathryn. Which, of course, made her all the more interesting and desirable.

Peter knew exactly why Erik had warned him away; the Council was dangerous, and Kathryn was part of its inner sanctum. But, this was also his chance to rise to the top. To be his own man, away from the almost overbearing Erik. Peter knew that Erik meant well, but after the first few months of recklessness, he had become incredibly dull. Again, Peter knew why, but that didn't mean he wasn't bored out of his mind.

To say he remembered the moment exactly was a lie. He remembered the story that Kathryn had told him. He saw it through her eyes, it was like an out of body experience.

He was stood in the sunbeam, standing stock still in the middle of a swarm of dust particles. Apparently, he had been mid-sentence and had just stopped talking. There had been no more words, no more movement, for a good, solid two minutes. With no small amount of curiosity, Kathryn had studied him, knowing almost immediately what was happening. It was something she had spent a good portion of her ample life fearing.

As she watched, it was like Peter suddenly came back to life. In modern day terms, it was like he'd 'rebooted' and it was the way Peter referred to these episodes now. But, only ever to himself. Although he was sure Erik had his suspicions, he avoided telling outright.

Returning to the land of the living was something that Peter could remember, as it involved excruciating pain. Headaches like that were a sign that something terrible was happening to him, Peter knew it and Kathryn confirmed it.

'Have you heard of The Rot?' she said, swirling the last dregs of her coffee around in her cup. Caffeine didn't have much of an effect for werewolves, but both Kathryn and Peter liked the taste, the texture and the smell. Having heightened senses meant that these kinds of things were important.

Peter tried to raise a quizzical eyebrow, but his headache was only just receding. 'I've heard of rot... in general.'

'I'm talking about The Rot, capital letters on the T and the R.' Her southern drawl making it sound like The Rot was something Peter wanted to hear about. It wasn't. 'It's pretty much one of the only things that can hurt our kind.'

Peter made his way to the table and took a seat. A cigarette - another thing that had little effect on his physiology - found its way into his hand. Smoking had never been one of Peter's pastimes, but he'd copied the habit from Kathryn. She could make anything look classy. 'When you say 'hurt'...?'

'I mean 'kill'... There's no easy way to put this, Peter, but...' she reached across the table and took his free hand in hers. Her touch was warm, comforting, but he knew it wouldn't be enough to cushion the blow of her next words. 'You're dying.'

These were the kind of words that took a while to sink in. A lot of short statements starting with *'you're'* were like that. *'You're dying'*, *'you're fired'*, *'you're useless'* were all bad, but *'you're dying'* was probably the worst of the bunch. There wasn't a lot you could do about that. There was no potential killer that he could reason and negotiate with. His killer was something that was invisible, unfeeling and unstoppable.

'No, that can't be right.' They say that there are several stages of grief, and Peter was beginning to experience them. Over the next few decades, he would experience all them - and, possibly some new ones that he'd invented, very slowly over multiple occasions. For now, he was on denial. He would stay on denial for a very long time. If he was honest, he was probably still in that stage now and he wasn't sure if he would ever be out of it. 'There must be some mistake.'

'I doubt it,' Kathryn said in that no-nonsense way of hers. 'I'm very rarely wrong.'

For the first time, her confidence and self-assuredness irritated him. What did she know?

'I've been around a long time,' she said, as if reading his thoughts. 'I first heard of The Rot about three hundred or so years ago. I saw what it could do first-hand. It destroyed a very good friend of mine... ate him from the inside out. It's not a fate that I'd wish on many people.'

Peter poured himself another cup of coffee from the cafetiere. Not because he wanted it, but just so that he had something to do to distract himself. The liquid had started to cool, so the steam that Peter usually liked to watch emerge from the cup was notably absent.

'You don't have to believe me. You can ignore everything I'm saying and carry on as normal, but it won't change the truth.' She said, refusing to shut up. 'You're wasting away, Peter. It won't happen immediately, but it will happen.'

'So, I still have some time, then?' Peter was always able to see the bright side of things.

'Some, yes. Although I couldn't say how long to be sure. It could be a year. Could be one hundred. The Rot affects everyone in different ways.'

'Then why are we worrying about it? Apart from the odd headache-'

'And the memory loss.' She interrupted.

'Yes, and that.'

'And the mood swings.'

'What mood swings?' Peter said, confused. Surely, he'd remember mood swings. Especially if they were severe.

'Yes, you become a different person when you're having one of your moments.' She said with a tired sigh. 'Do you remember Martin?'

Peter thought that he recalled the name. 'One of the humans that works for you?'

'He worked for me, yes. Have you noticed that he hasn't been around for a while?' she said, waiting for Peter to catch onto the point.

'Erm... yes, I suppose.'

'You killed him, Peter. Tore him limb from limb. Made a horrific mess in my hallway.' Kathryn said, sounding more annoyed that she'd had to clean rather than at the loss of a human. 'And do you know *why* you killed him?'

'No, I have no idea.' Peter admitted.

'Neither do I, Peter.' Kathryn said. 'And neither did Martin. Or any of my staff. There's not a person alive who can give you a logical reason for doing what you did. Martin hadn't said or done anything to insult you. Nothing had happened to anger you, relating to our poor friend Martin or otherwise. There's only one explanation for what you did.'

'The Rot.' Peter started to understand the severity of his situation.

***

A long time was spent in front of the mirror on the day Peter had found out about his affliction. It was almost as if he had to see it to believe it. The time spent studying his reflection was even longer than that he had spent when he had first been turned. Back then, hours had passed as he gazed into his new, perfect, beautiful golden eyes. Now he'd spent close to day and much of an evening starting at the mirror image of his naked body.

It didn't matter how long he stared, or from what angle he looked, he couldn't see any sign of the legendary - and terrifying Rot. This meant, if Kathryn's theory was to be believed, that all The Rot was in his head. It was invisible. This made it easier to ignore - especially since Peter wasn't a fan of the alternative. He didn't want to think about what was happening to his brain. Was The Rot just an over dramatic name, invented and spread to shock and scare a part of the population with little else to fear? Perhaps even dreamt up by an ancient version of The Council? Or was the name accurate and descriptive? Could he really be rotting away? Peter felt like he had been cheated. He'd signed up to live forever, but now he had been short-changed. It just wasn't fair.

***

The more she thought about it, the more Kathryn was sure that Peter was riddled with The Rot. It was the only explanation to fit his behaviour, the headaches and the memory loss. Before she had given her diagnosis, she found that she admired him. Now that admiration had turned to pity. And a small amount of disgust and revulsion. Whenever he spoke, she found it hard to focus on his words. Instead she was focused on what was going on inside him, deep beyond his skin and skull. What was his brain like now? Was it damaged beyond repair? How long would it be before he simply stopped being Peter anymore?

Kathryn couldn't be around Peter's inevitable deterioration. Their plans to get him into "*The Six*" had come to an end. He was a liability, one that could fall apart at any given moment. Plus, there was the greater concern that haunted and nagged at her... what if The Rot was contagious?

***

Many years ago

Blades were wielded. Skin was flayed. Flesh was studied. With every rat he dissected, Daniel's thirst for knowledge and destruction grew. One rat lead to another… and another… So many secrets were hidden in corpses and Daniel wanted to learn them all.

CHAPTER TWENTY-THREE

Present day.

The last couple of days had passed at a snail's pace. But, equally, they had also raced by. Time was moving oddly for Shannon. Every minute that flew by seemed to hammer another nail into Christine's coffin. While the lack of any real news felt like time was crawling lethargically, it was running out. It was enough to drive you to madness, and Shannon could feel her sanity slipping away.

The police had found nothing. They had no leads and there were no signs of a struggle at Christine's flat. Apparently, they'd paid a visit to a pub that Christine had visited and found nothing untoward. According to them, this meant that it was increasingly likely that Christine had taken off on her own. Shannon could still remember the conversation with the police officer now.

DCI Madison Severson had seemed nice enough, but she had been as helpful as a chocolate teapot.

'You think she's run away? To where? The fucking circus?' At the time, Shannon had found it hard to believe what she was being told. It was still impossible to swallow now.

'Yes,' DCI Severson replied in a steady, calm voice. 'It's the only logical explanation. There's just no evidence to point to anything untoward happening.'

'I'm her best friend.' Shannon said, somewhat meekly, that feeling of hopelessness visiting her once again. 'She would have told me if she was leaving.'

'Maybe. But, maybe there's a side of her life that even you don't know about. Perhaps she had a secret boyfriend - or girlfriend - and they've runaway to get hitched in the sunshine somewhere.' If DCI Severson had been talking to Shannon about just about anyone else, she would have believed her. But she knew her friend and she knew that something was wrong. She could feel it gnawing away at her gut. It felt like a family of rats had infested her stomach and were in the process of jogging around in it, nibbling and biting at whatever took their fancy. The policewoman was wrong, Shannon knew it without doubt. She just couldn't prove it.

'What happens next?'

'Nothing at our end.' DCI Severson said. The statement felt cold, like an icicle being slowly plunged into Shannon's chest.

'Right.' Shannon's voice was quiet. 'Fine. Is there anything that I can do?'

'We don't want you take the law into your own hands, Miss Moore. Please don't go doing anything stupid.' The policewoman's demeanour had started to change. Before she had been slightly standoffish, but still kind. Now she gradually switching to cold and defensive.

‘I have no intention of doing anything like that. Besides, you said that you didn’t think that anything bad has happened to her.’ Shannon said. ‘Look, I just want to find my friend.’

‘I understand.’ DCI Severson said, warming slightly. ‘The best thing you can do is keep an eye on your social media. I’m sure that in a couple of days some wedding photos, or photos from a spur of the moment holiday, will appear on Facebook or Instagram. You’ll see. Christine is fine. She’s probably off getting a tan and cocktail as we speak.’

‘You’re probably right.’ Shannon said in what she hoped was a convincing tone of voice. She still thought that the police were completely wrong, but she’d wasted enough time on this conversation and on waiting for them to do something. It was time for Shannon to act and it was time for her to ignore DCI Severson’s warning. What Shannon was planning probably would involve taking the law into her own hands. And it definitely involved her doing something stupid.

CHAPTER TWENTY-FOUR

'I'm so sorry.' Kit said, unable to remember the last time he had sobbed like this; he must've been a child. Alone, he still stood in the cell, with no-one for company except for his guilt and the ghost inside his head. 'I couldn't control myself. I know it's not an excuse, but I couldn't stop myself. There was nothing I could do.'

If Kit was waiting for a response, some words of comfort or forgiveness, he was disappointed. Even the shadow voice had disappeared, if it was ever there. Was any of this actually real? It still felt like it was removed from reality, like it was an exceptionally vivid nightmare. But, Kit knew otherwise. He was down to two possible explanations. The first was that everything was as it seemed: he was a werewolf and had just devoured another human being. The second was that he was losing his mind and had possibly murdered a human being. Perhaps even eaten her. Neither was an especially appealing option. Kit wasn't sure which one he was hoping was the truth. Did it even make a difference? The end result was still the same. He was still a killer. He'd still crossed that line, and, in Kit's mind, there was no going back from that.

Sinking to his knees, he let out another sob. Tears cascaded down his cheeks and dropped to the dirt floor below. Kit had never felt so wretched in his entire life. Maybe he should just end it, here and now. Maybe that was the best option for all involved. As far as he was concerned, he stood no chance at redemption, but at least it would stop him from hurting anyone else.

But, then came the question.

How do you kill a werewolf?

If what was happening was really happening, wasn't he immortal now? Did the same rules from the movies and the books apply here?

'Kit?'

Kit jumped at the sound of his own name before looking over at the cell's doorway. Erik stood there, illuminated by candlelight.

'Are you alright, Kit?' Erik asked. His voice seemed kind, but he was a friend of Peter's and, at this point, any friend of Peter's wasn't a friend of his.

'What do you think?' Kit said, snarling.

'I think that you feel awful. I think that you're currently feeling consumed by guilt and I think that you're trying to find some way to end it all.' Erik said, hitting the nail on the head completely. 'Am I close?'

'Actually... yes.' Kit said.

'Don't forget, I've been where you are. I've felt the things that you're feeling. Please remember, we're not all like Peter.' Erik found himself a spot on the floor that didn't have too many dried bloodied smears on, sat down cross-legged and made himself comfortable. Given that Kit wasn't meant to be joining them for long - he was merely supposed to be Peter's fall guy - Erik wasn't sure why he'd returned to the cell to check on him. He guessed that he felt responsible. No matter how many years passed, he still felt accountable for Peter's actions.

'I think Peter was always meant to be a werewolf.' Erik continued, not caring if Kit was paying any attention. His words were there to comfort himself as much as they were there to comfort the newbie. Kit's situation had brought back a whole heap of memories. Memories that he tried to keep buried. He didn't like the idea of them running around in his head. 'Sometimes I think he may have been a killer before I met him. I'm not sure if he'd done a spot of game hunting here and there, or if he was a full-on mass murderer, but there was definitely some blood on his hands. I sensed it the first time we spoke. I guess it was what drew me towards him.'

'So, you, er... created him?' Kit said, already enthralled by Erik's story, but unsure of what terminology he should be using.

'Yes, I created him... in the werewolf sense.' Erik said, smiling sadly. 'I'm to blame. Especially since, on some level, I knew it was a bad idea. But, I was still a young man then - in werewolf years, and human years - and I was angry. So very angry. I wanted to watch the world burn... and Peter was just the kind of person to help me do it. I'd just... I'd just done something awful. I understand that now. It was misguided. But, once I'd done it, there was no going back.'

'What did you do?'

'You're angry now, aren't you?'

Kit nodded, so far Erik was spot on with his assumptions.

'And you blame us for your current situation?' Erik's guesses were still right on the money. 'I felt the same when it came to my makers.'

***

Victorian London.

Stepping across the threshold, Erik came to a decision. He'd long ago discovered that he had neither the guts nor the knowledge to be able to kill himself and end this never-ending cycle of murder and monstrosity, but that had changed. In fact, it had changed that very afternoon. While stalking some potential prey for a feed later that week, Erik had been approached by man. A man who made no attempt to conceal his amber eyes.

'Greetings,' said the man. 'You're Erik, aren't you?'

'That's correct, but I'm afraid you have me at something of a disadvantage.' Erik said, reaching out a hand to initiate a handshake. Having no clue of who the man was didn't mean that he couldn't be polite. Being polite was very important to Erik these days. Now that he no longer lived on the streets and had access to a small fortune courtesy of his new family (he referred to it as 'blood money', but necessity made him spend it anyway), he made sure that he looked, acted and spoke in a certain way.

'My apologies. My name is Daniel Griswold.' the man took Erik's hand and shook it, before tilting his head to look under the brim of Erik's hat. 'And I think we suffer from the same affliction.'

'I think we do. I didn't realise that there were more like us.'

'That means that you haven't heard of the Council.' Daniel said, and Erik shook his head. 'That's disappointing. The Council are very important, they govern our kind. They make sure that we aren't discovered. They keep us safe.'

'Are you in the Council?' Erik asked, feeling naive.

Daniel laughed, although not unkindly. 'I'm part of it. Someday I hope to be a member of "*The Six*" - they're the ones who run the whole thing.'

'That sounds like a lot of responsibility.'

'Yes, it is. But I think I'd be good at it... if I ever got the chance.'

'How can you get the chance?' Erik said, intrigued by this secret world that he'd known nothing about until a few moments ago. It never even occurred to him that Daniel may be lying. It was like he was able to sniff out the truth. Maybe that was one of his abilities.

'You need to challenge an existing member.' Daniel said. 'Either to a physical duel, which undoubtedly leads to the death of one of the combatants. Or by... er... convincing someone to leave, through blackmail. Or finding some way to get them kicked out.'

'I see.' Erik said, unsurprised, but still disappointed that this Council was run by bribery and murder.

'You seem disappointed.' Daniel said, leading Erik away from the crowds and back towards Erik's home. The stalking would have to wait until later. 'It's how we have to live if we are to survive.'

'I've been told all about that. That killing is a necessity. It doesn't mean I have to like it.'

'But, you can live with it.' Daniel said, flatly and knowingly.

'Yes. I suppose so.'

'I think I can help you.' Daniel said, struggling to contain a smile that tugged at the corners of his mouth. 'If you'll do something to help me.'

'How can you help me?'

Daniel looked around, as if checking that no-one was listening in. 'Just as I already knew your name, I also know who turned you. Judging by your views on our ways, I'm assuming that you're not too happy about your current predicament. Is that right?'

'Yes...' Erik said, wondering where this was going.

'Revenge would help, would it not?' His voice was quiet, but his words shook Erik to the core. Revenge would be perfect. He wanted revenge more than anything. Not trusting himself to speak, he simply nodded.

'I can tell you how to kill them.' Daniel said, pleased that Erik was taking the bait. 'Is that something you'd be interested in?'

'Er... yes, it would.' Erik said. 'But what would I need to do in return.'

It felt like he was about to sell his soul to the devil. Perhaps he was.

'As I've said, I want to join "*The Six*".' Daniel said, his hand now resting on Erik's shoulder, ready to share a confidence. 'And I'm going to do it in a way that I think you'll approve.'

'What's that?'

'Democracy, my friend.' Daniel grinned. 'There's going to be a vote.'

'And you need me to vote for you.' Erik was starting to understand.

'Yes, that's all.' Daniel said. 'It's a good deal.'

Erik wasn't sure if that was true, but the promise of revenge was too sweet to pass up. 'I'll do it. I'll vote for you.'

'Marvellous!' Daniel said. 'As a sign of good faith, I'll give you my side of the bargain now. Don't forget that you owe me, Erik.'

'I won't.'

***

Present day.

The two men still sat across from each other, although Kit had now mirrored Erik's cross-legged pose.

'So, what's the secret?' Kit said. 'How do you kill a werewolf?'

Erik ran a hand through his hair and laughed quietly. 'It wouldn't be in my best interests to let you in on that little secret, would it?'

'What if I promised to spare you?' Kit said, the words tumbling out of his mouth before he had the chance to think them through.

'You'd spare me, would you?' Erik said, suddenly angry. 'It would serve you well to remember that I am older than you. I am older than Peter. And with age, comes experience. There have been numerous attempts on my life over the years - I guess it comes with the territory - I'd destroy you before you even came close enough to try.'

Kit shuffled away slightly, ready to defend himself if needed. Not that he believed he'd be successful if such an event arose. He raised his hands in what he hoped was a calming gesture. 'Okay, you're right... I'm sorry.'

'Right.' Erik said, relaxing quickly. Anger wasn't in his nature, not lately anyway. It was a fire that had long since burned itself out and was now just smouldering deep inside. 'Let's move on, shall we?'

'Yes.'

Erik continued his story.

***

Victorian London.

Erik stood in the hallway wondering if he could go through with it. Having the knowledge and actually putting it into practice turned out to be two very different things. His hatred for what Jack and Ida had done to him had grown steadily over the last couple of months, but he had kept up appearances in order to continue living in their home. He'd grown used to a certain lifestyle now. He hated them for that as well.

The house was their safe haven from the world outside. Even though they were deadly predators, if the world ever discovered them, it would be at their door with pitchforks and fire. One on one, a werewolf would always be victorious against a human, but big groups were difficult. They were dangerous and unpredictable. A scorned werewolf with a hunger for revenge and the means to get it was also dangerous and unpredictable. The idea that Erik was bringing danger into such a sanctuary did not sit well with him, even though he had thought he was doing it for the right reasons. No, it had to be done. Music disturbed him from his dark musings, someone was playing the piano. Erik made his way to the house's largest room, the sitting room, where the piano was kept. They'd spent many a night in that room, gathered around the piano while Jack played. They'd sang, they'd danced... they'd devoured the bodies of the innocent. They were heady times.

The music grew louder the closer Erik got to the door. He had to admit that Jack was an accomplished musician. In fact, aside from the fact that he had ruined his life, Jack had a lot going for him. He was a doctor who, despite being a werewolf, still served his community. He helped out at a local orphanage. He fed the poor. Erik had to admire the man for trying to atone for his atrocities. But, was it enough?

Jack's piano playing stopped and Erik listened as the stool creaked. Just as he'd held his breath, readying himself for whatever was about to happen, the music started again. This was a new tune. One that Erik hadn't heard before. Was Jack composing his own pieces now? It was possible, he did have an ear for this kind of thing. Letting himself become swept up in the music for a moment, Erik closed his eyes and a single tear dropped from one of them. The piece was absolutely beautiful. There was no doubt about it, it was a masterpiece. But, the rest of the world would never hear it, for Erik had a job to do. He put his hand on the door handle as the piece reached a crushing crescendo and hoped that Ida was in there with Jack. It would be easier if they were together. Erik didn't think that he'd be able to convince himself to do this again. Jack's fingers played the final notes and Erik opened the door, reaching for the weapon that was hidden in his waistband.

Closing the lid over the keys of the piano, Jack sighed. He didn't even look up. 'I know why you're here.'

A quick search of the room told Erik that Jack was alone. It wasn't ideal, but he couldn't back down now. Could he? The thought of giving up on the whole plan crossed his mind. Did he really need revenge? And he could still vote for Daniel even if he didn't kill Jack and Ida. He had the knowledge now, that was what mattered.

'You don't have to do it, you know.' Jack said, turning to face Erik. His soft voice trying to calm Erik. 'You can always leave if you're unhappy, we won't make you stay. If you leave now, you'll be gone before Ida gets home. Then you won't even feel the need to explain yourself.'

Erik thought about Jack's offer. It was a solution, but Erik realised that it wouldn't do. Part of him still wanted revenge. Even if he walked away, he'd still be consumed with thoughts of justice. Before he knew what he was doing, the gun that Daniel had given him was raised level with Jack's head.

'It's loaded with what I think it's loaded with, isn't it?' Jack said, his eyes locked with Erik's, searching them. Erik nodded. Mirroring Erik's movements, Jack nodded too, seeming to accept the situation instantly. 'I suppose this was inevitable. We went about this the wrong way. We should have told you first... about what you were getting into.'

'Yes, you should have.' Erik said, the gun shaking in his hand. He'd never fired a gun before, he hadn't even thought of practicing with this one first. What if it backfired? Sweat broke out across his body as he realised how hideously ill prepared he was. 'I wouldn't have agreed to it though.'

'That may be the case, but someone may have.'

'Maybe.' Erik said, but he didn't agree. Who would want this? Who would volunteer to become a monster? 'But we'll never know.'

Looking back now, the irony was not lost on Erik. He had told Peter all about what would happen and what he would become, and he jumped at the chance.

'Before you do what you're here to do, may I ask two favours of you?' Jack asked as he stared down the barrel of the gun. 'Please tell me that I'm entitled to that much?'

'Entitled? No, but I'm not the villain here. Say what you need to say.'

'Spare Ida. Just let her go. She doesn't deserve this.' Jack began and then reached for something in his waistcoat pocket. 'And give her this. Tell her that I ran out of time.'

A ring sat in Jack's outstretched hand. It was simple, yet beautiful, and in the time that Erik had lived with the couple, he knew that Ida would have loved it. Jack was planning to propose. Erik started to realise what he was tearing apart, but they'd brought it on themselves. He took the ring from Jack's hand and put it in his own pocket.

'I'm sure you know already that I had planned to kill you both.' Erik began, and Jack hung his head. 'But, I'll do as you ask. Besides, knowing that her soulmate is gone forever may be a worse punishment than a quick death. What do you think? Am I letting you off too lightly?'

Jack lifted his head to make eye contact with Erik. 'You're a vicious man, Erik.'

'You made me this way.' Erik said, his voice little more than a whisper, and pulled the trigger. The bullet flew through the air between them and tore its way through Jack's skull. His corpse fell against the piano, blood and brain matter dripping over the instrument.

Erik was never the same again.

***

Present day.

'So, what? I just need to shoot you?' Kit said, amazed that after his initial outburst, Erik had still told him how he had murdered his maker.

'There's a little bit more to it than simply firing a gun, Kit.' Erik rose to his feet, indicating that the history lesson was over. Holding out a hand, he beckoned Kit to stand with him. 'Come on. Now you know that you're not alone in these feelings. They are normal, as are you.'

Kit stood, ignoring the hand. It wasn't much, but he still wanted to retain some level of independence. 'Thanks, but I'm a myth and murderer, not an angsty teenager.'

This caused Erik to laugh. 'Ah, that may be so, my friend. But, it's still a tough transition. It still applies. So, remember, if you need to talk to someone, I'm here. Don't go feeling that you need to kill yourself.'

'I wouldn't know how to anyway.'

'Indeed.' Erik turned on his heel and made his way to the doorway, inspecting the bloodstains and general dirt and debris on the way.

'Why was it so awful?' Kit said, stopping Erik in his tracks.

'What do you mean?'

'Why was killing Jack so awful?' Kit said. 'It's what you wanted, wasn't it?'

'We must always be careful what we wish for, Kit.' Erik sighed the words, more than he spoke them. 'It's an old lesson, but one that I thought didn't apply to me. I regretted my actions the moment I pulled the trigger.'

Kit stared at Erik, urging him to continue. There had to be more to the story. Kit just couldn't accept that Erik had simply had a change of heart. As if reading Kit's thoughts, Erik nodded. 'Shall we sit back down again? Perhaps you would like to go somewhere a little more comfortable? Away from… all this.' Erik gestured at the abstract blood painting that decorated the walls, the floor and the furniture. Kit's eyes followed Erik's hand. It was a grotesque place to hold a civilised conversation, but Kit wasn't feeling very civilised any more.

'No, we'll stay here.' Kit said. 'It doesn't matter where we go, she'll still follow me.'

'Who? The woman?'

'Yes. She's all I've been able to think about since you and Peter woke me up. Well, her and our demise, of course. It's like she's still here, watching me. Waiting for the perfect moment to destroy me.'

Erik reclaimed his original spot on the floor. 'You know that ghosts aren't real, don't you? And even if they were… how could she hurt you? She's… well, she's pretty much nothing.... and you're a big strapping werewolf.'

'I don't know.' Kit admitted. 'I just know that she hasn't gone anywhere, and she's extremely pissed off with me. Staying in this room a while - making myself look at the mess - makes me feel like I'm atoning for my sins in some small way. I'm making myself suffer, I guess.'

'I suppose that makes sense,' Erik replied. '... In a warped way. I've been around a long time and I can promise you: ghosts do not exist. If they did, I would have seen one. Or smelt one. Or heard one. God knows I've extinguished enough lives to incur a wrathful spirit or two. All you're feeling is guilt, and the longer you live this life, the less guilt will come to visit.'

Erik paused, waiting for Kit to take his words in. They did make a certain amount of sense, but Kit didn't know if he wanted to stick around long enough for it to get to the stage where guilt was no longer a problem. In truth, he didn't know what he wanted. Two days ago, he had been jobless and broke, but now - reading between the lines of Erik's story - he had access to a new home and seemingly limitless funds. Never having to worry about money again was a big perk.

Plus, there was this immortality. Or, at least, near-immortality. Erik was probably around a couple of hundred years old. Imagine the things he'd seen, the people he'd spoken to, the changes he'd witnessed. Werewolfism was a remarkable gift when you looked at it that way. Its price was steep, but you get what you pay for.

'I'll try to get over it.' the sentence may have seemed sarcastic moments earlier, but now it was sincere. Besides, there was little else that he could do but try his best to get over it. It was pretty much the only option open to him.

Erik smiled. 'I'm glad to hear it.' Shuffling slightly to get comfortable, he continued. 'In answer to your previous question, I regret killing Jack for a few reasons.

The first, probably most obvious, was that despite the fact that he turned me against my will… or at very least, without my express permission, Jack was a good man. I have no idea how he and Ida ended up as werewolves, but I think he just wanted a safe a friendly community for them to live in. He tried his best to help regular people - human people - but he never quite shook the feeling that he was different. He even developed contact lenses, something that wasn't around back then, to change the colour of his eyes. He didn't want people to fear him while he was working, he was a doctor, after all.

My second reason follows on from that. Because of my… er… situation, I had it in mind that Jack was evil. But, since killing him and then experiencing involvement in the Council, I've come to realise otherwise. I killed the wrong werewolf that night, Kit.'

'You mean that you should've killed that Daniel bloke?'

'Exactly. Although, it's nothing personal against him. The Council just has the ability to twist people… to change them into the worst possible versions of themselves. I suppose it's the power that does it… corrupting them from the inside out. I'm sure you'll discover that for yourself soon enough.'

Kit nodded, understanding that the subject of the Council wouldn't be discussed further, for now at least. This story wasn't about that. 'What about Ida? What happened to her? Did you kill her as well or did you keep your promise?'

'I kept my promise to Jack.' Erik said, with an intense look of sadness on his face as he pulled a chain out from under his shirt. An engagement ring hung on it, sparkling in the candlelight. ‘I kept one of my promises anyway.’

CHAPTER TWENTY-FIVE

'I am old' she thought, as she stared at her reflection, studying the wrinkles and reading the years in her eyes. The statement was not one of dismay, nor was it full of anger or resentment, it was just a fact; she had grown old. Time had not spared her. She had been lied to, but she no longer cared.

Immortality was, after all, a joke. No-one got to live forever. You could try; there were ways and means (hell, she was proof of that), but eventually everybody dies. Eventually everything ends.

Willow Meade had known this for some time, witnessing a number of changes to her body over the last century or so. Wounds took longer to heal, and the transformations were starting to take their time, which was never fun when she was desperately trying to change back into her human form as the sun rose.

That's something they refrain from telling you when they're giving you the werewolf lifestyle hard sell. It's not the golden dream that they try to convince you it is. Immortality is a lie; it just delays the inevitable for a little while longer.

The beast rots from within.

It's gradual and, at first, you may not even notice it, but it is happening. Once The Rot sets in, there's no stopping it. Willow was past the point of worrying about it, figuring that she may as well ride the wave and see it through to the end.

In fact, Willow was grateful for it. And the shadows that had become her constant companions were grateful that she was grateful.

The trouble with so-called immortality is that there's so much time. Perhaps even too much time. There's no need to rush to get anything done if you always have tomorrow. And the next day. And the next. Willow had found that it was hard to be productive when you thought you were going to live forever.

That was why she was so happy.

There was nothing like a looming deadline to light a fire under your arse.

The dog snoring next to her brought her back to the moment. Jake was Willow's Staffordshire Bull Terrier and, more importantly, he was her best friend. Now that The Rot was really starting to take hold, Willow wondered if she would manage to outlive Jake. It was an odd thing to think about, considering she'd outlived so many other companions, both human and animal. The most recent of which being a cat called Clyde, whom she missed more than most people. Jake had been with her for almost four years. His energy and enthusiasm kept her in the present, reminding her that even though her time was winding down, it was still valuable.

Willow couldn't remember exactly how long it had been since she'd last spent any significant time with a human - or werewolf - companion. She had long ago lost any interest in any physical relationship, happy with the company provided by her pets. They were loyal, always happy to see her and, quite frankly, adorable. Fair enough, they didn't have a lot to say, but that was by no means a bad thing. Given how important Jake was to her, she'd have to make sure that she had a plan in place for if she did go first. He deserves to keep living in a good, safe home. She gently stroked Jake's side and he woke up, tail wagging instantly. There were many things in life that scared her, but leaving her dog with no home and no-one to care for him frightened her.

'We've got work to do, Jakey-boy.' she said softly, and Jake turned his head to nuzzle her hand. Her heart ached. There were times when she was convinced that the dog understood every word that was said and everything that was going on. Now wasn't one of those times. Now, Jake looked at Willow like she was a god; like she would live forever. Looking away from his deep, trusting eyes, Willow tried to think. It soon occurred to her that the last few decades of her long existence had been lonely. As much as the thought of leaving Jake alone worried her, she had no-one - no friends, no neighbours who she knew well - to take him on.

Willow could only hope that she would have enough time to make sure that he was safe before the end came. The trouble was, she wasn't sure how she was going to go about fixing this particular problem. As she tried to work out how she was going to find someone trustworthy enough to look after her best friend, she noticed the dark clouds at the edges of her vision were moving closer. Inch by inch, they closed the distance, wrapping around her. Closing her in.

It wouldn't be long now.

It wouldn't be long at all.

For the first time, death scared her. Willow wasn't ready to go.

***

At six o'clock in the morning, the park was neither hot nor busy. Birdsong filled the air and the only people to be seen were those walking dogs or going for a jog. Jake bounced along at her side and Willow couldn't tell if he was happy to be an important part of her disguise, or if he was completely oblivious. Probably the latter. It didn't take long to spot Daniel, he stood out like a shark in a fish tank. Obviously, he had ignored her advice to dress like a jogger and blend in, instead opting for his usual tailored suit. *Typical*, she thought. She'd never spoken to the man before, but she was sure that she hated him. She had been told many stories about Daniel Griswold and not a single one of them was good or complimentary. As he drew closer, Willow pasted a smile on her face.

'Mr Griswold?' Although she had heard stories of the man, she had never actually met him in the flesh. She had been expecting a monster. Instead, she was greeted with an incredibly normal looking man. This was a man who had apparently murdered and tortured hundreds over the years - both human and werewolf alike - and he looked... average. Willow would have liked to have thought that she would have sensed the evil on him, like it would have given off an unmistakable stench, but there was nothing. All Willow's heightened sense of smell could pick up was that Daniel had recently showered.

'The very same. And you must be Ms Meade?' He took her hand and kissed it. It was an old-fashioned gesture that was probably meant to come off as charming, but Willow found it creepy. Under other circumstances, she may have insisted that he call her Willow, but this meeting was purely business. She just needed to pass information on. Daniel was a means to an end.

'Yes.' Willow snatched her hand away. If Daniel was slighted by her reaction, he didn't show it. Willow got straight to the point. 'You may be aware of a multiple homicide that happened in Carshalton recently.'

'Yes, due to the nature of our kind, *"The Six"* - and the Council as a whole - make it our business to investigate... or, at least, monitor... any crimes like this. Violence of this magnitude usually suggests that a werewolf was involved.'

'Exactly, that's what I thought.' Willow said, momentarily forgetting who she was sharing the information with. She just wanted to share her findings. 'And I believe I know who the culprit is.'

'Oh, really.' Daniel didn't seem too impressed. Willow wanted to slap him. 'What makes you think that you've solved this mystery before the Council could?'

'I believe it's the work of someone I've kept a close eye on over the years.' Willow suddenly became aware that her surveillance may be perceived as strange. The phrase *invasion of privacy* sprang to mind. Still, she was here now. There was no going back. Willow had her reasons for following the actions of these particular werewolves, but she didn't need to reveal them to Daniel. Besides, once he found out what she had discovered, he was unlikely to give a shit why she was doing what she was doing. All he needed to worry about was her results, and what he could do with such information. 'It's the work of Peter Smedley, I'm sure you've heard of him.'

'Yes, I remember the name. It looked like he was going to try to knock one of us out of "*The Six*" for a while, but then he changed his mind. Most unusual.' Daniel looked down at Jake, who was currently studying the man, his head tilted to one side. 'What makes you think it was him?'

'As I said, I've been monitoring his movements over the years.' Willow kept a tight grip on Jake's leash. Even though she couldn't smell the evil on Daniel, it looked like Jake was close to picking something up. 'I occasionally visit their little pub. It's called The Hound & The Philosopher Inn. I'm always careful to make sure that they don't spot me, but I recently got close enough to hear the details of a rather interesting plot.'

'You have my attention. I had an inkling that they may have been involved. There was a familiar stench at the crime scene.' Any hint of charm had disappeared from the man's voice. Now he was all business too.

'Peter wants to overthrow the Council. This murder was meant to be reported in the media - it was meant to reveal the existence of werewolves to the general public.'

'Didn't he realise that we'd just kill him if we found out? It's a risky move... I'm not convinced-'

Willow cut him off. 'They've turned a new werewolf. A young man called Kit. Peter is planning for him to take the fall if things don't go quite to plan.'

Daniel seemed to accept this as an explanation. Nobody just walked away from power like Peter had. Not when they had come close enough to taste it. The way that Peter had laid down his proverbial sword and disappeared had never made any sense to Daniel. Was it possible that he had thought of this plan all those years ago when he was plotting away with Kathryn? Daniel had never trusted her. Then again, Daniel made a point of never trusting anybody. 'Tell me, Willow. Who are *they*?'

'Peter Smedley and Erik Haugen.' She answered without hesitation.

'Thank you, Willow. You've been most helpful, and you've confirmed what we already thought. You will be rewarded.'

Willow shook her head. 'I've got no desire for any rewards. Simply knowing that justice will be done is more than enough.'

'That's very honourable.' Daniel nodded. For a man like him, it was difficult to understand honour. He'd seen it in other people over the years, but it wasn't something he had himself. Nor did he want it. Daniel only looked to self-preservation, self-advancement and self-promotion. Some, Daniel included, considered his way of life to be selfish. But he had lived for centuries, so he was obviously doing something right. Especially when you consider that these honourable ones usually ended up dying for some cause or another. 'Thank you for your time, Ms Meade.'

'You're welcome.' Willow shuddered as Daniel turned and walked away. She'd be happy if she never had to see that man again for the rest of her life, but she knew that wasn't to be. She released her grip on Jake's leash. Now that the man was walking away, the dog seemed to relax.

That encounter had been a strange one, and Daniel thought it over as he walked. The information seemed good, perhaps even completely true, and it confirmed his own conclusions. He was glad that he had already thought to give Peter a call, the other man would be panicking by now. But there was something about that woman that made him feel uneasy.

Daniel was sure that he'd seen her somewhere before.

CHAPTER TWENTY-SIX

The coffee shop was busy; packed with sweaty bodies still determined to get their fix from a hot, caffeinated beverage. The noise, heat and stench of body odour was overwhelming, but Shannon supposed that the throng of people was a good thing. Nobody was going to notice one person. Even so, she held a much-loved paperback in her hands, occasionally remembering to turn a page to make it look like she was reading. She'd planned this stake-out as much as she could, even going so far as to take a book she knew well, should anyone ask her about the plot. Not that anyone would, but she wanted to be ready for anything. As she thought about being prepared, her mind flicked to the contents of her backpack. She had a torch, some rope, a knife, her phone and some pepper spray. Having no idea what awaited her in the pub on the opposite side of the road, made it difficult to know what to pack. All she knew was that it was dangerous. Shannon was already regretting her decision, but what else could she do? She had to do *something*. Nobody else was. No-one else seemed to care.

Draining her third coffee, she came to the decision to leave. She couldn't sit here forever, looking out of the window. Sooner or later, she'd have to move. And, it would have to be sooner as the coffee shop wouldn't be open for much longer. Shannon dropped the book into her backpack and pulled it over her shoulders. It was reassuringly heavy, the weight of the huge torch contained inside rested comfortably on her back. Weaving her way through the crowd, she made her way out onto the street. It was still hot outside and people were still walking around, either on their way home from work or on their way to somewhere exciting. The looks on their faces told her that they were either happy that England was still experiencing tropical temperatures, or grumpy and irritable because they were sick of sweating.

Shannon took a breath and held it before starting her walk across the road. She let the breath out slowly, trying to keep calm. What was she getting herself into? Once on the other side of the road, she looked back at the coffee shop. It looked so normal. Full of normal people doing normal things. Safe things. She was willingly walking away from safety.

But she had to do it.

She had to help Chrissie.

But what if she was too late?

Shannon couldn't shake the feeling that something terrible had happened to her friend. Why wouldn't she have called otherwise? Or come home? Or updated her Facebook status? Shannon found that she both wanted to find answers, and she also wanted to remain ignorant.

She looked at the door of the pub - The Hound and The Philosopher Inn - and tried to imagine what lurked on the other side. It looked like a normal pub. It could have been any number of pubs that Shannon had visited over the years. The only thing that set it apart from many was that it didn't seem to belong to a big, national chain. In normal circumstances, that would have worked in its favour, winning her over instantly. But, now that just made her feel even more alone. It gave her the ridiculous notion that if they didn't have a Head Office to answer to then they wouldn't take her seriously if she tried to speak to them. Or, maybe they were running a sinister human trafficking operation. Shannon thought about walking in with a weapon in hand but thought that may draw more attention to herself. That wouldn't do at all.

The door opened, and Shannon nearly jumped out of her skin. But, no monsters or hockey mask wearing serial killers emerged from the gloom. Two men, in their mid to late twenties, stepped out into the early evening warmth. Laughter followed them as they walked. It was like they didn't have a care in the world. Maybe the pub wasn't such a bad place. Even if the pub itself wasn't involved in Chrissie's disappearance, someone in there may be able to point her in the right direction. If Christine had gone in there that night, someone would have seen her. Maybe they'd remember talking to her. Shannon hoped that there would be someone in there who'd spoken to her friend and she'd told them that she was going to go and visit her family for a few days. Didn't she have a sister who lived in Cornwall? Shannon could only hope.

She'd now been standing in front of the pub's door for a few minutes. Any effort she had put into looking inconspicuous was wasted. She had to go in. It was now or never. With that thought bouncing around her head, urging her on, Shannon held her head high and walked through the door into the air-conditioned room within.

CHAPTER TWENTY-SEVEN

The pub was normal. From the comfy looking booths, to the beers on tap, to the drunken giggling, it was normal. Not only was it massively unnoteworthy, but Shannon felt surprisingly comfortable there. She didn't feel odd about entering the establishment by herself, as she had done previously in other pubs. She didn't even feel the need to get her decoy book out of her bag. Shannon felt sufficiently happy, and at ease enough to just sit and people watch. So what if someone noticed her? She wasn't breaking the law.

But something wasn't right. Despite this intense feeling of contentment, she felt odd. Perhaps it was because of the intense feeling of contentment that she felt so unusual. Was it unnatural? While she tried to figure it out, she started to take in more of her surroundings. Everyone here seemed relaxed and happy. There were no drunken disagreements about football scores or misunderstandings about texts sent the previous night. Nobody was drinking away a broken heart. Everyone was sickeningly cheerful. It didn't add up.

The sound of a door creaking open and then slowly closing again drew her attention. A door that was labelled for staff had just opened and closed, and out of it emerged a smartly dressed gentleman. The barman immediately ran over to him but approached him very cautiously. It was like he was in equal parts eager and scared to speak to him. This seemed to be bizarre behaviour as the gentleman seemed so kind and welcoming.

But, why did she think that? She had never met the man before. Suddenly feeling the need to be secretive, Shannon tried to watch the two men from the corner of her eye. They spoke for a few moments, with the gentleman looking calm and collected, while the barman tripped over his words and generally looked flustered and nervous. Again, she felt like the gentleman must be a wonderful person to talk to. It was like he had some kind of magnetic pull. It was almost too much to resist the urge to walk straight over to him and engage him in conversation. Shannon had no idea what they'd talk about, but she was convinced that anything he had to say would be incredibly interesting.

But, wait.

Why did she think that?

The gentleman briefly looked around the room, while he waited for the barman to get to the point and to hand him a small slip of paper. As he gazed at the pub's customers, he locked eyes with Shannon. She froze. Her breathing momentarily ceased. Her brain stopped mid thought. Had he spotted her? Did he know that she was watching him? His eyes continued to roam around before returning their attention to the barman in front of him. Although she no longer felt like she was under scrutiny, she was shaken. Even the bizarre atmosphere in this place couldn't do anything to relax her. Getting caught in the act of watching someone wasn't necessarily that bad, and it wasn't that which was troubling her.

It was the man's eyes.

They were yellow. She was sure of it. Another look was required to confirm her suspicions, so she used a trip to the bar to cover her tracks. As she walked over, she was able to get a full-on view of the man's face. There was no denying it, he definitely had yellow eyes.

Chrissie's dream hadn't been a dream. Whatever nightmare she'd described was real. Shannon felt a combination of dread and guilt swamp her. She should have believed Christine from the beginning. But, how could she? The whole thing was absurd, and Christine hadn't even known what to think herself.

'What would you like?' the barman's voice startled her; he had appeared almost the second she'd touched the bar. Or, maybe, she'd just been too swamped in her own thoughts to notice his approach. It was clear that whatever had kept him on edge while talking to the gentleman with the yellow eyes was now gone and he now possessed a relaxed confidence. The barman now seemed to be in charge of the room.

'Oh, ummm… just a glass of your house wine… please.'

'Red or white?'

'White, please.' It didn't matter what she chose - not because she was a fan of both (which she was), but because she had no intention of drinking it. A clear head was needed to formulate the next stage of her plan and the glass of wine would simply be a prop, a reason for her to be hanging around the pub.

'Is that all?' the barman said, and Shannon nodded, so engrossed in her own thoughts that she'd temporarily forgotten that she had the ability of speech. 'That's £3.55, please.'

The coins jingled around in her purse as she tried to sort through them, making far too much noise. Her hands were visibly shaking; this was not the behaviour of someone who was relaxed. This was not the behaviour for a normal punter out to unwind with a quiet drink or two. Surely the barman would notice? Trying her best to smile, Shannon handed him the money and collected her change and the glass. It felt oddly heavy in her hand, its weight imitating the weight she imagined to be carrying on her shoulders. In order to sell her act, Shannon rose the glass to her lips and took a small sip. The barman smiled, and she nodded back, before returning to the table where she had sat before. She placed the glass in front of her and removed her paperback from her backpack. She'd need to find a pot plant or something to dispose the wine into at some point, but it was serving its purpose for the moment. Opening the book to a random page, she pretended to read.

What she needed now was a plan. First, she decided to run through the things that she already knew.

One: this pub was seriously weird. Either everyone was high, or there was some weird invasion of the body snatchers shit going on here.

Two: Chrissie had mentioned that a man who had yellow eyes and who was a bit of a snappy dresser had come to visit her right after she'd been in this pub and witnessed a weird non-incident with a drunk guy.

Three: A smartly dressed man with yellow eyes was in this pub.

Four: She had no idea how to defend herself if things went wrong.

No sooner had the fourth point crossed her mind, did she have the overwhelming feeling that she was being watched. Slowly, she turned her head towards the direction of the bar and, sure enough, the barman was looking right at her. Under normal circumstances, she may have passed this off as him people watching. Or maybe she intrigued him because she was on her own. Or maybe it was because she wasn't a regular. Or, there was a possibility that he was a fan of the book she was reading. She took a quick glance at the cover. It was a damned good book. And who didn't like a bit of fantasy with dragons? A dragon would have been a useful ally right now. No-one in their right mind would dare mess with a dragon.

It was true, the barman could have been looking at her for any number of reasons. But, Shannon just knew that nothing good could come of it.

No plans had jumped into her brain and, now that fear and unease were creeping through her veins, any kind of rational thought - beyond fight or flight - had fled out of the window at high speed. Trying to appear as aloof as possible, Shannon packed away her book and made to leave the pub, not bothering to try and dispose of the wine. The barman was watching her anyway. Besides, for all he knew, she could have just realised that she was late for a train or something. That was, of course, assuming that he couldn't read minds.

By the time she left the pub, darkness had fallen. But stepping out into the night didn't feel as threatening as remaining inside the confines of The Hound & The Philosopher Inn. The street was not without its issues though, and one such issue was standing on the opposite side of the road, just outside the now closed coffee shop that Shannon had visited earlier.

A figure drenched in shadow and accompanied by a dog watched the pub from afar. Somehow, Shannon felt that shadow's eyes look directly into her own, even though she could make out no details. Unsure if they were friend or foe - but assuming that they were probably the latter - Shannon decided to make a hasty exit. She hadn't managed to solve the mystery of her friend's disappearance, but it had been a successful fact-finding mission in some respects. As she walked so quickly that she was nearly jogging, she could feel the unknown figure's stare on her back, and she had the oddest feeling that some of the shadows that had been surrounding the figure had broken away to follow her. Her pace quickened along with her heart rate. The world was a creepy and unsettling place.

***

The barman watched as the woman left, leaving an almost full glass of wine behind. She had been a strange one; jittery and on edge. The whites of her eyes were a little too visible, her smile a little too forced. Whoever she was, she had been unaffected by the drugs generously supplied by his employer and had even felt it when he'd been studying her. She was definitely an enigma. But, what did it mean? Was she some other kind of supernatural being that Peter and Erik had neglected to tell him about? Was she another werewolf? Maybe someone from the Council, here to spy on Peter? Perhaps they suspected that he was up to something.

The barman may not have known who or what the woman was, but he was fairly certain of one thing. She was definitely trouble. Now the only question was should he mention it to Peter and Erik? He wasn't feeling particularly appreciated at the moment. Maybe it was time things were shaken up a bit for those two.

The barman had decided: he wasn't going to say a word.

CHAPTER TWENTY-EIGHT

'Shall we?' Erik gestured towards the open doorway. Staying in the cell wasn't doing them any favours. 'We can't stay here all day.'

Kit nodded and got to his feet. Erik had succeeded in helping to exorcise some of his guilt. Most of it still remained, but he planned to hide that, burying it deep inside and using it to fuel him. At least until he'd had the chance to learn about what killed his kind and then put it into practice. After their little chat, he wasn't sure if he'd spare or kill Erik. In many ways, he seemed like a good man. A good man who had been in a few bad situations, but a good man nonetheless. Perhaps he'd find a lesser punishment for him. Something that would still feel like he was paying off a huge debt but allowed him to continue with his life.

Peter, on the other hand, appeared to hold no redeeming features. At that moment, Kit made himself a promise. He would make sure that Peter paid for what he'd done.

The two men started to walk through the tunnels, tunnels that were beginning to feel more and more like home the more time Kit spent in them. Kit assumed that he would be invited to live with Peter and Erik in the flat, but if he found that he couldn't hack it, he'd make his excuses and set up camp down here.

With the blood.

And the ghost.

Kit didn't care what Erik said, he was sure the woman was still down here, haunting him. He could feel her. At times, he was certain that he could smell her. Surely it was only a matter of time before he started seeing her. And hearing her. Would she try to communicate with him before she destroyed him? He wasn't sure. One thing he was sure of was that he couldn't keep referring to her as “she", “her” or “the woman”.

While Kit had been contemplating living arrangements and ghost roommates, Erik had got a few paces ahead of him. They were fast approaching the stairs up to the pub, and away from any further chances for private conversations for the immediate future. 'Erik…’

Sensing Kit's tone, serious and brooding, Erik paused, but did not turnaround to face the younger man. 'Yes?’

'What was her name?’

Erik hid his eye roll well. It was a skill that he’d perfected over many years of living with an over dramatic, obsessive creature like Peter. He understood Kit's guilt, but he also knew that such feelings were self-destructive and futile. They held no productive element. No purpose. And Erik knew this all too well. 'Her name shouldn't matter to you. I know it's harsh but try to think of her as just food. You wouldn't want to know the name of the chicken whose wings you coated in hot sauce and then ate, so you don't need to know hers.'

'I know it seems strange now, but I think knowing her name will help me… I need to process what I did. And who I did it to.'

Now Erik turned. Their eyes met, and he measured his words carefully. 'Are you sure? Because if you are, I will tell you. But, only if you're sure it will help you to get past it.'

'I'm sure.'

'... Because lying to me won't do you any favours.' In truth, Erik didn't care if Kit was lying to him. He just wanted to make sure that the kid still had all his marbles and would be able to function well enough. During that time together in that cell, Erik, like Kit, had come to a decision. Kit wouldn't be Peter's fall guy. They'd have to come up with a new plan or find someone else.

'I said I'm sure.' Kit's stare was cold and solid. He knew exactly what he wanted, he just didn't know how to get it. Not yet.

'Very well.' Erik turned and started to climb the stairs. His foot paused before landing on the next step and he held onto the banister. 'Her name was Christine.'

'Thank you.'

***

Walking through the door into the pub, Kit felt like he was traveling between worlds. Here was the world he'd always known; normal, mostly predictable and comforting. Beyond the door that he'd just came through lay a world of bloodshed and monsters. Kit supposed that this was his 'normal' now and, in spite of his reassurances to Erik, he still wasn't keen on his new role as horror movie villain. But, it was something that he was going to have to live with... until he could fulfil his promise.

'Hello again, gentlemen.' The greeting felt a bit forced, but Kit's entire catalogue of interactions with the barman had been unnatural, so, at first, he didn't think too much of it. Studying the man, a little more closely, Kit noticed that he'd changed since he'd last seen him. There was a thin layer of sweat covering him, his body apparently ignoring the bar's air-conditioning. He seemed somewhat skittish and even a little sickly, even though Kit was unable to smell any kind of disease or ailment on him. There was definitely something amiss though, but Erik didn't appear to notice. Or, if he did, it didn't bother him.

'Evening.' Kit said. As the word left his mouth, he became aware that not only had something changed about the barman, but something had changed in their dynamic. Kit held the power. He was a wolf now, a state of being that the barman coveted, despite perhaps trying to suggest otherwise. The stench of sickness may not have been on the man, but the fetid bouquet of jealousy was definitely there, hanging around him like a particularly persistent cloud. Kit despised every inch of the man standing on the opposite side of the bar. Not only was he an envious, smug, dishonest little creature, but he was also more than a little bit involved in wrecking Kit's life. The barman had performed no small part in this. Kit would have gone as far as to say that he was directly responsible for Christine's murder. Maybe even more so than Kit himself. Or Erik. Or, even Peter. Kit, Erik and Peter were, after all, werewolves. Physical changes as extreme as completely changing your species for a limited amount of time, were bound to have some effect mentally. Kit most certainly hadn't been in his right mind as he'd chowed down on Christine's internal organs. He had been more beast than human at that point. And, beasts couldn't be held responsible for their actions. He was merely doing what came instinctively. The barman - hadn't Peter called him Mr Lawson? - was the only human being in this bizarre motley crew. He should have shown some compassion, but he hadn't. Along with Peter, Mr Lawson was now on Kit's 'To Kill' list.

'Can I get you anything?' The barman was oblivious to the thought process in Kit's head.

'What's the point? It's not going to do anything for me, is it?' Kit said, earning him an approving chuckle from Erik. 'I can't enjoy beer any more, can I?'

'Er... n-n-no...' the barman stuttered. It was the first time that Kit had made him feel nervous. It was like he suddenly remembered what their new acquaintance had become. 'No, you're right. I'm sorry. Is there anything else I can get for you? Any errands you need me to run?'

'No, Mr Lawson. You've done quite enough.' Kit watched as the barman gulped. 'We were just leaving anyway.' With that, Kit headed towards the door leading to the flat. He didn't wait for an invitation from Erik to enter. He didn't feel like he needed one - he was family now, wasn't he? They were all one big happy pack of wild dogs.

***

With a confidence that he didn't know he possessed, Kit opened the door to the flat, not caring about how Peter would react to him being there. Peter was sat in one of the armchairs and looked as if he was going to say something important as Kit came striding in. Instead he settled for 'Oh, it's you.'

Walking calmly a few steps behind Kit was Erik. 'Kit's feeling much better now. Aren't you, Kit.'

'Yes,' Kit took up residence in the other armchair. 'I realise that what I did is all part and parcel of what I am now. I've just got to accept it.'

'Just like that?' Peter snapped his fingers to emphasis the speed of Kit's change of heart.

'Well...' Erik began, but Kit interrupted him. He needed to face Peter himself. It was good practice for later.

'Well, no. I'm taking baby steps... but, you'll be pleased to know, that they're baby steps in the right direction.' He had no idea if Peter would be pleased to know this, it was more likely that he wouldn't care less either way. But it was all part of the act that Kit was trying to sell. He picked an imaginary piece of lint from his borrowed t-shirt.

'It's true.' Erik said. 'It may take a little bit of time, but Kit's starting to take it on board.'

'Fair enough.' Peter said. Kit had thought correctly, Peter didn't care. 'Erik, I need to speak to you about a matter of great importance. In private.'

One look at Peter's face told Erik all he needed to know. Shit was about to hit the fan, if it hadn't happened already. 'Kit, I know you've just come back up here, but would you mind going back down to the pub? Just for a little while.'

'No worries. I think I'll go to the tunnels, though. I know he's your friend, but that barman guy really pisses me off.' Kit was taking a gamble with that statement, but the words were out before he'd had the chance to vet them. Luckily it was met with a small laugh.

'Don't worry, Kit.' Kit was surprised that it was Peter talking. 'Personally, I find Mr Lawson incredibly annoying. I was only saying something along those lines to Erik earlier today. I want to get rid of him, but I think Erik's a little bit attached.'

Kit met Peter's smile with one of his own. Now, this was interesting. Very interesting indeed.

***

Once Kit had disappeared through the door, Erik returned his attention to Peter. 'So, what's happened? I'm guessing it can't be anything good.'

'Daniel Griswold called.'

Erik tensed his jaw. Daniel's name still made his blood boil. Peter may have been selfish with a questionable moral code and even evil incarnate, but Daniel was in a league of his own. If Daniel was calling, it meant bad news for them. Not only did it confirm that "*The Six*" were aware that they'd been up to something, but it meant that Daniel would take great delight in finding out exactly what they were doing. While most detectives would have favoured evidence and following clues, Daniel only ever relied on one thing.

Pain.

Torture was Daniel's friend. Erik had found out just how close a friend it was shortly after he'd shot Jack in the head.

***

Victorian London.

The day that Erik had shot Jack, he'd left a note for Ida and then walked for miles. The words written on that note were embedded into his mind for all eternity. They moved around his head as they wandered.

'Dear Ida,

As I sit at this piano with Jack's blood pooling around me, I feel a sadness. I want you to know that I never expected to feel like this. I thought that killing you both would make me feel happy. I thought that revenge would sooth the part of my soul that screams all night, every night. But, once I looked into Jack's eyes and pulled the trigger, I knew that was wrong. My soul will still scream tonight. And for every night.

I do feel like some form of retribution was needed though. Which is why, to a certain degree, I still think my actions were justified. I don't, however, feel that it's necessary for both of you to die.

Both of our lives are ruined. You now have to live without your love and I will have to live with this curse that you have bestowed upon me.

Do not worry, you will never see me again.

Regards,

Erik.'

His hand had shaken as he wrote, leaving some of his handwriting almost unreadable. A tear fell onto the paper, smudging a word. It was the word 'soul' and Erik felt that was rather appropriate. Now his soul was smudged both in real life and on the page. He folded the note and placed it on top of the piano, being mindful of any substances that had escaped from Jack. Despite a tinge of sadness and a touch of regret, Erik had convinced himself that the note was Jack's fault.

It was Jack who had approached him on that night.

It was Jack who turned him.

It was even Jack who taught him to read and write.

'Goodbye, Jack.' Erik left the room and reclaimed his hat and coat from the hallway. The sound of the front door closing behind him had a sense of finality about it. The air outside was cold and the afternoon sun was a little too bright. Erik squinted as he tried to make a decision. Should he turn left or right? It didn't make any difference, as long it as got him to where he needed to be. And Erik needed to be anywhere but here.

So, he walked. And walked some more. He walked until the sun started to set and then he walked some more. Blisters formed on his feet, burst and then healed.

At some point during the night, Erik stopped. He didn't need to rest, he was just drawn to the sight of running water in a river. A small amount of waning moonlight bounced off it, making it glisten, but otherwise there was darkness. The water looked inviting. Erik could imagine wading into it and sinking underneath. A welcome respite from the trappings of the day. But, alas, it wouldn't be forever. Drowning wouldn't kill him. It might be incredibly uncomfortable for a while, but he wouldn't die. Water was not something that could kill a werewolf. The thing that could was currently hidden in the waistband of his trousers. The gun's cold steel felt reassuring against his back. There was one bullet left. It had been intended for Ida, but he hadn't been able to go through with it. However, sitting there, enveloped in darkness, the bullet felt like it was meant for him and him alone. It was fate. He had made Jack pay for his sin, now Erik had to pay for his own.

Reaching around, Erik's hand closed on the gun's handle. He pulled it from his waistband and held it in front of him. It looked unfeeling and unnatural. Up until that day, Erik had never seen a gun, let alone held or fired one. Now he had murdered someone with it and was about to kill himself. He put the barrel of the gun in his mouth and rested his finger on the trigger. Erik's eyes widened and his hand shook. The task was simple, he just needed to squeeze. But, knowing what to do and actually doing it were very different. It was much harder to be your own executioner than Erik imagined, even if you thought it was what you needed, or what you thought should be done.

The gun was snatched from his shivering grip, chipping his tooth as it was wrenched away from him.

‘Not so fast.’ the voice was familiar and entirely unwelcome.

‘Daniel.’ It wasn’t a question, Erik knew exactly who was standing just behind him. He turned, running his tongue over the jagged edge of his broken tooth. ‘What are you doing here?’

‘I think the question should be, what are *you* doing here?’ Daniel put his hand on Erik’s shoulder, gripping tightly. It wasn’t a gesture of support, it was to make sure that he wouldn’t run away. ‘You’ve caused me some trouble.’

‘I don’t understand.’ And he didn’t.

‘You were meant to kill them both, Erik. What stopped you?’

‘I couldn’t go through with it.’

‘Evidently not.’ Daniel started to lead Erik away from the water’s edge. A horse-drawn carriage awaited them a short walk away. Erik was amazed that he hadn’t heard them arrive, but he had been distracted. They climbed into the carriage and sat on the soft seats within. Daniel was clearly a man of means. ‘You left one alive and she raised the alarm. Did you know that your friends Jack and Ida were trying to live out of sight of the Council? They didn’t like the things we do or the way we do them. But, by shooting her sweetheart, you’ve drawn Ida straight to us. She reported the werewolf on werewolf killing faster than I would have thought imaginable. She told one of my esteemed colleagues all about it. Do you know what this means?’

‘No.’

Daniel leaned across him and pulled the small curtain across the window, shutting the night outside. ‘It means that the Council are going to investigate. When they investigate, they are going to ask Ida questions. Do you understand that?'

'Yes...' Erik replied, not sure where this was going.

'Did you tell her about me?'

'I barely know you. You had just given me the gun and she wasn't at home when I shot Jack. How could I have told her?'

'Apparently, you left her a note.'

'There's nothing about you in it.' Erik realised that the man was paranoid. A feeling of terror started to simmer below the surface. A few moments ago, Erik had wanted his life to end. But that had been on his terms, when he had been in control. Daniel was a rogue element, one whose intentions Erik was unable to guess at. 'Just read the note and you'll see.'

'I can't read the note, otherwise I would have done.' Daniel was frustrated, on edge and unpredictable. 'One of my colleagues is at the house at the moment. She'll be reading the note soon and I need to be prepared for whatever it says. If I'm implicated in any way, I need to get my story straight. So, Erik, tell me exactly what the letter said. Word for word.'

Erik nodded and recited the words that he had left for Ida. The words were still etched into his retinas.

'That sounds fine. A little melodramatic, but fine.' Daniel said, but the look set on his face suggested that he wasn't completely pleased with Erik's retelling. 'But how can I be sure that you're telling me the truth?'

'You have my word.'

'I don't know you, so I have no idea how much your word is worth.' Daniel shuffled along the bench seat, ensuring that there was no escape for his passenger. 'I need to know for certain.'

'How will you do that?'

'Don't worry, Erik.' Daniel smiled a smile that chilled Erik to his core. 'I have my ways.'

Erik had no desire to find out what Daniel meant by that, but he had a feeling that he was going to find out very soon.

'What will they do to me?'

'Who?'

'The Council. Are they going to hunt me down?'

'Are you hoping they'll do your dirty work for you?'

'Perhaps.'

'Then no.' Daniel said. 'They don't know who *you* are, even with your note. Jack and Ida were off in hiding, remember? You don't officially exist.'

'But my name is on the note.'

'You aren't the only werewolf called Erik.' Daniel said, smiling as he realised the effect his words would have. 'Some other werewolf will pay for your crime.'

More blood to coat Erik's hands. The guilt numbed him.

***

Physically, the journey in Daniel's carriage had been surprisingly comfortable - perhaps even luxurious - but Erik had not been able to relax. There was a glint in Daniel's eye that spoke of violence. *Is this what my future holds?* Erik asked himself. Would his inner werewolf force violent tendencies out, even when he was in human form?

No, that couldn't be right. Jack never showed signs of this. Neither had Ida. Daniel must have been born that way. Although he didn't know it at that time, Erik would soon meet another man with such tendencies. But things would be different with him. Peter would be on his side. Most of the time, anyway.

There was a knock on the carriage door. ‘Mr Griswold?’

‘Yes.’

‘We’re here, sir.’

‘Thank you, Baxter.’ The door was opened from the outside and a man - Baxter - was waiting on the other side. During his time with Jack and Ida, Erik had met people who had servants and he had spoken at length with those who served, but he had never seen anyone quite like Baxter. Baxter was a brute of a man and possibly would have given Erik a run for his money even if he had been in his wolf form. It certainly looked like he’d had the experience of a fight or two. A long scar ran the length of his head, starting at his hairline. It ran through his right eye - the cause of the scar had rendered that eye unusable - and then down until it travelled underneath his chin.

‘I take it this is ‘im?’ Baxter’s low gravelly voice suited his scared face perfectly.

‘It is indeed.’ Daniel stepped out of the carriage and beckoned for Erik to follow. With no other options open to him, Erik did as was expected and stepped out into the night. He found himself standing in the grounds of a large manor house. Sculpted hedges surrounded him, looking over him ominously. ‘Take him to his room.’

Baxter manhandled Erik along the driveway. As they approached the front door, it opened immediately, as if whoever opened it was waiting for them to arrive. The man in the doorway - presumably another member of Daniel’s staff - stepped aside so that Baxter could push Erik in with no obstacles in the way. Erik fell to the floor, bashing his chin. His broken tooth stabbed into his lip and his mouth filled with blood. It was not the best way to start his first visit to Daniel’s house.

‘Now now, let’s be careful.’ Erik heard Daniel’s voice and the sound of his perfectly polished shoes on the tiled floor. 'I don't want him too roughed up before we get started. That will spoil all the fun.'

'Right you are.' It was Baxter's voice now and Erik felt someone grab his collar and pull him upright. He stood in front of Daniel and licked his lip. He could already feel it healing.

'Take him to the basement and make sure he's secure.'

'Will do.' Baxter pulled Erik along and they descended a staircase together, Baxter with an arm around Erik's shoulders while Erik stumbled. In other circumstances, it may have looked like Baxter was helping a drunk friend down a tricky set of stairs.

A singular oil lamp was struggling to light the vast basement room. The room held little apart from a chair, a table and a large brown trunk. The trunk looked well-worn and well-travelled. Erik wondered where Daniel had been and what he had been doing.

'Sit.' Baxter pointed towards the lonely chair. Erik sat, not fancying a physical altercation with the man, and watched as his wrists and ankles were tied to the chair with leather straps. They were tight, but he knew he would be able to escape from them. Which was strange, surely Daniel would also know that he would be able to escape. All he needed to do was turn.

'Wait.' Baxter was a man of few words. Erik waited.

Soon enough, Daniel came down the stairs, whistling and smiling. He appeared to be much happier now that he was in his own territory. 'Let's begin.'

Daniel opened the case and pulled something out. Erik struggled to see what was in the man's hand.

'Don't worry, Erik.' Daniel said over his shoulder. 'There's no need to strain your neck, I'll show you. It is a gift for you.'

Daniel turned around and showed him a small glass vial. It was similar in shape to the one that had contained the worm that Jack had used, but it was smaller, and the glass was stained blue, obscuring its contents.

'Sniff.' Daniel said, holding the vial under Erik's nose.

Erik sniffed.

And things when dark.

***

Pain, hot and sharp, roused him from an uncomfortable sleep. 'Wh-'

The pain intensified as he tried to speak; something sharp was penetrating the flesh under his chin, while something else was digging into his chest.

'Did you know that human beings are a sick bunch?' It was Daniel's voice, filled with glee. 'Do you know how many methods of torture there are? All there to help collect information, or to punish. I need to collect information from you, Erik. I hope I don't need to punish you as well. Although, if I do, there's an assortment of methods I could use. I've tried many of them over the years. Some work better than others... but they're all entertaining in their own way.'

Erik didn't respond, he was too busy trying to block out the pain. It didn't make sense, he was a werewolf, he should be able to withstand this. That was a point, he was a werewolf. He should change. Right now.

Since the day that Jack had changed him, he'd trained him to control his transformations. It wouldn't do to suddenly change into a monster in the middle of the street in broad daylight. To stop a transformation, Erik had been taught to take slow, deep breaths and close his eyes. Jack had shown him how to perform a small meditation. It seemed simple, but it worked.

Luckily, they had also worked on how Erik could force a transformation. All he had to do was work himself up. Focus on the anger he felt and let his wolf manifest from it. Forcing the pain from his upper chest and under his chin from his mind, he concentrated, imagining his anger to be a physical entity that needed to be pounded and moulded into shape. It was a technique he had used maybe one hundred times before, and it worked every time.

But not this time.

Instead of changing into the magnificent, blood-thirsty, barbaric beast that he could be, Erik remained in human form. If anything, his pain had increased. The tensing of his muscles and straining against the leather straps had caused them to begin to tear into his flesh. Blood was also now dripping from his chin. Another thing struck Erik as being odd; he wasn't healing. Usually he could cut himself and then watch - and feel - the skin knit together before his eyes. None of that was happening now.

'You look confused.' Daniel knelt in front of him. 'Did you try to change? Did you really think that I wouldn't have anticipated you doing that? I've been around a very long time, Erik. Far longer than you. Far longer than your friends Jack and Ida.'

Daniel gave whatever was underneath Erik's chin a slight tap with his finger and a fresh jolt of pain ripped through him, making him scream through clenched teeth. Opening his mouth would have forced whatever *that thing* was further into his skin.

'Aww, did that hurt?' Daniel laughed. Not a small chuckle, but a big belly laugh. Even if the man was enjoying himself, the laugh seemed over the top and out of place. Something wasn't right with him. 'Don't worry, it's supposed to hurt. That just means it's working.'

Daniel stood and wandered back over to the table where his trunk awaited him. For what felt like an eternity, he just stared into it. Erik could only imagine what items were holding his attention for so long. Finally, he turned back around. No new objects were in his hands.

'I bet you're wondering what's in there, aren't you?' Daniel's eyes locked with Erik's. Erik felt like ignoring the man would cause more pain for him, so opted for a non-committal *'mmm'* noise. 'Then allow me to explain.'

The man seemed to enjoy his long, dramatic pauses.

'I was just starting to tell you about human beings and their love of torture, wasn't I? Until you hurt yourself trying to transform. I'll continue... Over the centuries, human beings have put a great amount of effort into developing tools and methods explicitly designed to cause as much pain as possible. In honour of that commitment, I've spent a large amount of time adapting some of these methods for our kind. One day, once I'm in "*The Six*", I'll bring my knowledge to the Council, so that we can use them to keep order. Until that day - and, make no mistake, that day will come - I'll just have to use them for my own personal enjoyment.'

Despite the pain, Erik couldn't help but notice that Daniel referred to anyone who wasn't a werewolf as human beings. He was correct in some ways, that is what they were. But the way he said the words made Erik think that he thought he was above them. He'd been a werewolf for so long that he could no longer remember being human. Any empathy that he once felt for them was long gone. That's if there was any there to begin with.

'Do you remember how I said that I'd been around a long time? Of course you do, it was only a little while ago. Unless you're suffering with The Rot, then I doubt that you would have forgotten about it already.' Had Erik been listening properly at that point, he would have had some clue about what The Rot was, and he might have been able to identify it in his soon-to-be friend earlier. But it was difficult to concentrate on every little detail when you were in constant pain. 'I was even around, slaughtering humans, when they invented the device that's currently snuggling up to your chin.'

He moved forwards again, as if he was going to touch it. The thought definitely crossed his mind, but somehow, he refrained. Erik had no idea why. 'That device is called a Heretics Fork. It's rather beautiful in its simplicity, but I have to show it to you for you to really appreciate it. Don't worry, I won't remove your one, I have a spare in my trunk.'

Back Daniel went to the trunk and this time he returned with a small, metallic object attached to a leather strap. The object had a fork at either end and the meagre light in the room made it sparkle majestically. The Heretic's Fork looked every bit as evil and barbarous as it felt digging into Erik's flesh.

'This, my friend, is the Heretics Fork.' There was an element of wonder in his voice. In spite of his feelings about the human race, he did seem to be in awe of whoever dreamed this item up. 'It was mainly used during the Spanish Inquisition... Its purpose was to get heretics and witches to confess... and, do you know, almost every single one of them did. It's remarkable really. Many of them were not even guilty. I guess the pain was just too much to cope with. Is that the case, Erik?'

Erik grunted, anything else was too painful.

'I wonder... If I left you like this for a while, what would you confess to?' Erik watched as Daniel scratched his chin with the other device in a thoughtful gesture. 'Do you think the words in your note would change? The note you left for Ida. I wonder if I left you here, like this, for a week, would you tell me that you told her all about me? Would you tell me that you told her that it was my knowledge that killed her beloved Jack?'

Erik grunted in what he hoped signified a negative answer. How long could he stand this? Why the fuck wasn't he changing or healing?

'You remember how I told you that you'd need a special bullet to kill Jack?' Daniel was jumping from subject to subject. 'Any old bullet wouldn't do, it had to be silver. Used in the right way - when it's mixed with something special and is administered correctly - silver can be deadly to our kind. When used in other ways, it can cause a lot of pain. Does it excite you to know that the Heretics Fork that I've used on you is made of silver? It certainly excites me. It's the reason why you can't change. You are completely at my mercy. If I wanted to kill you, I could. Just remember that.'

Abruptly, he walked away. Erik heard the man's footsteps disappearing up the stairs. Was that it? Was it done? How long was he going to be left like this? Erik had to agree, the Heretics Fork was an effective method of causing maximum pain with very little effort or equipment. Any movement he made, renewed and redoubled the agony. He wasn't sure that he could endure this misery for another hour, let alone a week as Daniel had eluded to. Insanity would surely claim him before that. What would happen if Daniel left him here for that long? Would he confess to things he had never done? If he did, what would Daniel do with him? He had, after all, mentioned that the torture devices that he was so fond of where made for both interrogation and punishment. Erik was sure that execution was included in Daniel's definition of 'punishment'.

Earlier that night, Erik had wanted to wander into the darkness and never return. He wanted to everything to end. He wanted to die.

Now he knew that he wanted to live.

Ignoring the combination of different levels of pain around his body, Erik once again tried to escape, struggling against the leather straps. It was futile.

'It don't matter.' A gruff voice filtered through the shadows. Erik hadn't even noticed that Baxter was still in the room. 'Even if you run, 'e would find ya. Besides, nobody ever escapes.'

Erik heard the sound of footsteps, then he heard the sound of breathing behind him. Baxter was close enough to snap his neck.

'Sometimes I think 'e wants 'is prisoners to escape. It's like it's all a game to 'im. Like a dog chasin' a rabbit. Or, a cat with a mouse. Cats play with their prey, don't they? Yes, 'e's more like that.'

The big man's breath was on Erik's neck, he could feel it moving his hair. Had he been able to, he would have gulped. Would Baxter kill him? Erik was utterly helpless. He couldn't move, so he couldn't defend himself. He couldn't speak, so he couldn't reason with the man. Erik felt like an ant waiting to be crushed by a shoe.

He felt Baxter move closer.

***

'Whatever it is that Daniel wants, it can't be good.' Peter's voice wrenched Erik from his memory. Peter was doing his best to wear out the carpet by pacing up and down. Erik took a seat in the armchair that Kit had vacated.

'Have you called him back yet?'

'Of course not! And I have no intention of doing so. He called on the pub's number... maybe if I don't return his call, he'll think that we've moved.'

Erik shook his head and let out a small laugh. 'That's not going to work.'

'I know... but what can we do? I know what that man is like. You've told me all about it.'

Peter had never had the pleasure of dealing with Daniel on a one-to-one basis – not properly. Up until now, he had only spoken to the man when either Erik or Kathryn had been present, and that had been enough to tell him that Daniel was deranged. In fact, the first time he'd met him when he was when he was with Erik and that had been enough to solidify that opinion.

'If you don't call him, he'll come here. Do you want that?' Erik was trying to think of a solution, but he knew that none existed short of running away and going completely off the grid.

A twitch flickered across Peter's face, as if an idea had just been dropped into his mind. Which, in a way, it had. 'Let him come. When he does, we'll go with the original plan.'

'No.' Erik said, unwilling to hand Kit over to that man. Anyone but him.

'We'll tell him that Kit did it all and hand him over. Daniel will be happy with his new toy and we'll live to see another day.'

'I said no.' Erik's words were slow and defiant. Peter knew that his friend meant business. 'I see potential in him. And nobody deserves what Daniel will do to him... except maybe Daniel himself.'

'Then what do you suggest?'

'I really don't know.'

***

Baxter crouched down so that their faces were level. His crooked yellowed teeth bit into his lip and his eyes darted this way and that, as if he was trying to come to a decision. The scar that ran down half his face and through his eye looked angry, the skin around it looking puckered and ruined. 'I don't know what Mister Griswold wants ya to tell 'im, but if I were you, I'd give it up quick. He don't mess around.'

Erik grunted, still unable to talk.

'Ya tryin' to tell me somethin', mister?' The big man took a quick look around the room, and a slightly longer look at the staircase. Happy that they were alone, he turned back to Erik. 'Raise your 'ead, I'm gonna remove that fork for ya. So's ya can talk.'

Erik raised his head and Baxter was true to his word, undoing the leather strap and pulling the fork away. Erik was sure that some of his skin went with it, but it was a relief not to have it touching him anymore. 'Why are you helping me? Won't he kill you when he finds out?'

'What makes you think I'm helpin' ya? You were tryin' to talk to me. I figure that you're going to die soon, unless you tell the boss what 'e wants to know. I'm just giving ya the chance for a few last words.'

'Fair enough, but won't he be angry that you removed that fork thing from me?'

'Probably... but, then, 'e did leave me alone down here with ya. Sometimes I think 'e's testing me... or that 'e wants me to do stuff like this. I do stuff like this a lot, I just can't help it. The people he brings here always have somethin' to say when he disappears. They like talkin' to me, so I let 'em.'

'And do you tell Daniel what they say?'

'I do now. How do you think I got so pretty?' Baxter ran one of his sausage-like fingers along his scar. 'It ain't just you wolf-people 'e plays with.'

Erik thought he knew what was going on, even if Baxter didn't. The brute was just a pawn in Daniel's game. A pawn that Daniel would no doubt punish for his complicity. Even so, Erik had to make the most of it. If an opportunity to escape presented itself, he had to take it. 'Say, Baxter... it is Baxter, isn't it?'

‘Yeah...’ For a moment, the larger man looked like a gorilla trying to complete a particularly tricky algebra problem as he attempted to work out where this was going.

‘Baxter, can you undo these straps?’

‘No way, the boss definitely wouldn’t want me to do that.’

‘How can you be sure? You said that you think he’s left you down here as part of his game. Maybe he wants you to release me? Maybe he wants me to run, just so that he can chase me again.’

Baxter rubbed the stubble on his chin. ‘He does enjoy the hunt.’

‘That he does.’ Erik’s plan seemed to be working. ‘So, you’d just be doing what he likes.’

‘I suppose that makes sense.’ Baxter’s hands moved towards the leather strap holding Erik’s left hand in place. ‘But, can I come with ya? Let’s say the boss ain’t happy about it... I’m a dead man.’

‘Very well, you can come with me. The more the merrier.’

‘And, if ‘e does hunt us down - which ‘e definitely will - and ‘e finds us...’ Baxter seemed to be struggling to find the words he wanted to use, and his fingers had paused in their task. ‘If ‘e finds us and it all looks hopeless, put me out of my misery before ‘e gets me.’

Erik was astonished. He hadn’t expected Baxter to want to leave or to want to die rather than be caught by Daniel. The man obviously didn’t treat his staff very well. ‘I agree, but... if you’re unhappy here, why don’t you just leave?’

‘The boss always finds deserters. The world ain’t big enough to hide in.’ A shudder sprinted down Erik’s spine as Baxter undid the straps. The feeling of urgency that he’d had since Baxter had started talking to him turned itself up a few notches. Time wasn’t on their side.

Daniel could return at any moment. His heart started to race, and he felt a change coming on, but he took a few deep breaths and put a stop to it. While he was able to control when he transformed, he wasn't yet completely able to control what happened after that, and he didn't want to tear Baxter limb from limb. Not after he'd risked his life to save him. Besides, it seemed that Erik's first impressions had been wrong, Baxter wasn't so bad after all. The poor man was in a similar situation to Erik, pulled into a world that he had no intention of even visiting.

'We 'ave to move.' Baxter also shared Erik's sense of urgency. His chunky fingers kept reaching for his scar, constantly reminding himself of what could happen if he got caught. Baxter was a formidable looking man, the kind that people feared instantly, even before he'd had the chance to carry out one of his master's despicable commands. He looked like he could knock the living daylights out of even the biggest foe with a well-placed punch… and he could. But he was also in a state of perpetual fear. Never knowing if his actions were part of an elaborate game that Daniel was playing was exhausting and the thought of what would happen if he did something wrong was enough to keep his nerves on edge permanently. Seeing his master show up with Erik had set the cogs in his head in motion. Erik was a new werewolf, recently turned. By Baxter's logic, this meant that he was nowhere near as deranged as Daniel. Until he saw it for himself, and despite reassurances from the others in Daniel's employment, Baxter assumed that becoming sick and twisted was all part of being a werewolf. Perhaps their first torture session was a rite of passage, something to be celebrated with drinks and cake. Not that he had ever seen a werewolf consume either of those things.

Nodding his agreement, Erik got to his feet. His legs and neck were stiff from sitting in the same position for so long, but at least the wounds under his chin and on his chest were healing. It appeared that whatever effect the silver had on him, it wasn't permanent. For the first time that night, Erik felt lucky. It occurred to him that he had no idea what the time was. How long had he been there? The time between being knocked out by whatever Daniel kept in his little blue vial and waking up seemed like minutes, but there was a chance that it could have been a lot longer. Erik could have been kept in this basement for days before he'd woken. But, that didn't seem right. That would have given Daniel time to see the note for himself and would render Erik's incarceration pointless.

Baxter headed to the staircase at a pace that was surprising for his size. Daniel's right-hand man was built for both strength and speed. Once again, Erik felt lucky. He would have smiled had he not been fearing for his life. He made to follow, but he found himself pausing in front of the brown trunk. Despite the need for haste, part of him was desperate to know what Daniel kept in there. What depraved things had he been planning to inflict on Erik?

'There ain't no time for that.' Impatience and fear littered Baxter's gruff voice in equal measure. 'I'd bet ya that the boss will be along at any moment. An' if 'e's gonna be here, we've gotta be somewhere else.'

There was no arguing with that logic, so Erik chased Baxter up the stairs, being as stealthy as he could manage. The fact that he was now barefoot definitely helped. The realisation that his shoes had been taken while he was unconscious worried him. What else had Daniel taken from him? What else had he done to him? The feeling of violation made him want to vomit, but he held himself in check and continued to follow the bulky form in front of him.

At the top of the stairs, Baxter paused, causing Erik to almost walk directly into him. 'Shhh.' he said, putting a finger to his lips. With great care, he slowly edged the door open. The contrast between the world downstairs and the world upstairs was astounding. The light was brighter for starters and Erik had to shield his eyes until they adjusted. Baxter didn't seem to have any such problems, he was obviously used to travelling from one part of the house to the other. 'Follow me. Once we're through, don't stop for nothin'.'

The pair left the darkness of the basement and tiptoed through the house's hallway. Erik had only seen it in passing as Baxter had dragged him through it when he had first arrived, so he hadn't had the chance to properly take it in. The ceilings were high, the walls white. The marble floor was cold on his feet. *No wonder I hurt myself when I fell*, he thought. The walls were bare, aside from a large painting that hung adjacent to the front door. It was so huge, Erik wondered how he had been able to miss it before. An ostentatious portrait of Daniel himself took up most of the wall, and it was awe-inspiringly lifelike. The artist had captured every detail of Daniel's face, every nuance. They'd captured his character perfectly. Their only error had been to exaggerate the man's height, but Erik supposed that they preferred to avoid incurring Daniel's wrath, rather than focus on total accuracy.

'Keep movin'.' Baxter's whisper was harsh. He wanted to be out of here and Erik couldn't blame him. After checking around for any witnesses, Baxter edged the door open. Cold, night air entered; its frost welcome on Erik's skin. Holding in his urge to transform was making him burn up. Baxter slipped through the opening and Erik followed, freedom almost within his grasp. He didn't know how they'd get away from the house's grounds. They could steal Daniel's carriage or disappear on foot. Either way, the house would soon be a distant speck on the horizon. Erik couldn't wait.

BANG!

The noise disorientated Erik. What was it? What was the wet substance on his face? Who was that figure? Where was Baxter? Erik's ears rang, and his blood pumped quickly. There was no denying this transformation now.

And it didn't matter anyway. Baxter lay on the porch in front him, his brain leaking from his head. Even a man of Baxter's size and strength couldn't walk that one off. For a moment, Erik pitied the man. Baxter had proved himself to be a good man, perhaps even honourable, in the last few minutes. However, grief at times like these didn't last for long. It was pushed deep down inside of him, along with his other human thoughts and feelings. There was no stopping it. Erik changed and howls rang through the night.

CHAPTER TWENTY-NINE

Clothes tore, skin ripped, and blood flowed. To an onlooker it may have appeared that something had gone very wrong, but this was all part of the metamorphosis from man to wolf. Erik howled and howled again. The sound - lonesome in the darkness of the night - may have seemed mournful to anyone listening in, but Erik was removed from any such feelings. At the moment, he knew only that he needed to hunt. And he needed to hunt the figure standing in front of him. Erik didn't ask himself why he had to tear apart that particular being, nor did he wonder why that being was not running away. At this point, Erik was all about action. He leapt into the air, claws and teeth baring down upon whoever was still standing their ground.

***

Daniel stood, watching Erik's wolf form come flying towards him and readied himself. His legs were shoulder width apart, ready to absorb the shock of the incoming werewolf and his hands were ready to wrestle the beast's muzzle away. Changing into a wolf himself was an option, but he didn't need to. He wanted to make sure that Erik realised that he was the alpha dog even when he wasn't a wolf. Taking down the other man like this would be the ultimate act of dominance.

Erik's huge mass crashed into him, knocking him to the floor. Teeth gnashed at his face and at his neck, but Daniel had been prepared. In just a few moves, he had wrestled the wolf's mouth away from his face and flipped him over. Erik now lay on the porch with Daniel straddling him. Still fighting for the upper hand, Erik thrashed and bucked beneath him, trying to escape. Trying to do anything to inflict a bit of pain. Daniel remained where he was, his face a stoic mask. He was almost calm - serene even. Taking a chance, he let go of Erik with one of his hands. Erik tried to seize the opportunity immediately. He was fast, but Daniel was faster. In a split second, Daniel reached into his waistcoat pocket and pulled out the blue vial. Using the same hand, he used his thumb to flick the cork out. It bounced across the porch and came to rest in Baxter's blood. The dead man's glazed eyes stared at it intently. Being careful not to spill a drop on himself, or inhale the fumes, Daniel wafted the vial under the wolf's snout. The frantic movement stopped immediately.

As Erik slowly started to change back into his human form - bones breaking and flesh ripping itself only to rebuild again - Daniel stood and surveyed the damage, taking a large amount of time to stare at the corpse of his former servant. Baxter's betrayal had been inevitable. So much so, that Daniel had been counting on it. It was why he'd left the man alone with his prisoner and why he'd been waiting on the porch with a gun and a small blue vial. The man's death had served no real purpose, except to provide another opportunity for Daniel to demonstrate his power. If good ol' Baxter had been thinking about switching sides, it stood to reason that others had been thinking about it too. In one swift movement, Daniel had showed his entire staff what happened to traitors. He'd also shown them that he had little problem in wrestling a werewolf with his own bare hands. If his staff were not scared of him before, they would be now.

Over the years, Daniel had seen many different kinds of leaders. Some he had followed, others he had defied. He'd overthrown them all in one way or another. Some like to lead by making their subjects love them. They wanted to be admired and fawned over. It was a method that worked in its own way, but one that made Daniel feel physically ill. People who said that they loved their king were liars. How could anyone love someone who was born into - or who married into - power and then sent them off to war to die on a battlefield? It was all so terribly fake. And, yet, he'd seen many a leader try to employ this tactic. The other method that Daniel had witnessed, was those leaders who lead through fear. If someone is afraid, they know where they stand. Best of all, the leader knew where they stood. There was no pretending. No niceties. Everyone hated each other, and that was fine by Daniel. He didn't need people like Baxter to love him; he just needed them to do what he told them to do. He didn't care what his servants said about him behind his back, so long as they knew that if they tried to stab him in it, they would swiftly meet their end. It was usually a good incentive for loyalty, but there was always the odd handful of Baxters who needed dealing with. It was surprising that the man had lasted as long as he had. Daniel had been sure that he would have flipped the day he found out that Daniel had raped and killed his wife. Now that he thought about it, Daniel found it quite remarkable how Baxter had held it together for so long. The thought of what his master had done must have ripped his heart out every day. And, yet, he still did what he was told. Even when he didn't realise that he was doing as he was told. Just like tonight.

Scraping his shoe, Daniel wiped something - most likely a piece of Baxter - onto the porch. One of his frightened, yet incredibly well-behaved, minions would need to clear that up soon. Daniel wondered how long it would take them to show the initiative and come out here and start using their scrubbing brushes. In their minds, they were probably trying to wait the optimum amount of time before emerging from the house. They didn't want to come out too late and risk their master's wrath, but they also didn't want to come out too early and step into his murderous rampage. It was quite the conundrum for them. The funny thing was that Daniel was nowhere near rampaging. A wave of calm washed over him. He could even be described as happy.

Turning his attention to Erik, he nudged him with the toe of his dirty shoe. A bloody mark was left on Erik's side. 'Let's get you back inside. You'll miss all the fun out here.'

Stepping over Erik's unconscious form, Daniel went back into the house. He was aware of eyes watching him through the gaps between doors and doorframes, or through the banisters. His servants may have hidden themselves, but he knew they were there. And, more importantly, he knew that they'd seen everything he needed them to see.

'Bring him in!' he shouted, in a voice that suggested any argument or delay would be an incredibly bad idea. 'I'll be downstairs. Don't keep me waiting.'

Daniel returned to the basement, eager to continue his work.

***

Once again, Erik woke up tied to a chair in Daniel's basement. It was getting to be quite the habit, and one of those really bad ones. Erik so desperately wanted to quit it. There was no fork this time, so maybe things were looking up. He tried to strain against the leather straps, but soon realised that was hopeless. The leather straps had been replaced with handcuffs and shackles. And, if the burning in this wrists and ankles told him anything, it was that these particular pieces of equipment were crafted from silver.

'Daniel,' Erik couldn't see the man, but he knew he was there. He had to be. 'Just tell me what you want from me.'

'You know what I want.' Daniel said, stepping into the light, like an actor stepping into a spotlight. 'I just want the truth.'

'I've told you the truth.'

'But, I just want to be sure. I have trust issues, you see. I mean, you've met Baxter. I thought he was my friend.' Daniel's words cut through Erik like glass and he felt another change coming on, but, thanks to the silver, the feeling waned as quickly as it begun.

The Heretics Fork was in Daniel's hand. He twisted it this way and that, admiring it in the meagre glow provided by the oil lamp. Dull splotches tainted the silver where Erik's blood had dried.

'In order to make sure that you are telling me the absolute truth, I'm going to need to take something from you.' Daniel said as he moved in close. His breath smelt sour, just another repulsive thing about the man who Erik had first thought could be a friend. How could he be so wrong? Was he that poor a judge of character? 'Just to make you aware, all the time I'm using my tools on you, and the secret recipe in my vial, you won't change and - best of all - you won't heal.'

'I've already told you the truth.' The thought of what Daniel could be capable sent a wave of terror through Erik. Sweat broke out on his brow and under his armpits. He was entirely vulnerable. He was at Daniel's mercy and, after the way he had executed Baxter, Erik wasn't sure that he was capable of mercy. Erik's mind race as he tried to decide if it was worth making up a lie. The truth didn't seem to be enough for Daniel, in spite of what he repeatedly said. There had to be something more he could say. Something that would spare him any further pain and, hopefully, let him walk away with his life intact. But, a new problem presented itself. What if he said the wrong thing? His lie could be the thing that sent Daniel over the edge. His tormentor wasn't doing a particularly good balancing act at the moment as it was, one word taken out of context could sent him spiralling out of control. No, that wouldn't do at all. Erik would have to stick to his guns and hope for the best.

'So,' Daniel cupped Erik's face in his hands and Erik experienced the formerly bizarre sensation of the cold silver of the fork burning him. Flesh sizzled and a smell, not too dissimilar from pork cooking filled his nostrils. 'Do you have anything to add to your story? Anything to change? Anything at all?'

Daniel's eyes searched Erik's for answers. They looked for a tell, something to suggest that Erik had been lying. Erik couldn't tell if Daniel had thought he'd found something or not. The man was utterly unreadable. His face was blank, betraying no emotions at all.

'Last chance.' he said, his face unchanging. The lack of any external emotion was unnerving. This man was not normal. Not even by werewolf standards.

'I've told you everything that was in the note,' Erik's pulse quickened, and he knew that Daniel could tell that he was petrified. Erik wished he could hide his emotions as well as Daniel. 'I told you what it said word for word. There's nothing else to say.'

'Is there not?' Daniel said. 'I disagree. I think there's more. I think you could tell me so much more. You just don't realise it yet.'

Without any further questions, Daniel's right hand left Erik's cheek. It was the hand that was holding the Heretics Fork.

'What… What are you doing?' Words were difficult to form, Erik's tongue felt huge and awkward in his mouth. He wasn't sure if it was down to something Daniel was doing to him, or just a by-product of his fear.

'I'm torturing you, my friend.' Daniel said, smiling and allowing his mask to break. 'I thought that much was obvious.'

Looking back, Erik was never sure if he started to scream before or after the edge of fork was sliced through his ear. Other than that, he could remember that event in unbelievable detail. The squelching as the ear slipped away. The plop as it dropped to the floor next to Daniel's smart shoe. The warmth of blood flowing down his cheek. The iron taste as some blood crept into the corner of his mouth. And the pain. The pain was made all the worse due to the fact that under normal circumstances he would be able to heal. Now, screaming did nothing to reduce the pain. Now, Erik had no idea if he would be disfigured for life.

'I really hope that you've been *listening* to me.' The stoic mask was well and truly gone now; Daniel was enjoying himself. The man most definitely was not normal. 'Are you able to *hear* me, loud and clear, Erik?'

'What have you done to me?' Erik's voice was shrill with panic.

'Calm down, friend. You don't want to start crying now… it's terribly undignified.' Daniel said. 'And, besides, *'what have you done to me?'* is not the answer I was looking for. I guess we'll have to try again.'

Taking Erik's ear with him, Daniel stepped away towards the trunk. 'I have all sorts of things in here that will encourage you to be more talkative.'

'I swear, I've told you the truth. There's nothing else!'

'Nothing? Are you sure? Think back, Erik. Think back to when you walked into the house. Did anyone see you?'

Erik thought. It was amazing what a bit of pain could do to focus the mind under these circumstances. He didn't have a photographic memory by any means, but he was fairly confident that nobody had seen him. 'No, no-one saw me.'

'Good. You're doing well now. I'm proud of you.' Daniel said, walking back towards him. Erik wasn't sure if he was pleased that the man had walked away from his trunk or if he should be concerned about what he was going to do now that he was in such close proximity again. 'But, I think there's more you can tell me.'

'There really isn't.' Erik felt like crying, but he took notice of Daniel's advice and somehow managed to refrain. His eyes burned with unspent tears, clouding his vision, distorting his view of his tormentor. 'There's nothing else I can tell you.'

'And you're sure?'

'Yes, yes, I'm sure!'

Daniel leant forward and one of his hands - the one not still occupied with the Heretics Fork - grabbed Erik's naked thigh, Erik could feel Daniel's grip bruising his flesh. The other hand moved painfully slowly, until it rested the tip of the fork on Erik's scrotum. The burning sensation felt more intense in that area. Erik felt the skin start to sizzle and break and the heat singed Erik's pubic hair.

'There's nothing else to say!' Erik's voice was high-pitched, frightened. Removing his ear was one thing, but his balls? That was something else. And, what was to say that Daniel would stop there.

'No, I think there's more. Now, I know what you're thinking. You're thinking that I couldn't be that cruel.' Daniel said, not seeming to know at all what Erik was thinking. Either that, or he was toying with him. Teasing him. Erik suspected the latter. 'But, if I tried really hard... I mean, if I really committed to it... I think I could make this fork penetrate your crown jewels quite effectively.'

'I don't know what else you want from me.' Erik's voice shook as much as his body. 'There's nothing else I can tell you.'

'Oh yes, there is.' Daniel said, pushing the fork into Erik's testicles. Not enough to pierce the skin, but enough so that Erik would notice - and be able to focus on very little else. 'I need to make sure that my colleagues in the Council will never tie me to the murder. They can't know that I'm giving away trade secrets like that.'

Racking his brains for another titbit of information, an epiphany came to Erik. 'You want to make sure that you're in the clear.'

'Exactly.'

'You are, I never mentioned you to Ida. I never mentioned you to anyone.'

'Excellent,' Daniel said. 'You're getting the hang of it now.'

‘Are you happy now?’ Erik tried to squirm away from the weapon, but he had nowhere to go.

‘Nearly. So very nearly.’ Daniel stared at the fork, as if he was wondering whether to use it regardless of what Erik told him. ‘I just need to know a couple more things.’

‘Yes, whatever they are, I’ll tell you.’

‘Have you spoken to any other members of the Council?’ Daniel asked, still staring at that fork.

‘No, I haven’t even spoken to any other werewolves...’ Erik said. ‘Besides yourself, Jack and Ida. You have nothing to fear.’

‘Good. That’s very good. Now, my last question.’

‘Yes?’ Erik said, eager to get the interrogation over with.

‘What would you do if I did this?’ Daniel asked as he raised the fork into the air and hammered it down onto Erik’s most private of areas. Erik’s screams were a mixture of pain and disbelief as he felt the fork tear away part of his body. A wet, flopping noise, met his eardrum as something soft fell against the ground. Erik passed out, unconscious once again in Daniel’s basement. ‘So that’s what happens...’

Not bothering to even wipe it down, Daniel took the Heretics Fork to his trunk and placed it inside. A contented sigh escaped him. Apart from one or two mishaps, today had been a good day. Daniel took a key from the trunk and returned to Erik. It only took a couple of seconds to remove the handcuffs and the shackles. The silver burnt his skin a little as he worked, but it was a pain that he had become used to over the years. In fact, in small doses like this he almost enjoyed it. The handcuffs and shackles fell to the ground, making a clattering noise, but nothing woke Erik. The poor man needed a lot of sleep. He had a lot of healing to do. Now that the silver was removed, Daniel watched as the man's wounds started to knit together. A new set of balls started to grow. Slowly, but surely, a new ear started to form. He could have made Erik's disfigurements permanent. He could have even killed him. But he chose not to. Erik had told the truth, and that's all Daniel had ever wanted from him. So, as a sign of his gratitude, Daniel would let him walk away. In one piece. Daniel may not have been normal, but he lived by his own code.

***

Many years ago

'The boy ain't normal.' Albert Griswold had found one too many mutilated rat carcasses for his liking. A small pile of rodent corpses sat on the ground in front of him. Tiny little eyes looked upon him for explanation. *Why did he do this to us?* they almost seemed to say.

'Maybe the boy's just curious. Wants ta see how they work or summat.' Emerald Griswold said. Daniel was her son and she refused to admit that there was anything wrong with him. Insanity lit Daniel up like a beacon, and there was no denying his cruelty, but Emerald would never admit her concerns to anyone outside of the family.

'Curious? Curious ain't the word for it.' Albert gently scooped the tiny dead bodies into a sack. 'He's a menace, Emmy.'

'He's no menace, he's our boy. Don't go saying things like that, people will hear.'

'There's no-one here.'

'Don't risk it.'

'Emmy, I know you don't want to hear it-'

'You're right, I don't.' Emerald replied. 'Let's change the subject.'

'I hate it too, but we need to do something. If the others find out what he's like, they'll kill 'im. We can send him away.'

'We can't just leave him somewhere.' Emerald wrung her hands as she was prone to do when she was nervous or worried.

'At least he'd be alive.' Albert and Emerald exchanged glances. Now that the truth was out, there was no way they could hide it again. The choice was harsh, but simple; stay together and watch as their son was murdered, or banish him so that he might live.

Another rat carcass was dropped into the sack and Emerald's eyes were drawn to the bloodstain that the little body left behind. They'd need to cover that over, they couldn't have people asking questions. Finally, she spoke again. 'Tomorrow. We'll need to do it tomorrow.'

Her husband nodded, biting his tongue and catching words that were eager to leave his mouth. *The sooner the better*, he thought. *Before he switches from vermin to people.*

Hidden just out of sight, Daniel listened to every word his parents said.

***

Present day.

A plan had started to form in Erik's mind, one that he had no success in carrying out before, but this time was different. He now had years and wisdom on his side, and he knew that Daniel's way with words wouldn't sway him now.

'Call him or don't, it amounts to the same thing.' He said. Peter wondered what his long-time companion was plotting. He knew that Erik knew just how bad Daniel was, but even in all their years together, he had never given him the full story. In some ways, Peter thought that may have been for the best.

'And what's that?' Peter asked, fearing he knew the answer to his own question.

'Daniel will come here.' Erik stood from the chair. 'Let him come.'

***

Victorian London.

Erik awoke to the sound of a doorbell ringing mixed with the soothing melody of birdsong. He was in a bed, in a bedroom with a large open window. Instinctively, one hand when down to gently cup his balls, while the other tested the side of his head for the missing ear. There were no missing parts. He was complete.

A muffled voice could be heard through the door, someone was talking to whoever had rang the doorbell. Erik's keen sense of hearing picked up what was being said.

'Ah, so you're here to join my staff?' It was Daniel's voice. He seemed happy, jovial even. Not like a man who had viciously tortured someone recently. 'I see you have good references.'

'Yes, sir.' The voice was calm and brimming with confidence. It was the voice of someone who knew no superiors. It would make him be a terrible employee. If Daniel was expecting another Baxter, he'd have another thing coming with this one.

'Take a seat, I'll be right with you.' The sound of footsteps told Erik that Daniel was moving further into the house. Now was his chance to escape. Dressing in the clothes that had been left out for him, Erik left the room and sped down the staircase. He soon arrived in the hallway at the front of the house, where a young man was sat on an incredibly ornate, yet highly uncomfortable looking chair. He looked very much like a naughty school boy waiting outside the headmaster's office.

'Are you here to work for Daniel?' Erik said, feeling like he should at least give the man some warning. He couldn't let him wander unwittingly into his demise, no matter how confident he sounded.

'Who are you?' The man said. 'Are you a friend of Mr Griswold's?'

Erik wondered how to answer. Both the truth and lies held an equal amount of pain in this house, so this time he opted for a lie. 'Yes, I am.'

'Then it's lovely to meet you.' The man said, holding out a hand. 'My name is Peter Smedley.'

Taking Peter's hand, Erik gave it a firm shake. 'My name is Erik Haugen. It's a pleasure to meet you.'

With formalities out of the way, Erik considered how best to tell his new acquaintance that his soon-to-be employer was a psychopathic werewolf with a torture chamber in his basement. As he thought, his eyes roamed around the hallway, eventually coming to rest on a pile of books that had been left on the bottom stair. Erik was surprised that he hadn't tripped over them on his descent. Peter followed his gaze. 'Mr Griswold left them there.'

'Did he now?' Erik said, picking the top book up and flicking through its pages. It was a small, leather-bound journal, full of Daniel's careful handwriting. After reading a few lines, Erik knew that the book would prove itself to be very valuable and he pocketed it without a second thought.

'You're not Mr Griswold's friend, are you?' Peter said, already knowing the answer.

'No, I don't think anyone is.' Erik said. 'Well, I best be going. You're welcome to come.'

'I suppose I'd better now.' Peter replied, showing Erik a cocky smile. 'I doubt my chances of employment are particularly high now that I've stood by and watched someone steal one of Mr Griswold's personal effects.'

'No, I suppose you're right.' Erik returned the smile. 'It's probably for the best.'

The two men left the house, leaving the door open. They didn't want the sound of it closing to alert Daniel to their departure. They needn't have worried, he watched them leave from the bedroom where Erik had recovered. It would, however, have pleased Erik to know that it took a while for him to notice that his journal was missing.

CHAPTER THIRTY

Present day.

Eyes followed her as she walked away, she could feel them piercing her back like laser beams. An open gate caught Shannon's attention. It looked like it lead to the back of the pub and she decided to seize her chance. Taking a quick step to her right, Shannon disappeared from the road and the prying eyes of the ominous figure and into the area behind The Hound & The Philosopher Inn. Dark and barren, aside from a few crates and beer barrels, it seemed completely at odds with the pub it lurked behind. From her position, she had the option of two doors. The first looked like a rear entrance to the pub, so she dismissed it. The second appeared to lead to a different part of the building. And, as luck would have it, it had also been propped open with a brick. Shannon's rational mind knew that it could be a trap, that whichever nefarious characters had taken her friend, may also use this opportunity to trap her as well, but the chance was too good to miss. Shannon had to know more. Making sure that the door was on the latch and ignoring the nagging thought that whoever left the brick could have also done this to prevent the door from locking, Shannon picked up the brick and went inside. She hoped that she wouldn't need it, but the brick could be a useful weapon.

Inside, it looked like the decorator had gone to town, doing everything they could to make the interior look foreboding. Shannon was greeted with a candlelight corridor that sloped down underground. With the brick gripped tightly in her fingers, she followed the dirt floor. A more intense claustrophobic vibe descended upon her as she took the slope down. She was definitely below ground level now. And she was in a tunnel. Again, the whole area was lit by candles and Shannon wondered if this was a design choice or if whoever owned the place found installing electricity to be too much of an effort. But, the candlelight did secure one thought in her mind, there was no way this area was used as storage for the pub. No way at all. Health and Safety would have had a field day with it.

A muffled voice stopped her in her tracks. She froze, as if even the slightest movement would draw the owner of the voice to her. If she was brave, the tunnel offered plenty of hiding places in the form of tiny rooms that jutted off from it at irregular intervals. Shannon just had to find one that wasn't currently occupied and lay low until the danger passed. Plans like this one always seemed so simple, but Shannon's body already wanted to betray her, wanting to run away screaming and forget about this little mission. Wasn't it a waste of time anyway? What could she do even if she found something.

No, she wouldn't let herself think like that. She had to do something productive. It's what Christine would have done for her, if the roles were reversed. Shannon made herself ignore the fact that she was thinking about her friend in the past tense and stealthily stepped into the nearest room. “Room” was a generous description for it. Everything about it screamed “cell”, even down to the bars on the tiny window in the door. It further confirmed what she already knew: things were not good. Not good at all.

'I’m going to do the right thing.’ the muffled voice, which was now rather less muffled, reminded her what she needed to focus on. Whoever it belonged to was close by. Possibly even in the adjacent cell. How many people had the man with the yellow eyes kidnapped?

'Christine, you have to believe me.’ Shannon could barely believe her own ears. It sounded like her neighbour was talking to her best friend. This was definitely a promising sign. Excitement and hope started to form inside her. This was it, she was going to find Christine. She was going to find her friend.

'Hello?’ Shannon spoke softly, her voice little more than a whisper. Despite this rush of hope, she still didn't trust this place.

'Hello?’ the voice echoed. Nobody else joined in, Christine didn't seem to be talkative. ‘I knew Erik was wrong. I knew it. I could sense you.’

‘Sense...?’ It was an odd word choice. Shannon felt her guard starting to build up again, while the little monument to hope that had started to form in her heart was dismantled piece by piece.

***

To say Kit was surprised when Christine answered him was an understatement. He had definitely got the feeling that she was still around - her spirit wanting to complete some unfinished business, namely revenge on him - but to actually hear her speak was a shock. Ghosts were real. Werewolves were real. It was an odd time to be alive.

'You... you do know what you are, right?' Kit approached the subject in a gentle and, what he hoped was tactful, way. She seemed confused. He hoped that he didn't have to explain what had happened to her. But, that would have been comforting in its own way. Maybe all the spirits of those who had died violent, pointless deaths had no idea what happened to them. Maybe they just thought they went peacefully. Or, judging by the tone of Christine's voice, maybe they had no idea that they had died at all. Perhaps there was a spirit world running alongside the living world. The idea both pleased him and creeped him out. How many ghosts were in this room with him?

'What I am?' The question confirmed Kit's suspicions. The poor girl had no idea what had befallen her.

'I hate to tell you this...' he started the sentence, hoping that he would be able to see it through to its conclusion without chickening out. 'I'm so sorry, Christine. There's no easy way for me to put this. There's nothing that I can say that's going to make this sound any better. You're dead. You're a ghost.'

***

Learning of Christine's death was a bitter pill to swallow. Shannon had known that this was a possibility. She'd known as soon as she hadn't been able to reach her friend on the phone that something was wrong, but to find out like this was especially unnerving. Shannon had walked into a world where people had yellow eyes and talked to ghosts. What if it was the yellow eyed man in the other cell? Whatever happened next, Shannon would have to be careful. She couldn't afford any mistakes.

'I was murdered.' Shannon had very little idea when it came to the details of what happened, but it was a fairly safe bet to assume that Christine had met a grisly end.

***

'Yes.' Kit said, his voice barely a whisper as guilt threatened to choke him. He badly wanted the chance to talk to his victim, to explain to her that he had no control over his actions and maybe find a way to repent, but now that the opportunity was represented to him, it was a lot harder than he'd imagined. Talking to himself about his sins had been painful, but easy. This was different. Now he was trying to confess murder to the victim. It was insane.

Maybe none of this was real and he was insane.

'I couldn't control myself.' Even if it was all in his head, Kit decided that he was going to see it through. It might be cathartic. 'I'm not used to all this yet.'

'That's no excuse.' Christine's voice said, and she was right. It was no excuse. Kit was just hiding behind a smokescreen. Of course, it wouldn't have been easy to stop, but if he had tried harder, he could have done it. He wasn't completely at the mercy of the beast that he became. He knew that now. After all, both Peter and Erik went through life without killing everyone in sight. They even planned their kills - that was the whole reason why they had this pub. It was the whole reason why they had cells like the one he was currently stood in. Kit's vision swam, and his knees went weak. Werewolves may not have been able to get ill in the strictest sense of the word, but Kit had made himself sick. He was sick with guilt. It was eating him alive.

'I know that now.' Kit sank to his knees, not trusting himself to stand any longer. 'I should've tried harder. But... you were my first...'

'And that's supposed to make things better?'

'No... no, not at all...' He held his head in his hands and massaged his temples. 'They told me that I needed to do it. I was going to die if I didn't.'

'Why didn't you do that?'

'What?'

'Die. Why was it okay for me to die, but not you?' Christine's voice was no longer confused and quiet. It was getting louder and angrier. Kit wondered what vengeful spirits were capable of doing. Would she start throwing objects around the room? Would she possess him?

'You're right, it wasn't okay...' Kit said. 'But they made me do it. I really had no choice... but I'm so sorry. I'm so, so sorry, Christine.'

'Who are they?'

'Peter and Erik.' Kit said. 'The other werewolves. The ones who turned me.'

***

'Werewolves?' Shannon was sure that she couldn't have heard that correctly. The shock of the word made her take a step back from her current spot, and her foot collided with a bucket that someone had used as a bedpan in the not too distant past.

'What was that?' she heard the voice on the other side of the wall say. Then she heard footsteps.

He was coming.

There was nowhere to hide.

***

Kit leapt up from where he had been kneeling on the floor. While he was expecting the ghost to do something - maybe to try and knock him out with a table - he hadn't expected to hear the sounds of a metal bucket being knocked over. It was far too mundane. In two strides, he had left the cell and was in the tunnel.

A figure stood in front of him.

'You.' Kit snarled.

***

The barman stood in the tunnel, blocking the only path between Kit and the woman. He'd watched the woman leave the pub. He'd even watched the other figure watch the woman as she walked away. As soon as she'd shown up on his CCTV for the tunnels, he knew that he had to step in. It wasn't that he'd suddenly gained a conscience, or that he actually wanted to help anyone. He just knew that the werewolves had had their day. It was time to bring them down and this woman might be able to help him do it.

'Yes, just me.' He said. 'Sorry, I didn't mean to disturb you.'

Kit studied the barman's voice as he spoke. There was no way that he was the one that he had been conversing with. That meant that maybe the ghost was real after all. 'Were you listening in?'

'I didn't mean to, I was just cleaning up.'

'What did you hear?'

'Not much.' The barman said, lying. 'But, I heard her too.'

The barman thought that it couldn't hurt to nudge Kit's insanity in the right direction.

'You did?'

‘Yep, I’ve never heard anything like it before.’ The barman was careful not to cast an eye into the cell. He had to make sure that Kit’s attention was not drawn there. ‘But, I suppose I should have seen it coming. If werewolves exist, then why not ghosts?’

‘That’s what I thought!’ Kit said, temporarily forgetting that he hated the barman. Maybe they had more in common than he realised.

‘What are you going to do?’ the barman said. ‘I mean, as lovely as she is, she can’t stay forever.’

‘But... I don’t know how to make her leave... I wouldn’t even know where to start. Or what to do.’

‘I’d imagine it’s quite simple,’ the barman said, amazed at how easy this was turning out to be. ‘Next time you communicate with her, find out what it is that she wants. Then, make sure that it is done. She’s only here for unfinished business, right?’

‘Right.’ Kit said, trying to imagine a form of unfinished business that didn’t end with him dying painfully. Nothing sprang to mind. The barman was smirking at him. Gone was his fear from earlier. Something had changed. Perhaps he thought he had the upper hand because he’d heard Kit either talking to a ghost or himself. The reason for his sudden increase in confidence didn’t matter. What mattered was that Kit knew that he could crush the little man like a bug. All he had to do was change and go at him with tooth and claw. It would be so easy.

And, yet...

He didn’t do anything about it. For starters, he’d been told that they needed to keep this guy around. Although, Kit couldn’t think of a single reason why, and Peter also wanted the man gone. But, the main reason why he didn’t change into his wolf form and utterly obliterate this man was because he wasn’t sure if he could. Not yet, anyway. He needed to learn how to control his new-found power, and that meant that he had to stare at that irritating face for a little while longer. Kit made a noise that was close to a grunt, sounding more animal than human and barged past the barman, still feeling the need to demonstrate his dominance, even if he wasn't going to be decimating him just yet.

'Bye!' the barman called, his voice taunting and echoing along the tunnel. His sing-song tone mocked Kit all the way up into the pub. Even long after Kit had left the tunnel, he still heard that voice.

The barman had to go.

CHAPTER THIRTY-ONE

'Come out, come out, wherever you are!' the barman called into the cell where he knew the woman was hiding. Nothing stirred from within. The barman took a step closer to the door. 'Come on, love. I'm on your side. I stopped the scary man from finding you!'

That may have been true, but there was nothing to suggest to Shannon that the owner of this chipper voice wasn't another scary man himself.

'I know you're there. If it helps we've already met.' The barman stopped in the doorway, blocking the only exit. 'I'm the barman here... My name is Caspar Lawson. What's your name?'

The barman's question was met with an overwhelming silence.

'It's clear that you know that... *something* is going on here.' the barman continued. 'And, judging by the things you said to our friend Kit there, I'm guessing that you're not a fan.'

Another minute was wasted waiting for a response. Silence remained.

‘I’m not a fan of what they’re doing either. I think we could help each other.’ The barman stared into the darkness, wishing that he had the same super-powered eyesight as Peter and Erik. And Kit, for that matter. He had to remember that Kit was just as powerful as the other two. It wouldn’t do to underestimate him, even if he was still learning the ropes. This suggestion seemed to interest the woman, as a slight shuffle of her foot betrayed her position. The barman’s eyes calmly moved in her direction, but he didn’t move. ‘Come on out, I won’t hurt you.’

There was another shuffle, but there was also hesitation. More coaxing was required.

‘It’s okay,’ He said. ‘Just think... If I wanted to hurt you, I could do it at any time. I just want us to work together. To take down a common foe. What do you say?’

‘I...’ the woman’s voice carried through the darkness with surprising clarity, she was closer to him than he had thought. Before he could find out what the rest of her statement would have been, a blinding pain wrecked through his head.

***

Shannon’s brick now had a slight coating of blood and a small amount of hair attached to it. She should have run then. There was no doubt about that. She should have run away and never looked back. Over time, she would eventually have found a way to deal with Christine’s murder. What could one woman do on her own anyway?

But, then, she wasn’t alone anymore.

Now she had an ally. He wasn't someone she felt she could trust. And, after being in that pub with him - even if he was just serving the drinks - she had found him quite creepy. But, what was the saying? Two heads were better than one.

So, instead of leaving her eerie dungeon like accommodation, she stayed... and waited for the man she'd just knocked out to wake up again, hoping that he'd still be keen on collaborating. She didn't have to wait long for him to regain his wits, but she had now been in this macabre chamber far longer than she had wanted to.

'What... What the fuck?' The barman - Caspar said - reaching for the wound on the side of his head. It had stopped bleeding but was still sticky to the touch. 'What was that for?'

'I wanted to get you before you got me.' There was logic there, Shannon hoped.

'But, I said I wouldn't hurt you!' The barman said, wincing. Raising his voice even a little hurt his head; he'd have to be quiet from now on. Besides, a bit of stealth wouldn't hurt them. It certainly wouldn't do for Kit to overhear this conversation, like Caspar had overheard his. 'Why are you still here, anyway? If I'm so bad, why didn't you leave?'

Shannon sat down beside him and, at some point while he had been incapacitated, she had pilfered a candle from the tunnel. The candlelight danced around the room like a mischievous sprite eager to cause trouble. The comparison made Caspar smile; it was something he could relate to. He would cause more than a bit of trouble for his employers before this was over.

'I had a change of heart.' she said after a slight pause. 'If you really do want to work together - and this isn't some kind of trick... or trap - then I think we should.'

'That's good to hear.'

'But,' her voice was sharp. This was one of those school teacher, don't-mess-with-me voices. Caspar rather liked it. 'if I so much as think that you're going to betray me, I won't think twice about bricking you over the head again... and next time I'll make sure you won't wake up.'

Shannon hoped her threat was believable. In truth, she had no idea if she could actually stomach killing someone like that. She supposed that it would depend on his level of betrayal. If it came down to him or her, he was definitely going to go.

'Understood.' Caspar replied. 'So, you know who I am... Who are you?'

Shannon wasn't sure if she should make up a fake name, but she also wasn't sure if it would make any difference. It wasn't like she was a superhero and was trying to protect her secret identity. 'I'm Shannon.'

Caspar held out a hand, then noticed there was blood on it, so swapped it for another. Shannon took it, handling it like it was a dangerous animal or something coated in toxic waste. The handshake was short and definitely not sweet. It all seemed so unnecessary. 'Good to meet you. What brings you here?'

'Someone here - the guy I was talking to...'

'Kit. His name is Kit.' Caspar said.

'Kit murdered my friend.' Now that she knew that was the case, the truth hurt. Saying it out loud to another person was more painful than she had imagined.

'You're a friend of Christine's.' Caspar said, nodding slowly so as not to aggravate his sore head. He choose his next words deliberately and meticulously, careful not to implicate himself in what happened to the young woman. 'That poor girl. The three of them deserve to hang for what they did to her.'

'Kit did mention that someone else was involved.'

'Yes,' Caspar said. 'Two someones actually. And I believe you saw one of them in the pub.'

'The gentleman with the yellow eyes.'

'Absolutely,' said Caspar. 'But there's no way in hell that he's a gentleman.'

Shannon stared at the candle's flame, almost hypnotising herself with it. It was oddly calming, given her current predicament. 'So, what's your story?'

'Revenge.' Caspar said. 'Plain and simple revenge.'

Caspar's tone suggested that he didn't want to go into any further detail, leaving it to Shannon's imagination. Thinking that he had lost someone at the hands of these maniacs warmed her to him. He suddenly seemed less like a creep and more like a comrade. They had something in common, even if it was a murdered friend.

Relief swept over Caspar as he realised that Shannon wasn't going to probe him for more information. He doubted she'd hold much empathy for him if she knew the real reason for his desire to get even. 'Kit told you what he was, didn't he?'

'What do you m-' Shannon said, while playing the conversation back in her head. 'Oh, you mean that. Is he deluded or something? Are they all on drugs?'

'I know it's hard to believe,' Caspar said, looking her directly in the eyes. 'but it's true. Werewolves exist... and we're currently sat underneath a pub owned by three of the bastards.'

'You're kidding me.'

'I shit you not.'

'But... it's not possible.' She said.

Caspar got to his feet, aware that he had probably been in the tunnel long enough. He didn't want one of his employers to come looking for him. 'Stick around if you want, I'm sure you'll see something to confirm it.'

Shannon thought about it but decided that she'd rather not. Following Caspar's lead, she stood too. 'I'll leave it for now. What do we do next?'

'I'll call you.' he said. 'What's your number?'

CHAPTER THIRTY-TWO

The first thing Willow noticed as she entered the pub was the general hubbub of conversation. The Hound & The Philosopher Inn was much like any other pub in any other town. To the untrained eye, there was nothing to suggest that this one was owned by werewolves. Even to someone who knew what they were looking for, there were very few tell-tale signs. The only thing that Willow could pick up on was the slight smell of death. It didn't matter how many times you washed clothes, carpets or upholstery, something always stayed behind. Lingering, refusing to leave. For someone such as herself, it wasn't an unpleasant smell, but it was a clear giveaway that, at the very least, murders took place here. Despite his clear excitement at being in a new place, Jake behaved himself and stayed by Willow's side.

The second thing that Willow noticed about the pub was that there were no bar staff. Willow knew this was unusual as whenever she'd risked a look inside the pub on previous occasions, the same barman had always been on duty. Whoever he was, she knew he was in on it. He had to be. No-one could be this close to werewolves for this long and not have a clue. As she was considering how much the barman knew, he emerged from a door labelled "*Staff Only*". Smiling to himself, he made his way back to the bar.

'Can I help?' he said, looking down at Jake on the other side of the bar.

'Oh, sorry... Am I allowed to bring him in here? He's very well behaved.' Willow said, hoping that the barman wouldn't make a big deal out of it. Not only was Jake a terrific companion, but he also helped to mask Willow's scent from other werewolves.

'Oh, don't worry about it at all.' The barman said. 'Would you like me to bring a bowl of water for him over to your table? Where are you sitting?'

'Yes, that would be great.' At first, Willow was surprised at how helpful he was, but then she realised that it was his job to be useful like this. It wasn't a good way to judge his character. 'I don't know where we're sitting yet.'

'No problem. Now we've got your doggy friend sorted, what would you like to drink?'

'A pint of this, please.' She said, pointing at one of the local ales that the pub had on tap.

'Great choice.' he said as he poured the drink. Willow exchanged her money for the pint and made her way to a nearby table, unknowingly picking the same one that Shannon had used a short while earlier. The barman followed her over with a bowl of water for Jake. Even though it was only water, Jake could barely contain his excitement. His tail was wagging so much that his whole body was wagging with it.

'Thanks.' Willow said as the barman set the water down on the floor. Jake had his tongue in it immediately, lapping it up like he had never seen water before. Willow took a sip of her ale and waited for the barman to leave. But he didn't leave.

The barman cleared his throat, making it obvious that he wanted to speak to her. 'Can I help?' Willow said, echoing the barman's first words to her.

'Erm... yes. Yes, I do believe you can.' He said. 'I saw you watching the pub from across the road. I know what you are.'

Willow subconsciously ran through her appearance; this guy didn't look like a werewolf, but Jake should have stopped him from sniffing her out anyway, she wasn't covered in the blood and guts of her latest victim and she was fairly sure that she had remembered to put her brown contact lenses in before she left the house.

'And what's that?' she said.

The barman leaned in close and whispered in her ear. 'You're a werewolf.'

'What? Have you lost your mind?' Willow tried her best to sound shocked and indignant.

'You can drop the act. I've been around your lot long enough to spot you. The contact lenses are a great touch though. You almost had me fooled.'

'How did you work it out?' she asked.

'May I?' the barman asked, gesturing towards the chair opposite.

'Go ahead.'

'I almost didn't and, to be honest, I wasn't completely sure until you confirmed it just now.' The barman looked around, making sure that they weren't being watched. 'I've just noticed that a few people have had eyes on this place lately. I figured that there was a chance that at least one of those people was a werewolf. I know one definitely wasn't.'

'The woman from earlier.'

'Yes,' the barman said. 'You were watching her too, weren't you?'

'Not intentionally. I was watching this place and she happened to be lurking around as well. Who is she?'

'I'll get to that in a minute. First, I need to know who you are.' the barman said and then lowered his voice to little more than a whisper. 'Are you on my side or not?'

'Fair enough.' she said, trying to work out the barman's angle. 'I suppose that depends on what you're after.'

'Do you know my employers?' The change of subject didn't feel like he was evading the question. It felt like he was building up to an answer.

'I know of them. I know their reputation.' It was almost the truth. Depending on what the barman told her next, she thought she might fill him in on all the details later. Taking another sip of her drink, Willow gestured to the barman to keep talking.

'So, you're not working with them? Or here to meet them?'

'No, definitely not.'

'So... Is it safe to assume that you're the opposite of a friend to them?'

'That's a safe assumption.' Willow wondered if the barman would ever get to the point.

'Wonderful.' the barman said. 'Welcome to the team. My name is Caspar. Caspar Lawson. Although, most people can't be bothered to learn my name - they usually just refer to me as "the barman" .... because, hey, I'm a nobody.'

'Well, it's good to meet you, Caspar.' Willow said, glad that events were taking this turn. If Caspar was telling the truth, he might come in useful. 'I'm Willow. And I take it that our mystery woman is also on our team?'

‘She is indeed.’ the barman said. ‘A lovely young lady by the name of Shannon. Seems she has a score to settle. One of the guys here ate her friend.’

‘She’s a friend of that family Peter murdered?’ Willow said, leaning close. Any concern she had about this man were gone. It wasn’t because she trusted him - she definitely did not - but he was an amazing source of information. Not only that, but if it turned out that he was trying to trick her, it wouldn’t take her long to dispose of him.

‘Family? What? No.’ Caspar said, genuinely surprised. ‘You know about that? Wow... I don’t know if that means that crazy bastard’s plan is working or not.’

‘What’s his plan?’

‘He wants power. By making werewolves mainstream, he reckons it’ll take power away from the Council. I’m not sure how that means he’ll get power. To be honest, I only know the parts of the plan that I’ve overheard.’

‘Interesting. It’s a bit risky though, isn’t it?’

‘I guess.’ Caspar said.

‘What if the Council found out about it before the press could? Wouldn’t they just execute Peter?’

‘Ah, yes. Peter had a backup plan.’ Caspar said. It was weird, but he was enjoying this. Willow seemed to be hanging on his every word, she was interested in what he had to say. For the first time in a while, he felt valued. Swapping allegiances was definitely one of his better ideas. ‘That’s why they turned the new guy. He’s gonna take the blame. Of course, he doesn’t know that.’

‘I see.’ She said. ‘It’s an interesting plan. I don’t see the point though. Not really. If Peter dislikes the Council so much, why doesn’t he just go off grid?’

‘Peter doesn’t always make sense as a general rule.’ Caspar said. ‘Like I said, he’s a crazy bastard.’

Willow took a couple of mouthfuls of her drink while she mulled that piece of information over. 'Has he always been like that?'

'I guess. I mean, obviously I haven't known him that long in werewolf years, but he's always been a bit unhinged.'

'Does he ever seem like he's in pain?'

'No... but...' Caspar said as he tried to recall a memory. 'I didn't think much of it at the time, but I caught him rubbing his temples once. You know, like he had a headache or something. But, werewolves don't get sick, do they?'

A wry smile appeared on Willow's face. 'We don't get sick like humans get sick, but there is one illness that every werewolf fears. It's called The Rot, and it pretty much does everything that the name suggests. It breaks you down, from the inside out. Hurts like hell. It kills you, eventually. The silver lining is that the pain goes when you die.'

'You have it?' Caspar said sensing that he already knew the answer to the question.

'Yes.' she said. 'I've had it for a while now.'

'I'm so sorry, Willow.' Caspar said. To his credit, he looked sympathetic. And, although Willow couldn't have known it, he was. He'd finally found someone - and a werewolf to boot - who spoke to him like he was an equal and she was rotting away. 'Do you know how long you have?'

'No, I don't. But, it's a lot less than the eternity I thought I'd have.' She said, ending the sentence with a little laugh. 'And, do you know what? Aside from the moments of pain - and I mean intense pain - it's not that bad. I used to think that I wanted to live forever, but over the years I've learned that isn't natural. Things should end. They need to.'

'You're not afraid?' he said.

'No.' The lie came easily. The truth was that she was petrified, but she was also ready for it. She knew that she was only afraid because life was all she knew. People - and werewolves were still people - always feared the unknown. Death would be a whole new adventure. One where she didn't even know if she'd be sentient. The worst part of facing your impending doom was that you didn't know what was on the other side. Sure, some had their religions that told them what to expect, but no-one really knew for sure. Everyone lived in some kind of cosmic joke where no-one had the full story.

'You're a braver person than me.' Caspar said. It wasn't meant as a form of flattery or as an attempt to flatter the woman. It was simply the truth. By nature, Caspar feared a lot of things, but death ranked highly on his list. Pretty much every decision he made was to prolong his miserable life. 'What makes you think Peter has this?'

'It's as you said, werewolves don't get sick. Peter's headaches - and I'm using the plural because I'd bet everything I own that his headache was more than a one-off... they can only be the result of one thing. The Rot is in his brain. He's probably had it for years. I'd wager that this is why he acts so impulsively.'

'That makes a lot of sense. Do you think he knows?'

'Oh, I'm sure of it.' She said, and then remembered the other woman. 'Sorry to change the subject, but who is Shannon avenging?'

'Her friend. I think her name was Christine.' Caspar said. He was about to withhold his part in what had happened, but then he remembered who he was talking to. Willow was a werewolf, she was bound to have done some questionable things. 'My job is to find people for my employers. Some of them are... well, sustenance and others are turned. Kit was the first one they've turned for years. The first one that Peter's ever turned. I get the feeling that he had to beg Erik for the knowledge on how to do it.'

'Christine was dinner, then?'

'Yes, for Kit. To complete his *Om grutt.*'

'How did Shannon find out about it?'

'I have no idea.' Caspar said. 'She has some impressive detective skills. I think she'll come in rather handy.'

***

Finally, Caspar felt like he belonged. In his little makeshift team, he wasn't just 'the barman', or even Mr Lawson, he was valued. And, if he was being honest with himself, that's all he ever wanted. Isn't being able to belong to something all anyone ever wanted?

After Willow had left, he promised himself that he would make any input of his into their joint venture count. The question of how he would do that remained unanswered.

'Isn't it about time that you closed up, Mr Lawson?' Erik appeared as if from nowhere. If Peter was a crazy bastard, then Erik was a sneaky one.

'Yes, of course.' Caspar said and rang his bell. 'Last orders, folks! Almost time to go home!'

Unlike any other bar, the patrons of The Hound & The Philosopher didn't complain. Nor did anyone buy any more drinks even though they could have. Instead, they all grabbed their coats, called out a polite goodbye and left the premises. Some of them even brought their empty glasses up to the bar to save Caspar from cleaning up so much. Those drugs the werewolves pumped through the air-con certainly had their advantages.

'It was a good evening, I take it.' Erik said as he watched the barman counting the money from the till.

'Yeah, I suppose... it was pretty average really.'

‘Any interesting characters tonight?’ Erik said. Caspar tried his best not to react and kept his eyes on the cash in his hands. What did Erik know? He couldn’t face the possibility that this new chapter of his life was over before it had begun.

‘There are always interesting characters in this pub.’ It seemed as good an answer as any. If he’d answered negatively and Erik had any idea of what was going on, then he was screwed. If he was too enthusiastic, then Erik would want more details. It was as close to a happy medium as Caspar could manage.

‘I noticed.’ Erik must have noticed that Caspar was trying not to look uncomfortable and was failing miserably. ‘You know, you are allowed to have a life outside this bar. In fact, it’s important that you do. So long as you don’t let anyone in on what’s going on here.’

‘I don’t know what you mean.’ He really didn’t. This conversation was taking an unexpected turn.

‘I saw you talking to a woman a little while ago. You should pursue a romantic endeavour... only if you wanted to, of course. Life should be varied.’ Erik wasn’t sure if he was just talking to the barman, it was advice that he should follow himself. The barman had now finished counting the money and was making sure the door was locked properly. ‘I think we forget that there’s a world outside those doors. We’re so caught up on what goes on in here.’

‘I know there’s a world out there. I live out there.’

‘You know what I mean, Mr Lawson.’ Erik thought he was being respectful referring to Caspar as Mr Lawson, but Caspar felt like he was being pushed away. It was another reminder that he was not one of them. He could work as hard as possible, pour his blood, sweat and tears into every task set out for him, but he would never belong. ‘We wouldn’t stop you... you must have needs. Everyone has needs.’

Caspar nodded. 'Thanks, I'll give her a call. Go on a date... not that I know what to do on a date.'

'I'm afraid I can't help you there. My knowledge of the dating world is probably as rusty as yours.' Erik was being honest. In his long existence, he had only been in two non-platonic relationships and both had ended badly. One had been with a human woman and, even though paranormal romance novels would have you believe otherwise, it was a disaster from start to finish. Especially at the finish. Literally devouring your partner was a sure way to kill the mood. As level headed as he was, he believed that his lack of luck in that department was due to destroying true love on the day that he'd blown Jack's brain across his piano. Jack and Ida had been the real deal. Now, not only was he cursed to walk the earth as a werewolf, but he was also cursed to do it alone. A prime example of a lone wolf. 'Well, everything seems to be in order here. Make sure you do give that young lady a call. I think it would be good for you.'

'I will.' Caspar said, agreeing with Erik. Speaking to Willow would be good for him, just not in the way that Erik had in mind. 'Goodnight, Erik.'

'Goodnight, Mr Lawson.' Erik headed back towards the door to his flat.

'Caspar.' Caspar whispered.

'Pardon?' Erik turned back towards the barman.

'Caspar. My name is Caspar.' He said, feeling slightly foolish.

'My apologies.' Erik said, nodding in understanding. 'Goodnight, Caspar.'

'Goodnight.'

Erik had tried, Caspar had to give him that, but it just wasn't the same. It wasn't enough. He knew that as long as he stayed there - in that pub, working for those people - that nothing would ever change. The realisation came to him that no matter what name they called him, it wouldn't change what they thought of him. He would always be their lackey, doing a job that anyone could do with the right persuasion. The sad truth was that he would always be seen as disposable. And that was a threat that they would always hold over him like the sword of Damocles. Death was only ever a heartbeat away in this job. It was an exhausting way to live, one that Caspar had lived for far too long. It was time for a change. As Erik closed the door, Caspar found himself reminiscing about the first time he set foot in The Hound & The Philosopher Inn.

***

A few years ago. Perhaps longer.

All his life, Caspar had been a nerd; an outcast that never seemed to fit in anywhere. So, he spent a lot of time alone. Having so much time on his own meant that he had to find things to occupy himself with. One of those things was reading, particularly books about the occult. Caspar read those books like there was no tomorrow. He consumed everything he could, the weirder and more dangerous the better. One cold November day in a year that he couldn't really remember, he found a book that would spark a new obsession. Caspar had been perusing the old books in a second-hand book store in London when one book with a green cover caught his eye. At first, Caspar wasn't sure what had drawn him to it. The unassuming tome's cover gave no clue as what he would find inside, so there was no suggestion that his appetite for the occult would be sated. Adding it to his pile, he bought it without even opening it. Upon reading it in the privacy of his own home, he became convinced that a creature that had been confined to myth, legend and horror movies was real. Caspar was convinced on the existence of werewolves. Although he didn't know it then, it was all downhill from there.

One thing that should be made clear is that, although he'd read a lot of books about the occult, he didn't necessarily believe any of it. Until that point, he didn't believe a word. To Caspar, those books were just an extension of the horror novels he loved. But, this odd little green book was different. While most of the books in Caspar's collection read like encyclopaedias on how to summon demons or step-by-step guides on how to become / kill a vampire, this one did everything it could to dispel the myth of werewolves. *It doth protest too much*, thought Caspar as he read page after page. He vowed then and there to find out more.

So, he followed rumours, studying newspaper reports of violent, unsolved murders - the grislier the better - and, even though the internet was still in its infancy, he used it to read so-called survivor's stories. Throwing everything together created an interesting picture of the myth-come-reality in Caspar's head. The more he researched, the more the creature was fleshed out. It felt real. He was sure of it.

On one of his many trips to the second-hand bookshop, he met a man who would change his life. As he scoured the shelves for another book that made his heart race as much as the green book did, he heard the little bell on the front door ring, announcing the arrival of another customer. Usually, he would just ignore the interruption and continue his search, but this time he was drawn towards the man who was currently approaching the shop's counter. The smartly dressed man was talking to the shop's owner, but Caspar couldn't make out the words. But, it didn't matter. There was something compelling about that man. And, any man who wore sunglasses indoors had to have a story to tell. Rather than strike up a conversation with him, Caspar decided to follow him, lurking several paces behind him at all times after he left the shop. After all, what would he say to the man otherwise? Social skills were not his strong point. Those would come later.

Caspar followed the man all day, as he went about his errands and spoke to friends and he never seemed to notice his newly acquired shadow. It was all going rather well. Caspar even considered a career change into the world of espionage, so pleased was he with his success. Following the man into a pub, Caspar took a seat at an empty table and planned to people watch for a little while. He pulled a book from his bag, so that he didn't look like a weirdo who was sat in a pub on his own. Now he was a weirdo who sat in the pub on his own with a book. The book that emerged from his bag was the now well-thumbed green book, known to Caspar (rather imaginatively) as The Green Book. He couldn't remember packing it, but he did refer to various pages in it rather a lot, so it didn't surprise him that he would have it to hand. Opening it at a random passage on a random page, Caspar began to read. He was soon completely engrossed in the book he'd read countless times, so much so that he didn't notice the man standing in front of his table.

'I wouldn't believe everything you read.' A voice said, making Caspar jump. 'Sorry, I didn't mean to startle you.'

Caspar sat opened mouthed, it was the man from the bookshop. The man he had been following for the entire day. Unsurprisingly, he looked exactly the same as he had for the last few hours - the same suit, the same slicked back hair - the only difference was that the man had removed his dark sunglasses.

Yellow eyes studied him.

'Er...' Caspar wasn't very talkative at the best of times, usually preferring to listen, but now he had been robbed of speech completely.

'I believe you wanted to talk to me.'

'What... I.... No...' Caspar's words failed him, refusing to join together to make any kind of sense. He started to sweat. Panic started to set in.

'I know you've been following me.' The man said, taking a seat opposite him. 'Go ahead, ask me anything.'

'Are... Are those contact lenses?'

'No.' The man said, staring intensely at Caspar. 'No, this is my natural eye colour... and I believe you know why.'

'I do...?'

'Yes, you do.' The man said. 'The internet is fun, isn't it? It's a wonderful invention; one of my favourites from this century. You can read about anything on the internet. I know what you like to read about.'

'What's that?' Caspar's mouth felt dry and he wished that he'd actually bothered to buy a drink.

'Werewolves.' The man said, flashing a devilish grin. 'Werewolves just like me.'

Under normal circumstances, Caspar would have dismissed the man's claims as those of a madman - like so many of the ones he'd read online. But circumstances felt far from normal. He was currently sat in a pub that he didn't know, talking to man he didn't know, after having followed him for most of the day. Add the fact that the man appeared to have yellow eyes and it all built a compelling case.

'Why should I believe you?'

'Because you wouldn't have been following me if you didn't think I was.'

'That would make sense if I knew why I had been following you, but I don't.' Caspar was surprised that he had managed to get so many words out in one go. He was starting to relax now, although he couldn't pinpoint any reason why that was.

'You were looking for werewolves. First, you read a book with a green cover. Isn't that right?'

'Yes, the Green Book... How did you know that?' Caspar said, forgetting that the book in question was currently sat in his shaking hands.

'I've been trying to track that bloody book down for years. A member of the Council... I mean, someone - a werewolf - wrote it as a way to throw normal people off our trail. I happen to think that it does the exact opposite.'

'I agree, I never thought that werewolves existed until that book went to great lengths to convince me otherwise.' This was beginning to feel like the most natural and comfortable conversation that Caspar had had in years.

'Exactly. So, I've been trying to track it down. I finally got word that it was in a local bookshop, so I went to make a purchase... only to find that someone had already bought it.'

'Me.'

'Yes, you. Although, I didn't know who you were then. I suppose that I don't really know who you are now, but we'll get to that. That's a point, we haven't even done introductions yet, have we? This conversation is completely arse about face. You should have stopped me.' The man said and laughed as if knowing that there was no way that a timid little man like the bookish stalker sat in front of him would dare to interrupt him. 'My name is Peter Smedley... and I take it that your real name is not really *VanHelsing666*, is that right?'

Hearing his own internet handle said out loud felt strange to Caspar. Strange and embarrassing. *VanHelsing666…* What had he been thinking? The internet felt like another world, existing within its own parameters, and yet, here was this complete stranger referring to him by a horribly cheesy username that he'd come up with late one night when he was signing up to online forums. 'How do you know that name?'

'We've spoken before.' Peter said. 'And, when someone introduces themselves to you, it's polite to introduce yourself in return. Maybe even offer a handshake and a 'nice to meet you'. But, I can't tell you what to do.'

'Oh, I'm sorry.' Caspar replied. Half of him still feeling unusually relaxed, while the other half started to feel ill at ease. 'I'm Caspar... Caspar Lawson... and it's nice to meet you, Peter.'

The two men shook hands and Peter continued talking. This was a man who enjoyed the sound of his own voice. He clearly liked to be centre stage. 'Caspar, what a wonderful name! So, as I was saying, we've spoken before. You've recently joined a website called *hellhound-uk.com*. I own that website, Mr Lawson. I'm hoping to find... er... sympathetic people to work with me on a project.'

Caspar knew the website well. There had been something about it that made it different from all the others. Something that made it seem legitimate. Now Caspar knew why that was.

'Are you willing to help, Mr Lawson?' Neither of them noticed at the time, but Peter was no longer addressing Caspar by his first name. He would only refer to him by that name a few times during their relationship.

While Caspar wasn't thinking about what Peter was calling him, he was thinking about the idea of a werewolf owning a website. And, regardless of whatever danger he was in, he found it hilarious. Laughter erupted from it as he found he could no longer contain it. His body shook as giggles took their hold. Tears streamed down his cheeks.

'Is something funny?' Peter said, smirking. He found the man's reaction quite amusing.

Caspar tried to compose himself. It took a while, but gradually he managed to catch his breath and stifle his laughter. 'I'm sorry. It's just... there's something absurd about a werewolf owning a website. Not that there should be... I mean, werewolves can do whatever they like... but... it's just... It's just quite strange. Unexpected. That's why I found it funny. I guess it's not really funny at all, is it?'

'Don't worry, Mr Lawson. It is funny in some ways. Especially if you're not used to the notion that werewolves are real.' Peter instantly put Caspar at ease again. Caspar knew that his emotions shouldn't be so easy to manipulate - that there was definitely something amiss here - but he didn't care. 'So, Mr Lawson, would you be interested in helping us?'

Now that he was composed again, Caspar was paying better attention to what was being said to him. 'What would it involve? What do you need me to do? I don't really have any skills.'

'Oh, don't concern yourself with that. We can teach you everything you need to know. You'll be fine.' Peter leant forward, and Caspar found himself doing the same. Their noses were only inches away from touching. Peter's eyes glanced quickly from side to side, as if checking that nobody was listening in on them. The rest of the pub was carrying on as normal. Conversations about football, TV shows and failed relationships could be heard in all directions. The smell of beer and bar food covered everything like a cloud. Caspar found himself wanting a beer and burger. Content that no-one was listening in, Peter continued. 'Tell me, have you ever worked in a pub? We need a barman.'

The level of secrecy did not appear to match with the questions that he was being asked. Caspar felt like he was missing something. 'A barman?'

'Yes, a barman. Someone to run the bar here and... perform other tasks for us.'

'But, I have no experience... and I don't have the people skills for this kind of work.' But, as he looked around the pub, taking in the sight of the relaxed customers and the welcoming glow of the lights, Caspar had the feeling that everything was going to be just fine. A sense of belonging crept over him, wrapping him in an embrace and hugging him close. It was like he was born to be here.

'As I said, we'll give you all the skills you'll need.'

'And, there's something else.'

'What's on your mind, Mr Lawson?'

'I find werewolves fascinating, but I have no desire to be one. Will you have to bite me and turn me into... y'know, one of you?' Caspar asked. 'No offense.'

'None taken.' Peter said. 'It's useful to us that you're human, so we won't be changing you. But, I feel I should point out that werewolfism is not passed on through the bite. That's a fallacy. You'll find that much of what you think you know about us is incorrect, but everything will fall into place in due course. Working here could be beneficial to both of us. You'll manage the bar for us and, in return you'll get somewhere to live and have the chance to study us. Of course, you won't be able to publish any of your findings, but I don't think that will bother you, will it?'

'No, not at all.'

'That's perfect. I think we're going to get on famously, you and I.' Peter said, flashing his teeth in a grin that should have chilled Caspar to the bone. Instead, he found himself grinning along with him. It didn't take long for Peter, along with his friend Erik, to turn Caspar into the perfect barman. Caspar became an expert at pouring drinks and picking out perfect victims for his employers. He knew full well that every person he introduced to Peter and Erik was about to come to a grisly end, but he wasn't bothered. What had the human race ever done for him? Nothing. He didn't even bat an eyelid when it came time to pick out a human for them to turn. The gore of the *Om grutt* fascinated him. The procedure was incredible and surprising surgical. all those books and websites that he'd read couldn't have been more wrong.

But, as the years went on, Caspar found his sense of belonging waning. He wasn't part of the team, he was an employee. The only way that he was going to become part of the inner circle was if they changed him.

But that would never happen. They needed a human.

CHAPTER THIRTY-THREE

Many years ago.

Blood was sticky. It was one of the first facts that Daniel had learned during his experiments and it was a fact that was being proved once again. The cape, which was as much - if not more - of Albert Griswold's flesh and blood as Daniel was, continuously clung to the backs of the boy's legs. The constant sticky slaps to his calves were not unpleasant, but they did slow him down. Not that he had anywhere in particular to be.

Daniel was alone now.

Almost.

+ *He is for us* + he could hear the shadows talking again, but this time they spoke of him, rather than to him.

+ *He is only a child* + another said.

+ *Have you ever seen a soul so dark?* + a third spoke up.

+ *Perhaps he is too dark.* +

+ *Impossible.* +

+ *He must join us.* + The first voice said.

+ *Send him to the wolves.* +

***

Present day.

They were both on edge, there was no denying it. But they were both trying to appear relaxed. Neither wanted to appear weak in front of the other.

'How do you think he'll react to seeing us again?' Peter said. 'Do you think he knows that we took his little journal?'

The way Peter described the journal made it sound like a book of secrets kept by a lovesick teenage girl, but nothing could be further from the truth. Daniel's journal held the secrets of their kind; what could make them and what would break them. It was how Erik had learned how to turn someone and, once Peter was ready, he had passed that knowledge onto him. Erik had also learned how to kill a werewolf, and that was a secret he still kept. He had no doubt that it was known by others, but he didn't want to risk such knowledge falling into the wrong hands. While Peter had been his companion of many years, there were times that Peter's hands would definitely be the wrong ones. It was just safer for both of their sake if he remained in the dark. Sure, Peter knew that silver was dangerous - there was no hiding that one - but he still wasn't aware of the secret ingredient that was needed to go alongside it.

'I'm sure he knows. Who else could it have been? Although it wouldn't surprise me if he tortured and killed his entire workforce once he realised it was missing.' Erik said, finding himself thinking of the journal for the first time in about a decade. He was careful to keep it locked away, far from prying eyes and curious minds. 'I'm sure he'll be unnervingly professional, especially if he brings someone with him. He may be a psychopath, but only behind closed doors. He prefers to cause pain and suffering in the comfort of his own basement.'

'Well, that's a turn up for the books. Every cloud has a silver lining and all that...' Peter said, becoming aggravatingly positive once again. It was an act though, and Erik could see through it. Anxiety coursed through Peter's body, making him nervously rub the back of his neck. At least Peter's worm was getting a bit of attention and a small massage out of it.

The conversation came to an abrupt halt as the door opened and Kit entered. 'Apologies gentlemen. I had an unwelcome visitor in the tunnels.'

'Our friend the barman?' Peter said, already knowing the answer. 'Maybe it is time we traded him in for a newer model.'

'He should be closing up by now.' Erik said, nudging Kit out of the way. 'I'll go down and check that everything's in order.'

Once Erik was out of earshot, Peter lowered his voice. 'I don't know why Erik wants to keep that little worm around. It's not like we can't get another one.'

Peter's word choice shook Kit. He'd used the exact word to describe himself only a few days ago. Could Peter have known that? No, that was impossible. Peter was smart, manipulative and a werewolf, but it was unlikely that he could have read Kit's mind. Werewolves couldn't read minds.

'I'm sure we can turn him over to our point of view.' Kit said instead of voicing the thoughts in his head. Just like Erik and Peter before him, he was now also hiding any hint of weakness. The battle to become the alpha dog was constant.

'I like that can-do attitude of yours, Kit.' Peter said. 'Listen, we've got a visitor coming in soon. For whatever reason, he's never liked me. I can't think why... as you know, I'm delightful. So, when he comes, would you mind entertaining him?'

'Just keep him busy?'

'Yes, pretty much.'

'If he's that much of a nuisance, can't we just... y'know...'

'Kill him?' Peter said and then sighed. 'If only it were that easy. Unfortunately, we can't dispose of this gentleman quite like that. He's one of us.'

'Why does that matter?'

'Good question.' Peter said. 'The way to murder a werewolf is a secret that is kept under lock and key and is, as far as I know, only known by select members of the Council. I guess they want to keep individuals like us from going on a murderous rampage and claiming absolute power for themselves. Which makes a lot of sense. I'd certainly keep it a secret if that was the case.'

'Didn't Erik kill his maker?' Kit asked, before having a chance to think. He may have been able to use that information if he hadn't blurted it out. 'At least, that's what he told me.'

'Yes, he did. But, he only fired the gun. The elements of the bullet that it contained are still a mystery.' Peter said. 'Even to him.'

'Are you sure?'

'Of course, I'm sure.' Peter didn't like it when anyone doubted him. Least of all pups like Kit. And especially when they made him doubt himself. 'If he knew, he would have told me. We've been friends for years.'

'Of course. Forget I said anything.' Kit replied, sensing that something wasn't quite right. Werewolves had a lot of secrets. It was starting to feel like there were more politics here than out in the so-called normal world. On the occasion when Kit had thought about werewolves prior to the last few days - not that thinking of werewolves was a regular occurrence for him - he always thought that they were savage, animalistic creatures. Beasts that were controlled by blood lust and basic urges. The complexities of werewolfkind surprised him. And now he was part of it. Kit's life had certainly taken a bizarre turn after that job interview. His mind spun in a cycle of *what ifs*: what if they'd given him the job there and then? What if he'd gone straight home afterwards? What if he'd gone to a different pub?

But, none of the answers to those questions really mattered.

***

After he had checked on the barman and made a mental note to call him Caspar more often, Erik started to make his way back to the flat. He would need to wait for the barman to leave before he could enter the bar again. He needed to check that the journal was still where he'd left it. The mere mention of it had made him feel anxious. All hell would break loose if it was discovered. If Daniel didn't kill him then Peter certainly would - if only to prove a point about why he shouldn't have kept the secret from him in the first place. It would make sense in Peter's warped mind and it wouldn't matter that he would just be confirming Erik's concerns. Peter's brain didn't work in the same way as everyone else's. It hadn't for a long time, if ever.

Erik entered the flat, wondering what had been decided in his absence. There was no doubt that Peter had set up some scheme or other. Probably one that used Kit as bait or a bargaining chip.

'Kit's going to entertain Daniel for us.' Peter announced as Erik walked in. It was just as Erik had predicted. As much as he enjoyed being right, there were moments when he wished that he wasn't. It was rather tedious. Peter was playing a dangerous game and they were all pawns in it. Erik felt an unusual sense of foreboding. It wouldn't be long until the proverbial shit hit the fan.

***

Finally, some time alone. The early morning sun caressed his skin and birdsong reached his ears, fumes of stale beer and petrol lined his nostrils. He let out a sigh. Peter was exhausted. Confessing it to anyone else was out of the question, but he felt like he'd gone too far this time. He'd bitten off more than he could chew. You don't outsmart the Council - especially not *"The Six"* - they have eyes everywhere. Hell, they were already on his trail. Peter had hellhounds on his trail.

Running was an option. He didn't even have to pack a bag, he could leave right now and be gone before Daniel even set foot through the front door. But, then, where did that leave him? Where did that leave Erik? They didn't even see eye to eye, but that didn't mean he wanted to chuck him under a bus. Or a steamroller. Daniel was apparently more like a steamroller; unrelenting, crushing everything in its path. Peter had always wanted outsiders to refer to him in terms like that. He wanted to be someone who was feared from afar. Feared, yet celebrated. It was a delicate balance and, standing in that backyard behind the pub, leaning on an empty beer keg, Peter realised that he had failed on all counts. Kit didn't even seem to fear him anymore. The previous night he had spoken to him as if they were equals. It wasn't fair. At least the barman feared him. There was that. It wasn't much though. It wouldn't surprise Peter if the barman was afraid of the dark.

A distraction was needed, something to take the edge off and then help him to focus again. He hadn't killed or fed properly since that family in thc house, it all felt so long ago now. Yes, that's exactly what he needed.

Not wanting to invite thieves into his establishment by leaving the door wide open, he made sure that the back door was closed before leaving. The streets called his name, eager to have him prowling them once more. He'd relied too heavily on the warm bodies procured by the barman. Peter was a predator by nature and he wanted to hunt. He needed to hunt.

***

Success had come easily and now his prize occupied the same cell that Christine had spent the last days of her life in. It was funny, he had thought that he had all the answers then. He didn't know if it had been *The Rot* affecting his brain, or if he was just plain overconfident, but he had thought he was in control. The message from Daniel had been a stark reminder that there were other players in the game. Those who had almost unbeaten records. Those who were older and wiser than he. It was a hard lesson to learn. One that left him feeling depressed and deflated. Luckily, he now had just the thing to cheer him up.

In front of him lay a man. Homeless, from the smell of him. Dirt caked his skin. Lice lived out their days in his beard and hair. The man was a mess. Peter even entertained the thought that he was doing him a mercy by bringing him here. Then he laughed. Of course, he wasn't.

The bearded man groaned, slowly coming to after the swift blow to the head that Peter had dealt him. The poor bastard had never seen it coming. Slurred speech followed the groan. Peter wasn't sure if it was the result of the man's recent concussion or too much booze. He was willing to bet the latter. 'What's goin'... What's goin' on?'

'We're going to have some fun!' Peter said to the homeless man. The man's eyes were still tightly clamped shut.

'I ain't seen ya. If you let me go, I can't tell no-one about ya.'

'Oh, I'm not worried about that, Mr... er....' Peter moved closer to the man's face. Close enough so that he could smell his breath. He was in dire need of some mouthwash. 'What's your name?'

With eyes still closed, the man answered. 'If I tell you, will you let me go? Will you let me live?'

'No.' Peter said, moving away once more. The man's rancid stench was offensive.

'Then what's my incentive?'

'If you tell me, I'll let you die quickly.' The realisation of just how bad a situation he was in hit the man and a dark patch of urine formed on the crotch of his tatty trousers.

'And if I don't...?'

'You'll die slowly. And painfully.'

'Fine. You win.'

'I always do.' Peter replied, some of his old confidence returning. 'In the end, I always do.'

'My name is Ron.' The man said. 'Please have mercy on me.'

'Open your eyes.'

Ron did as he was told. Instantly, his eyes locked on the devastating yellow of Peter's own. It was fortuitous that his bladder was already empty, otherwise Ron would have pissed himself all over again. Shitting himself wasn't completely out of the question though. 'What are you?'

'For you, Ron, I am Death.' Peter said, feeling as if he had won the lottery. Things were going swimmingly. Now that everything was in place, he could finally get to work. Leaving Ron on his own for a second, Peter crossed the cell and unlocked a cupboard on the other side. Only one item awaited him on the inside: a toolbox that looked like it had seen better days - before it had been chucked down several sets of stairs and then trampled on by a herd of elephants. The toolbox didn't look like anything else that Peter owned. Everything else had an upper-class element of style to it, while this was little more than an old tin box. Peter had chosen it for that very reason. It was a way of hiding it from Erik, or anyone else who chose to look at it. Looking at it, it couldn't possibly belong to him. He wouldn't touch something like that with someone else's hand. Lord, no. It obviously belonged to someone else. Peter was good at hiding things, and The Rot hadn't been the first thing he'd hidden from those closest to him.

With his box in hand, he strolled back to Ron, who was still lying helpless on the manky old bed. The box's contents slid around inside, clanking against the tin walls. 'What do you think we have in here, Ron?'

'If it ain't gin, then I ain't interested.' Ron answered without missing a beat.

Peter couldn't help but laugh, but Ron's attempt at levity did little to stop him in his tracks. It wouldn't be long before one of the others awoke and wandered down to the tunnels to see what he was up to. He had to be quick. But that didn't mean he couldn't be thorough. He set the toolbox down on a nearby table and opened it. The box's contents were not too dissimilar to those in Daniel's trunk, but Peter was ignorant to that fact. He had no idea how much he and Daniel had in common.

He pulled the first item from the box with a flourish, like a magician producing a white rabbit from a top hat. Ron's eyes fixed onto the item. It was small, wooden and screw-shaped. Somewhere in the back of his mind, his inner voice told him that it looked a bit like a buttplug. Ron hoped that this - whatever this was - wasn't going in that direction.

Sensing the man's interest in the object, Peter turned back to him. 'This, my friend, is what was known as a mouth gag. Surgeons in the late 1800's used to use them on their patients to stop their airways from closing... the patients were unconscious, obviously. It's ingenious really, isn't it. Such a big, important job for such a small and simple looking device.'

'Fascinating.' Ron said, his mouth dry. The thought of that thing being forced into his mouth was not a pleasant one.

'It is, isn't it? Do you know what else is fascinating?' Peter asked. 'I was around in the 1800's. That's a bit of a mind-fuck, isn't it?'

'Yeah.' Ron replied, feeling like he was well and truly screwed. This guy was nuts on every possible level.

'You don't sound very enthused, Ron.' Peter moved ever closer, brandishing the wooden mouth gag in his hand. 'I'm sorry, am I boring you?'

'No, not at all.'

'I suppose we had better get things started anyway. Time's running out.'

With an unexpected, almost super-human strength, Peter jammed the mouth gag into Ron's throat. Ron's gag reflex kicked in immediately. Vomit tried to force its way past the gag.

'I know it's called a mouth gag, but you didn't have to take it quite so literally.' Peter said, giggling as he reached the punchline. He ripped the gag back out, tearing the inside of Ron's mouth. Holding the device up to a nearby candle, Peter examined it. 'Blood. Isn't it strange to think that just moments ago, this was inside your body. It was wet and warm, and it travelled through you. Now it's here, drying and dead. Just another stain in this room of stains. Blood is so precious to life and, yet, whenever I've ended one - a life that is - there's always plenty of blood around.'

Ron shit himself. He wasn't embarrassed by it. In fact, it seemed like the right course of action at that moment. Maybe it was even a little overdue.

'Charming. Now that's a bodily excretion that I don't find interesting at all. But thank you for contributing.' Peter said, heading back to the table. 'I think it's time for another toy.'

Peter checked his watch. Seven AM was fast approaching. Erik didn't have anything that he needed to do at that time of day, but it wasn't unknown for him to get up early, and Peter didn't know Kit well enough to know his routine. Every second that passed was another second closer to being discovered. As fun as this was, Peter would need to hurry it up. Explaining this, and the contents of his toolbox, would be an awkward conversation. One that was best saved for another time. Preferably never. Apparently, regularly turning into a huge wolf and chowing down on innocent people was fine but taking pleasure in carefully - or violently – torturing, dissecting and killing a human being while you were still in human form yourself was a big taboo. If he was caught, he could always blame it all on The Rot he supposed. It was a complete lie, of course. He was like this long before Erik had turned him. It was the reason why he had gone to work for Daniel in the first place. His previous employer had recommended him. Dr Wilson believed that Peter's talents and interests would complement Daniel's perfectly. Things could have been very different if he hadn't met Erik that morning. He could have had a place on the Council - maybe even as one of *"The Six"* if he'd stuck around. Or would he? Would he still have got The Rot regardless of which path he took? Life was full of what-ifs. It was irritating like that.

His hand hovered over the toolbox, occasionally gracefully touching the individual items within. Eventually it came to rest on one particular tool. It was one of Peter's favourites. He was so fond of it, he had named it Old Faithful some years ago. Any occasion where he could use Old Faithful was fun and memorable.

Ron screamed as he saw the rusty old hand-cranked Skull Saw in Peter's hands. Although Ron had no idea of what it was, he found that his imagination was doing a pretty good job at filling in the blanks. It resembled a chainsaw, albeit a primitive, hand-cranked version of one. Its blade was littered with stains. Some of them could have been rust, although Ron doubted it. Peter's hand clamped over his mouth. 'Shhh.... shh... you'll wake everyone up. We don't want that, do we?'

The mouth gag was shoved back into his mouth before Ron could answer. Holding Ron's head still, Peter slowed his own breathing and listened. He counted to ten. He could hear nothing. It didn't seem like anyone had heard Ron's cry of terror.

***

In a way, Peter was right, Ron's scream had not disturbed anyone. It had not lead anyone to come down to the tunnels and investigate. Ron's scream didn't alert anyone to Peter's actions, as an investigation was already underway. Shannon hid in a cupboard, directly next to the one where Peter had got his toolbox from. She hadn't stayed in the tunnels all night but had returned in the early hours of the morning when she couldn't sleep. Her brain wouldn't let her, it just kcpt playing Christine's last moments over and over again. Or, at least, its own interpretation of them. So, rather than twist and turn for another couple of hours, Shannon had decided to get an early start. Although he had been trying to be stealthy, luckily Peter had made enough noise when he returned from his hunt for her to know he was close by and for her leap into the nearest hiding place. Her heart had nearly leapt from her throat when he came close. Knowing what she knew now - for she had been texting with Caspar for most of the night - she was amazed that Peter hadn't been able to smell her. Maybe the tramp's odour masked everything else. All at once she was both thankful and scared for the man called Ron.

Peter's depraved nature had surprised her. Not because she thought he was better than this, or more stable, or anything like that. It was because when she was informed that he was a werewolf who tore people to pieces and ate them, she imagined that was the worst possible thing there was. Then she stumbled upon this. At least the killing and the eating served some kind of purpose. At least it provided a bit of sustenance. But, this...? This was wrong on just about every level. There was no way you could defend this, not even to the most sympathetic of juries.

The overwhelming urge to do *something* grabbed hold of Shannon. She needed to do something, anything to help Ron. But, what could she do? She was just a normal woman, devoid of any superpowers or secret agent gadgets and Peter was the stuff of nightmares. Even if he hadn't been a werewolf, he was still evil and psychotic. Shannon had no doubt that he would have been that way whether he occasionally turned into a big howling mutt or not. She thought about texting Caspar, wondering if he would be able to save her again like he did when Kit was on to her. But, the thought of moving and making any kind of sound terrified her. Surely Peter would hear even a hint of a sound. Not only that, but Caspar had said that Kit was new to this. Peter, meanwhile, was an old-hand. Even if Caspar were to come down here, he'd just end up getting himself killed, rather than saving her. Shannon was willing to place a rather large sum of money on that being the case. The only thing she wasn't sure of, was if Caspar would be treated to a fast death - such as being eaten alive by a mythical beast - or a slow death, much like Ron was sure to experience. No, Caspar wouldn't be able to help her this time. She was on her own. Upon that realisation, the urge to do something subsided. Instead, she watched through a crack in the cupboard's door and listened, unwillingly becoming a strange voyeur to almost certain death.

***

The Skull Saw felt reassuringly heavy in his hands. He'd had the instrument for so long and used it as often as possible that it had started to feel like a security blanket to him. No matter where he was, no matter what was going on in the world, as long has Peter had that

Skull Saw, and was able to use it, everything would be fine. Only this time was different. This time the wonderful sereneness was fleeting. There was an imbalance in Peter's world, but he couldn't quite put his finger on what it was. He stopped what he was doing and remained completely still.

He listened.

Peter's impeccable sense of hearing picked up nothing. Absolutely nothing. It was almost too quiet. Like the lull before the storm. It felt like someone was watching him, studying his every movement and judging him. And if their judgement found him to be unworthy? What then? The hairs on the back of his neck stood on end and he had to fight all his instincts so that he wouldn't turn around and look through the doorway behind him. Part of him was sure that someone was there. Another part scalded him for being so stupid and weak. One of his hands released the Skull Saw and reached for the back of his neck, caressing it gently as he tended to do when deep in thought or in need of comfort. Both of those reasons were applicable at this moment.

Again, he listened. Now only Ron's sobs disturbed the silence. Other than that, nothing had changed. Even so, Peter felt like whatever was in the tunnels with him had moved closer. Suddenly, a thought occurred to him. He then knew what he felt like, and it was something that he had witnessed so many times in others. Peter felt like prey.

The hunter had become the hunted.

Peter knew which expression he was currently wearing. It was the same one that he had seen on Ron when he woke up, and it was the same as that on the faces of any number of his victims over the years. His wide eyes would be skittishly searching his environment for anything that may betray either where his predator lay in wait, or for anything that might help in escape. Peter refused to compare himself to his victims any further. He would deal with this issue in his way; he would remain in absolute control. Besides, there was a good chance that this was just The Rot giving him a friendly remember that his brain was gradually disappearing. It occasionally did things like this, making him hallucinate, making him hear things that weren't there. Reality was very fluid for Peter.

Closing his eyes, he grounded himself. Reminded himself who he was and what he was capable of doing. He was Peter Smedley, werewolf, amateur surgeon and all around badass. There was nothing he couldn't do. No foe that he could not conquer. He was Peter Smedley and he was ready for anything. He opened his eyes, half expecting to see someone - or something - right in front of his face. Hadn't Erik mentioned that Kit was scared of ghosts? Was that what was happening here? Was he finally being haunted by a disgruntled snack? But, there was nothing awaiting him beyond his closed eyelids. Even Ron wasn't looking up at him from the bed - his eyes were closed in pain. Maybe Peter had imagined the whole thing? Maybe it really was The Rot reminding him that it was there?

He cranked the saw, enjoying the way the candlelight bounced off the blade. Revelling in the squeaks as the mechanism whirled around. Savouring the smell of oil from the last time he'd oiled it. The Skull Saw was beautiful, functional and downright scary for anyone who happened to look upon it. Cranking the saw reminded him who was in charge here. He was. He was the alpha male in this room. In fact, Peter firmly believed that he was the alpha male in most rooms, regardless of who else was in them. The thought reassured him and refocused him on the task at hand.

SCRAPE.

The noise was loud. It was alien. Most unnervingly of all, it felt deliberate. Peter's silent watcher had finally made themselves known. A new game was afoot.

SCRAPE.

The noise came again. Peter felt like it was testing his resolve. Whoever was behind it wanted to see if he would run. They wanted to see if he would breakdown. No matter what happened, Peter promised himself that he would never give them that satisfaction. Besides, he was the alpha male, whoever dared to challenge him would be unceremoniously shoved back into their place. Maybe they'd even tumble a few more rungs down the ladder. It would all depend on how generous Peter was feeling when this was all over.

SCRAPE.

SCRAPE.

SCRAPE.

The gaps between the noises were closing in. Whoever was responsible wanted him to know that they were getting closer. Ever closer. It wouldn't be long now.

SCRAPE.

‘If you wanted my attention, you could have just knocked.’ Peter said with just enough swagger to appear unafraid. That was the thing, Peter *was* afraid. Surely if it were Erik or Kit, they would have said something by now, no matter how disgusted they were with his behaviour. If it was the barman, he would have pissed himself and runaway. Peter was dealing with an unknown. There were too many variables to plan properly, so he would just have to wing it. At least it would be a good workout for his improvisational muscles.

There was no response to Peter’s words. *Of course not*, he thought. He hadn’t asked a question yet. You had to ask a question to get an answer. ‘Can I help you?’

Silence followed. Even Ron had shut up again, sensing that something was going on. Possibly something that would be his escape from death and his ticket to freedom.

‘Speak up, dear.’ He tried again.

Silence.

‘Come on now, you’re just wasting time.’ Peter said, finally turning around to face the doorway, his curiosity was finally getting the better of him.

The doorway was empty. Only a blanket of darkness stood before him, cold and unyielding.

‘Hello?’ he called, into the black. Silence followed once more. Peter let out a breath, not realising that he had been holding it. ‘You may as well show yourself, I know you’re there.’

SCRAPE.

Peter got the distinct impression that he was being toyed with and, although he had done comparable things to numerous people over the years, he didn’t appreciate being on this side of things. Peter was used to being on the winning team. This, right now, did not feel like the winning team.

'Come on,' he said, 'It's getting boring.' The reality was that this moment in time was anything but boring. It was the opposite of boring. It was interesting. Absorbing. Suspicious.

'Careful what you wish for, Peter.' The voice was so quiet, that Peter almost didn't hear it. His ears had to strain against the sound of his own breath and now racing heart to listen to the words. He felt like he was being manipulated into doing exactly what his hunter wanted him to do, and he hated it.

'Enough's enough.' he muttered to himself and waltzed straight through the doorway and turned left. Instead of seeing the familiar, albeit unwelcoming, tunnel in front of him, he saw a man.

'What's enough?' The voice said. It was louder now, fuller somehow. Especially now that Peter knew it had come from the imposing shape in front of him. 'Get back in the cell, Peter.'

For possibly the first time in his life, Peter did as he was told without argument or question.

Inside the cell, with Ron forgotten, Peter looked at the man. His wide shoulders filled the doorway, blocking any chance of escape that Peter may have had. But, in spite of his large muscular frame, the man dressed impeccably. Peter pitied the tailor who had to take his inside leg measurement, especially if the poor mite was given the look that he was getting now. Something somewhere between hatred and annoyance. However, it wasn't the man's size, build or demeanour that worried Peter the most. The worst part was that he had recognised him instantly.

'Good morning, Daniel.'

Daniel looked at the Skull Saw in Peter's hands and nodded. 'A lovely item. I have a similar one at home.'

'Er... Thanks.' Out of all the things that Peter expected Daniel to say, that wasn't one of them. 'I have other stuff too. I like to collect things like this.'

'You may have noticed that I've brought my own little item for show and tell.' Daniel held up his hand and showed off the contents. It was a sharp blade with a big, dramatic curve, rather like a crescent moon. A small layer of dust coated the sharp edge of the blade where it had been dragged against the wall. 'Do you know what this is?'

Peter studied the item. 'It looks familiar. I'd say it was an amputation knife.'

'And you'd be right.' Daniel said with a smile. 'It's from the 1700s and it was brand new when I got it. Every notch on the blade, and every stain on it were all caused by me. I'm the only one to have wielded it.'

'Impressive.' Peter said, not really knowing what else to say.

'Yes. It is.'

A silence opened between them, feeling like a huge chasm. Peter felt like he should say something, but - for once - he was at a loss for words. Daniel had a look in his eye that suggested that silence was dangerous when it came to him. It was as if words distracted him, but now Peter could think of nothing. He coughed. It was meant to sound like he was clearing his throat, but it came out like an awkward, deranged dog bark. Daniel raised an eyebrow. *Yes*, thought Peter, *I'm getting him back on side. Things can still work out okay.* For a moment, Daniel looked like he was going to say something, but instead he moved at lightning speed. The blade moved through the air in a strong, clear arc. It looked like a movement that Daniel's body had performed countless times before. The impulse to move out of the way didn't quite escape Peter's brain and reach his limbs in time to make a difference. The blade sliced through Peter's neck with ease, severing an artery as it did so. Blood gushed from the mouth-like wound, spurting into the air and covering both Daniel and Ron.

With his body twitching on the floor, Peter tried to talk. It was impossible in the state he was in.

'Don't worry,' Daniel said. 'You'll heal soon enough. But, in the meantime, I need you to sleep.' The man produced a small vial from the inside pocket of his coat. Holding it at arm's length he pulled the stopper out and brought it to Peter's face. Strange fumes invaded Peter's nostrils, so thick it felt like they were oozing their way inside him. Vapour tendrils snaked through his respiratory system. Belatedly, he tried to cough, forgetting the gaping hole in his throat. Then there was only darkness.

***

Daniel pulled his mobile phone from his pocket and placed a call. Whoever was on the other end answered almost immediately. 'Bring the van around. I've got a souvenir.'

Using the toe of his expensive looking shoe, Daniel nudged Peter. He didn't react. Blood had started to coagulate beneath him, while the wound on his neck had started to heal. As Daniel had promised, it wouldn't take long for Peter to return to normal. Daniel's lackeys would have to work quickly.

A group of three, two men and a woman, rushed into the room. They operated like quiet church mice, their feet didn't make a single sound. One of the men held a suit cocooned in a protective plastic cover. Daniel was pleased, he hadn't even needed to ask for that. This little group thought of everything. They were the best batch of servants that he had ever had. 'Thank you, please hang it on door over there.'

The man did as he was told, while the other two got to work dragging Peter away. Even as they left the room, the first man was cleaning up the mess Peter had left behind. While his servants worked, Daniel stripped and changed into the new suit. His soiled clothing was squirreled away almost as quickly as it had hit the floor. Soon enough, almost all the evidence of the altercation between the two men was gone, wiped from existence. As if noticing him for the first time, Daniel turned his attention to Ron, fixing him with a stare that would have frozen him to the spot had it not been for the fact that he was still strapped in place.

'UGH! UGH!' Ron said, the sounds straining against the mouth gag. A well-manicured hand pulled out the device that was lodged in Ron's throat.

'What is it?' he said.

'Thank you!' Ron said. It was hard to talk, his throat bruised and torn, but he had to show this man his gratitude. And, hopefully convince him to let him go. 'Thank you so much! You're a hero.'

'I wouldn't go that far.' Daniel said, examining the mouth gag and the minuscule bits of flesh hanging onto it. 'And I wouldn't be thanking me, if I were you.'

'You're not going to let me go?' Ron never should have got his hopes up. He'd known that Daniel was bad news from the moment he'd walked in. Hell, he knew it from the sounds his knife made against the wall before he'd even seen him. The question was: was he worse than Peter?

'Good guess. You're a smart one, aren't you?'

'Please don't put that gag back in my mouth.' His words were pleading, his throat raw.

'I suppose I could grant that wish for you.' Daniel said, switching his gaze between the gag and the man. 'But we can't have you shouting your head off can we?'

Ron didn't like the way that Daniel kept looking at that gag. 'What about another gag? Something made of fabric. That would shut me up.'

'So helpful!' Daniel looked around the room before appearing to have an idea. A shoe was torn from Ron's foot and a filthy sock soon followed it. 'Found one!'

The thought of having that dirty sock shoved into his mouth - even if it was his own, because he knew where it had been - was repellent, but it was better than the wooden mouth gag. Plus, by his reckoning, all the time he was quiet and helpful, he was alive. The longer he was alive, the more chance he had of escape. Taking a deep breath, he braced himself for the sock caked in several weeks' worth of sweat and grime to be rehoused in his mouth.

'Hmmm...' Daniel considered the sock for a moment and then switched his attention to his hand. 'I don't know if that's enough.'

Right before his terror-stricken eyes, he watched as the man's hand started to vibrate. Bones moved beneath the skin, breaking and reshaping themselves. Fingers elongated, and talon-like claws replaced fingernails, tearing through the man's skin. Coarse hair covered the hand. The rest of the man remained the same.

'Impressive, isn't it?' he wagged his clawed fingers. 'It's one of the first party tricks you learn when you're changed into one of my kind.'

Ron didn't have the chance to ask what he'd meant by that, although he probably could have made a fairly accurate guess. They were monsters. They were monsters even before Daniel had done the weird hand thing. That weird hand thing raced towards his face, like a snake going in for the kill. The sharp, deadly claws explored the inside of his mouth, wrapping around his tongue. Ron's panic started anew. At several points during that morning he thought he was the most scared he could possibly be, then something else happened to prove him wrong. He was now willing to bet that you could always be more scared. His tongue was wrenched from his mouth in a firework display of red. Pain radiated from inside and there was no way he could move to lessen it. Screaming wasn't an option; his throat filled with blood. Daniel swallowed the tongue whole. Ron started to choke.

'Oh no you don't.' Daniel turned Ron's head to the side so that the blood would run out onto the filth-encrusted bed. 'It's not your time. Not yet, anyway.'

Now that Ron wasn't going to drown on his own blood, Daniel gently, but firmly, put the sock in his mouth. He looked down at his suit. 'Now I'm going to have to change again. Blood's a bugger to get out.'

Then he left.

CHAPTER THIRTY-FOUR

A white van almost ran him over as Caspar tried to enter the backyard to get to work. He was about to swear and give the culprit his finger, but then he saw their faces. Pale, drawn and focused. And then they were gone. Something about those faces chilled Caspar's soul. A vibration brought him back to reality and his checked the display on his phone.

COME TO THE TUNNEL. I'VE SEEN SOMETHING AWFUL.

Shannon. She was here. Or, at least she had been when she'd sent that text. Caspar could only hope that she was still there and not with the translucent zombies in the white van. The door to the tunnels had been left ajar and Caspar approached it with extreme caution. What had she seen? Was one of his employers down there? If they were, and they were doing something awful, Caspar wasn't sure what he could do to stop them. But, new team-player-Caspar had to try. Shannon and Willow were the closest things he had to friends - that he had ever had to friends - and now one of them needed his help. He couldn't bail on her.

The further he got into the tunnel, the more he smelt a combination of unwashed bodies, blood and the hint of bleach. Caspar wasn't sure what this meant, until he saw the unconscious tramp lying on a bed. In fairness, he still didn't know exactly what was going on, but at least he'd solved the unwashed body smell riddle. Standing in the centre of the room, he spun on the spot, checking for any other signs of life. There was no sign of Peter. No sign of Erik. And no sign of Kit. He appeared to be safe for the time being.

'Shannon?' he said, his voice a bizarre urgent whisper. It was difficult to make sure you were heard and make sure that you were quiet at the same time. 'Are you in here?'

A rattling sound made him jump out of his skin. One of the doors on a nearby cupboard opened and gradually, foot first, Shannon emerged. 'You have no idea how glad I am to see you.'

'What happened?'

'I'll tell you in a bit. We have to go. NOW. I have the feeling that they're coming back at any moment.' She raced past Caspar, speeding towards the outside world. She reached the door in what felt like record time. The morning air on her face felt divine. The blue sky was a miracle. Even the sounds of the adjacent traffic were stunning. Even though neither Peter nor Daniel had spotted her, Shannon felt lucky to be alive. If she'd fidgeted or sneezed while hiding in that cupboard, she may not have been here now to appreciate the morning sounds of a South London road.

'Where are you going?' Caspar asked, catching up with her. 'What about that man back there?'

'We can't save him. Not yet, anyway. They're coming back and if he's gone when they do, they're going to start looking for reasons why.' Shannon replied, pushing the guilt she felt down deep and knowing that it would fester inside her. 'And, in answer to your first question: we're going for a coffee. I'll fill you in on everything. We've got problems. Big problems.'

Shannon gave Caspar every detail that she could remember about that morning, while she savoured the most amazing tasting coffee she had ever had. It was hot, strong and she had laced it with sugar, which was something she didn't usually do. But, she figured that a brush with death was a fair enough reason to momentarily break away from her diet. Someone had once told her that the ideal coffee should be hot as hell, dark as night and sweet as sin. This one ticked all the boxes.

***

Jake sat at the bottom of a huge oak tree, barking at a squirrel. The squirrel was teasing him by running up and down the trunk, always remaining just out of his reach. Willow revelled in the cool morning breeze. It felt like the weather was starting to turn. Summer was over, and autumn was just around the corner. Autumn and spring had always been Willow's favourite seasons. For her, they symbolised change, constant and eternal as it was. And now, not only would this autumn signify a change in weather, but it would see a change in her too. Daniel was due to be paying Peter, Erik and their new recruit a visit soon, and hopefully it wouldn't be too long before he started to dish out his punishments. Once those punishments had been administered - assuming they were of the right magnitude - Willow could relax as her mission would be complete. Being so close to the end was an amazing, but frustrating feeling. She was so close to success that she could almost taste it. She wanted to reach out and grab it now, but she was reliant on Daniel. Could she trust him to do as he was supposed to? No, and this was precisely why she was spending the next few days hanging around close to The Hound & The Philosopher Inn. If something were to happen and Daniel couldn't finish the job, she would do it for him. She just had to be ready. She had thought about just marching over there and killing Erik and Peter outright, but that seemed too quick. It would be over before they even realised what was happening, and that just wouldn't do. They needed to suffer. The trouble was that Willow didn't think she had it in her to be that sadistic. Not on her own anyway. That's where Daniel came in.

***

'I didn't expect Daniel to show up so quickly.' Caspar was still digesting Shannon's story. 'And I certainly didn't expect him to get so close to Peter without him realising.'

'He realised eventually... it was just too late by then.'

'That's an understatement.' Caspar said, before being struck with a thought. 'I've just remembered, I've got something to show you.'

'What is it?' she said as Caspar reached into his backpack. A relatively small, leather-bound journal was placed between them on the table. 'What is this?'

While Shannon was curious about the book, she didn't reach for it; something about it screamed at her, telling her to stay away. There were things written within its pages that weren't hers to know. Forbidden things. Dangerous things.

'It's a little perturbing, isn't it?' Caspar said, recognising the expression on Shannon's face. 'It's like it's basically telling you to fuck off. Clever really... but not as clever as what's written inside it. This is a game changer.'

'What do you mean?' Shannon's eyes were still fixed on the book, watching it warily.

'It tells us how to make them.' Caspar said, looking around to make sure no-one was spying on them. 'And how to break them.'

He didn't need to explain to Shannon who he meant when he said 'them', nor did he have to explain any part of his statement. If what he said was true, and providing what was written in the book was fact, then Caspar was right. This was a game changer. Shannon couldn't believe their luck. It was almost too good to be true.

'What do we need to do? How do we kill them?' Shannon asked, becoming quite animated. Caspar gave her a look, signalling her to calm down. She lowered her voice. 'What do we need to do to finish this?'

'We shoot them.'

'Is that it? I could have come up with that.'

'With a silver bullet.'

'About a gazillion horror films could have told us that.'

'But silver has to be blended with aconite.' Caspar said, leaning back and smiling, knowing that he had just played his winning hand.

'What the hell is that? It sounds weird... are we going to have to break into a secret government lab to get some?' Shannon asked. 'Shit, are there werewolves in the government? The real one, I mean. Not their Council.'

'Well, I don't know if there are any werewolves in the government,' he answered. 'But I do know what aconite is.'

‘Oh, for fuck’s sake, Caspar,’ Shannon said, not angry with him, but starting to get frustrated. ‘Out with it! Spill the beans!’

‘It’s another name for wolfsbane.’ he answered. ‘I should have realised it sooner.’

‘Don’t be silly, why would you? Because it’s got ‘wolf’ in its name?’

‘No, that’s not why.’ Caspar stroked his chin, wondering how he could have missed this. ‘Before I came here, before they employed me, I read a lot of books. Weird ones, really. I read stuff about the occult, magick, witchcraft - which, by the way, aren’t all the same thing. It’s how I ended up getting caught up in this world in the first place. I found a book that tried so hard to tell me that werewolves didn’t exist, that it basically confirmed to me that they did.’

‘Was the wolfsbane thing in that book?’

‘It was in another one. A book I’d read a few years before. I guess it has been long enough for me to forget it, but I’d have hoped that I was intelligent enough to connect the dots.’

‘Don’t beat yourself up.’ Shannon said, reaching across the table, her hand touching his. She was warm and real. Best of all, she was looking out for him. She was on his side. That was something worth fighting for, the best kind of reason to put a stop to Peter and Erik’s reign of terror.

‘I once read this thing...’ Caspar said, continuing. As he spoke, he passed Shannon a handful of wolfsbane infused silver bullets. Caspar had been busy. ‘it was called *‘Rede of the Wiccae’*, but some refer to it as *‘the Counsel of the Wise Ones’*. It’s rather like a long poem, with lots of rhyming. Some of it makes sense, but the rest doesn’t. Or, it didn’t. Not to me... and not back then. There’s a line in it that says, *‘Widdershins go when Moon doth wane, An the werewolves howl by the dread wolfsbane'*. I can't believe it was there, in my head, for all this time.'

'If it makes you feel any better, it didn't say anything about a silver bullet.' She said, admiring one of the bullets.

'That's true... But it would have been a step in the right direction.' Caspar said, almost wistfully. 'I could have worked everything out years ago. I could have stopped this.' But Caspar knew he wouldn't have stopped it. At least not right away. Old Caspar would have just used the information as a bargaining chip to further his own agenda.

'Maybe.' Shannon said. 'Maybe not. Either way, it doesn't matter now. Let's go get what we need and go and kill some werewolves... the whole damned lot of them.'

Shannon stood, and Caspar made to follow, before remembering something else that he needed to share. 'Maybe we shouldn't kill *all* of them.'

'Why not?' She asked. 'They're all murderers, aren't they?'

'Well, yes... but one of them is helping us.' Caspar said. 'Her name is Willow.'

'Willow?'

'Don't worry, she's on our side.'

'If you say so.' Shannon remained unconvinced.

***

A collection of kings and queens had sat on England's throne since Daniel had last been in the same room as either Erik or Peter. Granted, he had watched them from afar, it was always worth keeping tabs on those who had wronged you, but he had avoided conversing with them for some time. This wasn't because he feared them, or because his anger prevented him from talking to them, he was simply waiting for the optimum moment. He needed his presence to cause as much of an impact as possible. Timing was everything.

And, it appeared, that the ideal time was now.

The woman - Willow - had given him quite the titbit of information. It was still rumour and conjecture, but all he had to do was prove it. Daniel had been waiting for a moment like this for years. Early this morning, before dawn broke, Daniel had grown sick of waiting and he'd decided to go hunting. Yes, the ideal time was definitely now. Of course, it did help that one of the pair was currently hogtied on the floor of his basement. The servants - his A Team - had left him to it, knowing that they had to focus on cleaning the blood from his two suits and preparing themselves for Daniel's official visit to The Hound & The Philosopher Inn later that day. Daniel praised himself on getting an early start that morning, it meant he could be so much more productive.

For once, he turned the overhead light on. The basement was illuminated by a bright, daylight bulb. It was a stark contrast to the scene that he usually set for his visitors. Candlelight or pitch darkness usually provided the correct atmosphere, but Daniel had the feeling it wouldn't be enough for Peter. After all, Peter was a kindred spirit. A fellow torturer, and a former surgeon's apprentice to boot. He'd know all the tricks of the trade. Daniel was going to have to be creative with this one. Fortunately, Daniel did enjoy a challenge; he knew that he'd rise to it and succeed. He always did.

Peter started to stir. The gash across his throat had fixed itself. The man was as good as new.

Rat-a-tat-tat.

The basement was invaded by the harsh noise, breaking Daniel's concentration, shattering it into tiny, fragmented pieces. He sighed. The moment was gone. At least he knew that if one of his A-Team was knocking, it had to be something important. Decades had passed since he'd vowed to get revenge on Erik and Peter for slighting him, a little bit longer wouldn't hurt.

'We're ready, sir.' A voice called down.

'I suppose it would be best to keep to the schedule. Make sure that our friend here is kept safe and secure.'

'Yes, sir.'

After taking one last glance at Peter, Daniel left the basement.

***

+ *He's going to do it again. The pack are not supposed to torture each other. They're not supposed to torment each other. That's our job. It's our right. We have earned this right. We deserve it.* + The shadow that spoke was the same shadow that had worried about the depths of Daniel's evil when he was a child.

+ *Then he will be perfect to join us. When the time comes.* + One of the others said.

+ *No, he won't join us.* + the first voice said. + *He'll want to control us. Own us.* +

For a moment there was silence as the shadows contemplated Daniel's strengths and weaknesses.

+ *We'll find another.* + the second voice said.

+ *Yes, another.* +

***

Rat-a-tat-tat.

There was something about the fact that his team always knocked on the door in the same way that both pleased and amused Daniel. This time they were knocking on the currently locked doors of The Hound & The Philosopher Inn. Although Daniel had accomplished a fair bit that morning, it was still too early for the pub to be open. The door opened inwards, slowly. A face - a human face - appeared in the gap.

'Good morning.' The face said, as he recognised what Daniel was, if not who, and opened the door fully, allowing Daniel and his team to enter.

'Yes,' Daniel said. 'It is, isn't it?'

PART THREE

CHAPTER THIRTY-FIVE

After the coffee with Shannon and a brief chat with Willow over the phone, Caspar was ready for Daniel's visit, but he was still surprised that he had made it back to the pub so quickly after Peter's kidnapping. Not that he had mentioned anything to Erik or Kit about that. That was for them to find out later. The door creaked as if in protest as he opened it to let Daniel and his entourage in. Caspar made a mental note to oil the hinges later. That was, of course, assuming that there would be a later. Caspar wasn't entirely sure about how long this would take. Would it be over in ten minutes or would it require a bit more time and a lot more work?

'Are your employers around?' Daniel said as he wandered around the pub. Caspar had begun the process of opening up, so the lights were on and chairs had been taken off the tables, but they still had around an hour before the doors opened. Daniel wiped a white gloved finger across one of the tables and inspected it for dust.

Bizarrely, Caspar found himself more worried about what Daniel would do if he wasn't happy with his cleaning, than he was about what would happen to him if Daniel did decide to slaughter Erik and Kit right there and then.

'Yes, of course. I'll get them for you.' Caspar said, racing behind the bar to the phone. 'Please make yourselves comfortable.'

As Caspar pressed a button on the phone's receiver, Daniel took a seat at the table that he had inspected. Apparently, it had passed his cleanliness standards. The rest of his team remained on their feet. Whether they stood or sat, Caspar's guests listened to every word he said into that receiver.

'Good morning, Erik.' Caspar said, not having to fake his cheeriness. 'You have some visitors.'

Daniel listened to the one-sided conversation and waited, wondering if Erik knew that his little buddy had disappeared. He supposed not. Not yet, anyway.

'It's Daniel.' Caspar said, answering Erik's questions on the other end of the line. 'I think he wants to see all of you.' Caspar was careful not to say *both of you*. That would have given everything away, and it was too early for that. Hanging up the phone, he turned to where he knew Daniel was waiting for an update. 'They'll be right down.'

'Splendid.'

'Can I get you anything?'

'No, thank you.' Daniel said, tapping his foot to a rhythm that nobody else could hear. The action reminded Caspar that he would need to put the music on for when the pub opened, but it didn't seem appropriate at the moment. What if putting his playlist on disturbed Daniel's inner soundtrack? That wouldn't do at all. If there was one thing he didn't want to do, that was piss Daniel off.

Erik and Kit emerged from their flat quickly, faux nonchalance plastered on their faces. Caspar knew they were nervous. In fact, he reckoned they were probably shitting themselves.

'Good morning, Daniel. What a pleasure!' Erik said as he greeted the older man. Fake sincerity mingling with the fake nonchalance. 'I'm sorry to say that it looks like you're a little early for Peter. He's not up and about just yet.'

'Oh, that's a shame.' Daniel said, adding his own fake disappointment to the mix. Both men knew that Peter wasn't still in bed, but only one of them knew where he was. 'I'm sure we can have a chat without him. Actually, it may work out well. You see, I need to talk to you *about* him.'

'I see.' Erik said, taking a seat at the same table and nodding to Kit to do the same. A chair squeaked against the floor as Kit moved it and took his place at the table.

'I'm sure you know what the problem is.' Daniel said. 'Peter's most recent activities can't have escaped your notice.'

It wasn't a question.

'I'm aware that he has made some questionable decisions...' Erik said, choosing his words with the utmost care. He knew that Daniel - and, by extension, the Council knew that he had knowledge of Peter's suburban adventures, but he didn't want to implicate himself too much. He had to show that he wasn't involved.

'We have a choice, Erik.' Daniel pulled off a glove and examined some dirt underneath his nail. Caspar wondered if it was Peter's blood. 'There is only one way that this will end. Peter will have to be eliminated. We can, however, choose how this is done. One option is that I could do it.'

'And the other option?'

'The other option is that you can do it. It would go some way in redeeming yourself in the eyes of the Council, Erik.'

'I see.' Erik said, it seemed to be his go-to phrase when he couldn't think of anything else to say.

Daniel rose from his chair and started walking towards the door, his entourage following close behind. 'You can have some time to think about it. We know this is a tough one.'

'Thank you.'

'You have until tonight.' He opened the door. 'Until sunset seems fair.'

***

Jake growled, low and deep while staring at Daniel. The little critter had always been a terrific judge of character. Willow's attention turned from the pub's window to the man now stood beside her. She hadn't planned on talking to Daniel, at least not yet, but it was no great problem. As far as he was concerned, they were currently, and bizarrely, playing for the same team.

'Good morning.' he said, ignoring the dog. 'Enjoying the show?'

'Just making sure that my concerns are being dealt with appropriately.' Willow said, facing Daniel head on, unwilling to let him intimidate her.

'And are you satisfied?'

'I suppose so. Although I do have one question.'

'Ask away.'

'When sunset arrives, and Peter's executioner is determined, how long will it be before the sentence is carried out?'

'Worry not, this will all be put to bed very quickly. Let's just say that, whatever happens, Peter will not be around tomorrow.'

'It's a step in the right direction. What of the others?' Willow said, keeping a tight grip on Jake's leash. The growling dog was determined to let Daniel know that his presence displeased him. Jake's efforts were going unnoticed though, he was still being ignored by the man.

'I've a few options for them. Nobody's walking away from this without paying some kind of price.'

'Very well.' Willow said before turning and walking away.

Daniel watched as she walked. The feeling that he knew her from somewhere still nagged at him.

CHAPTER THIRTY-SIX

Victorian London.

Silence.

Silence was the only thing filling the house as far as Ida was concerned. The furniture - the belongings that she and Jack had collected over the years no longer seemed to hold any substance and the ticking from the grandfather clock no longer reached her ears. The words in the tear-stained confession left by Erik rang hollow. There was nothing in this house apart from the body of her soulmate and the silence. That godforsaken silence. In that moment, Ida couldn't even be sure that she really existed. Her limbs were numb. The only thing she was aware of was a pressure building in her head. It pushed against her skull, demanding that she either scream or cry.

A tear fell unhindered, but the scream was internal.

Ida couldn't bear to break that damned cursed silence.

Taking one more look at Jack's lifeless body and the blood and gore splattered piano, Ida picked up her bag and left the room - and the house - behind her. Outside, night had fallen, welcoming her into its dark embrace and shielding her from any would-be onlookers. No-one would see her puffy eyes, nor the pain and anguish etched across her face. It was better that way. If someone was to try and comfort her, Ida wasn't sure if she would thank them, embrace them or tear them limb from limb.

So, she walked. In much the same way as Erik had wandered the streets before her, Ida wandered relatively aimlessly, her feet not caring which direction they took or where they'd end up. Only her thoughts had focus.

Jack's death was inevitable. In spite of their attempt at immortality, Ida knew in her heart that - sooner or later - both of them would cease to be. In reality, eternal life just wasn't possible. Part of her had wanted to believe it, just because endings were always difficult to process, but most of her knew that it was a work of fiction; a bedtime story to help them both sleep at night. It didn't matter what they'd done that day, there would always be tomorrow to put it right. And the next day. And the next. Suddenly, little mistakes or lapses in judgement no longer mattered when you had an endless supply of tomorrows at your disposal. But, she'd always known that they were kidding themselves. Ida had just been happy to play along. It was a good dream, but one that had to end sooner or later. She just didn't think it would be so soon, nor did she think it would have been in this way. To have him *taken* from her - and by someone she had almost come to trust - really stung. It was a wound that felt raw. Ida knew that it was a wound that would never truly heal. Betrayal begs for revenge, and revenge rots a hole in even the kindest of hearts.

Mere hours had passed and already her heart felt tainted. Ida knew that there was no going back for her. She had to have her revenge and, while she may not have an eternity, she did have plenty of time to make sure that her revenge was as absolute as possible.

CHAPTER THIRTY-SEVEN

Present day.

Rosa Ward stood at her post at the top of the stairs, just outside the locked door that lead to the cellar. Having been one of the team who had aided Daniel in retrieving his prize that morning, it stung a bit to be left behind while he taunted the other two rebels back at the pub. While others, like Riley, Howard and George, were in a mood because they always wanted Daniel to take notice of them, Rosa was annoyed because she'd miss what was going on. It was an opportunity to learn and, while she had spent a long time studying Daniel, learning about him and discovering the reasons why he did what he did, there were many things about her employer that were still a mystery, but - unlike her colleagues - she knew what he kept in his special little vials. And she had a good idea of what they did. No, she had no desire to be Daniel's favourite. Rosa had other plans. She was going to go off on her own one day.

There was only one problem - she was still waiting for her change. Daniel turned one of his team once in a blue moon and Rosa felt like she was running out of time. But, this whole situation with Peter, Erik and Kit had given her hope. The knowledge was out there. She just had to get it for herself. There was no doubt in her mind that going back to the pub would help her with that. Although Daniel pretty much controlled every single second of their day, Rosa planned to find a way to sneak out. A moan came from beyond the door.

'He's awake.' Riley Sanford said, stating the obvious. She had also been tasked with guarding the door. She wasn't sure if it was to prevent Peter from getting out, or to stop someone else from getting in. Either way, she wasn't opening that door for anything.

'Clearly.' Rosa said. 'Do you think we should check on him?'

'Nope. Not a chance. No-one gets in. No-one gets out.'

'What if Howard or George do something to him and Daniel finds out that we did nothing to stop it?' Rosa said, watching her question work its way through the other woman's mind, causing trouble and suggesting doubt.

'Like what? What could they do? It's not like they can hurt him. He's a werewolf.'

'I don't know.' Rosa started to think through what could happen. One idea shone through from all the rest. 'What if he convinced them to free him?'

'I suppose that's possible... but what could we do about that? Remember... he's a werewolf.'

'True, but... there's just the two of them down there. Think about it, it's easy to convince two people to free you... but four? That's gotta be tough. We could be the voices of reason.'

'Hmm....' Riley turned to look at the door. 'We could be the voices of reason. I think Daniel would appreciate that, wouldn't he?'

'Yes, I think he would.'

'Maybe there would even be some kind of reward.' Riley said, reaching for the door handle.

'Definitely.'

Riley opened the door.

***

Howard Eastcott looked at his phone for the third time in five minutes. It was pointless, you could never get a decent signal in the basement. On the other side of the room, George Tucker yawned.

'Why couldn't we go to that pub? I hate all this waiting around.' George said. Complaining was one of the things he was really good at and he had been demonstrating to Howard just how good he was all morning. 'I wouldn't even care if we couldn't go to *that* pub. Any pub would be fine by me. Why have we been stuck with babysitting this guy?'

'Why? Because Daniel said. That's why.'

'Doesn't this bother you?' George said, starting to pace.

'Of course it does, but there's not a lot we can do about it.' Howard said, putting his phone back into his pocket, but knowing that he would probably be getting it out again in two minutes. Phone addiction was a very real thing when it came to Howard. 'And bitching about it won't change anything, so shut up.'

George rolled his eyes and sighed. 'Why couldn't I have been paired up with one of the others? Even Rosa is more fun than you.'

Howard looked back at George and smiled. 'For the same reason that we're not harassing Erik at the pub at the moment. Because Daniel said so.'

Shaking his head, George let out a humourless laugh and Howard reached into his pocket for his phone again. As Howard was trying to get some signal to look at Twitter, the man secured to the chair in front of them groaned. The two men exchanged glances, unsure on whether or not they should speak. Peter was a prisoner, that much was certain, but he was also a werewolf. As far as Howard and George were concerned, werewolves were higher than them in the food chain. George cleared his throat nervously and Howard fumbled with his phone.

'Excuse me, gentlemen, would you mind untying me?' The captive man was surprisingly polite. Howard looked into his eyes. Even though the silver in his binds were preventing him from changing, he was sure that he could still see the power lurking in their depths. It was like a coiled spring.

'We... We can't do that... sir....' George said.

'Of course, you can!' Peter said. 'Think positively! You can do it! I believe in you!'

'That's... not what I meant...'

'I know that's not what you meant, Mr... er....'

'I'm George.'

'Okay, George.' Peter shuffled in his seat, trying to get comfortable with the limited range of movement that he had. 'You're just Daniel's lap dogs, aren't you? You can't decide to do things for yourselves.'

'We're not mindless drones...' George began, well aware that Peter was trying to manipulate him, but unable to help himself. Before he could utter another word, the door opened, and two sets of footsteps descended the stairs. Howard didn't appear to notice, his eyes transfixed on Peter. George turned as Riley and Rosa appeared at the bottom of the stairs. 'You're on the wrong side of the door.'

'Are we?' Riley asked, looking from George to Peter and back again. 'Having a nice little chat?'

'No-one in, no-one out.' George said, repeating Daniel's instructions. 'You've disobeyed.'

Being accused of violating Daniel's rules was basically a death sentence on a normal day, but both Rosa and Riley believed that today was anything but normal. For Riley, it would be a chance to show-off to her boss. It was a chance to be noticed and elevated above her peers. While for Rosa it meant that she was moving ever closer to her dreams of the *Om grutt*.

'Naughty girls.' Peter said, receiving looks as sharp as daggers from both women.

'Daniel will thank us for it.' Riley said, focusing back on George and deciding that Peter was arrogance personified. She supposed that could happen to a person after decades of getting their own way.

'If you say so.' George said, not noticing that Rosa was taking herself on a little tour of the basement, taking in all the sights that it had to offer; Daniel owned a collection of "tools", including a baseball bat and a deadly looking bucket of molten silver. Rosa couldn't guess what that bucket was made of, surely the silver should be melting through it? Meanwhile, Howard noticed nothing. The trunk that Rosa thought of as Daniel's "toolkit" was close by, open and waiting for her to take a look inside. She knew that Peter had a tin toolbox filled with very similar items and wondered if he had borrowed the idea from the older man. Or maybe Daniel had stolen it from his would-be protege? Or maybe it was just one of life's coincidences. Rosa supposed that it didn't matter much.

'You two should go back to your post.' George said, reminding Rosa that she wasn't in the room alone. 'Before Daniel gets back. I won't say anything. I promise.'

'Why do you two want to be alone with him so badly?' Riley said.

'Because that's the job that Daniel gave us... Duh!' George said, showing his age and lack of maturity.

'If I may interrupt...' Peter began, not actually caring if he was interrupting or not. 'I don't care who goes or who stays, I just want to get out of here. As a couple of you may know, I've left a somewhat sensitive little project tied up in the tunnels under my pub... that is, of course, assuming that your delightful boss hasn't introduced him to his demise. Now, would someone let me go?'

No-one answered. Riley looked to George and he looked right back at her. Howard continued to stare. Rosa was still completely transfixed on the trunk.

'Wonderful.... You there!' Peter said, trying to get Howard's attention. 'One Thousand Yard Stare Chap. What's your name?'

Howard didn't answer. He didn't even move a muscle. He was so still that Riley wondered if he was still breathing. Even though she had often put an end to someone's life, the idea of hanging around in a room with the still standing corpse of someone she knew made chills run through her body. George made as if to answer, but Riley caught his eye again and shook her head. He remained silent.

'Fair enough...' Peter said. 'I can make it worth your while. Any of you. The one who helps me gets whatever they want.'

Rosa's ears perked up. 'Anything?'

'Absolutely. All you have to do is name it... once I'm free.'

‘What if we all help you?’ George asked.

‘Then I’ll owe each of you a favour, won’t I?’

It was a tempting prospect for each of them, particularly Rosa. This could be the moment that she had been waiting for. The *Om grutt* was almost within her grasp and, yet, it didn’t feel quite right. It felt like a trap. Peter may have been a werewolf, but he was also a desperate man and desperate men were prone to making bargains and offering treasures that they either didn’t have or couldn’t afford to give. Besides, Daniel’s toolbox - his torture trunk - was calling her name. Rosa could only imagine the things she could do with the items held within it. Her heartbeat quickened with excitement and Rosa’s mind was made up. Peter wouldn’t be freed by her hand.

Without a word, Howard sprang into life, as if someone had just activated the power switch in his head. If anyone ever had the opportunity to ask him what he had been thinking about before his switch was turned on, Howard wouldn’t have been able to tell them. It was almost as if he had ceased to exist for a few moments. He had become a blank slate, ready to be rewritten and reprogrammed by anyone with the means and inclination to do it.

***

This was new. Maybe it was the one single perk of being ravaged by The Rot. For the first time ever, Peter could read minds. Or, at the very least, one mind in particular. Now that he had focused on him, the One Thousand Yard Stare Chap’s (or Howard as he now knew him to be) mind was an open book - and Peter’s ticket out of Daniel’s hell hole. Once Howard was galvanised into action, Peter had to restrain himself from yelping with glee. It would have been terribly inappropriate.

***

With all the charm and grace of a mindless zombie, Howard lumbered over towards Peter. One hand flailed in the general direction of the chains holding Peter's arms in place, while the other rooted around in his jacket pocket for the key. The clumsy movement made it look like Howard had never used his fingers before - like they were a new form of technology that he was ill-equipped to understand. As if to further confirm this image, Howard grunted - bringing a mental image of a Neanderthal to everyone else in the room - as he dropped the precious keys on the floor.

With the same finesse that he had possessed when moving towards Peter, Howard dropped to his knees to reach for the keys. His index finger brushed against them, but before he could pick them up, a blunt object hit him on the head from behind. Howard collapsed, silent and still, onto the floor. Peter looked up at the person wielding the baseball bat - the person who had stolen his means of escape.

'When I get out of this... and I will get out of this... you'll pay dearly for that.'

Rosa shrugged. 'If you say so.'

She walked back over to the trunk and admired its contents in much the same way that Peter fondly examined his own tools. Peter recognised the look. This one was dangerous.

'Then again...' He said, realising her potential and trying to gain access to her mind like he had with Howard, but with no success. 'I could do with someone like you. Someone who does what they need to do to get things done.'

Peter couldn't help but think that this feisty young woman would be the perfect candidate to replace that godforsaken barman.

'What makes you think I'd wanna work for you?' Rosa asked, getting close. Her face was now level with his. 'I already work for a werewolf. Why would I switch one egotistical maniac for another?'

Even though both Riley and George agreed with her, they winced at the description of their leader. There was always the chance that he had some way of listening in. He was a bit like Santa Claus in that respect; he could see you when you're sleeping, and he knows when you're awake. Most importantly, he always seemed to know when you were doing or saying something you definitely shouldn't be. There was a very good chance that this would end terribly.

'Not work *for* me.' Peter said, changing tact. 'Work *with* me. We could be a team... Partners.'

'Equal partners?'

'Yes.'

'How can a human and a werewolf be equal?'

Peter nodded, she had a point and he understood now what the young woman wanted. The price of his freedom would be to bless another young soul with the joy of *Om grutt.* A small price to pay for escaping with his life intact.

'You're right. Get me out of here and I'll change you. You'll be strong. Powerful.'

'And we'll be equals.'

Peter nodded again.

'I will not become one of your underlings.' Rosa said, reiterating her point. 'It doesn't matter if I'm a werewolf or not.'

'Agreed. It's as good as done.'

Rosa toyed with the bloodied baseball bat that was still in her hands. She didn't think that she could trust

Peter. Actually, she was one hundred percent certain that she couldn't trust him. But, it really didn't matter. This was the best option that had come her way for quite some time. She knew that she had to grab the opportunity with both hands. She also had to reach down and grab the keys from the floor.

'NO!' Riley shouted, panicking as Rosa's hand closed around the cold metal. If one of them betrayed Daniel - and it didn't matter who - each of them would be forced to pay the price and Daniel wasn't known for his leniency. Having worked for Daniel for almost two years, Riley had seen former colleagues tortured and killed for even the most minor of indiscretions. Daniel was always dreaming up new cruel and unusual punishments. If she closed her eyes, she could still recall the sights, smells and sounds of one unlucky team member - Johan - as he was boiled alive. His agonised screams had echoed around this house for what felt like hours. At the time, Riley had thought that it was never going to end. The poor man had been conscious almost until the end, feeling every moment of his body being cooked. The worst part was how she had reacted to the smell of Johan's cooking flesh and organs; her stomach had rumbled. She tried to fool herself into believing that it was because it was almost dinner time and she had missed lunch completely - and, in fairness, that may have had some influence on the reaction - but, Riley knew the truth. The truth was that Riley thought Johan smelled delicious. Luckily, the sight of his red, blistered skin and clouded, sightless eyes had completely put her off sampling the freshly prepared meat.

Riley didn't want to find herself experiencing the same fate. Nor did she want something to happen to Rosa. Even though they didn't always see eye to eye, Riley had grown attached to Rosa after the last two years. She wouldn't go as far as to say they were friends

- Rosa seemed determined to keep everyone at arm's length - but she did like her. They even occasionally had a laugh. George and Howard were nice enough too, although Riley had only recently started to work closely with them. Daniel like to keep mixing things up. It stopped his employees from forming relationships or plotting uprisings.

'Rosa,' she said, hoping that the use of Rosa's name would make sure that she paid attention. 'Don't do this. Please.'

'Hmm...' Rosa rubbed her thumb against the key, apparently weighing up her options.

'Put the key away.'

'It's too late.'

'No, it isn't.' Riley said. She didn't believe it, she thought they were all doomed, but there was no point in making matters worse. 'There's still time to put this right.'

'Right?'

'Yes... right.'

'There is no right and wrong, Riley. Especially not here.'

A smirk crept over Peter's face. Rosa was correct. The concepts of right and wrong were overrated. George shifted on the spot and, although Peter wasn't able to read his mind, he could tell that Rosa's words were giving him cause to think. Maybe even re-evaluate his position in Daniel's organisation. Or not. Beyond the fact that he was thinking, George was unreadable. Peter needed to find a way to get him on side, and fast. He was becoming a risk.

'George.' Peter said, deciding to talk to him directly. The two women paused their discussion. 'Where do you stand on this?'

George didn't answer, instead he barged by Rosa and focused on the trunk. 'So, there's no right and wrong here?'

'True.' Rosa said before Riley had the chance.

'That means we can do whatever we want.' His voice was excited, like a child when presented with a sweet treat or a new toy. Rosa followed his line of sight to the trunk - the trunk that had held her captivated only moments earlier.

'What's the plan, George?'

'No plan. I'm sick of plans and rules.' he reached into the trunk and pulled out an odd-looking device. It was one that none of the team members had ever seen Daniel use, but Peter knew exactly what it was. It was a medieval torture device known as a "Head Crusher" and it did exactly what it said on the tin. Peter's skin crawled. If George decided to use this on him, there was a chance that he'd never get out of this basement alive. Peter inwardly cursed the silver binds on his wrists and ankles, not wanting the others to know how scared he was. If they knew that he was now consumed with fear at the thought of his own demise - especially a demise as a result of a Head Crusher yielded by a mere human - he would lose any power that he had.

'What the fuck is that?' Riley said.

George shrugged. 'I can take a guess on how to use it. Let's experiment!'

'Wait.' Rosa said, giving Peter some new hope. He'd been right to try to appeal to this one.

'Why?' George asked, examining the Head Crusher. 'You were all for breaking the rules earlier?'

'Think about it, George. We've got an opportunity here. Peter is going to pay me back for my help and I'm sure he'll do something for you too. Isn't that right, Peter?' She turned her attention to the man in the chair.

'Yes, of course.' He said. 'What do you want?'

George seemed to weigh up his options for a moment. 'What if I don't want anything?'

'That's fine... it's a lie, but it's fine. Everybody wants something. But, even if you insist that you don't want anything, think about what Daniel is going to do you when he returns to find out that you've killed Peter. You know how much he was looking forward to spending some time with his new toy. You know he loves his projects.'

Again, George paused. His hands explored the Head Crusher, testing it and working out how it functioned. Turning the screw at the top, pushed the bowl-like part down. Peter knew that the bowl-like part was a cap to put on the victim's head, but he wasn't going to say anything. The trouble was that it looked like George had already worked it out. Unbeknownst to his current companions, George had always been quite quick to work out how to use gadgets and tools. His mind had always been technically inclined. As a child, he'd spend hours and days of his school holidays taking things apart and putting them back together again.

'He'll kill me.' George said, his tone was very matter-of-fact, as if he had already come to terms with the consequences of his future actions. 'But, it doesn't matter. I don't think any of us are getting out of this alive.'

'Really?' Riley said, the prospect of her own death was now feeling very real.

'If we work together, with Peter, we stand a chance.' Rosa said, looking between George and Riley, trying to get them both onside. Riley stared intently at the floor, while George continue to fiddle with the object in his hands. The Head Crusher squeaked as he cranked the screw once more, stiff due to a lack of use. The noise was like nails on a chalkboard, making Rosa, Riley and Peter squirm. Their involuntary reactions were completely at odds with George's. George smiled. It was a small smile, barely perceptible, but it was definitely there. It was the smile of a man who had made up his mind and was content with it. It was the smile of someone who was about to do something that had - up until this point - been denied to them, forbidden even. George smiled because he was about to inflict excruciating pain, and perhaps even death, upon someone who under normal circumstances would have overpowered him in an instant. It was like he, a mere mortal, was about to go up against a god. The thought alone was intoxicating. Was the act worthy of the death sentence he had bestowed upon himself? George certainly thought so. Everybody had to go sometime, he may as well check out having done something that many would have believed to be impossible.

Taking barely two strides, George closed the distance between himself and Peter, slamming the Head Crusher device onto Peter's skull before he had even come to a stop. Peter thrashed about in the chair, trying to get as far away from almost certain death as possible. Blood dripped from Peter's face as his lip split against the device. George laughed, his cackle was void of any humour, the only thing that lurked within it was insanity.

Both Rosa and Riley raced to Peter's aid, each helping the werewolf for their own separate reasons. Guided by Riley's hand, the Head Crusher came off Peter's head and clattered to the floor. The noise alone was enough to silence George's laughter. It stopped short. The sound ending abruptly. Meanwhile, Rosa rugby tackled her colleague, forcing him to the ground and knocking the wind from his lungs. The pair lay on the floor for a few moments, catching their breath and contemplating their next moves. Peter sucked on his split lip, realising what a close call that had been. He owed these two humans his life and he would make good on his promises to them, whether or not Erik approved. All he had to do was get out of this basement before Daniel returned. Peter would have loved to wait for Daniel and then kill him when he walked through the basement door, but he had still not been given the secret. He didn't know how to extinguish one of his own kind. His years of experimentation through torture had given him some ideas, but he didn't hold the full answer. Not unless he could force him into this chair and then crush his head while he was bound with silver. That might work. Then again, it might not. But, if it did work, would it be too quick? No, Daniel's death would not be swift. It wasn't something that Peter could do right here and now. Peter wanted to savour it. He'd need to experiment. Practice. Practice makes perfect...

Leaping into action, and forcing his way over Howard's unconscious body, George leaped back into action, aiming for the Head Crusher. He was fast, but Rosa was faster. With a grace and athleticism that she didn't know she had, Rosa overtook George and grasped the device. George's yell of frustration was loud and unholy. The look of determination on his face was fierce as he tried to wrestle his prize from her grip. The torture device was all that mattered to either of them. For those moments, it became their whole world. The fight became a tug of war, with neither party willing to give up. Each party matched their strength with their opponent's. The pair was well-matched. It was a battle that seemed to have no end. Riley wondered if it was possible for anyone to win. A fight like this could surely go on forever. Maybe there was a chance that they'd just tire themselves out. She suppressed a smile; the thought was almost laughable. She wanted her teammates to take naps like small children, rather than tearing each other apart.

Riley dragged Howard out of the way, not wanting him to suffer further injuries and wondered if she should try to intervene. If she did, what could she do? Both Rosa and George were better fighters than she was. She swallowed, not quite sure what to do. Decision making had never been Riley's strong point, she was the kind of person who struggled with what to have for lunch. She was fantastic at following orders and getting the job done but making a choice - no matter how trivial - was near enough impossible. Over the years, she had discovered something important; sometimes doing nothing was the best choice. It was the choice that she made at that moment.

Rosa kicked at George, not aiming for any part of him in particular but getting him square in the chest. The force pushed him away from her, but it wasn't enough to knock him to the ground. It did slow him down though. Taking full advantage of this, Rosa charged towards her adversary, screaming as her feet pounded against the floor. Every footstep echoed the sound of her heart pounding in her chest and the pulse in her ears. The scream was primal, a savage war cry from her Neanderthal brain. A declaration of bloodthirsty intent. Her brain knew that it was kill or be killed, and it did not want to lose. George met her scream with one of his own as he stepped up to interrupt her charge. They came together in a clash. Limbs flailed, punches connected, and skin bruised and tore. The fight went by in a blur, neither of them was really sure when the winner was decided, or how they had achieved it.

Rosa's primal brain was still in charge and it was only after she had fixed the Head Crusher to George's head that she realised that her fight was won. She was victorious. With sadness, she realised that she had only won the battle. She couldn't let George go. She couldn't let him live. He was a danger to all them. Rather than allowing herself any time to talk herself out of it, Rosa forced the metal plate underneath George's jaw and started to turn the screw. Using his hands, he tried to pull the device from his head, but the pressure from the screw was too much. He wanted to stand, but his legs wouldn't let him, his knees buckled and the pain in his skull prevented any rational thought. There were no thoughts in Rosa's head either, her mind was focused on the task at hand. Riley and Peter watched with equal parts fascination and disbelief.

The screw was meeting more resistance now and she had to use almost all her strength to continue turning it. George's screams became gurgled and there was an audible crack as his skull began to shatter. His face was now a mask of crimson. Both eyeballs popped from their sockets.

George stopped screaming. In fact, he stopped doing anything.

Rosa let go of the Head Crusher and both George and the device clattered to the floor. It was over. She looked at her hands, covered in blood and brain matter, and knew that it wouldn't matter how often or how thoroughly she washed them, they would never be clean.

'What... what have you done?' Riley said, her heart in her throat.

'She did what she had to do.' Peter said. 'Now, let's get out of here. I'd rather not be sat around this basement when Daniel returns.'

Rosa nodded, burying her feelings of remorse. She *had* done what she needed to do. It was a matter of life or death, of him or her. She was sure that George would have done exactly the same thing had the roles been reversed. Once more, she reached for the keys that would free Peter from his binds.

'Stop.' It wasn't a request, it was a demand. Rosa looked up from her task to see Riley standing over them, a cold steely look unlike any expression she had ever worn dressed her face. In addition to that unwavering look, she also held the bucket of molten silver that had been bubbling away all morning like a witch's cauldron. Rosa felt the heat radiating from it before she saw it.

'Riley...' It was barely a whisper. Rosa's mouth felt dry. Peter didn't need to turn his head to know that something bad was occurring behind him. 'What are you doing?'

'What needs to be done.'

'You can't...'

'I can, and I will. Step back, Rosa, there's no need for you to die as well.'

'Daniel will kill me.'

'Maybe, but I don't want to. Step aside. Please.'

Rosa got to her feet, looking Riley dead in the eye at all times. 'Put the bucket on the floor. Carefully.'

Riley didn't move. She didn't speak. Rosa took advantage of Riley's lack of action and moved closer to her, closing the distance between them. If she could just lower the bucket to the ground, then they should be alright.

In one swift movement, Riley elbowed Rosa away and began to pour the silver.

'SHIT!' Rosa yelled, realising that she had both misjudged her strategy and underestimated the other woman. She barrelled into Riley, knocking her out of the way. Screams and the smell of burning flesh filled the room. It was too late; Peter was covered in the silver. Skin began to melt from his face, dropping from his skull, no longer solid, but not quite liquid yet either. Rosa raced over to him, eager to undo his bonds and end the nightmare. If not for his sake, then for her own.

'Water.' He said, the word barely forming and his lips disintegrating before Rosa's eyes. Covering the distance between her current position and the sink at the far end of the basement, Rosa filled another bucket with water. Peter both sighed and sizzled as she chucked it over him. Relishing the feeling as it splashed over his body, Peter took a deep breath. Wasting no time, Rosa undid the binds and Peter got to his feet. His body shook, trying to morph itself, but failing. Between the silver and The Rot, Peter was all but done. His breath was ragged. His skin was either missing or had turned a greyish-blue colour. One eye had been transformed into goo. Peter looked down at his body, taking in what he could of his new appearance, watching it change right in front of his one good eye. The silver was speeding up whatever decomposition that The Rot had started. Would his flesh be reacting in this way if he wasn't already riddled with that disgusting affliction? Riley would pay for this. Everyone would pay for this. Even though the water had stopped the silver on the surface, the liquid that had made its way inside him was still going strong. Peter was going to die, and soon. He sure as hell wasn't going to go alone. He raised his arm and one almost skeletal finger sought out Riley.

'Ooogh!' he said, his voice a rasp. He didn't need lips to form the word properly to get his thoughts across. He could tell by the look on Riley's face that she knew he meant her. Her body visibly trembled in response. *Yes, you,* he thought as he strode towards her. Rosa stood, gaping, unable to speak and unable to move. Peter's new appearance really took your breath away. Peter grabbed Riley by the throat and lifted her as if she weighed as much as a rag doll.

Riley looked into the hideous face in front of her as she struggled for breath. It was like she was in a nightmare and a demon fresh from the sulphur-laden, fiery pits of hell had caught her. She tried to breathe. She tried to talk. Her fingers grasped at the hand around her throat, nails tearing through the damaged skin, pulling it from the bone like an abhorrent pulled pork. If her actions bothered Peter, or harmed him in any way, it didn't show. Making sure that he held eye contact for as long as he could, Peter tore off Riley's head. Her body slumped to the floor and Peter discarded the head by throwing it across the room. It came to rest next to George's corpse. Peter's revenge had begun.

Rosa thought about running. But, even in the state he was in, she had the feeling that Peter would have been able to catch up with her without too much effort. Instead, she stayed where she was, hoping that her actions up until this point were enough for Peter to let her keep her life. The *Om grutt* suddenly seemed unimportant.

Peter faced her head on and cocked his head like a confused zombified puppy. He looked from her to the prone form of Howard and back again. Grunting, he turned from them both and left the basement. Rosa had no idea if he had let them live because they'd each tried to help him, or if he simply didn't think they were worth the effort to kill. It didn't matter either way, Rosa was alive. And she would only stay that way if she got out of the basement - and the house - before Daniel returned. Grabbing Howard under the armpits, she dragged him towards the stairs. She couldn't let Daniel find him, she'd been responsible for enough death already that day.

CHAPTER THIRTY-EIGHT

'We should be the ones to do it.' Kit said. He'd been able to think of nothing but Daniel's offer since the man had left. 'It's the best option for us.'

'I don't disagree.' Erik said, pacing backwards and forwards across the flat's living room. 'It's just that I don't think I *can* do it.'

'Then let me.'

'No.' Erik said, quickly, almost snapping. 'You can't.'

'Why not? I wasn't close to Peter. It won't affect me like it will you.'

Collapsing into one of the armchairs, Erik sighed. 'But you don't know how to. I've told you, killing a werewolf isn't a simple process. Well, I suppose it is… but only if you know how… which you *don't*.'

'Then tell me,' Kit said. 'Let me help you.'

'I can't.'

'Yes, Erik... Yes, you can!' Now it was Kit's turn to pace. 'I'm going to find out how to do it sooner or later, so you may as well tell me about it now when I can actually use the knowledge to do some good.'

'No.'

'I promise I won't kill you.'

Erik laughed wryly. 'That's not what I'm worried about, Kit. Death doesn't scare me. If I'm honest, it's probably high time that I met my maker. The reason why I don't want you to have this knowledge is because I don't want to burden you with it.'

'That's bullshit.'

'No, it isn't.' Erik said. 'If you knew how to kill our kind, the Council would be setting to work at utilising your knowledge before Peter's blood had even dried. The only reason that they hadn't roped me into being one of their assassins, like Daniel was, is because officially they don't know that I know.'

'Then why ask us to kill Peter?'

'Daniel knows I have the knowledge; he gave it to me, after all. But, I assume that the rest of the Council are expecting to fill us in tonight and then recruit one or both of us. Or kill us if they don't recruit us. Either that, or they've known what I did all along and are just playing a little game with me. Quite frankly, either way is likely.'

Even with Kit's limited experience with werewolves, he could easily believe that they'd play a game like this. It was just the kind of sneaky and devious thing his new species would do.

'Would working for the Council be so bad?' he said, interested. 'Being an assassin sounds kinda cool.'

There was nothing about this that seemed to be a burden to Kit. Becoming an assassin did hold a certain appeal, especially when he considered that his first werewolf kill would be Peter. It felt poetic. Kit even went as far as to believe that it was meant to be. Other than that, how busy could an assassin employed by The Council be? There couldn't be that many werewolves requiring death sentences running around. Could there?

'Your life won't be your own.' Erik said, either unaware or ignoring the fact that Kit was now lost within the thoughts in his own head. Nothing Erik could say would sway him. His mind was made up and he'd never been surer of anything. This felt right. And, if his new job got a little too busy, he would just disappear and live off grid. It was all deceptively simple, and appealing. Sadistic werewolf mind games, or no sadistic werewolf mind games.

'Maybe we should just leave.' Erik was saying. 'Find Peter and go. That's a point, have you seen Peter today?'

Now that he thought about it, Kit realised that he hadn't. This was most unlike the other man, usually he would be throwing his weight around or firing obnoxious remarks at whoever had the misfortune of being in the vicinity.

'I haven't seen him all morning. Maybe the barman's seen him.' The word "barman" was said with a sneer, as if saying it caused Kit physical discomfort. Erik noted that kit was becoming more and more like Peter, even if the man would never want to admit it.

'Caspar.' Erik corrected him.

'What?'

'The barman's name is Caspar.'

'Why is that important?' Kit said, not really caring if there was a reasonable answer. A wolf shouldn't have to bother to learn the names of sheep. Especially when the wolf planned on dragging said sheep to the slaughter.

'We need to know the names of our friends.' Erik said. 'And, right now, we need all the friends that we can get.'

For a while, Kit refused to dignify that with a response. The man responsible for pulling him into this mess was never going to be his friend.

'Don't worry,' Erik noticed the look on Kit's face. Undisguised hatred covered it. 'I'll talk to him. You, pack a bag. We'll leave as soon as we can.'

Kit shook his head, slowly. 'Not a chance.'

'You want to talk to Caspar?'

'No.' Kit said. 'I'm not leaving. You can run and hide all you like. I'm going to stay here. I'm going to kill Peter and become an assassin.' There was a twitch in the back of his neck as he spoke and thought about the promise of violence. He'd almost forgotten about the worm. The worm was excited. Kit felt the same way.

'You have no idea what you're getting yourself into, Kit. Whatever you're imagining, it's wrong. No matter what you do, The Council will find some reason to punish you. Maybe they'll take offence because you've been living here with us. Or, maybe one of them will just take an instant disliking to you. You've only got to have a face that reminds one of "*The Six*" of someone they hate... or someone they loved too much... and you're done for. You could execute Peter and they could kill you straight afterwards. Come with us, Kit. We'll start afresh. All of us.'

It wasn't so long ago that Kit had wanted to end it all - Christine's murder had weighed heavily on his conscience, threatening to overwhelm him completely - but now the prospect of dying didn't seem as appealing. He was starting to feel comfortable in his new skin and wanted to be able to fully explore his new life. But, while he couldn't trust The Council, he wasn't about to ride off into the sunset with Erik and Peter. They may have started to build something of a rapport, but he still hadn't forgiven them for what they did - or for what they made him do. That first kill had been soul-destroying, but, oddly, the idea of more was exhilarating. What had he become?

To think, all this started because he'd had a crappy job interview. It had only been a few days ago, but it felt like it had happened years ago, and to someone else. That version of Kit was a complete stranger to him. He didn't even miss him. Then, for the first time, he wondered if anyone out there missed him. He never had got around to calling his Mum back. The last time he had spoken to her, she'd called him "Bernie" and practised some interview questions with him. It had all seemed so important at the time. Now that it was on his mind, it felt even more important. A lump started to form in his throat and he quickly turned away from Erik so that he couldn't see the tears forming in his eyes. At that moment, Kit truly understood what loneliness meant. Perhaps that was the curse of his kind. Not being murderous animals, not having to transform into hellish creatures, but being alone. Perhaps that was why Erik was clinging so desperately to this ill-matched, pathetic excuse of a family. It certainly explained why he had put up with Peter's behaviour for so long. It even went some way in explaining why both Erik and Peter tolerated the barman. To be so alone must be a terrible thing, especially when you have near enough an eternity to experience it.

'Kit?' Erik looked at the back of the younger man's head, trying to sense what he was thinking. All he wanted was to keep them together, to keep them safe. And, most importantly, to make sure that he wasn't alone. To be alone would be to face what he really was. It didn't occur to him that this was the exact thing Jack and Ida were attempting to do all those years ago.

'Yeah?'

'Everything alright?'

'Yeah.'

'So, what do you say? Will you come with us?'

Kit turned, semi-confident that his was a face of a strong man / werewolf and not that of a boy who missed his mother. There was nothing wrong with mourning the life he could never return to, and the people in it, but he couldn't let Erik know what was on his mind and tearing a hole in whatever remained of his soul. There was no doubt in Kit's mind that - even with the best intentions - Erik would take that vulnerability and shape it so that it fit in with his plans.

'Yes.' Kit said, the lie coming easy.

'Thank you, Kit. I promise you won't regret this.' Erik put his hands on Kit's shoulders and embraced him. Kit allowed him this moment of believing his little faux family was staying together, unable to decide if this false hope was a kindness or a punishment. And, he couldn't decide which answer he'd be happiest with. Kit pulled away, putting an end to the kindness / punishment.

'Okay, go find out where Peter is, and I'll pack.'

Erik nodded, smiled a little and left the flat. The sound of his highly polished shoes on the stairs echoed around Kit's brain along with a slight pang of guilt. He would be packing a bag - he had no intention of spending another night in the pub - but it wouldn't be to follow Erik. Kit had his own path to take.

***

Downstairs, the barman was putting the final touches to the pub before opening the doors, whistling as he worked. The tune pausing as he heard the sound of footsteps on the stairs.

'Caspar.' Erik said as he strode through the door. That had been the second time that he had spoken to him using his name. Caspar wasn't sure how to feel about that.

‘I’m sure you heard our exchange with Mr Griswold.’ Erik said, knowing that he had.

‘I did, yes. I don’t envy you at all.’ Caspar said, and it was true. He may have desired revenge, but he didn’t envy Erik this particular choice. ‘It’s a tough decision. I imagine you’re going to need some time to think it over.’

‘Not at all.’ Erik said, looking around the pub as if seeing it for the first time. Or the last. ‘I’ve already come to a decision. I’m picking neither of their options.’

‘What are you going to do?’

‘I’m running. We all are... and that includes you, dear boy, if you’d like. I was thinking about rewarding you for your unwavering loyalty as well. Were you still interested in being turned?’

‘Wait... What?’ Caspar had heard Erik’s words perfectly clearly, he just needed a moment to think it through. A week ago, he would have leapt at the chance, but now things had changed. Caspar was finally happy being human. He had friends and purpose. Throwing that away for a romantic, and probably naive, notion of becoming a werewolf was pure insanity.

‘The *Om grutt...*’

‘Yes... That’s very kind of you, thank you.’ He said. Erik had known that Caspar had wanted the *Om grutt* for years, a sudden change in heart would raise his suspicions, and they were too close now. ‘I’d like that very much.’

‘Then it’s settled.’ Erik said. ‘Pack your things and get ready to move out. We’ll be gone as soon as I’ve spoken to Peter. Have you seen him this morning?’

‘Umm... Yes.’ Caspar wondered how much he should say. ‘In the tunnels.’

‘Ah, yes, I should have checked there first.’ Erik started to head towards the “*Staff Only*” door. ‘Thank you, Caspar. Don't forget to pack. And don't bother to open up today, there's no point.'

'Right you are.' Caspar watched Erik leave and wondered if he should follow his employer's advice. Not to go with him, but to pack a bag. The events that were due to take place that evening, whether Erik ran or not, would change his life completely. It was unlikely that The Council would let him keep the pub. If Caspar was honest with himself, it was unlikely that The Council would let him keep his life. Packing a bag or two seemed like a very good idea.

***

The tunnels smelled like a person had exploded. The smell of just about every bodily function and the sharp pang of bleach hung around in an offensive bouquet. Erik paused at the bottom of the stairs, allowing himself a moment to get used to the stench, his sensitive sense of smell reeling. As a werewolf, Erik was used to the smell of death and destruction, but this was different. Whoever was down here reeked, and they were still clinging onto life. The air around him started to feel wrong. Everything began to feel wrong. Erik felt like he was off-balance. Something had happened down here, he just knew it. On legs that were unsteady, he followed the smell.

The source of the smell became apparent as soon as he entered the room. There, tied to one of the rickety old camping beds, was a man. He was completely still, but still hanging onto the tiniest bit of life. Erik could just about hear a faint heartbeat radiating from him. His hair and beard were matted; his clothes stained and ripped. Erik rightly assumed that this was a vagrant that Peter had picked up from the streets. Although why he had left him like this, he didn't know. Blood had dried on the man's face where it had dribbled down from his mouth. Erik lent in closer to take a better look. Shallow breath grazed his face, weak, ragged and sour. Every moment that passed saw more life drain out of the man.

'What was he doing with you?' Erik said, turning to look around the room. Various tools that Erik didn't recognise littered the floor. Parts of the floor were suspiciously clean, stranding out from the usual stains; someone had done a hasty clean-up job. A cupboard stood with its door wide open. Peering inside, Erik sniffed. Someone had been in there. A human. Possibly female. *Yes, definitely female*, he thought. Were they hiding or was Peter storing them in there? He hadn't mentioned anything, but Erik wasn't naive. He knew that his friend got up to all kinds of stuff behind his back. The murder of the family that kick-started this nightmare was proof enough of that. The feeling that something wasn't right crept over him again. Where was Peter? Where was the girl from the cupboard?

From his crouched position on the floor, Erik turned and looked up, seeing the door frame for the first time. It looked like it was scratched. Standing slowly, Erik walked towards it, studying it as he got closer. His eyes followed the scratch, noting as it snaked around the door frame and along the wall of the tunnel. Peter was reckless, but it seemed odd that he would intentionally damage his own property. And, there was no doubt about it, this was intentional. Someone else had been here. Closing his eyes, Erik sniffed the air. Someone else had been here.

Another werewolf.

Now that he had picked it up, the scent was unmistakable. It was familiar, and its familiarity made

Erik tense. His hands turned to fists and he battled with every impulse and muscle in his body not to change then and there. He knew who had been down here.

Daniel.

'He took him, didn't he?' Erik said to the unconscious man, crossing back into the room. The man didn't reply. Erik tried to listen to his heartbeat, but now it was almost too faint for even a werewolf to hear. Erik leant in closer, staring intently at the man's face for any sign of movement. 'What did you see?'

Silence hung in the air as Erik's question went unanswered. Erik sighed as the reality of what was happening settled in. Daniel had Peter, and Erik's plan had been flushed down the toilet. The thought of running without Peter crossed his mind. Could he do it? He had to admit that there was a certain appeal.

The dying man's eyes snapped open, alert and wide. Their gazes locked and, upon seeing Erik's yellow eyes, the man screamed. It was all too much. Whatever Erik was using to compose himself crumbled away and he began to change; skin, flesh and clothes tearing rapidly. His animal self took control faster than ever before and, once it did, there was no stopping it.

There was little left of the homeless man when it had finished.

***

'Kathryn?' Daniel always liked to have the first and last word in telephone conversations. Kathryn couldn't have had time to have put the phone to the next to her ear yet, so his greeting was premature.

'Hello?' Her voice seemed distant, her tone distracted. 'Who is this?'

'Check your display if you don't recognise my voice.'

There was a slight pause before she answered. Daniel pictured her pulling the phone away again to read the display. 'Oh, Daniel. Good morning.'

'Yes, it is a good morning, isn't it?' Daniel's irritation was instantly forgotten as he focused on his reason for calling. Shuffling in the backseat of the car, he made himself comfortable, the leather seat cushioning his buttocks.

'Yes...' Kathryn said. 'Are you calling for any particular reason? As you know, we've a lot to prepare for tonight.'

'I know, I'm calling about that.'

'Spit it out, Daniel.'

'Fine... I have Peter. There's no chance of him running away now.' Daniel grinned, unable to contain it. 'No matter what, Peter will be dead before tomorrow. I told you it was a good morning, didn't I?'

'You did.' Kathryn said. 'Good work. Just make sure that you don't lose him before tonight. Remember how easily Peter and Erik ran away from you last time?'

'Why do you always have to bring that up?'

'Oh, don't be so sensitive.' Kathryn said. Daniel could feel her mocking him down the phone. 'Just make sure that he's ready for this evening.'

'Don't worry about it. He'll be there.'

CHAPTER THIRTY-NINE

The conversation with Kathryn festered in his mind as the car pulled through the gate and onto the driveway. He hated how the other members of "*The Six*" always mentioned his failures at any opportunity. Failures were not a common occurrence for Daniel, but the ones he had experienced tended to follow him around, leaping from the lips of his peers more often than he would like. Granted, he also did the same to them, but that wasn't the point. The sound of gravel under the car's tires reminded him that he was home and the car came to a stop.

'We're back.' The driver said. Daniel tried to remember his name. Was it Howard? Did it matter? Names were unimportant, and he hadn't put in any effort to learn the names of his employees since Baxter.

'Thanks for pointing out the obvious, Howard.'

'I'm Charlie,' the driver said, correcting his boss before he realised what he was doing. 'Howard is the tall, dark haired guy guarding the prisoner downstairs.'

'I don't care.' Daniel said, getting out of the car and making his way to the front door. Other members of the entourage scurried behind him, racing to get to the front door before Daniel did, so that they could open it for him. Their boss was in a bad mood and they didn't need it to get any worse. Nicole, the member of the team known for her speed, made it to the door first, opening it without flourish. Daniel barrelled through it, almost walking through before Nicole had opened it fully. His footsteps echoed around the house as he stomped through it. Framed photos rattled on the walls and ornaments shook on their shelves. Usually when Daniel was like this, his servants would rush to his aid, but no-one came. Even the team he had returned with kept their distance, self-preservation rating highly in their decision-making process. Daniel was too consumed with his bad mood to notice the lack of attention. Instead, he made his way to his office, looking forward to spending some time alone. The door almost flew off its hinges as he slammed it open. He slammed it shut with just as much force. Finally, he was alone.

Taking a deep breath, he surveyed his domain. A familiar stench reached his nostrils; he wasn't alone. Peter was here. Now that he was aware of the trespasser, he noticed that the high-backed leather chair was facing away from the desk and that someone was very obviously sitting in it.

'Peter.' he said, letting his former prisoner know that he was aware of his presence. He knew exactly who he was sharing the room with. The question was how the hell had he escaped?

The chair turned slowly, creaking as it moved to reveal its occupant, and Daniel was faced with the monstrosity that Peter had become. Skin and flesh had been pulled away, revealing bone, muscle and skull beneath. One eye was completely missing, the remnants of it congealed to whatever was left of his cheek. The skin that was left was turning blue. In spite of the many horrific things that Daniel had witnessed, including the many things that he had been responsible for, Daniel gasped. Taking in the sight, he realised that someone had poured molten silver over him. A lot of it. The silver Daniel had intended to use on Erik later that night, after the festivities. In all his years, he'd never seen someone - man or beast - that had survived being doused in that much silver. Even in this grotesque state, Peter was quite remarkable.

'Ugh.' Peter said, motioning towards a pen and a notepad on the other side of the desk. Daniel slid it over to him, careful not to touch the ruined man directly. It wasn't like he could catch the deterioration caused by the silver, but Peter now repulsed him. Not only that, but there were rumours that the man was infested by The Rot and, although Daniel was fairly sure it couldn't be transmitted by touching an open wound, he didn't want to risk it. And Peter was just one big, festering open wound now. In front of him, the festering wound scribbled furiously. Daniel read the words that were presented to him. The handwriting was in capitals, messy and desperate.

WHAT'S THE MATTER? I THOUGHT THIS IS WHAT YOU WANTED.

Shadows crept at the corner of Daniel's vision as he took in the words. At first, he dismissed them, but they were persistent. Invisible fingers caressed the back of his neck, terrifying the worm that had inhabited his body for centuries. It shook with fear and burrowed deeper into its host. He bit back a scream, aware that Peter was still in front of him; one eye studying him intently. Recognition dawned on him. Daniel knew these shadows. They had spoken to him when he was a child. They had guided him through his *Om grutt*. But now, they seemed different. Gone was the advice and curiosity. Hostility had been left in their place.

'The reality is rather more intense than I imagined.' Daniel said. 'It's amazing that you're still alive.'

Peter nodded at this and then averted his gaze to something behind Daniel. At first, Daniel just thought that he was looking off into space, contemplating his mortality or maybe he had seen the shadows circling him like greedy vultures. Were they after both of them? But then he noticed it. A small, almost imperceptible nod. Someone else was in the room. He hadn't noticed their scent over Peter's stench. Daniel turned in time to hear his office door being locked. The person responsible stood in front of him. Rosa. Unlike many of his servants, he knew her name. He had seen the same qualities in her that he had seen in Peter. Independence, an interest in the macabre and a lust for blood. His plan had been to eventually turn her and work together with her. She was to be his legacy. And it helped that he had a bit of a crush on her. Daniel may have been old, but he still had needs.

'Rosa, how could you?'

'I look after number one, Daniel.' She said as Daniel felt a hand on his shoulder. Peter had used his disbelief to get closer to him. Daniel had completely underestimated his opponent and the situation. His eyes worked their way to the fingers grasping him and creasing his shirt. They didn't look human and nor did they look werewolf. They looked dead. Peter should have been dead. But he very clearly wasn't. Daniel turned to face his main opponent, knowing that he still needed to find a way to keep an eye on Rosa as well. She was dangerous, it was why he liked her. Taking in the sight in front of him, he noticed that in Peter's other hand, he gripped one of the knives from his trunk. The knife was old, one of Daniel's favourites that he'd used many times over the years. The thought that it would be used against him bothered him more than Rosa's betrayal.

Peter nodded again, not bothering to disguise it this time. 'Ugh.'

Hands gripped him, Rosa's hands. They ran down his arms and forced his hands behind him. Silver cuffs were clipped on and Daniel was lead toward his leather chair. He sat without any further encouragement.

'I'm not getting out of here alive, am I?'

'No.' Rosa replied. Peter said nothing.

At the surprise of both Peter and Rosa, Daniel smiled. 'I chose well.'

'What are you talking about?' Rosa asked.

'I must applaud my superb judge of character.' Daniel said, his vision tunnelling. The shadows were preparing to claim their prize. 'At some stage, I'd wanted each of you to be my protege. I thought you'd be perfect killers. Perfect werewolves. And perfect torturers. It looks like I was right.'

'You were going to make me into a werewolf?' Rosa said, reaching into Daniel's jacket pocket for the vial that she knew would be there. This would complete the job that the silver would start.

'Yes.'

'Then why didn't you?'

'You weren't ready yet, Rosa. It wouldn't have been long though.'

If Peter was concerned about Rosa switching sides again, he didn't show it. He almost felt like he could take on *all* of them. Almost. He still recoiled when the shadows got near; he knew that he couldn't take on those critters. There was no doubt that they were going to take him eventually; he'd heard them chanting *'Om krell'*. *Om grutt* was the beginning, *Om krell* was the end. But, *Om krell* could wait. In his current mental state, he knew that he could take on both of them. Nothing would prevent him from achieving his revenge.

'It's too late now.' Rosa said, as Peter moved closer to Daniel. Daniel looked around, wondering if there was a way out. This wasn't how this was supposed to go. His survival of this day was supposed to be guaranteed. He had never even questioned the possibility that he wasn't safe. He could scream. Perhaps that would encourage the remaining members of his team to come to his aid, but he couldn't be sure that they'd remain on his side. Nor did he want his final moments on this earth to be full of the sounds of him screaming and begging for his life. Even in this most desperate of times, Daniel was still a proud man. His eyes stopped looking for ways to escape and instead focused on the shadows that moved ever closer, circling him like a pack of wolves. Those shadows were always there, lurking in the darkness, but most of the time Daniel - and most other werewolves - didn't pay them any attention. The only time they really came into focus was during the *Om grutt* and at death, or - in Daniel's exceptional case - childhood. None of Daniel's blood had been spilled, but they must have sensed his impending demise. Their presence chilled him, both figuratively and physically. Cold pervaded his body, his heart feeling like it might freeze. The shadows were hungry, their icy grip ready to snatch away his soul.

\+ *Om krell* + they chanted.

'Ugh.' Peter grunted, and Daniel sensed movement behind him. Rosa poured the contents of the vial into the bucket. The heat from the molten silver battled with the icy chill inside him even before Rosa had started to pour. The silver cascaded over his shoulders, eating its way through his torso and his thighs. Rosa had left his head untouched and, if pain hadn't been ravaging him at the time, Daniel may have asked why. A scream tried to escape from Daniel's mouth, but he suppressed it with the same amount of will that the silver suppressed his change. Pride was the only thing he had left to him. Peter's form filled his vision. And so did the knife.

Peter's remaining eye bore into Daniel's as if trying to communicate with him. Daniel couldn't get the specifics, but he knew that whatever came next would hurt, perhaps even more than the silver. Peter pressed the knife into Daniel's temple and started to slice. Pride slipped from Daniel's white-knuckled grip and he screamed. His howls reverberated around the office and were answered with the sound of his servants shaking the office door, unable to enter. At least one of them could be heard slamming into the door with their body. It wouldn't be long until they breached, but it was still more time than what Daniel had. His face felt raw, like it was being consumed by fire. There was a wet noise, but Daniel had long since closed his eyes, refusing to watch the events play out in front of him. He heard Peter grunt again, signalling Rosa. It wouldn't be long now. Seconds later, the silver coated his skull. The heat was unimaginable and when the cold reaper's grip finally came, Daniel embraced it.

The embrace only lasted a split second.

Daniel may have thought that he was prepared for death, but he was not prepared for what the shadows had in store for him. Icy tendrils wormed their way through him. Through what was left of his skin. Through his ruined flesh. Through his bones. Through his brain. They played with his thoughts and desecrated his memories. Even a man like Daniel had times to cherish, but the shadows took them and warped them, changing them into something twisted and perverted. They took their time, delighting in any pain and discomfort that they could cause. Reminding him of his sins. Forcing him to watch. Forcing him to watch his childhood. A human childhood.

Daniel tried to scream.

But he had no lips. He had no face. He had no body.

And, soon enough, he would have no soul. It was then that Daniel realised the true cost of becoming a werewolf. It was then that he really paid the price.

***

Many years ago

Albert Griswold hadn't put up much of a fight, cowering behind some trees like a terrified bunny rabbit. Disappointingly, he had even given up on running quite quickly. Instead, he'd pleaded and begged for his life. Snivelling and sniffing, and kissing Daniel's feet. But, Daniel's feet didn't need kissing. All Daniel wanted was to show his parents that he wasn't going to let them disown him.

He belonged here. With them.

If he couldn't have that, then neither could they.

'We're not gettin' rid of ya, boy. I promise.' his father had said. The words were of little consequence and Daniel had found himself focusing on the line of snot that was hanging from Albert's nostril. A familiar scent of urine hung in the air between them. Albert was a coward.

Daniel didn't like cowards.

The knife was biting its way through Albert's skin before either of them had the chance to realise what was happening. In flaying the skin of his still screaming father, Daniel found an odd sense of peace.

Eventually, Albert stopped screaming. He stopped doing much of anything. Silence wasn't able to retain its hold for long as soon Albert's screams were replaced with someone else's. Daniel's mother had found them.

'WHAT HAVE YOU DONE?' her voice was shrill, the sharpness of it making Daniel wince. 'You really are a monster… I didn't want to believe it… you're a demon.'

Daniel didn't move. No words came from his mouth. No shame reddened the skin of his cheeks.

Emerald looked at her son and took in the full extent of his crimes. Albert was gone. And her son was wearing his skin like a cape.

'I wanted to save you.' She said, her voice quieter now. So quiet that Daniel had to move in closer to hear her properly. 'I wanted to keep you here, but it wasn't to be. The others would kill ya.'

Again, Daniel said nothing.

'You're my son.' she said. 'I love you. I wanted you to live. The only way we could make that happen is if we sent you away.'

Daniel's face was blank, devoid of any comprehension. The sacrifice that his parents were willing to make was meaningless to the boy; it was beyond his understanding. Adult Daniel - dying Daniel - the one being forced to watch this - understood it. He finally understood it. Emerald and Albert had just been trying to do the right thing. His first murders, the first human blood on his hands, was a result of a misunderstanding. If Daniel could have, he would have wept.

***

Present day.

Charlie crashed through the door pausing just in front of the desk to hold his shoulder. The movies never showed you how much that actually hurt, and he was pretty sure that he had done some lasting damage to himself. Taking no notice of his injury, Nicole barged past him, eager to be the first one to reach Daniel.

But something stopped her in her tracks. Nicole stopped and stared. They all did. Charlie even stopped rubbing his shoulder. Each of them tried to make sense of the scene in front of them. On the other side of the desk stood a man - a man who was missing much of his skin - wearing a mask. The mask made him look like a waxwork of their boss, a waxwork that had started to melt. Gradually the team's eyes went from the man to the figure slumped in the chair. The figure in the chair lacked a face. In fact, it lacked much of anything. Soon enough, the pieces of the puzzle fell into the place. The man before them wasn't wearing a mask, he was wearing Daniel's face.

Collectively, the team screamed. The screams were stopped short as the man started to walk towards them. Daniel's remaining minions parted to allow him to pass. Rosa followed in his wake.

CHAPTER FORTY

The backpack was full, its contents straining against the seams. Caspar didn't have many belongings that he wanted to take with him into his new life, but he had more than enough to almost break the zipper on his bag. Over the years in the employ of Erik and Peter, he'd acquired numerous nick-knacks and a small library of books, but none of those items reflected who he was now. Those were the possessions of a man aiming to become a werewolf. Caspar was now a man hoping to become more human.

RING RING

Caspar jumped as the phone rang. Dropping the bag on the bar, he made his way behind it and grabbed at the phone.

'Hound and the Philosopher Inn?' he said, aware that it was likely going to be the last time he answered the phone in that way.

'Get Erik.' The voice on the other end was abrupt and clearly didn't want to waste its time or breath in talking to the likes of Caspar. From that, Caspar deduced that a werewolf was on the other end. Probably one of "*The Six*". And probably calling about this evening's events.

'As you wish.' Caspar wondered if the voice would notice his sarcasm oozing along the phone line towards her. Probably not. Covering the mouthpiece of the phone, Caspar turned towards the closed "*Staff Only*" door and shouted. 'ERIK! PHONE!'

The minute that passed while Erik made his way back up to the pub felt like it took an hour and Caspar was very aware of the presence waiting on the other end of the line. He thought about making small talk with her but decided that she wouldn't take too kindly to it. Eventually, Erik appeared, wearing spare clothes from the tunnel, meaning that he had changed unexpectedly. The usually calm and collected looking man appeared flustered and more than a bit panicked. He raced towards the phone, took a breath and moved the phone towards his head. Nodding his thanks to Caspar, he turned his attention to the voice awaiting him.

'Hello?' Erik's voice felt thick in his mouth.

'Hello Erik.' Kathryn's voice met his ears. 'I'm sure by now that you've realised that we have Peter.'

Erik nodded and then remembered that he had to speak. 'Yes.'

'I'm calling to give you the location for tonight's activities.'

'Go on.'

'There's an industrial estate on East Brady Hill.' Kathryn said. 'We'll be in one of the warehouses there. It used to belong to a toy company, so look out for the one with sign for Croft's Toys. Do you know where that is?'

'Yes.'

'Fantastic.' Erik could picture Kathryn's lipstick framed smile. 'Be there at 10pm. Don't be late.'

'Underst-' Erik started to speak, but Kathryn had hung up before he had the chance to finish.

'Bad news?' Caspar asked from his spot at the end of the bar. He'd busied himself with his backpack while trying to listen in.

'Yes. I'm afraid that we need to make a few alterations to our plan.'

'Oh yeah?'

'Yes, we need to rescue Peter.'

Caspar hoped that his look of shock was convincing. 'They've kidnapped him? I hadn't seen him all day, but I never would have imagined...'

'It's typical Daniel. I've been down to the tunnels and he was here earlier. Peter was already gone before Daniel spoke to us this morning. He gave us that choice, but he knew that no matter what happened, Peter would die. He was just toying with us.'

'How can we get to Peter?'

'He'll be at the East Brady Hill industrial estate tonight. We'll have to play along with them and then grab Peter as soon as we can.'

'Just let me know what you need me to do.' Caspar said. He was wondering how he was going to get to the event, but this was giving him a front row seat.

***

Reading through the text for probably the thirtieth time, Shannon started to come to terms with how *real* everything felt. Everything felt very real now. They had a time and a place. Peter's death was a certainty. All they had to do was make sure that Kit and Erik met their end as well.

Then it hit her. People were going to die tonight. And she was going to watch it happen, and it was likely that she was going to be directly responsible for at least one of the deaths. Once again, Shannon questioned whether she was up to it. The plan ran through her head for about the millionth time that day. They were going to the warehouse, they had to wait for an opportunity to steal a gun and then they had to shoot a werewolf - or many werewolves - with the special bullets that Caspar had made. It was a ridiculous plan. The fact that it relied heavily on liberating a gun from a werewolf was more than a little concerning. A knock on the door disturbed her thoughts.

Approaching the door like it was a wild animal, Shannon felt fear rising in her gut. Her hand rested on the door and she was somewhat surprised an electrical charge didn't course through her. Peering through the spy hole, Shannon confirmed that there was no-one there. She opened the door and looked around. There was no sign at all that anyone had even been there recently.

No sign, except the small cardboard box by her feet. Shannon picked it up carefully, like she was handling a bomb, and read the note that had been neatly written onto the box.

This is for tonight. Do what you have to do.
Willow.

Caspar had told her that they were working with a werewolf called Willow and Shannon hadn't been sure how comfortable she was with that. In her mind, all werewolves needed to be destroyed. She opened the box. Inside sat an antique gun and a small collection of bullets. At least she didn't have to worry about stealing a gun from a werewolf anymore, one had just given her one. Everything was falling into place.

There was no doubt in her mind now, she had to see this through. She owed it to Christine.

CHAPTER FORTY-ONE

'You should run, Jake.' Willow said to the dog at her feet. 'I don't think I'll be coming back from this. I wanted to find a home for you before this happened, but I ran out of time.'

The dog whimpered, seeming to understand his mistress' words. Jake didn't want to run, he wanted to stay with Willow. He was determined to protect her. They both looked down the hill at the industrial estate below. A cluster of run down warehouses, porta-cabins and vehicles littered the area. It looked so mundane. Ridiculously so, when Willow thought about what was about to happen down there. Within half an hour, it would be chaos, something akin to hell on earth. With or without the input of Willow and her new gang.

Death was coming.

Willow could feel its chill seeping into her bones, even on this hot summer's night. *It won't be long*, her thoughts were directed to the chanting shadows in the corners of her vision. They seemed to be sated by that thought, backing off a bit, giving her some space. Willow hadn't been strictly truthful with Jake a few moments ago. She didn't *think* that she wouldn't be coming back from this, she *knew*. The speed that The Rot was claiming her was increasing. Her head continuously ached. Her moods switched within moments. She felt broken. The *Om krell* was well underway.

No, it wouldn't be long now and, if she was going, she may as well go out with a blazc of glory. She turned to look out in the other direction, at the town beyond. Out there, normal people were getting on with their normal lives. Maybe they were planning to spend the evening having drinks with friends. Maybe they were having barbecues and beers in the last of the warm night air. One thing was for sure, most of them had no idea what was going on a few miles away; they weren't being harassed by shadows. But, for all its normality, the town didn't look peaceful. The sea of lights made it look like it was on fire. Willow thought that she would be quite happy to watch it burn.

***

The gun felt heavy in her hands. Shannon wasn't sure if it made her feel safe or if it put her in more danger. But, then, considering she was going to be spending the night hunting werewolves, she couldn't get into much more of a dangerous position. Not for the first time, Shannon questioned her sanity. What was she doing here?

She pushed the thought from her mind and paid closer attention to her surroundings. She was early, but she couldn't count on the werewolves not getting there early as well. Shannon needed to keep her wits about her.

Each of the warehouses wore a different sign. Some looked better maintained than others. It didn't take her long to find the one that she'd been looking for. Croft's Toys stood in front of her and Shannon gripped the gun even tighter. She should have tested it before she'd got here, but she had nowhere to test it and her neighbours probably would have called the police. Gunfire wasn't a common sound in her street. Shannon would have to take it on faith that Willow had supplied her with a gun that worked. It was almost more faith than Shannon had. After all, Shannon had never met Willow, and she was a werewolf. The enemy. Staring at the gun, she came to a decision; it did make her feel worse. But, she had to go with it now. Unless, of course, she could over-power one of those assassin werewolves that worked for The Council. How hard could that be?

After checking that she was alone, Shannon opened the door to the warehouse. It groaned a bit, demonstrating its lack of use and maintenance. Echoes surrounded her as she entered. The silence and darkness crowded her, but she pushed through. She needed to find a safe place.

BEEP BEEP

Her Casio watch's alarm made her heart leap into her throat. It reminded her that she only had fifteen minutes until showtime. The sound also served to remind her to turn off all alarms on her watch and to make sure that her phone was on silent. Shaking her head, she realised how close that was. What if she hadn't remembered and a text had come through while the werewolves were here? All this would have been for nothing. She couldn't believe that she'd been so careless.

After spotting a ladder that lead to a walkway above the main floor, Shannon knew where she would be hiding. Climbing the ladder quickly, but carefully, she reached the top in a matter of seconds. She checked her watch. There was still time. Using that time to her best advantage, she started to pull the ladder up behind her. There was no point in advertising her position. Clanging noises filled the warehouse as metal banged and scraped against metal, and Shannon closed her eyes and hoped that no-one else was in the vicinity just yet.

Shannon waited and, soon enough, the first batch of people entered. They were almost five minutes early. Shannon realised just how fine she'd cut it. Had they heard her moving the ladder?

Down below, around a dozen people milled around, checking for intruders and getting themselves ready. Shannon had no idea who was werewolf and who was human. But, there was one person she recognised almost immediately. DCI Severson. No wonder she'd be dragging her heels with Christine's case, she was in on it. The werewolf bitch.

***

Caspar slung his backpack over one shoulder and groaned at the weight of it. Deciding that there was no way that he was going to be able to carry it around like that all night, he switched it so that he was carrying the weight on both shoulders. Something dug him in the back. *Wonderful*, he thought, but there was no time to unpack and repack now. Kit and Erik were already walking out the front door. Erik paused and turned back.

'Are you still coming, Caspar?' he asked.

'Yep, just had to adjust my bag.'

‘No second thoughts?’ Erik said. ‘Now’s the time to say if you’ve changed your mind.’

‘No, it’s fine.’ Caspar said. ‘My mind’s made up. It’s just weird to be saying goodbye to this place.’

Both Caspar and Erik took a moment to look around the pub where they’d spent the last decade or so of their lives, each one reliving different memories, both good and bad. The pub, meanwhile, remained the same as always, not reacting in any way to the pair’s sentimentality. Rooms and buildings full of inanimate objects were a bit like that.

‘Erik.’ Caspar said, interrupting the other man’s reverie and shattering the silence.

‘Yes?’

‘Did you ever think about running? There’s a good chance that no matter what we do, Peter will die tonight. You could have just run, stayed alive and spared yourself some pain.’

‘I won’t lie, the thought had crossed my mind. Walking out that door and picking a direction at random does hold a certain appeal. But... it’s Peter. I couldn’t just leave him.’

‘But, why not?’ Caspar said, making his way to the door. ‘Would he do the same for you?’

A few moments passed, and Erik chewed on his lip as he considered his answer. ‘Probably not. But, that’s really not the point. Our actions should be our own, we shouldn’t let them be dictated by the actions of others. Especially when those actions are hypothetical. You never know, if our roles were reversed, Peter may come to my aid, even at the risk of sacrificing himself. He appears selfish and narcissistic but has surprised me more than a few times over the years.’

Caspar paused with his hand on the door handle, the level of his betrayal sinking in. Were his actions his own? Would Erik have saved him had he been captured by Daniel? Now that he thought about it, he probably would have.

'It's all about loyalty and integrity.' Erik was saying, joining him at the door. 'These things are important to me. They matter. What am I without them? I may as well remain a beast full time. Does that make sense?'

'Absolutely.' Caspar said, opening the door and entering the night beyond. For a moment, he questioned his plans, but it was all too late now. The wheels had already been set in motion.

***

The night felt electric, charged with an energy that Kit had never experienced before. It was like the whole world knew that something was about to happen. Impatience seized him while he waited for Erik and the barman. It felt like they were testing him. What could be so important that they had to discuss it now? Kit considered the options. They could be planning to put a stop to his plans, but, then, as far as Erik was aware, they were all on the same team. Then it dawned on him. Erik was likely offering to turn the barman and expand his little family. That wretch of a barman would probably agree and fall over himself at the prospect of becoming a werewolf. The fool. Still, at least Erik wouldn't be alone. Kit found that he didn't despise Erik quite as much as he thought he did. If the man escaped the night with his life, Kit wouldn't begrudge him a friend to take along for the ride. Just as long as Peter was gone. That's all Kit wanted.

Checking his watch for the third time since being outside told him that they were running out of time. *Tick. Tock. Tick. Tock.* Whether they were planning to rescue Peter or go along with "*The Six*"*'s* plan and execute him, they couldn't afford to be late. Just as he was about to call out for Erik, the barman emerged from the pub and Erik followed behind him. Kit watched as they locked the doors, noting that the barman looked sad to be leaving. Kit could understand it; The Hound and The Philosopher Inn had been his life. Perhaps he would have felt sorry for him if he didn't hate him so much. If there was one man who deserved the misery of becoming a werewolf it was the barman. Good ol' Caspar Lawson.

Darkness camouflaged the shadows, disguising their silent march. It wasn't the time to chant yet, but that time would come soon. They could feel it; it weighed heavily in the warm, night air.

CHAPTER FORTY-TWO

Feeling more than a little out of his depth, Kit followed Erik into the warehouse. Old toys still littered the floor in places, but other than that it was largely empty. Up until entering, Kit had been sure of himself. He'd had some idea of what he needed to do, but as soon as they'd crossed that threshold, doubt had started to set in. Would he be able to kill in cold blood? Kit the Wolf could tear someone limb from limb in the matter of minutes, but would Kit the Man be able to do the same? Despite the warm summer night, Kit shivered.

As they entered, they were ushered further into the warehouse by people that Kit had never seen before. Their eyes lacked the orange colour of werewolves, but they moved with efficiency and discipline. Were minions of this calibre a Council / "*The Six*" thing, or could any werewolf put together an army of assassins? If it was the latter, why had Erik and Peter settled on the barman? There was no way around it, they were massively outgunned. It was fortuitous that Kit planned to do exactly what the Council wanted them to do when it came to Peter.

'So, you made it. I thought you'd run.' one of the werewolves said, unable to hide her contempt for Erik.

'As you can see, we didn't.' Erik turned to Kit, who had somehow found himself in the centre of the warehouse, surrounded by stern looking werewolves and their minions. He counted three werewolves in total, aside from himself and Erik. There was no sign of Daniel or Peter. 'Kit, please allow me the pleasure of introducing you to Madison Severson, one of "*The Six*". Madison, this is Kit.'

'Hello.' Kit managed to say.

'It's a pleasure to meet you, Kit.' Madison said. She meant it too, she was looking forward to getting the events started. 'Four members of "*The Six*" will be in attendance tonight. There's Daniel, who you've already met. He'll be along soon, and he'll be bringing our guest of honour. This is Kathryn Hartmann.'

The woman to Madison's left nodded in greeting. Kit nodded back. The woman looked conflicted and Kit wondered how well she knew Peter and Erik. Madison took a few paces to the remaining werewolf who was standing closest to the door. 'And this is Joseph Newton. I know you're new, but I'm sure you'll treat them with respect deserving of their rank.'

'Yes.' Kit found that he could only respond in single words; sentences were currently beyond him.

'We're just waiting for Daniel to arrive. I hope you're ready.' Joseph said. 'I understand that Daniel left you with a choice earlier today. Am I to understand that you've come to a decision?'

The question was met with silence; Erik stared at the floor and Kit nodded.

'And what did you decide?' If Joseph was frustrated with this response, he didn't show it. If anything, he seemed to be enjoying himself. It was a game of cat and mouse and he was the mouse.

'I'll do it.' Kit managed to say.

'I knew I liked this new one.' Madison said. 'Now we just need Daniel and Peter to arrive. Has anyone heard from them? It's not like Daniel to be late. Especially not to something as important as this.'

'Goddammit, Daniel.' Kathryn said under her breath as she moved her mobile phone to her ear. Thc phone rang once. Then twice. Then three times. Each ring brought a new sense of alarm to Kathryn. Something wasn't right. Darkness tugged at the edges of her vision.

'Well?' Madison said, watching Kathryn's face as if trying to read it. 'Where is he?'

'There's no answer.'

'Maybe there's traffic.' Joseph said.

'Traffic?' Madison said, almost spitting the word out. 'Traffic? On the way to an industrial state that's barely used? At ten o'clock at night?'

'I'm just trying to help, Madison. Calm down.'

'I'll calm down when you stop being an idiot.' Madison said and then busied herself with getting a gun from the holster she wore on her left leg. Unable to look away, Kit stared intently at the cold metal in the woman's grip. Kit felt himself freeze as Madison looked up, her eyes locking with his.

'Is that it?' He said, his voice barely more than a whisper.

'If you mean is this the gun that's going to kill Peter, then yes, it is.'

***

Taking aim with her own gun, Shannon eavesdropped on the conversation below. Having never fired a gun before, she had no idea if she was doing it right. Shannon had never been so under-prepared for anything in her life. *What the fuck am I doing?*

The group below looked agitated. Something wasn't going to plan. Did this mean that their plan would fall apart at the seams as well? Shifting slightly, Shannon positioned herself so that she could see Caspar. Her new friend looked scared, his body was stiff, frozen to the spot. He hadn't even taken the time to look around his surroundings. Perhaps he thought that any movement would betray the fact that she was here. Whatever the reason, he was scared. The man looked pale, nervous and like he wanted the ground to open and swallow him. This was something that Shannon could relate to, but she hoped that he would still be able to act when the time came. They couldn't rely on her gun alone, and Caspar didn't even know that she had that.

Forcing all other thoughts from her mind, she returned to aiming the gun at Kit, hoping that - when the time came - she'd be able to pull the trigger. She also hoped that she'd know when that time was. It didn't look like Caspar was going to be capable of making any kind of signal. Just as a new set of nerves threatened to overcome her, two figures appeared in the doorway. The smaller one wasted no time in making sure that the doors were firmly closed behind them.

***

'You made i-' The words caught in Madison's throat. In front of her stood a man who had more in common with a decomposed corpse than any living thing. The decomposed corpse was also wearing Daniel's face.

Disbelief seized Erik. Various scenarios for how this night was going to go had played out in his head, but none had looked like this. This was beyond the realms of reality. 'Peter?'

Something wet and gloopy fell from the monster's face as it nodded. The Daniel-mask was starting to tear. Hope drained from Erik as he realised that Caspar had been right; Peter wasn't going to walk away from this. It was a miracle that he was still walking now. Bloodied blades stood ready in each of Peter's hands.

'What have they done to you?'

'Silver.' Peter's companion said before nodding in the direction of the other werewolves. 'And now he's here to pay them back.'

With that, Peter pounced onto Madison, knocking the gun out of her grip. Sharply dressed minions and werewolves alike sped after it as it skimmed the warehouse's floor. Eventually, it came to rest next to Kit's boot. Fate was calling him.

Voices surrounded him, and Peter felt like he could hear the internal monologue of everyone in the warehouse. Some wanted to kill him, and some wanted to run. But they all shared the same fear. Some of these people were werewolves and, yet, Peter was the scariest thing in the room. If he had possessed lips, he would have smiled. Picking out the human voices from the werewolves wasn't difficult, but it didn't matter; it was unlikely that anyone would walk away from this. Especially since he now knew that Kit intended to kill him, and Erik had brought him here. As far as Peter was concerned, the one person - human or werewolf - who was going to walk out of here alive was Rosa. *I wish I'd met her sooner*, he thought as he watched her taking on the minions single-handedly. They were dropping like flies.

Tracking Kit's movements with her gun, Shannon tried to get a clear shot. It wasn't that she didn't want to risk hitting anyone else, except for Caspar, but she didn't want to waste her ammo. Six wolfsbane covered silver bullets were at her disposal; she had to make each one count.

In amidst the panic, Peter could pick up individual thoughts and associated sounds. He heard Joseph running towards the door before anyone noticed and he threw himself at him. The member of "*The Six*" didn't seem so important and powerful lying face down in the dirt and dust.

'Please...' Joseph said as snot and tears pooled into the dirt. Peter could feel the man's muscles squirming against his skin. The change was upon him. 'Let me go...'

Not a chance, thought Peter. Blades tore into Jacob's back, slicing his clothes and flesh with ease. Allowing himself a moment to savour this victory, Peter dropped one of the knives and rummaged around in Joseph's fresh carcass. Bone was destroyed and blood covered Peter, but his arm quickly came free with its prize. Peter held up Jacob's heart for all to see. Shadows drew in close, infecting the corpse almost immediately. Peter could see them clearly all the time now.

Peter may have been deformed so much that he could no longer speak, but Kathryn could read his intentions loud and clear. No good would be had sticking around. As she had been the one to choose the venue for this outing, she knew every inch of it. Including where the back door was. Using the confusion to her advantage, she changed into her wolf form. Clothes tore, and skin ripped. In her panic, she nearly choked on her own tongue. Blood splattered anyone and everything around her. That change was unusually painful. It was like her body wasn't working properly. *The Rot*, she thought. *I've got The Rot*. Her days were numbered no matter what she did, but she still didn't fancy dying in this warehouse. Running like she was being chased by the Devil himself, Kathryn made her escape. Looking back, she would always be grateful to Erik for his distraction.

'Peter!' Erik called, shock wearing off and survival instinct kicking in. 'Stop! We have to get out of here!'

Erik wasn't deluded enough to think that he was going to be able to save his friend, but he did have to get out of the warehouse safely. He had to get Caspar out safely too. His eyes flicked over to where the barman was fighting some battles of his own and proving his worth. It was two against one and he was landing more hits than he was taking. Erik watched him grab a gun from one of the minion's holsters.

While Erik looked in the opposite direction, Peter made his next move. Grabbing his knife from the floor, he ran towards his friend. But his intentions were anything but friendly. His legs were still powerful despite falling apart, driven by vengeance, and Peter used all his strength to half jump, half fly towards Erik.

BANG!

The sound was like the universe was being torn apart. Bodies fell to the floor, looking for cover.

THUD.

Everyone turned towards the noises. Peter was dead. The smoking gun shook in Kit's hands.

***

Shadows surrounded Peter and their bitterly cold touch soon laid claim to him. Unlike when they'd taken Daniel, they didn't subject Peter to a corrupted version of his greatest hits. Peter was different. Peter was special. After the disappointment of Daniel, Peter was chosen.

The Shadows had infected Peter with The Rot almost immediately after Erik had turned him. They'd known that he was special then, and they knew that he was special now. Only one other werewolf had lived with The Rot as successfully as Peter. Most gave up or begged for help that wouldn't come. Not Peter. In retrospect, the shadows considered the idea that they should have infected Daniel on the day he'd turned. Perhaps things would have been different then. Maybe he could have joined them. But, he'd seemed so perfect already. It was a shame that they had needed to devour him.

Peter's soul was not devoured. It was changed.

Om va'ratt.

Peter's soul became another shadow in the dark.

***

A feeling of dread settled on Erik, wrapping itself around him like a funeral shroud. After years of being the hunter, it was a difficult adjustment when the tables were turned. His reaction was almost instantaneous as Peter fell beside him. His long-time companion's remaining eye was open, but its light had dulled. Even the amber was fading away. Erik had forgotten that Peter's eyes had once been a deep brown. Now that they were no longer able to see, this felt like an important detail, but there was no time to dwell on it or mourn yet. Erik could only hope that there would be time enough to brood on this later. Now he had to run, and run he did.

***

The sound of the gunshot seemed to give everyone else permission to start firing guns too. The unfortunate thing was that the minions Rosa had been fighting had already perished, their need for weapons diminished. Swiping herself a couple of guns, Rosa made for the exit. With Peter dead, she had little reason to be here. The rest of these guys could fight it out amongst themselves.

BANG!

Caspar was about to fire his newly acquired gun, but someone else had shot first. Missing half of his face, Kit lay on the floor in front of him. *She did it!* Caspar thought as he looked up to where he imagined Shannon would be hiding. His guess was correct. Their eyes locked and brief knowing smiles were exchanged. The remaining minions followed Caspar's gaze, easily homing in on their new prey. A cacophony of gunfire filled the night as everyone discharged their weapons.

Finally, silence reclaimed its territory.

***

Leaving their warehouse, the secret punishment chamber of "*The Six*", where shots were still being fired indiscriminately, Erik found himself outside - and easy to spot. He needed to get out of the open and find a new shelter. Another warehouse and two portacabins stood within stumbling distance - none of which belonged to "*The Six*" as far as Erik knew. Discounting the portacabins - if he was followed into one of them, he'd be trapped - he ran to the other warehouse. The surprise he felt at finding the doors unlocked was overshadowed by the relief of finding sanctuary.

Cardboard boxes and metal shelving surrounded him. As Erik started to take in his surroundings, music started. It was loud enough to make its presence known, but soft enough that he had to almost strain to hear it. It was both unusual and familiar, but soon enough, he recognised it. How could he ever forget it? Were ghosts real?

'Jack?' he called out, his voice reflecting the fact that his body felt like a bag of nerves. Confusion washed over him.

A light came on at the end of the warehouse revealing a hooded figure hunched over a table. The music was coming from a Bluetooth speaker. It seemed odd to Erik that a piece of music he'd last heard around two hundred years ago was being played on something so modern.

'No.' the figure - a woman - said. 'Jack is dead. You killed him, remember? Or are you losing your mind like Peter did?'

"Did" - she already knew that he was dead. It stood to reason that she was involved somehow - maybe another member of The Council, or a different foe entirely. He'd tried to escape, but he'd run straight into her lair.

'Ida?' he asked. 'Is that you?'

'I was Ida once,' came the reply and the woman removed her hood. 'I go by the name of Willow these days.'

I could make a run for it, Erik thought. Before he had even had the chance to act on his decision, he heard a loud noise. The temperature fell, and his vision started to darken around the edges. 'Do you feel cold?'

'Yes.' Willow replied. 'I do. The closer I get to the end, the colder it gets.'

'And the darker it gets.'

'Yes.' Willow said, knowing that it wouldn't be long until her revenge was complete. Now that the time had come, Willow didn't feel any pleasure. She didn't feel whole; she felt emptier than ever.

'This is the end.' Erik said, realising he had a hole in his gut. Lacking any kind of grace, he fell to the ground. 'This is the end.'

The last bit of life sparked out from Erik's eyes. Yellow turned to blue. The same blue eyes that Willow – or Ida as she had been then – had looked into all those years ago. It was then that she finally understood why Erik had done what he had done. She and Jack had changed him. They had damned him.

Willow turned off the speaker, the silence swamping the night instantly. She used the last bit of energy that she had left to get back to the top of the hill to sit with Jake.

***

Finally, after all these years, Erik felt free. It seemed right – poetic somehow – that Ida should be the one to kill him.

For the third time that night, the shadows began their work. Twisted images invaded what was left of Erik's soul. Erik tried to fight them back. He should have known that the peace would have been short. As if taking offence to Erik's unwillingness to submit, the shadows redoubled their attack. They forced Erik to watch as his younger self performed atrocity after atrocity. He'd levelled cities. Murdered children. Raped the innocent. Even though he knew that none of it was real, his soul absorbed the guilt. His soul started to tear, and the shadows reached for the pieces, eager to consume them. Soon there was very little left of Erik. He realised then that he was wrong before; the gunshot wasn't the end. This was.

Just as they reached the final piece, something stopped them. Erik watched as one shadow broke away from the pack, placing itself between Erik and the dark horde. It seemed familiar somehow and it seemed to know him.

A branch-like limb started to grow from the shadow until it reached the final part of Erik's soul. Erik fully expected it to grasp it and swallow it down so that he became nothing, but that didn't happen. Instead it reached towards the last soul piece and then flicked it away. The remaining piece of Erik's soul spun through the void before exploding in a blast of light. The peace he would find at the end of that light would not be short-lived; it would be eternal.

***

Each step from the industrial estate to the hill was agony, and Willow wondered if she was going to make it. She had to. She had to say goodbye to Jake. There was still one option left to her, Wolf Willow could take on this hill in a dozen strides. Using energy that may be better used elsewhere, Willow changed and loped towards the hill's summit. Following close behind her was a large crowd of shadows.

\+ *Om krell* + they chanted.

***

She had no idea who was living or dead in that warehouse at the moment. All she knew was that she was alive, and she had escaped. And that was enough for now. As she stepped into the night, she spotted one lone wolf running into the distance. Fingers tightened around the gun in her hand. There was one bullet left; it felt like fate.

Limping as it ran, the werewolf still moved faster than Shannon ever could. She could have let it go. Her mission was complete; Christine's killer was gone. Kit had died by her hand. Revenge had been claimed. But, Shannon knew that if she let this werewolf go, it would kill someone else, perhaps a child, maybe someone she knew. Shannon knew that she couldn't go through that again. The shot through Kit's head had been an extremely lucky shot and Shannon wasn't sure if she could get that sort of aim again. How many werewolves would she have to hunt and kill? She hoped that it would just be one more.

A small collection of trees waited for her at the top of the hill. No other signs of life were visible. A panic-inducing question sprang to mind: Am I being hunted? The night around her was still, an eerie hush had fallen over the wildlife. The gun felt like a dead weight in her hand. Part of her hoped that she wouldn't have to fire it again, while part of her knew that she would. Biting back the urge to call out 'hello?' like an idiot in a horror movie, Shannon scanned the area. Branches snapped behind her, and Shannon spun around searching the shadows for the silhouette of the werewolf that was no doubt planning to devour her.

There was nothing there.

It would have been easier if the creature had been there, staring at her with blood-lust evident in its eyes. At least she would have been able to get this over and done with, one way or another. Waiting was just painful.

CHAPTER FORTY-THREE

The bag was packed tight, but Rosa tore through its contents. As she had been waiting for the gunfight to come to an end, she realised that she was homeless, jobless and completely alone. Needing any supplies she could find, the backpack that had been on the back of Erik's human, seemed like a good place to start. Various items littered the floor around her. Most of the clothing wouldn't fit her, but the shirts and the hoodie might come in useful, especially if she had to sleep on the streets. At the bottom of the bag, Rosa's fingers grazed something hard. Pulling it out, she discovered that she held a book. A journal.

'Is.... is it over?' Erik's human was alive.

'Yes. Are you going to be trouble?' It seemed unlikely, the man was the proud owner of at least two bullet holes.

'No. Please help me.'

Rosa looked at him. It would have been easier to walk away, but if he was Erik's human, it may have been a friend of Peter's. 'Fine. I'll get you to a hospital.'

'Thank you.'

'What's this?' she asked, flicking through the book's pages.

Caspar thought about keeping the secret, but there didn't seem to be any point. Plus, this woman was going to help him. 'It used to belong to Daniel, but Erik and Peter stole it some time ago.'

'That must've pissed him off.'

'Absolutely.' Caspar said, as he rode another wave of pain.

'Listen, dude, I don't know you... and I don't know if you'll appreciate me being straight with you, but you don't look like you're going make it to the hospital.'

'No.' Caspar knew that she was right.

'Do you.... er.... want me to put you out of your misery?'

Now that death was facing him head on, Caspar was afraid. He yearned for the near immortality he had coveted for years. He could help Shannon and Willow if he was alive, but he was useless to them dead. That was, of course, assuming they had survived. Maybe he was on his own?

'There's one thing we could try.'

'Oh yeah? What's that?'

'In the side pocket of my bag, there's small vial. Use it. Follow the instructions in the book. It's the page where I've folded the corner down.' Caspar's breathing was ragged. Skim reading the page, Rosa's eyes widened.

'This is the *Om grutt*.' She said, unable to believe her luck.

'Yes.'

'If I do this for you, I need you to do something for me.'

'You want to change too.' He could see it in her eyes. Rosa nodded eagerly. 'You've got yourself a deal.'

***

Exhaustion threatened to claim her, she'd been in a state of fight-or-flight all night and all her body wanted to do was sleep. Her legs ached and threatened to give way beneath her. The grass looked oddly comfortable. But, if she slept, this werewolf would either kill her or escape. Probably both. A renewed sense of resolve replenished her. Shannon rubbed her eyes as if to clear them and searched the shadows again.

Twigs snapped again.

Shannon whipped her head around to face the noise.

A bird squawked, perhaps alarmed at being awoken so early, and took flight. The beating of its wings grabbed her attention and she turned again. Everywhere, ignorant to the fact that it was still night, the world was starting to wake up.

Then she heard it; the sound of running.

Shannon raised the gun and pointed it in the direction of the sound. It was impossible to aim properly in this darkness, so Shannon relied on her other senses. The source of noise emerged from the shadows. A dog. Shannon had never been very good at identifying dog breeds, so all she knew was this wasn't a big dog, but it wasn't a tiny dog either. It also wasn't particularly fluffy. Bending down, she examined its collar.

'Okay, Jake.' She said as quietly as she could manage as she stroked his head. 'You look as terrified as I feel. We need to look after each other.'

As she looked up, she saw *it*. And it was running.

Towards her.

It was huge. Fur that was more grey than black glistened in the moonlight. Its yellow eyes were wild, but focused. It knew exactly what it was doing. A hellhound had come to tear her soul apart.

'Shit!' she said as it barrelled over the grass towards her. The werewolf appeared to be slightly unsteady and its pace was slowed as it knocked into trees, sending flocks of terrified birds away from their nests and into the sky. Wings beat a tattoo into the night. When the beast was around six feet away, it stopped. Drool pooled from its mouth. Yellow eyes studied her. Sharp fangs glinted in the moonlight. For a moment, Shannon thought she saw intelligence in its eyes. Understanding, perhaps. But, that moment was short-lived.

A talon-tipped hand swiped at her face. Shannon's reflexes kicked in and she ducked, almost dropping to the floor. She regained her balance as quickly as she could. Falling down now would make her vulnerable. It was a death sentence.

The beast swiped again, missing and snarling in what Shannon imagined was frustration. Shannon backed away and the werewolf matched her step for step. Despite its frustration, it seemed to want to take its time. It could easily end her life instantly, but it was toying with her.

Those talon-like claws came again, this time just an inch from her face. As they passed by, a smell wafted into Shannon's nostrils. Rotting flesh. Whether it was the remains of an unsuspecting victim, or the animal itself, Shannon couldn't be sure. One thing she was sure of was that it smelt like death. She just hoped that it wasn't going to be foreshadowing her own. The stench made her gag. The world seemed to stop as regained her composure. Everything moved in slow motion.

The beast pounced.

The gun fired.

Jake barked.

EPILOGUE

CHAPTER FORTY-FOUR

Sunlight roused her from a slumber she didn't remember falling into and she had no idea how long she had been asleep. It took a few moments for Shannon to realise where she was. The trees on the hilltop still surrounded her. She had survived.

But what about the werewolf?

Getting to her feet, Shannon studied surroundings that didn't seem so threatening in the daylight. They seemed normal, almost mundane. A sigh of relief escaped her mouth as she realised that she was standing in the middle of gloriously mundane trees. They were beautiful. The tranquil nature of her surroundings was destroyed when she glanced in the other direction. A small distance away - no more than a few paces from where she had slept - there was a body.

The woman was naked and had a huge bullet hole in her chest. *The werewolf. Willow.* Shannon thought. The woman's skin was pale, a patchwork quilt of scars, discoloured tissue and rotting flesh. Even without Shannon's fatal shot, Willow did not look well. Had this been suicide-by-werewolf-hunter?

Next to Willow's body sat the dog from the night before. Guilt pulled at Shannon's heart, but she hadn't had a choice.

'Sorry little buddy.' she said to the dog. He made a small noise and then took a few paces towards her. 'I'll take care of you.'

She hadn't known Willow, but the woman had given her the gun that had probably saved Shannon's life, so she felt like she owed her. Looking after Jake would go some way in paying back that debt, but she also couldn't leave Willow's body on top of the hill like this. She felt like she had to bury her. Or, at least, cover her up. But, there was nothing in the immediate vicinity that would help her with this.

'There's bound to be something in one of the warehouses.' She said to Jake, already getting used to talking to the dog. Together, they started to walk down the hill, back towards the industrial estate.

A howl filled the world around them. Hungry, bestial and feral. It turned Shannon's blood to ice. Her fingers clenched, and she realised she didn't have the gun anymore. Even if she did, it would have been useless without any ammo. Jake turned and started to run back up the hill, past Willow's body and towards the town on the other side. Staying put would mean certain death, Shannon knew. Sometimes it was okay to run. Without any further thought, she followed the dog.

Another howl tore through the morning air in answer to the first.

How many werewolves will I have to hunt and kill? Shannon wondered, unable to shake the feeling her mission would never be complete.

***

As with Peter, the shadows added another one to their ranks. The *Om va'ratt* had been successful, and Willow accepted her fate willingly.

ABOUT THE AUTHOR

Lou Yardley is an Office Gremlin by day and an author by night (it's the best time, really, as it's when all of the monsters come out to play). "The Other's Voice" (published in 2016) was her first novel and she has discovered that this whole 'writing thing' is quite addictive.

She currently lives in an area that's close enough to London to be expensive, but far enough away to make it a pain to get to and from gigs.

Find her online at:
www.louyardley.com
Twitter: www.twitter.com/LouciferSpeaks
Facebook: www.facebook.com/louyardley
Instagram: www.instagram.com/louciferspeaks

BOOKS BY LOU YARDLEY

Standalone novels:

Hellhound (2018)

Books in THE OTHERS series:

The Other's Voice (2016)
The Others: A Bleak Reflection (2017)

Novellas:

Jingle Bells (2016)

Short stories:

Lydia (2016)

Flash fiction:

Wasted Time (2017)
Imps (2018)

Lightning Source UK Ltd.
Milton Keynes UK
UKHW03f1533050418
320581UK00001B/1/P